STORM
HOLT

THE GODDESS PROPHECIES

BOOK  THREE

ARAYA EVERMORE

STORM HOLT

Cover art by Deranged Doctor Designs

www.arayaevermore.com
www.joannastarr.com

This is a work of fiction.
All names, characters, places and incidents are the product of the author's
imagination and any resemblance to actual persons, living or dead, business,
events, or locales is entirely coincidental.

StarFire
Published by StarFire Epic Fantasy

Paperback Third Edition
ISBN-13: 978-99957-917-1-1

Also by Araya Evermore:

The Goddess Prophecies:

Night Goddess

The Fall of Celene

Storm Holt

Demon Spear

Dragons of the Dawn Bringer

War of the Raven

Acknowledgements

Thank you to Jon whose patience and support over the years have enabled this work to come to fruition. Thanks to John Jarrold for his excellent editorial work and advice. Thank you to Milo, Kim and Darja for their superb cover art.

Thank you to my precious Reader Team who make this work that much more fun. A special thanks to Ian for his unending enthusiasm and help in spreading this story to other fantasy readers.

Thanks to the Cosmos for making this work possible. I would also like to thank you, the reader, for joining the adventure.

For Fortitude

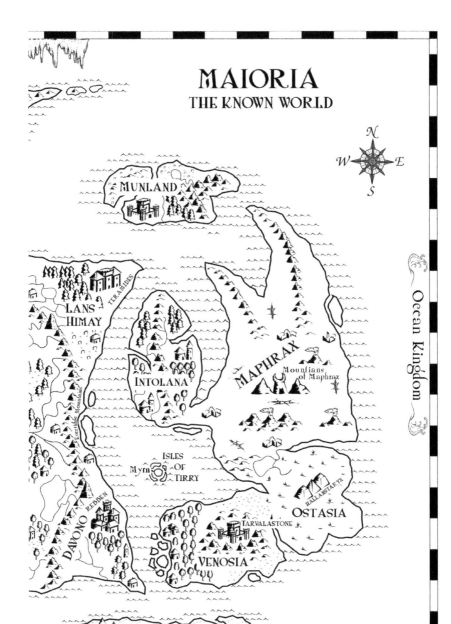

MAIORIA
THE KNOWN WORLD

CHAPTER 1

Demons

ISSA cradled the raven talisman in her lap. It glittered even in the darkness of night. Ehka dozed beside her, and together they sat alone by the stream. There were no moons tonight, and above the forests of Southern Frayon, the overcast sky blocked out the stars.

'Light,' she commanded.

The talisman responded and a soft indigo glow pushed back the darkness. It would respond to simple requests such as light, much like Freydel's orb and staff, but nothing else. Holding it in her lap did no more to reveal its powers than leaving it wrapped up and tucked in her blacksmith's belt.

She couldn't sleep, despite being exhausted. Every time she closed her eyes she saw Ely's face, ashen and lifeless in death, and then the pain and anger came. Finally, she'd given up and left the others sleeping, telling Palu'anth—who kept watch—that she would be by the stream if anything happened. That wasn't likely since they were hidden deep in the forest with only small animals busy in the night.

'It must do more than that,' she murmured, inspecting the glimmering stone closely. Ehka ruffled his feathers. 'Some help you are,' she said. He snapped his beak. She smiled. It was touching that he chose to come with her, rather than roost in the safety of a tree bough back with the others.

'We've been through a lot together, haven't we?' she whispered, and tickled his neck. He made a crooning sound. She yawned. Maybe she should go back to the others and lie down, at least she could just rest. But Ely's face would still be there to haunt her.

She looked back at the raven talisman. If it helped her enter the realm of the dead, perhaps it could also help her reach the sacred mound, where she might find answers about its powers. What harm could trying do? She had to learn how the talisman worked somehow.

'I have no spell to say aloud, Ehka,' she said, turning the talisman over in her hands. Without thinking too much, she closed her eyes and imagined the sacred mound. Instead of seeing Ely's face, the familiar ancient stones appeared before her. The entrance to the mound itself was pitch black and mysterious. She placed the talisman against the raven mark on her chest and spoke clearly.

'Take me to the sacred mound, the place I see in my mind.'

Her chest tingled, and the talisman turned so incredibly cold, that she gasped and nearly dropped it. *Is it really working?* She opened her eyes, and found herself sitting on the rich green grass with the talisman. Ehka was no longer beside her. She was still dressed in her undershirt, and the windless air was cool. The sky above the trees was a soft grey as if it were dawn or dusk, like it always seemed to be when she came here.

'Ha-ha. Great goddess, it worked, I'm really here.' She stood up grinning. Maybe with the talisman, she could reach the sacred mound whenever she chose, rather than only when it came to her. It would take practising. She stepped towards the mound, and peered into its dark, mirror-like entrance, straining to see beyond her reflection. Gripping the talisman, she took a deep breath and stepped forwards into the cold liquid surface.

Freezing blackness engulfed her, so cold she couldn't breathe for a moment. Then it was gone, and she stood in the dark, shivering and completely disoriented. She blinked into the black as the cold receded. Though she could not see the stone steps that led downwards, she knew they were there. Carefully, she stepped down them one by one onto the paved floor.

Light normally would have come by now, but it was still dark. What if it hadn't worked properly? What if she were somewhere else? How would she get back? Cursing her impulsiveness, she turned back towards the door but then realised she'd never left the sacred mound by going *back* through the liquid doorway. She walked up the steps and reached for the space where the door should have been. Her hands found only hard stone. She felt around the area with increasing haste, but there was no door. Her breath came faster. She gripped the raven talisman.

'Light,' she commanded.

Indigo light emanated from it. She breathed a sigh of relief and leaned her forehead against the cold stone. Moments later, brightness pulsed from behind her. She turned around. A yard away, a spinning vortex of energy formed in the blackness. It was a mass of swirling blue, white and grey energy, a whirlpool of storm clouds suspended in mid-air, about a foot wide and two feet tall.

Lightning flared erratically within it, but there was no sound, which she found strange given the ferocity of the moving energy. She could feel the Flow alive all around her, but it was in turmoil and moved in a wild, unpredictable manner. If she entered the Flow, perhaps she could calm it, *or perhaps it will break me.* Even now she dared not enter the Flow, not after almost losing herself in it on Celene. She was still so weak, and it was too dangerous. All she could do was observe and feel its chaotic movements.

The vortex began to grow, coming closer as it increased in size. She stepped away from it until her back pressed against cold stone. The vortex filled her vision and ballooned until it was only a couple of feet away. It had to be at least a yard wide now, and twice as tall. The frantic energy within it began to take on a magnetising effect, drawing into it the energy of the Flow and the light of her raven talisman.

She could feel it pull on her. She reached behind, searching for some nook or cranny to hang on to, but there was nothing. Hopefully it would pass. Its chaotic energy would soon burn itself out, it had to. She closed her eyes against the flickering spinning light barely a foot away from her face. She was being pulled towards it. She groped the wall again and tried to wedge her fingers between the tight fitting stones, but they slipped free. She clung to the talisman, hugging it to her.

'Make it stop,' she commanded, but nothing happened.

She closed her eyes and focused on where she had been by the river with Ehka, but she couldn't recall the details to form a clear picture because it had been so dark. It didn't matter anyway, the panic forced the concentration from her. Desperately she reached for the Flow, but that too slipped from her grasp. The very effort of trying exhausted her. The Flow could not help her, the talisman was a mystery, and even if she'd had her sword it would be useless here.

The pull of the vortex increased, its static energy brushing her arm and making her hairs stand on end. Her feet began to slip and she struggled desperately for balance. She lost the battle and screamed as she was dragged into the maelstrom.

If it had been silent before, then it was deafening now. She was spinning in the eye of a storm, lightning flashed everywhere and flickered all over her body making her judder. Thunder boomed in strange sonic waves that echoed forever or ended abruptly. Her ears were filled with the increasing noise of rushing wind and her own screams. A hundred different forces were trying to tear her body and mind apart. She curled up into a ball, hugging the useless talisman as she spun through the vortex.

Everything stopped; the noise, the wind, the spinning vortex. Silence. Light came. An unknown world appeared, one illuminated by a strange green moon. A massive plain of nothing but dirt and rock spread around her for miles, with not a blade of grass to be seen. Ahead was a towering spike of black rock that thrust over a thousand feet into the green-tinged sky. The air was hot and sticky. She released her death-grip on the raven talisman.

Her eyes fell upon a glowing white spear lying beside her—the same one she had seen in Zanufey's hands. The long haft was plain, and looked to be made of platinum. The spear tip was also white, and moulded into a beautiful but deadly sharp leaf-shape. What was it doing there lying in the dirt? She touched its surface. It was smooth and cold, but did not feel like metal, it felt more like crystal. At her touch magic flowed within it—a low, harmonious, ringing sound. The talisman grew warm in her lap. Then another sound echoed, blotting out the chime.

A deafening grinding noise came from the black spire. Her heart began to pound. She squinted and saw the base of the spire opening as if there was some giant door. Black shapes poured from the opening. To Issa, they looked like a plague of insects spewing out. Blood-curdling howls filled the air, and she broke into a cold sweat. The black shapes flooded in her direction, and she leapt up onto shaking legs. Some of the things coming out of the spire flew, whilst others ran. They moved fast.

Demons.

She turned to run in the opposite direction but faltered as she was greeted with another sight; a rising dust cloud of swiftly approaching riders. The ground shook under the pounding of the horses' hooves, and their neighs filled the air alongside the demons' howls. There were a dozen white horses, each carrying a heavily armoured knight, moving at break-neck speed towards her. She turned back to the demons. Though both they and the knights were a long way away, they were quickly closing the ground between them.

Are they coming for me? Or the spear? She looked back at where she'd left it. It was glowing furiously. She couldn't leave it there for the demons. She ran back and picked it up. The spear and the talisman pulsed in her hands as if trying to tell her something, or perhaps in response to the approaching knights and demons.

The demons were close now, especially the flying ones. She could clearly make out their hideous faces. Long black snouts, mouths filled with fangs, eyes gleaming hungrily for death. Some of them were huge, their bodies several yards wide and their wings casting a dark shadow on the ground below.

She tore her eyes from them. Why was she here? What was she supposed to do? The sound coming from the spear became louder, latent power flowing within it, and its pulsing sent increasingly stronger shock waves up her arms. It was becoming painful to hold and look upon.

'Why am I here, I didn't choose to come here,' she cried, her voice lost in the din of the ringing spear.

The knights and demons showed no signs of slowing. *The knights won't hurt me, I know that. Surely they can see me?* But if anything the knights came on faster, spreading themselves into one long line of charging horses. The man in the centre drew his sword and shouted. The other knights unsheathed their swords at his command, the sound of metal sliding easily against metal rang in the air. She whirled around to see the demons closing in. They too had spread themselves wide, a mass of hellish creatures coming straight for her.

It was too late to run, they would be on her in seconds. But surely the knights would avoid her? She whirled back to face them, but they didn't seem to have seen her at all. Sweat beaded on her face. She clenched the talisman and the spear, whirling to face the knights and then the demons. They would reach her at the same time, and she would be trampled or eaten alive.

They were only a hundred yards away—the pounding of hooves, the howling of demons, the shouts of the knights, and the ringing of the spear were deafening. She closed her eyes and screamed, slamming the raven talisman against her chest in a last desperate action.

CHAPTER 2

Into the Past

'WHY did you not take me through the Storm Holt?' Freydel shook the Orb of Death, desperate for an answer. Dark energy from the orb swirled with the pink energy from his hands. Nothing was solid in the astral planes, but certainly, life existed there, albeit in a less dense energy form.

He was somewhere in the astral planes of Celene, but it was hard to recognise the place when everything was immaterial and made of energy. The landscape looked like a painting drenched in water so that all the colours ran into each other and mingled.

He was not alone. All the time he felt eyes upon him from every direction—it didn't matter whether they were real or imagined, he still felt them. He was lost in a moving sea of energy, and he felt sick, he'd felt permanently sick since he'd been trapped here. His physical body was suffering in this unnatural place.

The orb remained silent.

'I wish I knew how to use you fully.' He raised his voice and it echoed around him. Echoed off what, exactly, he couldn't be sure. The hairs on the back of his neck prickled, which told him it was time to move and hide. Anger and frustration seemed to draw more attention from whatever existed in the astral.

He saw the hazy outline of dense trees ahead and walked towards them. His consciousness moved forwards and he had the strangest feeling that his body was following, but lagging behind as if there was a gap between his mind and his physical body. The trees were not distinct like in the physical realm but took the form of semi-solid energy. He moved between the flowing trunks and stopped, drew his energy close around him and became still. The attention he had felt before was no longer there. *I cannot do this forever, either he will find me, or my physical body will dissolve into pure energy in the astral planes.*

Why had the spell to take him to the Storm Holt failed? Something had happened, but what? He remembered falling through the vortex and escaping Baelthrom's grasp. The Storm Holt gateway he hated and knew so well had appeared before him, and he *had* entered it. Then his tower on Celene had appeared, and destruction filled the air. But how was that possible when there had been nothing but peace and calm when he'd left. How long had he been gone? All he had done was recite the spell to call the Wizards' Circle. Barely minutes had passed as far as he could tell. He stared at the orb deep in thought.

'Time moves differently…' he breathed, stroking its surface. 'But I had been gone only minutes.' Half an hour at most. In the dream state, entire dreams often took only seconds. But maybe in the astral planes, like the dream state, time was not so linear. Could it be that the orb had travelled forwards in time in the astral? One thing was for sure, the orb's power was purer here, unfettered by the constraints of the physical realm, and more powerful.

Freydel tugged on his beard, trying to ease his desperation to get out of here. The Storm Holt was the gateway to the demon worlds. The Murk was first, and it was one dimension below the physical plane of Maioria. The astral dimension was thusly two planes above the Murk. *Ahh. No wonder it didn't work, I was two dimensions away rather than one.*

His brain hurt. Understanding what had happened was at the limits of his intellect and power. He was treading the unknown; no wizard had ever been physically trapped in the astral. Or at least been trapped in the astral and survived to return and tell anyone about it. But had they ever pondered the time link? Time was of utmost importance. The longer he stayed, the weaker his physical body became and the less likely he would ever get out. It was all about time.

He peered between the tree trunks. There was nothing but blackened scars raking the land where Dread Dragon fire had seared. Smouldering black patches and rubble were all that remained of a village in the distance. *Celene is destroyed. Only the goddess knows where the people are.* But his sadness was numbed knowing his own survival was at stake. He was limited by magic and knowledge, and Baelthrom was hunting him and the orb.

The orb will do what it can to survive, perhaps this is how we have become trapped and moved in time. He had a thought and held up the orb.

'There is a stronger, older power at the Temple of Celene. Built as it was atop a sacred vortex millennia ago. Perhaps this power can help us now.' He closed his eyes and visualised the temple. 'Take me to the Temple of Celene,' he commanded the orb. It responded instantly.

There was the briefest feeling of motion, coolness, and then all was still. The Mother's Chamber materialised into hazy fields of energy. Two figures appeared in the haze, one dressed darkly and leaning over another dressed in white lying on the floor.

'Cirosa,' Freydel said aloud, recognising her instantly. Seeing her on the floor, he started towards her then paused at the look of cold fury on the man's face. Memory of that face stirred within him, but he couldn't place it.

'Cirosa, are you all right,' he called out, but the figures didn't respond, and all he could hear was an indistinct murmur as they spoke. It dawned on him then. *They cannot see or hear me.*

Two huge Maphraxies entered the room. Their deformed, heavily muscled bodies and twisted faces made him grimace. He shrank back from them, praying that they really could not see him. If they were here then Baelthrom was close, watching. They slung the limp form of Cirosa over their backs and then everyone left.

He let go of a long-held breath.

When they had gone, he sat in the darkness for a long time, trying to calm his racing heart. Baelthrom was certainly near. He had to get away. They had taken Cirosa. They would either kill her or make her one of them. She was lost. Why did they take her? The orb brought him here, could it show him why?

'Why did they take Cirosa? Show me,' he commanded the orb. It pulsed. The movement came again, and this time he felt himself moving distinctly backwards.

Now he was outside by the temple next to the old yew tree. It was dark and only a few lights from the dormitory windows lit up the night.

Ahead, he could just make out the large feathered form of a harpy and Cirosa sat opposite it. They were speaking. He shuddered at the sight of the bird woman and then froze. Harpies could use magic, who knows what they could see in the astral planes. He could not hear what was said, but the harpy tossed her a package.

'What is in the package?' Freydel breathed. He had not intended to command the orb this time, but it pulsed at his words and he moved forwards.

He felt dizzy as he took in Cirosa's office, with its book-lined walls and large desk. Cirosa was sitting down, staring deep into an amulet. He blinked. It couldn't be. But his eyes weren't deceiving him. *One of Baelthrom's bloodstones.* There was a look of rapture on her face.

'Is she in league with Baelthrom…?' he said in shock. The orb pulsed.

'Stop, enough,' Freydel gasped, struggling to comprehend what he had seen, and afraid of being detected after speaking Baelthrom's name aloud. 'Take me back to now.'

Forward movement came, but only briefly. He stood on rocks facing out to sea. Vertigo held him for a moment, and for some time after he did not know where he was. Ahead, the sea swirled as a mass of blue energy. Behind, stretched a jagged coastline of rocks being pounded by waves, high cliffs, and tiny sandy coves. He stared to his right where a small harbour and fishing village tucked deep into a cove away from the weather and waves.

'This is not Celene, this is Frayon,' he said, finally recognising Zeath, the most south-westerly village of the mainland. From Zeath, merchants travelled to and from the Sacred Isle to sell and buy wares. He looked to the horizon and could no longer see the once visible isle. *Where is Celene?* Cold dread made him shiver.

He sat down on the rock and wiped the sweat from his face. His body trembled and he wished the sickness would go away. He had to return to the physical world, he was dying here. He forced his aching mind to think. They had taken Cirosa. Had she betrayed them and joined Baelthrom? Why else would the harpy give her a bloodstone? Why she would betray them, he could not fathom.

He looked at the orb. He'd discovered a power within it that he had not thought possible. Time travel. At least in the astral planes he could travel to any time he wished with little consequence to himself, so it appeared. If he could time travel could he be safe from Baelthrom? Time travel was dangerous, a thing both desired by all wizards and feared in equal measure.

Only his good friend, the Master Wizard Grenahyme, had ever claimed to have successfully time travelled. Freydel was sure his late friend had started going grey at that point. Grenahyme had admitted he'd unwillingly seen his own death, having no real control over where he travelled to. That unsavoury thought had put all other wizards off trying. But if Freydel did not travel in time now, he would not just see his own death—he would experience it.

'So this is now,' Freydel said grimly to the orb. 'Celene is utterly gone,' *and my entire life's work with it.* But what was a life's work in the face of imminent death? He cradled the orb in his lap.

'If I die what will happen to you? Will you be lost to the world? Left in the astral planes waiting for Baelthrom to find you? That cannot be allowed to happen and you know it.' He stared into the swirling blackness and spoke carefully.

'You have your own will to protect yourself. Whatever the cost, take us to a place we can reach, where we are safe from Baelthrom. A place where I have a chance to return to the physical world.' *Or I shall soon die here.*

The orb pulsed darkly, and he felt himself being drawn into it. If he'd had anything less than a highly inquisitive mind he would have resisted, but this was the first time the orb had done anything of its own accord, with no power of his own. Then there came a fast backwards moving motion that lasted for a long time.

The place upon which Freydel stood was very different to the one he'd left. The air felt real as it filled his lungs, and everything was clearer and more solid. He rubbed his eyes and looked around. Had he left the astral planes somehow? Was he safe now? The thought excited him, but he had no way of knowing.

It was warm like Celene but arid like Atalanph, and there was a hot breeze blowing. He looked down. He was standing on a path made of crystal that shone white in the dark. It was night, but when he looked up at the stars, he recognised none of the constellations or the two small white moons in the sky. He stared at those moons for a long time.

Though it was night time there were human-like beings all around him, and this is where he struggled to comprehend what was happening. He stared at them open-mouthed. They were around two feet taller than he, slender, and with long skulls and faces that were aquiline in appearance. They had large almond shaped eyes, high cheekbones and small perfectly formed lips. They were completely hairless, and the colour of their skin ranged from smooth white to pale gold.

He stood there frozen in fear and awe. Would they attack him? Would they stop and speak to him? But the beings paid him no heed, and he couldn't imagine them attacking anything. He began to relax, but at the same time worried he had not left the astral planes.

Were it not for their hairlessness, height and colour of their skin, he would have sworn they were the Ancients, as he had seen them in the orb's memory. He glanced down at the orb. It was a swirl of black and the darkest blue. One thing was for certain; he was not on Maioria anymore.

The beings were all dressed in long robes of shimmering pearlescent material that he'd never seen before. It moved like fine satin only more sheer and floaty. Some of the beings spoke to each other as they walked, their voices soft and flowing, whilst most others gesticulated in graceful movements without uttering a word. He realised they were speaking telepathically—just as the Daluni spoke to animals, only this was far more advanced. *They have telepathy. It is said that the Ancients had telepathy.* As soon as he thought it a passing couple glanced in his direction, maybe even at him. He held his breath, but they did not stop and continued to walk past. *Perhaps some of them can see me.*

They all appeared to be of a similar height, and he could not easily tell the difference between male and female. Some had the barest of hint of breasts, and maybe some faces were rounder and smoother, but beyond that they were all similar, all beautiful and regal. They seemed to float as they walked, delicate and agile, and there was an air of peaceful calm and extreme intelligence about them.

A group of three walked past him in telepathic communion. The being in the middle held up his or her hands and spoke a word. Freydel felt the barest tinkling of magical energy and a glittering golden box appeared above the being's palm, intricate in design and totally flummoxing as to its purpose. The being took hold of the solid object, turned it around in their six-fingered hands as the others looked on, and then with another word demanifested the gold box.

Freydel stared. *They can manifest and demanifest solid objects at will?* These beings used magic that was far more advanced than anything he'd ever seen or heard of on Maioria. And yet he knew from the backwards motion of his time travel that he had gone a long way back in time, not forwards. *A pre-ancient race, but where in the cosmos am I?*

Not knowing what else to do, he followed the group of three. They seemed to be going where most of the other beings were going anyway. The crystal path led between sloping walls made of bricks twice the height of a man. He followed the wall up with his gaze until he reached the point towering far above him. *A pyramid.* The huge construction made him feel minuscule. He walked closer to the wall and noticed each brick was covered in symbols and beautiful text of flowing curving lines. A writing he had not seen before.

He held the orb up. 'Make sure you memorise all of this, I want to study it later,' he said, but the orb gave no response. Even so, he walked close to the wall and held the orb out, hoping it would record what it saw, just as he'd managed to record the contents of his books and spells in the past for easy retrieval whilst he was away from his study.

The crystal path was getting busier. The graceful beings all talked silently amongst themselves, so the only sound was the soft steps of their bare six-toed feet, and the swishing of their fine robes. They appeared to be worried or concerned about something from the solemn look on many of their faces. Everybody was now moving in the same direction and Freydel had nothing to do and nowhere else to go but follow them.

They rounded a corner and came into a vast open plateau made of the same white crystal as the path. Ahead there stood not just one huge pyramid, but several surrounding the plateau. Their majestic glistening peaks were quite a sight in the star-filled night sky, and there were several more pyramids beyond them. He was awestruck as he tried to comprehend the amount of wealth and effort put into creating this incredible place. They must have truly adept wizards to move all these beautiful stones. But when he looked closer at the beings, they didn't appear to act wealthy or adorn themselves with distinctive fine clothes, jewellery or crowns. Everyone was dressed the same, walked and talked the same, and they all seemed of equal status.

Suddenly the tip of the largest pyramid to which they were headed began to glow. Everyone turned to look up at it, their faces half-smiling, half-something-else. Freydel tried to pinpoint the emotion, but all he could come close to was worry, a shared underlying concern mirrored on all of their faces.

They entered a relatively small arched entrance, about a yard and a half wide, to the otherwise huge pyramid, and came into a wide long hallway. Inside they were surrounded by soft aquamarine light coming from the crystal walls, floor and ceiling. *The Ancients had crystal temples, but nothing like this have I seen in the orb's memory . . .*

The beings were illuminated, making them even more beautiful and otherworldly. Now and then, one of them would glance in his direction, look directly at him, and then turn respectfully away. Every time they did that his heart began to race, but no one ever approached him.

Perhaps some can see me. If I am in the astral planes and they can speak telepathically, who knows what they can see and sense.

However, he felt no threat come from them, only a serene peace. Still, he kept himself physically as far away from them as he could, and hugged the crystal wall. He didn't fancy anyone walking straight through him as if he were a ghost. The thought chilled him to the bone.

They walked the long crystal hallway and came to a huge open area within the pyramid. It was filled with beings sitting or standing on steps that also served as crystal seats. It looked like one of those amphitheatres they had on Lans Himay, except the central arena area was tiny. Only a handful of beings could stand there at the same time, and it was clearly not for games or sport.

Suddenly the beings crowding the theatre became still, and Freydel sensed the atmosphere grow silent as if he had subconsciously been hearing all their telepathic voices and now they had stopped talking. They all began to sit down, and Freydel followed suit.

From amongst the crowd, an extremely tall being walked towards the lowest middle point of the theatre. His dark blue robes shimmered as they swished, the colour of them instantly setting him apart from the others. Freydel felt the orb pulse hot against his thigh.

The being came to a stop in the centre and turned to look at those assembled around him. His skin shone like burnished gold, and his dark blue eyes gleamed in the crystal light. Freydel felt it instantly, the same feeling he felt when meeting a powerful magic wielder, only this one felt more powerful than anyone he had ever met. The Flow moved strongly around him, ready for his command. The being wore an amulet that glinted in the light, a blue stone so dark it almost seemed black.

Freydel gasped. Several faces turned in his direction, including the being standing in the centre, but he only half-noticed, all his attention was fixed on that horribly familiar amulet. *It is the same as Baelthrom's bloodstone amulets.* Save that this stone was dark blue and not blood red, and the metal surrounding it was silver, not black gold. But otherwise, the design was exactly the same. The same size, the same smooth oval cut of the stone, the same style of chain, and the same design of the amulet encasing it.

'That is uncanny,' he breathed, suddenly feeling afraid. More faces looked in his direction. He looked into the violet eyes of the being sitting next to him and held his breath. The being's smile reassured and calmed, and he turned back to the dark-robed figure. This only served to unnerve Freydel even more. They could see him, but why did they not talk to him? *Maybe I am but a ghost to them.* Perhaps they deeply respected non-physical, peaceful visitors.

Freydel also turned back to the dark-robed figure and found dark eyes watching him. For a moment he felt a probing of his mind. He pulled his energy closer, and the probing mind seemed to slip from him as if no longer able to detect his presence. Still, the being's eyes looked in Freydel's direction and he sensed darkness there which was absent in the other beings he'd so far seen.

The dark-robed being finally dropped his gaze and looked down at the crystal floor. He spoke words that Freydel did not understand in a deep voice and held his hand out, palm down. Freydel felt strong, pure magic move, and beneath the being's palm a crystal about a foot in diameter began to rise from the floor, stopping its ascent only when it reached his hand. He let his hand drop and stared at the crystal silently for a few moments.

He began to speak loudly for all to hear. Though the spoken words Freydel did not understand, the silent telepathic words that were put directly into his brain he did. He had never experienced anything quite like it.

'We have had communion with the Yurgha, and once again they urgently request our assistance.'

The crowd moved restlessly. Many shook their heads and frowned in consternation. Another being spoke from the other side of the theatre. The voice sounded feminine and somehow carried clearly. Freydel wondered if the room had been specially constructed to carry sound, much like the Ancient's legendary music halls had been. The one who spoke stood up and Freydel's eyes rested on a silvery-white skinned slender being.

'We know very well that the Yurgha require aid, they always will if they continue their dark ways and abominable experiments. But we also know they will trick us, they always have in the past. The Yurgha can never be trusted. Over the centuries we have lost thousands of lives trying to assist them, but always they turn back to their darkness.'

Agreeing nods spread across the crowd. The dark-robed being's face remained unreadable as he spoke.

'What if it were us that had been attacked by those beyond the light? What if we were the ones infected with the sickness of victimhood, revenge, competition and greed? How would we feel if no one came to our aid and, worse, turned away from our plight? Is that the way of the One Source? To leave others to fall into darkness? No, it is not, and well we all know it.' He frowned as he spoke—was it anger at the crowd or something else that disturbed him? Freydel could not tell, but the being seemed deeply troubled.

'We have already helped them so much, we do not trust their intentions.' A deeper male voice spoke from nearby. 'Even now they have doubt and worry burning in our minds, particularly yours, and you have helped them the most. We can see already how they have affected you, though you selflessly try to help them. They must be quarantined and helped from afar once we know *how* to help them.'

'Time is running out,' the dark-robed being said loudly, hushing all murmurs. Worry creased the foreheads of all those surrounding Freydel.

'The power of the sun is at its strongest, and our planet is at its energetic peak. Combined with the power of the crystal pyramids, much can be achieved. Our window of opportunity is only a few sunrises. I myself will go to them, alone if I have to, as I've said before.'

'They are pushing too hard. It must be the entire council's decision to decide how we will help them, if indeed we shall at all,' a commanding voice said from behind Freydel. 'Ayeth, you have already poured much of your heart and your spirit into helping the Yurgha. With all your powers and efforts we worry that we shall lose you too to their infected minds. Then we *all* shall be in danger of falling, just as the Yurgha have fallen. Do not risk yourself and our entire race for the saving of another. We will not risk our own race falling from the light. There must be another way.'

'They have not fallen yet,' the dark-robed being they called Ayeth said quietly. 'They may never fall if we only help them. Just one last time.'

'You must see that your love for Lona, pure and beautiful as it is, has blinded you,' the same voice said from behind. 'You risk all of us by being with her. We can all see the darkness that had entered your heart since you shared yourself with her...'

'Enough.' The dark-robed being spoke quietly, yet his command was absolute, and everyone fell silent. 'How can you heal the darkness if you do not embrace it and bring to it the light? Is that not what we have always said?'

Nobody spoke. Everybody frowned and looked at the ground or at each other.

Ayeth continued, 'All our powers are nothing if we cannot help others. And what if it works? Imagine our two races pure and powerful once more, standing in the light together. Imagine how many others we could help heal if we combined our powers together. We could banish the darkness and forever eliminate the possibility of falling from the light again.'

Freydel sensed the mood of the crowd lifting. The hope in Ayeth's voice moved him.

'There is hope, yes,' the older being conceded.

'Just one more chance,' Ayeth snatched onto the change in mood. 'One more chance to use the crystal pyramids. I will do it alone if I have to, but any others are welcome to join me in this grand healing.'

'If it fails, Ayeth, you must be quarantined until you have healed,' the older being warned.

'Of course,' Ayeth inclined his head, feverish hope inflecting his broad smile.

Freydel suddenly felt himself drifting, mentally and physically, and he felt beyond sick. He was somehow losing his grip on reality. Panic rose in his befuddled brain, and he reached inside his robe to grasp the orb. Many almond eyes stared at him, clustering his vision. The world tumbled, and then there was nothing.

CHAPTER 3

To Be a Coward

ISSA lay with her eyes closed for a long time. From the sound of the others sleeping, nobody was awake yet. A day had passed since she had returned unscathed from the demon world, but even now she was still shaken. The talisman had brought her back to the spot beside the stream, where a frantic Ehka flapped and a worried Palu'anth searched. He said he'd been searching for her for nearly half an hour.

The whole of yesterday had been spent convincing everyone she was all right, and promising Asaph that she wouldn't try that again. She wished there was someone she could talk to who knew something about the talisman or the sacred mound. Arla might know, she's the one who found the talisman after all.

Yesterday evening, they'd rendezvoused with more Karalanths of a different tribe. Rhul'ynth, Palu'anth, Diarc'ynth and Cusap'anth were now joined by four other deer people, all armed with quivers full of arrows and knives strapped to their bodies. They were keen to take up the rallying call and travel across Frayon to gather their exiled kin into one tribe once more.

Issa sorely needed a decent meal and a bed and some new clothes— Asaph and Coronos wanted the same. So the humans had decided to walk the distance to the nearest city, Corsolon, some twenty-five miles east. Rhul'ynth insisted that they travelled together. She was right, there was safety in numbers, especially after the Life Seekers attack, and no one wanted to take any chances. But the Karalanths would only go as far as the city, and so they'd camped out in a thick grove of oak trees a mile or so from Corsolon.

Though it was warm, Issa's back was stiff and sore from the hard ground, and this morning she really longed for a bed. A bed like the one she'd had on Little Kammy, or even better, the luxurious deep bed she'd had in Castle Elune on the Isle of Celene, a Celene that was no more.

All gone.

She kept her eyes closed. She didn't want to face the morning. Already the sorrow for Ely and all those lost was creeping closer. Already she was struggling with a reason to carry on on this painful path.

I should leave them, all of them. Slip away into the forest unseen, never to be heard of again. That is the only way they can be safe. Everyone who was close to her, or even knew her, was at risk from Baelthrom and his horde.

She suddenly hated the Raven Queen, the Dread Dragon-armoured warrior who haunted her, who became her when the blue moon of Zanufey was at its fullest. It was the Raven Queen Baelthrom wanted, not her.

I am Issalena Kammy from Little Kammy, and that is all. I should never have agreed to kill Keteth. I had no idea that I could. Now everyone is dead. Again. I risk the lives of all those close to me.

She should disappear. Asaph would find another to love, maybe a nice Draxian woman living in exile. Otherwise, he'd end up like Rance. Dead. If she went now no one would hear her leave, no one could stop her. She could change into a raven and fly far away. Live out her life somewhere remote. *And watch the world around me be destroyed by the immortals.* Baelthrom would destroy them all, no matter where she lived, whether he had her or not.

She clenched her eyes shut tighter, felt a tear run down her cheek. That left only two choices; to run, run forever, or seek revenge for those murdered. Soothe her anger and helplessness with retribution until her own life was taken. No matter how painful, an early death in battle would be better than watching all those she loved die around her. *I would be a coward if I ran away.*

A long sigh escaped her lips, and she wearily opened her eyes. The light of dawn was slowly brightening the quiet forest, illuminating the mist that clung in tendrils to the long grasses. Duskar lifted his head from a few yards away, mouth full of the grass, ears pricked forwards. So trusting. Even though he was still wary of Asaph, sensing keenly the dragon blood that flowed in the man's veins, they didn't need to tie him up. He wouldn't leave her side now. Not since the horrors he'd survived on Celene.

Did you know I had another horse, Duskar? She was taken from me too. Her eyes misted over. Memory of Haybear's gentle nature was replaced by the vision of a charred carcass in the smoking ruin of her home. She could not let it happen again. Ehka shifted his weight in the branches above, catching her attention. He looked sideways down at her, ruffled his feathers and yawned.

Asaph was asleep beside her. He sighed, the growing light dragging him from his dreams. As if sensing her eyes upon him he rolled over and blinked back at her. He must have seen the concern on her face, for he smiled encouragingly, a smile that always made the butterflies in her stomach flutter. She managed a weaker smile back. She couldn't bear the thought of him being with someone else.

How can I run? How can I turn away and leave them all to their fate? I will stay with them. I will die with them.

That left only the one choice. Revenge.

'Ow, I need a decent bed,' Asaph groaned, wincing as he stretched his sore back muscles.

Everyone was awake now and busy pulling food from their packs. Coronos nodded but said nothing. His face was pale and drawn, and Issa felt his pain for Ely's death alongside her own. She hoped he did not blame her for Ely's death, even though she blamed herself.

'You two-feet are soft,' Cusap'anth commented as he checked the string of his bow. Asaph snorted.

Everyone was tired and sore from travelling and the recent exhausting battles. The harpies had almost cost Issa her life, but thanks to Ely's bracelet her wounds healed quickly when she slept. As long as she got enough sleep, that was. The bracelet could not heal her magic reserves though, and she dared not even think about touching the Flow yet. She still felt lucid and not fully in the present after over-using magic in Celene.

They ate a breakfast of dried apricots, blackberries gathered en route by the Karalanths, and nut-buttered bread, which happened to be the last of their pack food. They planned to get more supplies in Corsolon and decide from there what they should do.

'We should see the mayor and city council, tell them what has happened to Celene,' Issa said and swallowed the last of her nut bread with a gulp of water from her flagon.

'They'll probably already know from their wizards,' Coronos said, puffing on his pipe. 'But we can give them the full details. To attack so far south… They must have a base somewhere.'

Issa's eyes went wide. 'Of course. They must be on the Isles of Kammy. I never thought of that before. How dare they be there,' she chewed her lip. The thought of those bastards on Little Kammy made her feel sick to her stomach.

'They won't stop at Kammy or Celene, and there is nothing but towns and fishing villages along the west coast of Frayon. Easy pickings should there be an attack,' Coronos said.

'Our northern cousins say the Feylint Halanoi are concentrated in the north,' Rhul'ynth said.

'There is nothing we can do but warn everyone, anyone,' Issa clenched her fist.

'We can tell the Mayor of Corsolon to send carrier pigeons or something faster to the Halanoi at Port Nordastin,' Coronos nodded.

'It may already be too late. How can they send an army so far west in such a short time?' Issa asked, but no one answered her. She sighed. At least there was no one left on Little Kammy for them to murder, but she still felt dreadful. 'I guess all we can do is warn the people.'

They packed up their things in silence as the sun finally tipped the treetops and began dissipating the morning mist. The sky was clear blue, and it was already hot in the sub-tropical forest.

Duskar refused to carry anything but Issa, despite her and the Karalanths coaxing him with their Daluni talents. Instead, he would prance and rear if anyone so much as tried to put their small packs on him. Asaph scowled at the horse, even without holding a menacing pack he couldn't get near the damn thing.

In the end, Issa got Duskar to take two packs instead of carrying her and they finally made their way through the thick green trees following narrow animal tracks. Four Karalanths led the way and four others trailed behind, all listening for danger and checking that nothing followed them. Issa prayed they didn't suffer any more attacks from foltoy or worse. She doubted she could even swing her sword right now.

Coronos said nothing the entire journey, and though he forced himself to move faster, everyone moved more slowly to match his pace.

Issa caught Asaph frowning. Usually, he commented on the flora and fauna, pointing out what was different in the Uncharted Lands, but this morning he'd hardly said anything.

'He'll be all right after proper rest and food,' Issa said. 'It isn't far to Corsolon.' She nodded at Coronos ahead of them and squeezed the younger Draxian's arm.

Asaph smiled at her. 'But only time can heal his heart, if it can at all when you lose a daughter.'

He took her hand in his, taking her by surprise. Tarry was the only boy who had held her hand before, but this felt different. Yes, Asaph's hands were bigger and stronger—a man's hands and not a boy's for sure, all calloused and rough from manual labour and sword fighting, but why did she blush and feel self-conscious? She dropped her eyes and carried on walking, surprised again when he didn't let go and instead matched her pace.

What if they could forget this whole thing and the war? Find a house somewhere in a nice village in Southern Frayon. They weren't warriors or trained Feylint Halanoi, they were just people who had been forced from their homes and lost those they loved.

'We don't have to do this,' she started and then wished she hadn't spoken.

'Do what?' Asaph's blue eyes looked at her intently.

If she stared hard enough she would see the dragon sleeping within. She swallowed and looked away. He was a prince of a once great and noble country, how could she expect him to live in a hovel with her? And what would they do? Toil the land day and night to feed their children and then die of old age? How could a prince, an exiled king, ever be satisfied with that?

'It's nothing, I meant nothing,' she sighed and looked up at the sunlight falling through the leaves.

'Tell me,' he urged, a frown creasing his brow.

'It's a silly thought. We don't have to do this, fight the enemy like vigilantes and warriors. We are so few, and they are so many. We cannot make a difference. Unless we join the Feylint Halanoi. I was thinking we could find a house somewhere in a nice village and live like everyone else does…' she trailed off, feeling foolish and weak.

He smiled. 'I like the sound of that, especially with you.' She blushed. 'But I don't think that will ever be enough for the Raven Queen, for one chosen by Zanufey.'

'I'm not the Raven Queen, I'm Issa,' she said abruptly and stopped. She tried to pull her hand away, but he wouldn't let go. He turned to face her and waited as the others passed until they were alone.

'I will not leave your side, no matter how hard this gets,' he said, his face serious. She looked at the floor, feeling like a coward running away, and ashamed to have mentioned such things. 'Zanufey calls to you whether you want it or not, and I think in your strongest moments you really are the Raven Queen—you've always been the Raven Queen, whatever that ends up meaning. Besides, for all that I want a quiet life with you, Feygriene calls to me also. Drax calls to me. The exiled sleeping dragons all call to me. I know they are out there, somewhere. I would not be content in a quiet, boring village either.'

Issa nodded. He was right, they would grow bored and old and probably go senile. He stroked a strand of hair back from her face. Whether she wanted it or not they *were* warriors now. He bent to kiss her then, his lips touching hers gently, taking her by surprise a third time that day. She responded without pause, almost instinctively, and definitely too eagerly, or so she thought.

It wasn't like the first kiss they'd shared, all fire and energy and passion. This kiss was soft and gentle, nourishing. For a blissful moment, all her worries and sorrows were washed away. He pulled her closer and her heart began to flutter.

There came a loud stamp, a rustle of leaves, and a cough. They pulled away reluctantly to gaze at Palu'anth. His majestic antlers looked rather impressive against the backdrop of the green forest. She steadied herself against Asaph, feeling dizzy.

'Love might have to wait,' Palu'anth winked. 'We've reached the edge of the forest, and the city is in view.'

They clustered at the forest edge, the Karalanths stayed back behind the humans to keep out of sight. To ensure their own survival they kept themselves as secret as possible, encounters between humans and Karalanths rarely turned out peaceful.

Patchy, sunburnt grass stretched down a long sloping bank towards Corsolon's city walls. In the distance within the walls stood a wide squat castle on an elevated position atop a gently rising hill. Surrounding it was a dense array of buildings with slate roofs, tall, thin chimneys and round turrets. The light grey walls gleamed in the sunlight, and above the west gate, the city's flag depicting five white crosses on a royal blue background swirled in the breeze.

Asaph turned back to the Karalanths, 'I guess this is where we part once more, though I'd prefer not to. Good luck in finding your cousins. Feygriene protect you.'

Cusap'anth nodded and then smiled. 'We will meet again, Draxian. Our totems will let us know where you are and if there's trouble.'

'Likewise the ravens,' Issa added, coming to stand beside Asaph. If she needed the Karalanths she could send Ehka, maybe even other ravens if they came when she called like before.

Rhul'ynth embraced her and she returned her friend's hug.

'I too would rather we didn't part,' Rhul'ynth said, reluctantly letting her go, 'but we must gather our kin. Those immortal bastards are everywhere, and who knows what they are up to.'

'At least we both know we have friends amongst our races,' Issa said. Rhul'ynth grinned.

Not wanting to draw attention to themselves they hid their weapons. Issa hid her short sword as best she could in her pack on Duskar's saddle, but Asaph's long sword was a trickier affair. Rather than put on his cloak in the sweltering heat, he instead wrapped it around his sword and Issa sneaked it under the other packs on Duskar's back whilst he was busy chomping on grass.

They didn't have a bridle, and so tied a piece of rope around Duskar's neck. He didn't need a halter since he never strayed too far from Issa, but a horse without a harness, and a fine looking one at that was ripe for stealing. The rope made them look poorer too—that and their dirt-stained, travel-worn and torn clothes hopefully meant no unnecessary attention would be drawn to them.

After a brief farewell, the humans departed from the Karalanths and headed towards the city. When Issa glanced back there was nothing to see but the thick foliage of trees. The Karalanths had already melted back into the forest. She immediately missed Rhul'ynth's company. The Karalanth woman's wit and warrior spirit had taught her much, but the Karalanths would be safer the further they were away from her. She turned back towards the city.

Issa stared at the thick line of people queuing to get into the city's West Gate. She felt nervous faced with such a throng, and following Coronos' lead, nonchalantly joined the long trail. She noticed Asaph looked equally uncomfortable. They had all been away from large groups of people for a long while, living amongst the Karalanths in the middle of the forest.

As they moved closer to the gate, it got busier. She realised she had never seen so many people or been to such a big city. Even Kammam, what she thought was a busy bustling port on Little Kammy, was only a tenth the size of this. Given the number of people flooding the gate, the city must already be bursting at the seams, and many more now joined the queue after they had. She found herself gawping up at the high walls and trying to glimpse that huge castle beyond them.

Asaph seemed to be gawping as well. Perhaps he had never seen a city or even a town before.

'They live in there? Within bricks and stone?' he said. Issa giggled. He looked at her. 'It just seems so unnatural, especially when you've lived a lifetime in tree houses. And look how many people there are. So many all crammed together and cut off from nature. How do they see the stars above? I guess it's exciting, though, being around so many people from all over the Known World.'

Coronos cleared his throat. 'Don't gawp so much you two. I haven't been in a busy city for over twenty-five years, so it's a shock to me too. I've never been one for crowds, but it's a relief to be back in the Old

World, with all its familiar ways.

'You are right, Asaph. The life of a city is busy and exciting. It reminds me of the thronging streets of Drax, and the bustling halls of Castle Draxa,' he sighed and smiled, but to Issa, there seemed a pained look in his expression too.

'Just relax and act normal, or at least like everyone else,' he added under his breath. 'We don't want to draw attention to ourselves. If we get searched and are found to be carrying weapons, it won't go down too well. Cities expect commoners to declare their weapons, but I won't be leaving my old sword at the gate. Not when they sometimes don't return a nice sword, and instead see an opportunity to arm themselves cheaply. I won't hide it in the forest for vagabonds to find either, or worse come under attack without a weapon. We also have the orbs to consider. Imagine those falling into the wrong hands. It simply looks like we're bringing a horse to market to sell.'

Issa stopped gawping, and Asaph gave a serious nod. They certainly couldn't risk losing the orbs at any cost. They were turning out to be more troublesome than she'd thought. Perhaps she should have given the Orb of Water back to the Wykiry somehow. If only she could find a place to hide it and keep it safe, but nowhere was safe from Baelthrom.

Dropping their stares they tried to match the mood of those around them, which was either boredom at being stood in a slow moving queue, or anxious to get in. Most people seemed to be buying or selling their wares at the markets, others possibly looking for work or going to work or looking for trouble.

The people themselves were mainly tanned brunette Southern Frayonesse mixed with some paler fair-haired northerners. She noticed a few black-haired swarthy looking Davonians who reminded her instantly of her music teacher on Little Kammy. She even spotted two tall, dark-skinned Atalanphians. The men had staves and were dressed simply in cream robes. Because of this, she suspected they were religious, possibly on a pilgrimage. She'd heard of the blue-eyed people from the desert continent but had never seen any. She knew they worshipped Doon, something she'd always found odd because Doon was the Lord of the Forest and Atalanph was not known for its trees, being a desert continent.

Remembering not to stare she dropped her gaze again. At least with such a mix of people she hoped they'd be unlikely to stand out. Though there were no other Draxians that she could see, and she also did not look like most other Frayonesse people either, being tall, dark-haired and pale. She wondered where her mother and father had come from. Tall, pale and dark-haired did not match any race description that she knew of.

Many walked pulling their loaded carts behind them, whilst the richer ones had their carts pulled by horses—either way, they all went the same pace.

They were close now, and she could see the guards checking everyone that entered the gates with as equally bored expressions as those they let in. She didn't envy them, their heavy chain mail tunics and helmets were already making them sweat in the morning sun, and they had a long day ahead.

A guard caught her with his gaze. She swallowed and carried on walking. His gaze lingered too long, making her angry, then Ehka landed on the turret above him with a loud squawk. The guard turned to shoo it away and stabbed his pike menacingly at the bird. Issa stifled a laugh. Ehka flew off. He would have to find his own place to stay tonight, she thought. She didn't need to worry about him, he was more capable than she was of looking after himself.

Now forgotten by the guards they passed through the western gate without pause or incident and made their way into the packed square.

CHAPTER 4

Marakon Returns

THE hooves of Marakon's horse thundered beneath him as he led his knights along a wide path through the jungle. He gripped the stone Jarlain had given him, fancying he could feel it leading him on. He could smell the sea and the scent of smoke from cooking fires somewhere in the distance. Soon they would be with the Gurlanka, where much-needed food and water would be consumed in great quantities.

He was jubilant. He had survived the Drowning Wastes and found his knights. The dark blanket that had covered all his days was now lifting. That sense of despair and loneliness, of searching for something he could never reach, was now dissolving. He felt clear-headed, clear-hearted. They all had paid the price for the evil committed that terrible day so long ago and were now free to walk the world once more. There was only one task left to do, destroy the demon wizard Karhlusus once and for all.

The raven appeared out of nowhere, swooping low and squawking loud, dragging him out of his thoughts. It was smaller than the one that had led their horses to them in the Drowning Wastes, and its pink tongue showed it was young. Its raucous warning sent shivers down his back. He looked ahead but could see nothing other than the dusty path and jungle crowding around them. Still, the raven squawked its warning.

'The ravens are on our side. It is warning us,' he shouted to his knights over the noise of thundering hooves. 'There must be danger ahead. Remember, whatever happens, those that look like us are most likely our friends.'

'I'm ready for anything,' Oria said, a keen, excited look in her eyes.

He grinned at her. He was certainly ready for anything. He sat up and spied for danger. The smoke he'd smelt was no cooking fire. Dark smoke billowed above the trees ahead. Worry for Jarlain suddenly gnawed at him, and he urged his horse faster. He was ready, but he prayed it wasn't Maphraxies.

The smoke grew thicker and the air became hard to breathe. Their horses didn't even flinch as they bounded into the smog. These were no longer ordinary war horses, he realised, they'd seen death, felt death, and returned to the living that much stronger.

Screaming and shouting came through the smoke. He squinted into the choking blackness and could barely see the ground beneath his horse's hooves. The sound of fighting was all around. He heard that familiar metallic ring as his knights drew their swords, and pulled his own free of its scabbard.

They plunged out of the smoke into bright sunshine. Mayhem filled his vision. In every direction, Gurlanka were locked in a struggle with Histanatarns. The enemies' nutmeg green fish-scale skin shone metallically in the sunlight, and their glassy yellow eyes gleamed. They flooded into the village in their hundreds, coming up the wide track that led to the ocean, stabbing with their knives or hurling their spears with devastating accuracy. For every Histanatarn felled by Gurlanka arrows, two more immediately filled their places.

'An old enemy,' Cormak growled. The oldest dwarf's face was fierce as he hefted his axe.

Marakon nodded. As small as this enemy was in stature, they more than made up for it in numbers and ferocity.

'They killed my entire crew just weeks ago,' Marakon said. He gripped his sword, he was looking forward to taking his vengeance.

Gurlanka herded together the elderly and young, moving them back to the safety of the trees. Everyone had thick curved knives almost as long as short swords. Marakon knew those blades were deadly sharp, a stark contrast to their pretty sheaths and hilts decorated with colourful weaving. Those with bows had climbed trees and rooftops, and they fired arrows so fast, Marakon could not see the shafts flying as they devastated the front line of the invading Histanatarns.

The enemy had started fires where they could. Houses burst into flames. Their wooden structures and bamboo roofs flared alight even if their solid mud walls did not. Burning rooftops sent the archers running as each house flared alight the one next to it. The fire spread alarmingly quickly. Fallen leaves and old trees caught light, hampering the old and young from being herded into the jungle.

Marakon danced his horse around bodies and spared a precious moment to take in the fearlessness and skill of the Gurlanka as they wielded their blades. They hacked and slashed without hesitation or error and moved onto the next. Every able-bodied man and woman, old and young, had a weapon, and all who could engaged the enemy. He had only ever seen these people at peace, but now the warrior spirit was alive within them, he found a greater respect growing. They could certainly teach him a thing or two.

A spear hurtled into the Gurlanka line. He saw a man fall, but another Gurlanka jumped in the gap where he'd stood, and blocked the enemy from breaking through. For a moment he glimpsed dark curls amongst the throng. He strained to see more. Saw Jarlain swing her blade and maim a Histanatarn just as another jumped on her undefended back. His heart skipped a beat as it brought Jarlain to the ground.

He turned his horse towards her and lunged forwards, running down the Histanatarn who jumped in his path. He reached Jarlain in seconds just as the enemy raised its sharp knife. He brought his horse to a skidding stop and grabbed the descending knife. With all his strength he crushed the Histanatarn's arm in his grasp and yanked viciously, feeling the socket come loose. He smashed his sword pommel into its face, the enemy sagged and he dropped its body.

Another screamed and rushed in, but Jarlain rolled and sliced his spine. She gasped, eyes wild with life and fury. She smiled up at him, her brown eyes warming his heart. She staggered upright, blood oozed from her thigh turning her tan clothes red. She was hurt, but still managed to stand.

'There are too many,' he said, breathing heavily. 'We'll cut them off at the trees. You're hurt. Stay safe,' he added the last, knowing that to convince her to seek shelter would fall on deaf ears, just as it had fallen on his Rasia's ears in battle so many times before.

The Gurlanka knew how to look after themselves. Jarlain nodded. He wheeled his horse towards his knights and glanced back, but she was lost from view. He prayed she would leave the battle and find shelter. The Gurlanka were heavily outnumbered, and all were beginning to fall back.

'Knights,' Marakon roared. 'Let's stem the flow of these bastards.'

He lifted his sword high and veered his horse towards where the Histanatarns were flooding in. His knights roared back and followed him, a line of white horses gleaming in the mayhem. Marakon smashed into the enemy line without pause, his horse's hooves trampling and stamping over their small, wiry bodies. He sliced his long sword in an arc, barely feeling the blade hit flesh as he decapitated two and wounded a third in the same blow.

He heard the battle cries of his knights behind him as they hit the enemy hard, and for the first time in his life he saw the Histanatarns hesitate. It must have been a long time since they'd faced mounted knights in armour. It lasted only a moment before they screamed and came at the knights. His horse slowed at the tree line, reared as he turned it fast around for another run through.

Three Histanatarns came on at once, two on one side and one in front. He cut the first down in a spray of blood. The second ducked, missing his sword, but not seeing his devastating backward swing. Red blood splashed over his face and the flanks of his white horse.

He wiped his cheek and turned to the other, seeing in his peripheral vision the strange gestures it was making in the air. Before he could react, it hurled glittering sand straight into his face. A thousand needles of fire pierced his skin and eye. He yelled. He couldn't do anything. *Curse all magic wielders!*

He raised his sword and hacked uselessly in all directions, blinking and rubbing his eyes as he pulled his horse back. Arrows whistled past, making him flinch. He squinted through streaming eyes and searing pain, readying himself for the inevitable thrust of spear or knife to finish him off. The pain began to dim. Finally, his vision cleared enough to see. All around him lay dead and wounded Histanatarns, Gurlanka arrows in every one of them. He looked to the trees, saw archers there. He raised his sword in gratitude. There was no time to pause.

Another Histanatarn caught his reins and swung itself up onto his horse's head, its scaly skin gleaming green. A blade lunged for Marakon's throat, but his horse flicked its head, trying to dislodge the thing clinging to its face. The blade scratched harmlessly down his breastplate. He crunched the pommel of his sword down upon its skull, crushing it and killing it instantly. He shoved its lifeless body down onto the blood covered ground and drove his horse forwards again.

His heart pounded in his chest, every fibre of his being was ready for fighting, and adrenaline flooded his veins. This is what he lived for; to stand on the edge between life and death, never knowing from where his end might come. A swift blade he did not expect, a spear he didn't see. Death could come at any time, and he would be waiting.

The Histanatarns fell back from his horse, wary this time, but his mount and sword were fast and two more fell under them before they were out of reach.

'Drive them back to the shore,' he snarled, struggling to stay mounted as his horse reared away from a stabbing spear.

Hooves crashed down upon the spear-wielding enemy, it wailed a strange high-pitched cry and fell to the ground. Despite their overwhelming numbers, the Histanatarns' small bodies, quick knives and light armour were no match for plate-armoured mounted knights, and for the first time in ages, Marakon was relieved to find himself on the side creating the blood bath. The only threat was to their horses' undersides and from spears launched with enough force to pierce armour.

The knights cut through the mass of Histanatarns, making their way towards each other until they formed one line again. They pushed forwards, and step by step forced the enemy back through the trees.

They emerged onto a long, white sand beach. The turquoise sea lapped at the shore. Marakon found the peaceful scene at odds with the clash of metal, sprays of blood and howls of rage. He led the centre and forced his way forwards until they formed an impenetrable arrow shape driving straight into the mass of shrieking Histanatarns.

'They're as vicious and relentless as always,' Hylion said beside him. His usually pale elven face was flushed and splashed with blood. He had a cut above his eye that was dripping down his face.

'Their numbers are thinning now. Push them back into the water. They won't stop until they're all dead or swimming,' Marakon rasped.

He stabbed his sword down at the Histanatarn trying to climb up his leg and sunk his boot into its face, splattering its ugly nose in a spray of blood. His horse's hooves now touched the water.

'This place is sweltering,' Lan gasped on his other side, sweat pouring down his brow. Blood soaked through his ripped leather gauntlet and over his sword hand, but still he showed no signs of weakening. The sea came up to their horses' fetlocks, but the knights fought on, pushing the Histanatarns further into the sea.

The Gurlanka rushed to their sides and behind, they must have overcome the Histanatarns in the village. The enemy was out-numbered, and the sea was turning red with their blood.

Only when they were waist high in water, did the enemy turn and dive under the waves back towards their boats. Marakon sliced two more before it got too deep. The ring of metal and cries of battle dwindled as what remained of the enemy fled. Arrows whistled overhead, taking out any that could be reached before they swum out of range.

Marakon grinned as he watched the Histanatarn's crawl into their boats and flee towards the horizon. He took in deep gulps of air. *That's for Bokaard and Lanac and Erylin, and all the others, you bastards.*

One by one the knights dismounted, and watched the enemy go. Behind them came the rising cheers of the Gurlanka. Marakon lifted his sword and cheered, his knights did the same. He washed the blood from his sword and face.

'Thank the goddess they are leaving. How many did they lose, at least half their number?' Ironbeard asked. Seawater came up to the dwarf's chest, washing the blood out of his beard.

'I reckon a thousand came here,' Ghenath said, cupping water in her hands and splashing it onto her bloodied face. 'But I see only a hundred fleeing. Look at how many empty boats there are,' she smiled. There was relief in her pale violet eyes.

Marakon nodded, taking in the mass of bobbing boats. He stopped washing the blood from his horse's flanks and looked at them each in turn. None had fallen, how could that be? He remembered them being good, the best even, but against an enemy so numerous? At least one should have fallen or been seriously injured. He rubbed his beard thoughtfully.

'How bad are our injuries?' he asked.

Most shook their heads. Lan held up a bloodied hand, 'I think two fingers are broken, but all are still intact.'

Hylion wiped the blood flowing from his cut. 'Something hit me hard, twice. I've got a headache, but I think food and rest will fix it.'

Marakon nodded. 'What are the odds...' he trailed off.

Ghenath understood where he was going. 'Against so many, one or two of us should have fallen—at the very least a few of us should have had more serious injuries,' she said. 'Perhaps Woetala protects us.'

'Not Woetala.' Cormak shook his head. 'Zanufey.'

'Or perhaps you just can't die twice,' Ironbeard said. They laughed.

'Do you think we'll live forever, that we've become invincible?' Nemeron asked.

Marakon instantly remembered he was the youngest knight there, but at only twenty years old he was still the quickest with a rapier any of them had ever seen. Although now he was thousands of years old.

'I don't think I want to fight forever,' Oria said, her green eyes staring off across the ocean.

'Zanufey most certainly protects us,' Marakon agreed and pointed to the raven circling above them, no doubt waiting to pick a chunk of flesh off one of the fish bastards. 'That is why we must no longer be called Knights of the Shining Star—that name is tainted and best forgotten and laid to rest.' The knights nodded, thoughts of the past hanging heavily over them. 'I was thinking, we should call ourselves Knights of the Raven, since the raven is sacred to Zanufey. It was the raven that found us from beyond the grave and united us together once more.' They all looked up at their new totem as it wheeled above them in the clear blue sky.

' "Knights of the Raven." It has a nice ring to it,' Oria said, watching the bird. 'And if that's what will keep us alive...' she shrugged.

Marakon nodded. 'My thoughts exactly. But before we jump to such divine conclusions and think ourselves invincible and immortal, I think we'd better see how we fare against a deadlier enemy.'

'Vicious and numerous and deadly as they are, Histanatarns are nothing compared to demons,' Lan agreed.

'And demons are nothing against Maphraxies,' Marakon said. 'But this, my honourable knights,' he spread his arms wide, 'is the first of our glorious victories, like those we used to have.'

They all cheered. On hearing them the Gurlanka cheered as well, raising their weapons high.

'Come, let's meet our new friends,' Marakon nodded towards the shore where the Gurlanka were clustering. He led his horse through the water and realised how odd he and his knights might look to a people who had never seen plate armour or mounted knights. Right now he longed to get the sweaty heavy stuff off.

He spied Shufen pushing his way to the front of the crowd, a big grin spreading across his bloody, muddy face. Marakon grinned back, wiping the blood and sweat and grit from his face. The two men looked at each other then embraced. Shufen wrapped his knuckles on the metal of Marakon's breastplate.

'Hard as iron on the outside, soft us mush on the inside,' Marakon grinned.

'Hah. I don't think so,' Shufen said. 'We definitely need something of this design.'

'Where's Jarlain?' Marakon's voice was hoarse.

'In the healing room,' Shufen said. Marakon smiled, relieved. 'And she is asking about you.'

Histanatarn bodies covered the beach and floated in the water. It took hours for the knights and unwounded Gurlanka to pile them up on the sand. As they worked they stripped the enemy of their weapons and whatever else they had of use, which wasn't a lot. The weapons would be remade into better Gurlanka ones.

No one spoke much during the bloody task, but Shufen said what every Gurlanka knew, that each dead Seadevil meant one less to fight in the future. They covered the bodies with dry forest matter, and then set them alight. The parched leaves and wood was quick to light, and the mound of bodies roared into a blaze.

Shufen, Marakon and the knights made their way through what remained of the Gurlanka's home. Some houses were burnt out holes whilst others were untouched. Most were somewhere between the two. The Gurlanka had already removed their wounded, but the blood patches that littered the ground and splattered the walls could not be taken away.

Marakon steeled his heart against the destruction as they walked. How many times had he seen the devastation of war? He had to harden himself against it.

One of the Elders came over to him, her wispy white hair blowing out behind her. Her face was pale and sombre, but she managed a brief smile and touched his arm.

'You came not a moment too soon, half-elven. You have our deepest gratitude.'

He shrugged. She passed him a welcome flagon of water, which he drank noisily, the cool water delicious in his parched throat. Then she led him and Shufen to the Elder's house. Marakon thought it a miracle that it had remained unscathed by fire and suspected magic.

Inside on the ground floor was a large room filled with many wounded Gurlanka, and unwounded Elders and townsfolk able to help. Incense kept the smell of blood and gore absent. A fire burned in one corner of the room where hot water was boiling and various devices being sterilised. At one end, Jarlain lay with her eyes closed, covered with a blanket on a low pallet.

'She's sleeping.' The Elder woman reassured Marakon. 'She was lucky. The knife went deep into her thigh. She's lost a great deal of blood, but we managed to close the wound quickly.'

'If only we'd arrived sooner,' Marakon murmured, gently stroking Jarlain's hair back from her forehead. 'I'm sorry for your losses,' he looked up at Shufen and the Elder.

'How could you have come sooner? We are lucky you and your knights came at all,' Shufen said. 'You fight nearly as well as the Gurlanka,' he grinned. Marakon chuckled quietly.

'I want to hear your story,' Shufen added. 'What really happened in the Drowning Wastes? Who are these warriors?'

'Pah, have you got a decade free? I'll tell you what I can later. All I can say simply is a curse was put upon us that has now been lifted by my return, and maybe something to do with the dark moon. After thousands of years spent damned in exile, these knights have returned so that a great wrong can be righted.'

Shufen looked at Marakon, all laughter gone from his face and he spoke in a serious voice. 'Then the first wrong has already been righted this day by driving back our shared enemy. May you have what you seek, Sarun.'

Marakon inclined his head at the term of respect. Sarun meant closest brother and was a word rarely used amongst the Gurlanka. 'It was an honour to fight at your side against the Seadevils. Maybe we will fight together again some day.'

'Maybe,' Shufen nodded, 'but not too soon.' Marakon smiled. 'I must help the others. Just make sure she wakes up.' Shufen left the room.

Marakon looked down at Jarlain who suddenly stirred. Her face was gaining some colour and after a moment her eyes opened. She looked up at him and smiled.

'We did it, didn't we?' she asked. There was warmth in her hand as she gripped his lightly.

'We did,' he replied and lifted her hand to his lips. 'They said you lost a lot of blood but the wound has closed well. How do you feel?'

'Oh, great,' she said, and grimaced in pain. 'Honestly, I'll be fine. Just a little weak.' Her usually rich voice was still faint. He worried about her, more than he wanted to admit, more than a married man should. A tall, short-haired Gurlanka woman came over bringing two steaming cups of spiced soup. He took the soup and thanked the woman, then set his own aside and helped Jarlain to sit and drink hers first.

'I remember you doing this for me not so long ago,' he said, remembering when Jarlain and Tarn had taken him in and healed his wounds. So much had happened since then, he felt a year had passed.

She nodded. 'You looked so frightening to us, with your weapons and your wounds.'

He smiled, took her empty bowl, and helped her lie back down. She closed her eyes as a wave of tiredness overcame her. He stood there watching her drift off to sleep again as he drank his own soup. Satisfied that she was comfortable and sleeping he went back outside.

The sun was setting and the wind had picked up, creating a welcome breeze. His nine knights were chatting with the Gurlanka as they washed their armour and weapons in the water basin meant for watering animals. Hylion and Lan were being cared for in the healing room. Though that desperate sense of urgency had disappeared since he had been reunited with his knights, he knew he had to call the boatman soon. They had to return to the Old World and there was much to be done, but right now they all needed rest, especially the injured.

He went over to them, unbuckling his armour as he walked. He eased off his heavy cuirass and sighed as the wind blew over his sweaty chest. 'Taking this stuff off has never felt so good,' he moaned and stretched amongst loud murmurs of agreement.

'I can't remember being anywhere so hot,' Ironbeard said, tugging his thick beard away from his clammy chest in irritation.

Marakon pulled off his shirt and dunked his head in the water basin. Spring water had been channelled away from the main stream and pooled into the large moulded stone basin before it trickled out the other end and was channelled back into the stream. He stood up with a gasp as the cold instantly cleared his head and splashed it all over his arms and chest. Only when he was done washing away the dirt and blood did he turn to talk to anyone.

'You look different to how I remember for sure, but it's uncanny for there is still a likeness,' Nemeron said thoughtfully. 'It's in your eyes, or should I say, eye, the set of your chin. The way you hold yourself and the way you speak. But despite all that, I do not remember you having that many scars.'

The other knights nodded and came closer as they polished their armour.

Marakon looked down at his chest, covered as it was in a network of lines, some fine, some thick, some white and some still red. They told the story of his life, and how he'd survived. 'And I doubt I had an eye patch, or a half-elven heritage before, either,' he grinned. 'Although, thankfully, I'm not a king, and I don't ever want to be one again.'

'You were a good king, before Karhlusus,' Oria said and gave a half smile of encouragement. 'And it seems ours is a bond that even time cannot break. We return, goddess knows, thousands of years later to right the wrong done to us.'

'Aye,' Cormak said, his eyes narrowing fiercely. 'Even if I'd died a hundred times, I'd still return to kill that bastard. I still see their faces before me, in my dreams and when I'm awake. Even little children...' he trailed off, looking horrified at his own hands.

Oria squeezed the dwarf's shoulder. 'You don't suffer alone. We were all there, we all murdered,' she said.

Marakon saw the suffering on his knight's faces as a reflection of his own. Knowing that you had taken innocent lives in a horrific manner, lost everything that you were and damned yourself to an endless hell of torment, was its own curse. And it had all been his fault. And he had killed the most. He swallowed a lump and looked to the tree line where the sky began to smoulder in the setting sun.

'We can be free,' he said quietly, his voice gruff as he nodded. 'We *will* be free. Today was just the first, the first victory of many. And we will stand by each other's side until our task is complete.'

'Here, here,' Ghenath said, and put an arm around Oria. They both smiled, a real smile, though the pain was still in their eyes.

'We are here together at the end of our damnation, to bring back our glory and make things right,' Marakon said. 'We have returned to claim our rightful place amongst the heroes of old.' The knights cheered at that. 'Whilst we have Zanufey's blessing, let us forget our old name. Let us be remembered as Knights of the Raven. Let us be bringers of justice and honour like once we were. We will train and teach others what we know; our creed, our skill, our expertise and our fortitude, so that they may become one of us. Maioria needs an army of knights such as we to set her free, an army of Knights of the Raven.'

Everyone clapped and cheered. The Gurlanka looked on intrigued and began to clap along, seemingly ever ready to join in a celebration.

'But first we need rest and sustenance,' he said when everyone had stopped clapping. 'Lan and Hylion are being treated for their wounds. But tomorrow we must leave. Let's meet on the beach at dawn. So drink, eat and sleep.'

He laid his armour and his sword beside the others. He needed a strong drink, they had to have something potent here. He went to search for one.

CHAPTER 5

Demon Trouble

GEDROCK squinted into the light of Zorock as it dimmed then turned orange. The setting moon of the Murk did that, turned a muddy amber as it slid beneath the horizon—a horizon of craggy rocks and squat trees with long finger-like branches that reached over the ground. Where it sank in the north-west were his enemies, the Grazen, and the homeland he and his kind had been driven from long ago.

Tonight, deep in the rocky swamp forests of Eastern Middle Murk, there was no breeze, and it was hot and humid as it always was in the underworld.

'Karhlusus,' Gedrock growled aloud the name of the half human, half greater demon abomination who drove the wars that divided the lesser demons apart. Their cousins the Grazen were enslaved, and they—the Shadow Demons—were hiding in exile like rats. Karhlusus was not even from the Murk, but he fully controlled it having successfully divided the Grazen and the Shadow Demons against each other. Now no lesser demons at all held the seat of power at Carmedrak Rock. Now their old kingdom was no longer called Carmedrak Rock, but Karhlusus Keep. And that made Gedrock's black blood boil.

'They cannot kill us all, my lord, not if we hide amongst the shadows as we Shadow Demons have always done since they came. They have tried for thousands of years to annihilate us, but clearly, they cannot,' Wekurd wheezed. 'And if they cannot destroy us then they can never fully take the Murk.'

Gedrock's old advisor came forward a step, his skinny lank frame bent over and held up by a gnarled staff. His bald head shone in the murky orange-green light and a lipless grin revealed three very sharp and surprisingly white fangs that stood out of his otherwise grey face. His long thin tail curled and uncurled around his right foot as it always did when he was vexed.

Gedrock grumbled in response. His advisor was right, but for a king to live in exile made his head pound with rage. He knew not to come up here because it always angered him, and he hadn't done so for several moons, but now something made him. For some reason he just had to see Zorock set once more over their lost kingdom.

'Let's go back into the caverns where we are safe. A new nest of wursels has been discovered, and their blood is fresh for drinking,' Wekurd said.

The thought of hot blood from a wursel softened his scowl, and he almost turned to go. Almost. Their lives, the future of the Shadow Demons, and their entire planet were more important than fresh blood from a wursel.

'Go. I stay.'

'I cannot leave your side when enemies might be close,' Wekurd wheezed.

'A moment more. Alone,' Gedrock growled in finality.

Wekurd knew better than to question his King when in this dire mood, and he limped off unhappily, his staff dragging between steps. Gedrock watched him disappear into the blackness of the cave, just one of the many entrances to their huge network of caverns, their place of exile.

Gedrock turned back to the darkening orange-green sky, and his scowl returned. Though it was a long time before he'd came into existence, Grazen and Shadow Demons had once been one, cousins united before Karhlusus came and opened the gates to the Pit, letting the greater demons into the Murk.

Karhlusus was not an ordinary human, and neither was the other half of him just any greater demon. Gedrock's Finder, the one who'd dug him out of the rock and brought him into existence, told him that Karhlusus the human was once a great black arts wizard from the higherworld, and this wizard was far more powerful than any demon he conjured up. He was stronger than the strongest greater demon. Which is how Karhlusus conjured up the great King Kull and held him in thrall until this day. King Kull himself was an ancient king of the greater demons—a demon who had managed to crush his enemies and dominate the entire greater demon world.

Knowing they were greater than the sum of their parts, King Kull gave Karhlusus more power than he could ever have had alone. In return Karhlusus gave Kull a physical human body in which he could move around the Murk and, more importantly, the higherworld Maioria. So they agreed to share one body. An abomination if ever Gedrock had heard one.

It was demon-possessed Karhlusus who broke through the demon tunnels from Maioria, coming through the Storm Holt gate into the Murk. It was from there that King Kull, through Karhlusus, opened the gates to the Pit and let the greater demons flood in.

Hope ended then for them—no lesser demon was ever a match for a greater demon. Gedrock clenched his fists. Now, when he looked at the moon of the Murk setting gracefully over the place of his enemies, he was reminded that they were doomed and their world was lost. It was only a matter of time. He knew from the images in the crystal shard that Karhlusus amassed a growing army of greater demons. Soon he would open the gates to the Pit, soon greater demons would come and destroy them all.

Blackness fluttered in his peripheral vision. Instinctively he melted his form into shadow, his whole body disappearing into darkness. The raven landed close and looked straight up at him completely unafraid. Though Gedrock had no form, the raven was not fooled. He was reminded that ravens could see what moved in the shadows. Ravens came from the higherworld, and that was the last thing Gedrock needed.

Of all the creatures that lived upon the higherworlds, and of those that resided upon the underworlds, only ravens could move at will between the two. Demons and wizards had to use gateways and tunnels of energy connecting the worlds, and only the most powerful and skilled could open a gate and navigate through. No lesser demon had willingly gone to the higherworld since the gates were sealed after the Demon Wars thousands of years ago. All gates, that was, except one.

When he did not materialise the raven squawked. Carmedrak was the lesser demons' god, and Zorock was his messenger. The raven belonged to a goddess not of their world, so why should he, King Gedrock, answer her messenger? The raven squawked again.

'We want nothing from your blinding world,' Gedrock growled at the bird, allowing only his face to appear out of the shadows. He caused his eyes to glow red menacingly and bared his fangs, but the bird was not fazed and instead took a step closer. It cocked its head expectantly. Curiosity at the bird's bravery made him materialise fully. That and wondering what hot raven blood tasted like. Blood from higherworld creatures was far more delicious and powerful than anything they could get in the Murk.

Gedrock reached to grab the bothersome bird, but as his clawed fingers brushed the bird's feathers pain exploded in his head paralysing him, preventing him from roaring aloud, preventing him from fighting or fleeing back into the shadows. The raven had a message for him, and he had to receive it.

The world began to spin, and he thought he was falling, but there was nothing to stop him. He lashed around and flapped his wings then, real as day, Carmedrak Rock loomed huge and ominous in his vision.

Gedrock, held aloft by unseen and unfelt hands, plunged through the thick, jagged black walls of Carmedrak Rock. He instinctively shielded his face from impending doom, only to be amazed that he passed unscathed through walls of stone. Then bright white light blinded him.

He howled as he recognised that which all demons fear; the white spear Velistor. Its horrific light seared his eyes and froze blood. He slammed his eyes shut but the light came even there, burning into his sockets, his mind and his black heart with its awfulness.

'Get it away from me,' he screamed.

The light went, and slowly he dropped his arms. It was night and he was no longer within Carmedrak Rock. Instead, he looked at it from afar. He glanced down from the rugged mountainside upon which he stood and took in the vast emptiness of Carmedrak Plain that surrounded the great spire of Carmedrak Rock. In the distance the rest of the mountain range that ringed the plain rose high into the dark sky, black and foreboding.

All of the Shadow Demons stood behind him. Tens of thousands of lesser demons shuffling restlessly, wings beating in anticipation, eyes flashing red with rage as they looked upon their lost kingdom.

Then Zorock tipped the mountain peaks to the east and his green light spread across the plain. There came a great noise of rock and metal grinding violently against each other and shaking the ground. Then the huge door at the base of Carmedrak Rock began to open like a great black cavernous mouth. Gedrock's guts squirmed as thousands of huge greater demons intermingled with their slaves, the smaller Grazen, spewed out from behind that door.

'The Pit Gates are open,' Wekurd's thin voice rasped in horror beside him.

'Karhlusus has opened them. We are doomed,' Gedrock replied, 'but I will not become a slave like the Grazen.'

Gedrock gripped his twin-bladed sword, lifted it high and spread his wings wide. With a howl, he leapt from the rock and all those with wings followed their king's flight. The others shifted into the shadows and melted down the mountainside, a great wave of darkness flooding into the valley to meet and wreak death against their cousins and the hated greater demons.

Gedrock dropped fast, twin-bladed sword leading his flight. In one motion he descended upon the left flank of a group of Grazen and decapitated a slower moving one. Its head slid between his two blades, barely slowing his descent. Thick black blood oozed over his sword and he swiftly melted back into the shadows as the Grazen's body turned to molten rock and moments later exploded. A hazard of killing any Grazen; if you weren't quick enough withdrawing your weapon, it would melt in the terrific heat and then explode, along with whoever still held the killing weapon.

Gedrock's thick claws raked into the dirt as he rematerialised. He spun, decapitated another and fell back. He swung his blades and smashed against the trident of a third Grazen just as the second exploded, showering them with burning ash and rock. They roared at each other ignoring the molten debris, once cousins and now despised enemies. Fury drove Gedrock's sword fast, and the third Grazen fell headless to the floor. Decapitation was the only way to be sure to kill a Grazen.

A Grazen exploded to his right, the shock waves stunned him for a moment and searing ash showered him again. To his left there came a gut-wrenching high pitched wail followed by a flash of black light as one of his Shadow Demons was speared through the heart. The Grazen holding the spear was not quick enough and Gedrock smirked as the Grazen turned black and then disappeared forever into shadow. Lesser demons never died alone and always sought to take a soul or two with them.

Gedrock raised his blades to counter the axe of another Grazen. Fury gleamed in his opponent's eyes and for a moment Gedrock wondered what lies Karhlusus had told his brethren to make them hate the Shadow Demons so. He hardened his mind and heart. The Grazen's axe fell between his two blades and in one motion Gedrock yanked the weapon away, disarming it, and swung back to slice off its head. He disappeared back into the shadows, feeling a flutter as the Grazen exploded and glowing rocks flew through his shadow.

A flying Grazen caught Gedrock from behind as his form solidified. It was a big one, bigger than he, and thick claws ripped into his shoulders as heavy wings beat upwards lifting him quickly from the ground. His cold black blood seeped from his wounds, making him even more furious. Through the pain he beat his own wings hard, driving him up into the underside of the Grazen that lifted him.

A trident struck down, three prongs speared his chest but not deep enough to kill. Howling in pain he gripped the trident, shoved it up, and drove his own sword into a leg that carried him. Cold blood spattered over his face and agonised screeches seared his ears. He twisted the sword hard and felt blades crunch through bones before dismembering the foot.

With only one clawed foot embedded, it was not enough for the Grazen to hold him. Gedrock ripped his shoulder from its grasp and flew upwards. In a swift motion he struck the head from the Grazen's shoulders. The Grazen plummeted. It turned to molten stone in mid-air and exploding as it hit the ground, maiming two of its own.

Ahead more flying Grazen came, their brown skin gleaming with a greenish tinge in Zorock's light. He'd been exposed, and they knew to look for and kill the leader of the Shadow Demons. But the flying Grazen never reached him.

A chain of burning spikes lassoed around his throat and dragged him through the air. Flapping his wings he spun around and glanced at his enemy, the huge pitch-black shape of a greater demon flapped its wings lazily. Its form was not solid, it was like a Shadow Demon part merged into shadow. Great horns curled away above its small pointed ears and its face was thin and long, terrifyingly long, its black eyes barely visible in the rest of its dark form.

Its wings spread wide and a long thin tail snaked around Gedrock's waist in a crushing vice. Gedrock shuddered, fear of the greater demon sapping his strength. He could not fight. Instead, he watched the battle unfold below as he was dragged through the air towards Carmedrak Rock. Dragged over a battle where the Shadow Demons were being slaughtered, towards a balcony where a hideous pale-faced demonic wizard stood grinning.

In a great iron cage behind the hated demon wizard was the spear, Velistor, shining so bright and so horrific Gedrock could not look at it. Above the cage perched the raven. Everything he feared had come to pass. The Shadow Demons were doomed. The Murk was lost.

CHAPTER 6

The Elders' Visions

MARAKON found Tarn. Tarn had been looking for him, and he thankfully carried a flagon of jungle spirits, so he called it. It turned out to be a clear, peach-coloured liquid that was more potent than any dwarven spirits Marakon had tasted. It scalded the throat, but after only a few sips Marakon felt his body relaxing. He felt he hadn't relaxed for days, or slept either. But he couldn't sleep now, never this soon after a battle.

The Gurlanka funeral pyre had been built, and now they were beginning to set light to it. People filled the area before it, around the drinking well and reaching to the steps of the Elder's house where Tarn and Marakon sat. No one sobbed loudly. Everyone was sitting or standing silently in deep, reverent thought.

'Did many die?' Marakon asked somberly.

'Yes, more than we have ever lost before,' Tarn said briefly. 'But no children, though some children now have no parents. They will be well looked after by everyone.'

'I'm sorry.'

Tarn looked at the ground. 'This is an old enemy, but they keep us strong. Our warriors have gone to the One Light, there's no shame in that,' he said the last proudly although his lips trembled.

'I had wondered at the quietness of your mourning,' Marakon admitted. There had been no sobbing wails, or inconsolable people amongst the Gurlanka, only a shared solemn silence. 'But I agree. When people said my father should leave the army and war behind, and live to a good old age, he used to say, "Better to die on the battlefield than to die an old man in bed." I have never found a reason to disagree with him. I have lost so many friends I find it hard to mourn anymore. I think I pity myself more for not having fallen.'

Tarn smiled, his eyes glistening with tears that did not fall.

'Is she your partner?' Marakon asked, indicating behind him to the Elder's house where Jarlain still slept.

'No, she's my older sister. Half-sister, we have the same mother. Her father was killed by Seadevils before she was born.'

'Ah, you seemed alike,' Marakon nodded.

'She likes you,' Tarn grinned. Marakon simply smiled back sheepishly. Knowing that pleased him.

Two of the Elders, the deaf High Elder he'd nicknamed Red Beard and a woman, joined them. The High Elder spoke.

'You fought bravely and selflessly today, half-elven. You did not have to help, but you did even after the horrors you faced in the Drowning Wastes. We thank you. You and your knights are always welcome as equals among us,' he said spreading his arms wide to include the other knights.

Marakon stood up. 'It is my duty,' he said. Even though the man was deaf, he could lip read and understand what was said in other ways. Something which Marakon marvelled at.

'The Seadevils took many from me before I arrived here. It was an honour to fight them alongside the Gurlanka,' he bowed slightly to the High Elder.

The female Elder smiled and said, 'There are things we need to speak on, Marakon half-elven. If you have time now, the sooner, the better for we know you will soon leave us.'

Marakon raised an eyebrow, how could they know he planned to leave?

'I have time,' he said. He'd given up trying to work out how they always seemed to know so much about him. Whoever these Hidden Ones were that they spoke to, they knew about a lot of things. She inclined her head and led him inside the house via another door that bypassed the sick and wounded.

Marakon followed the Elders up a winding wooden staircase until they came to the top floor. A large open room stretched out in front of them. There were no windows or doors, just thick wooden posts supporting the roof and a waist high protective handrail all the way around.

The climate was so warm that the Gurlanka did not need to shut out the weather, and welcomed the constant sea breeze. Huge purple flowers wound themselves around the supporting posts and balcony, scenting the breeze with their sweet fragrance.

The floor was made of orange wood polished to a high shine. The house was no different to the other Gurlanka houses in material, just bigger and of a slightly different layout.

A small pot atop a metal tripod under which a flame flickered stood to one corner of the room. From it steamed a delicate scent of incense that Marakon did not recognise. It mingled pleasantly with the smell of the purple flowers.

The other Elders came up the stairs, nodded respectfully to Marakon, then sat cross-legged in a circle in the centre of the room. He admired their flexibility despite their age. Red Beard motioned him to join them and together they sat in the circle. His stomach rumbled. He'd already had plenty of bread and soup but his hunger was insatiable today. He hoped they couldn't hear it.

They sat quietly in the circle. The minutes ticked by, but still, they sat, their breathing slowed, their eyes focusing in front of them but seeing nothing. He tried not to fidget and wondered if they were somehow communing silently. He never sat still and hated being alone too long with his thoughts, or at least he used to. Now he understood who he was better, sitting still with his thoughts didn't seem as bad, as long as they didn't turn into memories. He couldn't cope with memories. One of the Elder women spoke.

'We have seen in our future a sky without stars, a world without hope. You could say that we have seen in our future no future at all. Nothing. Have you seen our future, Marakon?'

'No,' he replied.

They were silent at that. They all began to hold hands and when Red Beard and the woman beside him reached for his, he tentatively took them.

'Then close your eyes and see,' she said.

He frowned and closed his eyes. What was it they were going to do? He was quite astonished. Behind his lids blackness stretched out around him. Not the enclosed dark that was normally there when he shut his eyes. No, this darkness was expansive, a huge open space of endless nothingness.

'I see nothing,' he breathed, taken aback by what they were somehow able to show him.

'And then in the darkness, a light grows...' she whispered.

Indeed, in Marakon's vision, he saw an indigo orb appear as a speck of light. Then it either grew bigger, or it was coming closer, for its soft blue light was expanding. Slowly that light revealed the gentle contours of desert sands under a night sky filled with stars. Everything was bathed in soft indigo light.

A huge glistening trilithon stood in the centre of the desert, so alone and out of place. Then a robed figure formed before the doorway created by the three stones. Her face was hidden in a hood, the swathes of her robe moved gently in the breeze. He had a strange longing to go and stand beside her, to be in her presence.

'... And she appears...' the Elder said, her voice tinged with wonder. 'She beckons to us.'

Sure enough, the robed figure lifted a slender luminous hand and beckoned to him. He started towards her and strained to see within the folds of her hood, but all he could make out was a smooth pale chin and perfect lips.

'... Then she is gone...'

The vision ended abruptly. He opened his eyes, blinking.

'Do you know what this means, half-elven?' the Elder woman asked, her clear brown eyes looked into his.

He shook his head. 'I have never seen this. I have never even seen a place like this in the Old World.' He wondered what it could mean for a moment and then spoke his ponderings aloud.

'Before I came here I met a man cursed to row a boat for eternity. He asked me whom I served, and I knew then when I had never known before that I had come to serve Zanufey the Night Goddess. I still don't know why I told him that, only that I know it is true. Since then her messenger the raven has often been with us. All I can say is that I think she is Zanufey, and I think she is calling you, but for what I don't know.'

The Elder woman smiled. 'Yes, that is indeed what we think. And that is what the Hidden Ones say. Zanu calls us. But why? We do not know either.'

'All I can say for certain is that Baelthrom and his Maphraxies are coming to every corner of Maioria, the Known World and the Unknown,' Marakon said, and leaned forwards. 'I think that is why Zanufey is calling to all those who would help.'

'Have you seen this... Baelthrom?' the High Elder asked.

Marakon shook his head. 'Few have seen him. But all know what he looks like because some of his horde take a likeness to his form. They are called Dromoorai, and they ride atop Dread Dragons.'

He closed his eyes as memory, of that last day with Bokaard flooded back to him. The screams of the Dread Dragons made his heart shudder now as it did then. The hands holding his clenched and sharp intakes of breath echoed around him. *They can see what I see?* He blinked open his eyes, everyone else had theirs shut so he closed them again.

'Yes,' several Elders answered his unspoken thought aloud, further shocking him. 'When we are joined like this and the memory is vivid, we can see what each other sees,' a strained voice said.

'Evil, greater even than that which destroyed our ancestral home, Unafay, moves upon Maioria,' the High Elder said. 'I see again our utter annihilation. Maioria will be no more, just as Unafay is no more. This is why the future is dark.'

Marakon half opened his eyes, saw the sorrow and anguish upon the faces of those around him. 'Yes. That's why I fight. It's all I can do. I wish I could tell you they will not come here, but that isn't true.' He closed his eyes again, not wanting to see their pain.

A black helmeted face flickered in his mind and his white eye burned behind its patch, making him gasp in pain. The eyes of Baelthrom were completely white as they glared at him from behind triangle slits. Fear grabbed hold of Marakon's gut and clenched painfully. He was dimly aware of the gasps of terror around him. He clamped his hand over his white eye and gritted his teeth. Sometimes it did this, burned with pain as fierce as when he got the wound, and always he wanted to claw it out of his face.

'I see him,' a woman's strangled voice said.

Slowly the pain dimmed and he forced his good eye open. The image of Baelthrom went along with the pain. He gulped air into his lungs and wiped the sweat rolling down his forehead.

The Elder woman opened her eyes, her face pale and drawn.

'We must consult with Jarlain every day, and ask her to see with her vision. This enemy is unlike any we've ever known.'

The other Elders murmured their agreement. They looked at the floor in silence, frowns of worry on all their faces. Red Beard spoke and an enigmatic smile spread across the old man's face, replacing his frown.

'The Hidden Ones spoke to me whilst you were in the Drowning Wastes, Marakon half-elven. The goddess moves in mysterious ways, but it seems you and your knights and we the Gurlanka share an ancient bond.'

Marakon frowned and then realisation dawned on him.

'Unafay,' he breathed. Speaking the name aloud with this growing understanding immediately brought a lump to his throat, he blinked through the mist filling his eyes. He remembered a land, a beautiful land of green hills and many lakes, warm summers and mild winters.

'Yes,' Red Beard said, and the others smiled. 'We were very different then. But sometimes, for all our ancestors' great advances, I think we are better now. Here we are more connected to Maioria and the Great Spirit of All than ever we have been. In our dreams, we all share a memory of a bountiful land, and our hearts ache. The Hidden Ones showed me that you were a great leader until the demons came.'

Marakon nodded, his mind drifting in ancient memories.

' "In the Valley of Death terrible things happened," ' he murmured aloud the boatman's words. 'That is why we have returned.'

'Your curse can never be fully lifted until you find the one that cursed you,' an Elder woman said, concern furrowed her brow.

'We will find him,' Marakon said resolutely. 'That is why we have returned.'

'When the demons came, our land was lost,' the High Elder said. Marakon nodded, he remembered that part all too well. 'Their evil destroyed our minds, hearts and bodies in ways only demons know how. The land was poisoned and turned against us. Those of us who survived fled west across the sea. There we became one with the small groups of people we had once traded with.

'Now the peoples of Unafay survive along the coast of this new land where food is abundant, and we spread as far to the north as one can go. We, the Gurlanka, are the most southerly of the tribes. Here we came and here we remain to this day.'

'Then you must warn the other tribes.' Marakon leaned forward and wrung his hands. 'Tell them there's a threat more deadly than all the Seadevils combined. An enemy more dangerous than the demons who destroyed Unafay. You must try to unite yourselves into one people. There's greater safety in numbers.'

'Yes, he's right,' one of the other Elder men said. 'It will take time but the half-elf warrior speaks wisely.'

'We must plan and plan now,' Red Beard nodded. 'But first know this, Marakon half-elf from the Old World. The Hidden Ones have told us that whatever has cursed you has cursed you well. Even now you bring danger even as you bring honour and justice. Until you are truly free, wherever you tread so too does danger. Be watchful and never let your guard down.'

Without another word they all began to rise and leave. Red Beard gripped his arm, stared into his eye and nodded, then followed the other Elders down the stairs. Marakon had the strangest feeling he would never see the wise old High Elder again, and that Red Beard knew this.

He followed the Elders down the stairs, helped himself to another bowl of soup and bread, and went outside into the open air, weariness settling once again in his heart.

CHAPTER 7

The Daily Brawl

THE square was a large courtyard about one hundred and fifty feet square. It was already filled and being filled further with colourful marquees, stalls and canopies selling all types of wares from food and spices, to gifts and exotic pets, wine, cider and beer, and a vast array of cloth and styles of clothing.

Issa immediately went to the first stall, dropping Duskar's harness and reaching covetously for a swathe of deep indigo silk.

'It's from Atalanph, Missy, the finest silk around. Make you look pretty,' a bent over, half-toothless woman crooned from inside the stall.

'It sure is beautiful,' Issa said stroking it.

'Usually three gold a yard but you can have a yard for two,' the old woman said.

Issa gulped. She doubted she even had that much in her pouch.

Asaph came over and took hold of her arm.

'When we're rich you can have all the Atalanph silk in the land. But not now,' he said quietly but firmly and steered her away from the stall. 'We need to eat first, shop later.'

Issa nodded in morose silence, ' "When we're rich," ' she repeated emotionlessly. The last nice piece of clothing she'd owned was that beautiful dress Ely had given her. She drove back a pang of sadness. Coronos gave her a half smile as he handed back Duskar's rope.

'Can't we magic up some gold?' Issa asked him.

He laughed. 'No alchemist in the land has ever been able to create gold or silver, and they have been trying since the dawn of time.'

Issa sighed and stared longingly back at the indigo cloth. Surely turning one thing into something else, like lead into gold, would be easy for a wizard. Isn't that what magic was for anyway? They'd be richer than kings if they could, but they didn't seem so rich, so she guessed they couldn't.

The smell of fresh baked bread wafted over to her and her stomach rumbled. She forgot about gold and being rich and moved towards the pastry stall, the others following close behind, hungry looks on both their faces.

'I've enough for a few meals and comfortable beds for all three of us tonight. If we can strike a bargain we can get horses and some clean clothes,' Coronos said reaching into his pockets. 'But after that, we'll need to go elsewhere for funds,' he finished with a frown.

'I have a little from my savings, though I've no idea how far it will stretch,' Issa said, also frowning. 'If we need money, I can earn some by healing horses or other sick animals and pets. Though we would need to stay in a town for a few days to find business.' She wasn't overly concerned with money, what she had would keep her going if she spent it carefully, and her healing skills were always much sought after.

'I have nothing. The Kuapoh don't use money, and I'm sure they are right,' Asaph said with a sigh. Issa raised an eyebrow and tried to imagine never needing money or needing to buy anything either.

'It has been a long time, but if the King of Frayon is still alive he will have kept my treasury,' Coronos said.

Asaph and Issa both looked at him, wide-eyed. He held up his hands. 'It's not much, but I was careful to never keep all my savings in one place, especially since I travelled so far to see Hari, and especially not with the Maphraxies attacking Drax. King Thaban and I were good friends, and I pray he still lives.' Coronos turned back to the pastries and licked his lips.

Issa forgot her stomach and thought about Ely's mother. She stroked the silver leaf bracelet on her wrist and recalled Harianna's face. She had seen her so briefly when Ely had given her the bracelet. *She made this, a healer's bracelet. Did she know I would one day wear it? Did she know of her own daughter's demise.*

'Issa?' Asaph said and stroked her arm. She looked up. 'What would you like?' he repeated. She turned her attention back to the pastries and forced the memories of Ely and her mother away. Coronos was smiling at her, a hint of poorly concealed pain in his eyes.

'I'll have what you're having,' she said with a shrug.

She'd lost her appetite, but as soon as she started eating it came back again. The pastries were delicious—soft on the inside, but flaky on the outside, spicy and sweet and very filling. She struggled to finish her own and couldn't believe it when Asaph went back for another. Afterwards, they began to hunt for the cheaper clothes' stalls.

'Hey, you there. You with that black horse,' a man yelled from somewhere.

Issa froze as a guard pushed through the crowd towards them. His domed helmet and nose-guard concealed most of his face, but his eyes were hard and thin lips set. Her heart began to pound. He knew she had a sword, maybe even the orbs too.

'You can't drag a horse through here. No one wants horse shit in the market area. If you are selling livestock, you need to be in the opposite quarter. If you are not selling then horses should be tied up in the stables by the South Gate,' the guard scowled.

'Yes, sir. Sorry sir,' Issa said meekly. Relief washing over her.

The guard turned away shaking his head and disappeared into the crowd.

'Phew,' Asaph said. Issa sighed and nodded.

They took their packs off Duskar's back, and she took him to the stables, grabbing a nosebag of oats for him on the way.

She reluctantly took him into a crowded stable. What if he kicked or bit the other horses? She'd be in trouble if he hurt a stable boy. She spied an empty one right at the end and took him to it. With his nosebag on he didn't seem to be too fussed about the other horses, although he did try to follow her when she turned to go.

'Stay, Duskar,' she said and ruffled his forelock. She chewed her lip. She was so used to him being there that she didn't want to be without him. A stable boy came running over.

'Yes miss, that stable is free,' he said panting. A man yelled from somewhere. 'I'll be right there,' the boy yelled back.

'I hate market days,' he said and wiped the sweat from his forehead. Issa grinned. He looked up at Duskar

'He doesn't like anybody but me,' Issa warned the boy. He and Duskar eyed each other warily.

'Yes, miss,' he said nervously but smiled when she gave him a copper coin.

Duskar would be all right, she convinced herself. It would do him good to be around other horses and he couldn't always be at her side.

On her way back to find the others she passed a stall selling cotton and linen clothing at a price far cheaper than she had seen in Kammam. After a quick look, she bought a sleeveless tunic dress that came to her knees. It was similar to what many South Frayon women were wearing, simple and light for the hot weather. She picked out a long-sleeved cotton cardigan of a similar length in pale blue. It would do for the cooler nights.

Her leather boots were still good and best for riding, but her feet were hot and sweaty all the time. She picked up a plain pair of sandals and put them on immediately. The ageing stall owner took a shine to her, and with a smile back at him she got the lot for a few pennies less. She left with a hearty "thank you," and hunted for the others.

Pushing through all the people was exhausting, but she eventually found them at a large armour stall. Asaph finished putting on his new brown boots and smiled approvingly at her sandals.

'I've had these old things for ten years.' He waggled his ripped and worn boots of a strange Kuapoh design. 'And now I have some armour too.' he proudly showed her his metal-studded gambeson and thick, similarly studded, sword belt.

'Frayon Highland Leather, it is the best in all known Maioria,' the merchant said from behind the counter. He smoothed his long black moustache and continued to extoll the virtues of Highland Leather without pausing for breath, eager to make a sale. Asaph added a pair of half-price, second-hand vambraces. Coronos paid the man, and they left before he could talk anymore.

Outside, Coronos showed her his new linen shirt and a cloak of soft grey wool. They had purchased nearly everything they needed apart from horses, dinner and a good bed for the night.

'I can't wait to wash and put on clean clothes,' Issa said, itching to be in her new clothes. When it was this hot she didn't mind wearing a dress. 'A steaming bath, soft bed and hot chocolate,' she added dreamily.

The others laughed.

'I don't think turning up at the mayor's place dressed like peasants would go down too well,' Coronos mused. 'And besides, it's getting late in the day. By the time we find a suitable inn it'll be dinner time. Let's go at first light tomorrow morning. Maybe the innkeeper, or the mayor himself, will know where we can find horses at a fair price.'

'The cobbler said the inns were better closer to the castle,' Asaph said.

They turned and headed up a wide cobbled path in the castle's direction. The crowd was thinning now and some marketers were beginning to pack away their wares.

'A present for you,' Asaph said as they walked, and passed her a pair of dark studded vambraces. 'From a stall selling sword training armour. I think they are for a youth and they are not Highland Leather but they're still good and strong. I couldn't find any in your size but these,' he explained.

'A present for me?' Issa grinned and took the vambraces. She never thought to buy armour. She pulled them on. They fit but were stiff and hot. 'Good in a sword fight but too hot for now.'

'They'll loosen up and flex with age,' Asaph said.

She smiled at him. 'Thanks, but I have nothing to give you.' She didn't even think to buy anyone a present, but now she thought of it she wondered what on Maioria she could have bought him. She would try to get him something another time.

'I don't need anything other than a wash… and a bed with you in it,' he grinned.

'How can you say that?' she yelped, feeling her cheeks flush. She hoped him buying her presents wasn't just to get her in bed. She glanced at him, but there was only genuine humour in his eyes.

Coronos pretended not to hear them, but she saw a grin spreading across his tired face. Seeing his frown disappear, however briefly, was enough to make her smile. He'd been frowning since they'd left Celene and she worried for him.

They headed to the north of the city, away from the market and towards the permanent shops and inns that lined the city walls.

' "The Corsolon", ' Issa said, reading aloud the peeling sign of the imaginatively named tavern. They all peered inside the darkened doorway, but the dirty glass door revealed nothing except a muddy reflection of themselves.

'Looks as good as any other,' Asaph shrugged. Coronos raised a sceptical eyebrow. 'Let's check it out,' the younger man said, intrigued. He stepped up the stone stairs and strode confidently inside. She followed him which much less confidence.

Blinking in the darkness from the brightness of day, the only thing that greeted her was noise. Lots of it. Angry shouts were followed by the sound of smashing glass and something heavy falling on wooden flooring. A strong hand grabbed Issa's arm and yanked her to the side as a chair came hurtling past where she had just been standing.

Issa blinked into Asaph's shocked face, her eyes finally adjusting to the dark. She glanced around at the mayhem. Two tavern girls were crouched behind a glass-covered, beer-soaked bar as the brawl continued in full sway. The stocky bar owner was busy in a fight against somebody she couldn't see because a table turned on its side blocked her view.

The tavern was filled with men and there were no women to be seen, apart from the hiding tavern girls. Many men were dressed similarly in simple cream shirts, caps and neckties, marking them out as sailors.

Others looked to be farmers or locals or both, and all of them were drunk and fully absorbed in the fight. There were tables and chairs everywhere, and many were smashed. Food and alcohol littered the floor making it incredibly slippery. A sailor and a mean looking man slipped over and came crashing to the floor beside them.

'Let's go,' Asaph said.

'Uh huh,' Issa agreed, letting him steer her protectively out of the door. They stood outside blinking in the sunlight.

Coronos was already there waiting patiently. He raised an eyebrow. 'A glance through the door should always suffice to tell you where the daily brawl is.'

Asaph coughed. 'You could have warned us.'

'It is better you learn the ways of the Old World for yourself,' Coronos gave a wicked grin. 'Let's take a side street off the main road. Maybe we'll find a quieter more respectable place. They took a small cobbled road leading east through a quieter part of the city. After a wiggle through old and precariously leaning houses, they came to a smaller tavern called The Goat Underwater.

'Sounds ominous,' Issa mused.

Coronos grinned at her and reached for the iron door handle. It turned with a screech and he peered inside. After a moment he looked back at them.

'Looks more our thing, and they even have South Frayon ale. I've not had that for over twenty-five years,' he grinned and looked ten years younger.

Issa and Asaph looked at each other, then followed him inside.

'Come in, come in. We have fresh ale and good food for all,' the jolly bar woman beckoned and greeted them with a big smile. She was short, fat and her light brown hair was tied back, although most of it was coming free in straggles that framed her shining red face. She smelt of wine, hence the red face, Issa thought.

There was a sunlit doorway on the other side of the bar, suggesting a beer garden and making it a lot less gloomy than the other tavern. Issa felt herself relaxing and heard Asaph give a small sigh of relief. There was only one other person there, a skinny old man bent heavily over his pint at the bar. He glanced at them, looked them up and down, then turned disinterestedly back to his pint. Perhaps the sour, partially drunk look on his face might be why the bar woman was eager for more patrons.

'Ah my dears,' she said in a soft Southern Frayon accent. 'Come eat, drink, there's plenty of space here or out in the garden, and it's a wonderful day for sitting outside. Food and drink to be had by all?' she gushed.

'Actually, we need a place to stay for the night, as well as food and drink,' Asaph said.

The woman's smile deepened. 'Well, we have only one room left tonight, if you don't mind sharing. Though I'm not sure it will be to your liking as there are only two small beds.

Asaph thought about it for a moment then glanced slyly at Issa who refused to meet his gaze.

Coronos gave a brief nod and said, 'We'll take it and make up a third bed with cushions and our clothes.'

'Splendid,' said the woman clapping her hands. 'Now take a seat in the garden and I'll bring food and drinks.'

A short time later Coronos was smiling down into his rich, orange-coloured South Frayon ale, whilst Issa and Asaph were enjoying a flagon of Corsolon wine. The wine was cold, sweet and refreshing as they sat under a frayed canopy, partially protecting them from the hot afternoon sun.

The garden was more of a paved area with a few rather sad dried up potted plants that had died a long time ago. Prickly cacti weeds with bright pink flowers pushed up between the paved stones, and she thought they actually brightened up the rundown place.

Lunch was a simple, but enjoyable salad of tomatoes, cheese, eggs, pickles and plenty of bread. Afterwards she stretched her back and yawned.

'Finally, a sit down on a proper chair, if you can call it that.' The rickety bench they shared creaked alarmingly as she wiggled. Coronos nodded in agreement and Asaph joined her yawning.

The wind had dropped and it was getting hotter. She pulled off her hot tunic. It caught on her undershirt as she did so and pulled down the front just enough to reveal the raven mark.

'What's that? You've hurt yourself,' Asaph noticed immediately, setting down his glass.

She pulled her shirt closed. 'It's nothing. Just a bruise.'

She'd been mulling over whether to tell them about the mark for days, but she really didn't feel talking about it right now. All she wanted was to have a normal few days enjoying a new city and forgetting anything bad had ever happened in her life. For the past few hours, she'd begun to feel like her old self again. She'd begun to feel like Issalena Kammy rather than the Raven Queen she was supposed to be.

'Let me look at it. Does it hurt?' He reached over to her and tried to see, but she pulled away grasping her shirt between her breasts.

'Please,' she said, louder than she meant to.

He pulled away, embarrassed as well. 'Sorry, I didn't mean to…' he let it trail off, whatever he was going to say. She could tell from his frown that he was caught between wanting to help and letting her be.

'The mark of the raven, if I'm not mistaken,' Coronos said as he filled his pipe with lintel weed. Issa looked at him, despite his age he had sharp eyes. 'Freydel would know more about that, but there are some things I've heard about. When did it happen?' he looked at her and smiled reassuringly at her worried look.

She released her grasp on her top and smoothed the crinkles.

'It happened after I returned the dagger to Karshur,' she began. 'I wanted to talk about it, but everything's happened so quickly since then. I told you about the dagger, and when Karshur took me to the Land of Mists, but I did not mention the gift. I didn't understand it, I still don't. Karshur's task was done, and in doing it he gave me a gift before he departed. A mark that is a raven,' she hesitated, wondering how to explain.

'Alongside Keteth's gift, the mark is a spell that allows me to physically go into the land of the dead instantly and return. I think there's more to it,' she added, remembering her abrupt return from the Murk. 'I didn't want these gifts, and don't want to use them, but it saved my life on Celene. It seems that ravens also have this gift, to move between the worlds.'

'Ravens can travel between the living and the dead,' Coronos nodded. 'A gift such as that will have hidden blessings I'm sure.'

'There's something else that happened, maybe the Karalanths told you,' she said, wondering if she should talk about it. She wanted to share the strange things that happened to her and didn't want to shoulder them alone.

'It's a bit like when Asaph becomes a dragon. When the foltoy attacked us in the forest, I somehow transformed into a raven to escape them. I'm not quite sure how it happens but I'm almost certain Karshur's gift, the raven mark, has something to do with it.' There, she'd said it now, and she went silent to see what their reaction would be.

She was relieved to see only looks of mild surprise on their faces, then annoyed—surely transforming into a raven was no small thing. She looked into her glass and drained the rest of the wine.

'There's far more to this world than even I can imagine,' Coronos said, shaking his head with a smile, 'and here I sit with two shapeshifters. You two really are becoming quite something.'

'As long as it doesn't hurt, I'm sure the mark is quite becoming,' Asaph grinned at her. His dimples made her blush. 'Maybe one day we could fly together.'

'I'd like that,' Issa smiled.

They finished their drinks as the evening drew on and the late summer sun faded.

'Let's get an early night,' Coronos advised, 'and hopefully see the mayor first thing before anybody else.'

They both nodded, already stifling yawns as it was.

CHAPTER 8

Beneath Doon's Light

'WE thought you were dead,' Shufen said, sipping his steaming soup as they sat outside the Elder's house. The light of the pyre illuminated those gathered there now that the sun had fully set.

'I was gone at most half a day. Possibly the worst half a day of my life,' Marakon said, gripping his mug between his hands.

'You were gone no less than a week, my friend,' Shufen shook his head. Marakon started at his words.

Shufen continued without noticing. 'We waited for nearly as long. I thought you were already dead but Jarlain did not believe it. Then she had a vision of you returning on shining horses that moved faster than the wind. Then she saw the Seadevils coming. If she hadn't had that vision, we wouldn't have been at all prepared for this attack. Thank the goddess you came, there were so many of them.'

'A whole week?' Marakon replied incredulously.

Shufen nodded. 'I warned you about that awful place, time moves funny there. What did you see?'

'I saw myself, of what I was many lifetimes ago. I'd never really thought about past lives, or if they were even real.'

'They're real all right,' Shufen nodded, eyes wide.

'Indeed. And now my knights of yesteryear, who died forgotten and alone and cursed to wander the Drowning Wastes as wraiths, have returned. Their curse has been lifted so that we may right a wrong and finish what we started.' Shufen looked at him with raised eyebrows.

'We must destroy the one that cursed us,' Marakon shrugged. 'How long I've wanted to be free of the darkness surrounding my days,' he shook his head. The memory of the ordeal in the Drowning Wastes, of the demon wizard Karhlusus, and of his past lives made him pale.

'Seeing you all fight…' Shufen voice broke his thoughts. 'I think you have powers beyond mortal men and women. I think the goddess has blessed you in spite of your curse. And now you have your first victory.'

Marakon smiled. 'The first of many.'

' "The first of …" what, did you say?' Jarlain's voice came from behind. She smiled down at them.

Marakon jumped up, surprised to see her up so soon when surely she should be lying down. She had washed and changed into clean clothes, but she looked pale and exhausted. Before he could stop himself he embraced her. She hugged him back, she felt weak. Her hair smelt of flowers and he found it quite intoxicating.

'I'll go see how my father is doing,' Shufen said and left.

'The first of many victories,' Marakon said huskily and drew back. 'Your stone, the one with the bear, it brought me back. It reminded me of the real world, of you.'

She said nothing, only smiled. 'I'm so glad you returned.' Tears glistened in her eyes.

'You should not be up. You were hurt badly,' he said.

She nodded. 'Yes, I lost lots of blood, but the Elders are learned and skilled. The bleeding has stopped, though it will take time to heal fully. Movement can help, and I was getting sore from lying down. I could sleep no longer.' He embraced her again and felt her sag weakly in his arms.

'Let's sit,' he said hastily, and helped her sit beside him, she leant most her weight on him. 'We should take you back to bed.'

'No.' She shook her head. 'I want to stay here with you.'

He stroked back a lock of her hair, noticed the smooth curve of her cheek in the light coming from the Elder's house. 'I cannot stay,' he said.

'I know,' she said without looking at him. 'That's why I don't want to go back to bed. I don't want to be alone.'

'I have a wife and children,' he began. Perhaps she knew already. A flicker of pain passed across her features. 'And I must return to them. I miss them and my home.

'The goddess calls us and we cannot ignore that call. I never really thought about the goddess much. I thought like most think, that she, in all her guises, had abandoned us to our fate. But now the dark moon of Zanufey rises, and because of it, because of her, my curse has been lifted so that I might right a terrible wrong I committed. I have to set my knights free for good.'

He said these things, the truth, and yet all he wanted to do was to stay here with Jarlain and the Gurlanka. Set down his sword and heal his warrior spirit once and for all.

'Tell me what you did. It's time to hear it all, I'm not afraid and I won't judge. I know you for who you really are. Who we were in the past is not who we are today,' Jarlain said.

Marakon looked at her and sighed. He didn't want to talk about it, but they had to know, she had to know. He finished his mug of spirits and stared at the burning pyre. Where to begin? The memories of that far away time rolled through his mind, and they were as clear as if it had all happened yesterday.

'A long time ago, I'm not sure how far back, but it was during the Demon Wars over three thousand years ago when I was king of the ancient sunken land of Unafay.' Jarlain leaned back to stare at him, disbelief in her eyes.

Marakon smiled. 'I'm not lying. It was your High Elder who revealed that part to me just a few hours ago.'

Jarlain looked away and curled closer into him as he spoke. He told her everything that he remembered; of his honourable knights and their battles against the demons, of his rise to power and greed for more, of being tricked by Karhlusus and slaughtering hundreds of innocent people. He told her as quickly as he could, thinking that if he spoke fast, the emotions would have no time to break through. She did not say a word, even for a long time after he'd finished. Eventually, she broke the silence.

'I wish I was cursed with you, like one of your knights,' she replied, jutting her chin forward and pursing her lips.

'No, you do not,' he said, shaking his head. His voice was hoarse from all the talking. He didn't want to think about the past anymore. 'I will miss you, terribly, and want you to come with me.'

She looked at the ground. 'My duty is here with my people. I must help rebuild our home and lives and heal the pain of those left behind.

One day I will become an Elder. And, if it is right and appropriate and the Hidden Ones speak to me, I will become the High Elder. I can take no husband.'

'I don't want you to have your ears broken,' Marakon scowled.

She shrugged. 'For the good of all, I would. But they say I already have a special gift, the gift of foresight, and if it is through that that the Hidden Ones will speak to me, then my ears need not be stilled.' Marakon felt a little relieved at that.

'Does it annoy you when they call you half-elven?' she asked, changing the subject.

'Yes,' Marakon said. She giggled.

'I like the sound of it, though, they seem brave and beautiful,' she said, looking at Ghenath as she sat talking with Cormak a few yards away. She was dressed in linens like the Gurlanka and her long hair shone gold in the firelight.

Marakon snorted. 'Beautiful, yes. But most turned out to be cowards. And a few,' he nodded towards Ghenath, 'are the best people I have ever had the honour to fight beside.'

Jarlain looked at him as if pondering something. 'I see the war within you. You are probably the strangest man I've ever met, able to see clearly the worst in people, but also the best. You are strong in many ways, but carry a painful past, and yet you fight so fearlessly and ferociously. After so many tortured lifetimes, and remembering them, I doubt I would have the strength nor the will to carry on.'

'I have no choice but to carry on,' he shrugged. He held her close, and they sat in silence, listening to the sound of the people talking before the pyre, the moans of the wounded behind them inside the Elder's house, and the sound of the sea in the distance breaking on the shore.

'When will you go?' she asked.

'Soon. We have already stayed too long. As soon as Hylion, Lan and everyone else has rested.'

'How will you go?'

'The same way I came. The boatman, Murlonius. I just have to call him, he is waiting for me. He too is cursed. He can never set foot upon mortal physical shores again, though that is all I know of it. I think he is ancient. An Ancient, even.'

'I would like to meet him. In this world, there's nothing but pain, sadness and loss.' Jarlain shook her head. 'I wish that Seadevil had killed me.'

Her eyes fill with tears. He bent to kiss her cheek, wanting to kiss away her tears, but instead he found her lips. She parted them and he kissed her. He kissed her harder, feeling her own need match his. She gave the softest moan with her eyes closed. His heart was pounding, his own desire surprised him. He should not want her the way he did, not when Rasia was waiting for him with his children, for spirit's sake. Was it possible to love two people equally? He drew away reluctantly.

'Take me into the trees,' she breathed.

He looked down at her. Her brown eyes stared unblinking up at him. He would leave soon, never to return. Could he deny her? Could he deny himself and forever wonder? Gently he picked her up and carried her into the dense jungle. Soon he would leave her forever, and that awful thought drove his actions and drowned out the voice of guilt.

Marakon stopped in a sandy clearing within the trees. The sea was only a few yards away, and the ocean lapped at the shore.

Rasia would like it here, he thought with a half smile. The white beaches and tall palm trees would remind her of her childhood home on the coasts of South Frayon. She would want to swim naked in the moonlight, her long copper curls floating out around her. He loved Rasia but he couldn't deny his feelings for Jarlain. He felt bad and confused.

He set her down on her feet and held her close. She looked up at him, tears filling her eyes once more, and he bent to kiss her, long and gentle. He could hold her and kiss her and enjoy these last moments together. Nothing more. Then he would be back in Rasia's arms with their sons running around them, where he belonged.

He pulled back, guilt and desire battling within him. *It is only a kiss,* he told himself, though he wanted more. It had been so long, months too long. He felt torn in his stomach.

After a moment, he pushed the guilt away and bent to kiss her with certainty. She drew him down to the floor smiling, making the tears curve around her cheeks. She lay down, her long dark hair spread out around her.

'You should have a husband, many will love you,' he said, stroking her stomach.

'I don't want one,' she shook her head. 'Children, maybe. Lovers, yes. But a husband, no, and it's forbidden for an Elder anyway. The only husband I would have is you.' She trailed her fingers up his bare arms as she spoke making his skin tingle.

He sighed at her words, trying not to think of his own family, wanting only these moments with Jarlain. The white light of Doon spilled through the clouds then, illuminating everything. He took her trailing hands and kissed them. She pulled his own hands down to stroke the soft skin of her thighs through the fold of her skirt. He let her take control as if by doing so it would somehow quell his guilt.

She undid his shirt and he let it fall free as he stroked her smooth skin, wanting to feel every part of her. She slipped off her own shirt, and his breath caught in his throat as Doon's light spilled over her full breasts and slender stomach. The moonlight shone like silver on her shapely body. He felt he should not be allowed to touch something so beautiful, and for a moment he hesitated. But when she drew his hands to her breasts he could not resist either, and it was then that desire flooded into him fully. He kissed her and fumbled for the cords of her skirt, letting it fall away. He touched the bandages of her leg where she'd suffered a knife wound.

'I don't want to hurt you,' he said pulling back, his voice deep with desire as she kissed and nibbled on his lip.

'You won't,' she reassured, and laid back down drawing him with her.

'Jarlain,' he breathed, as she pushed down his trousers and gripped his buttocks firmly.

He stroked her from her hips to her stomach to her breasts, feeling her skin turn to goose pimples in delight as he felt every curve. She gave a moan and he could delay no longer. He laid himself firmly against the inside of her good thigh as she shifted her legs apart. Gently but firmly he pushed into her, making her gasp.

With each gentle thrust, she pulled him deeper, and he felt as if a lifetime of tension was slowly being released. He began to lose himself then, falling into the excitement of desire as he made love to Jarlain. He was himself fully, but drifting in a sea of ecstasy. He wondered if she felt the same as she arched her back, half closed her eyes and moaned.

She tightened herself around him, and his bliss reached a new level. It had never happened before when he made love, this losing of the self, but with Jarlain something seemed perfect, divine.

They moved together and all else fell away, the sound of the sea, the light of the moon, there was only this moment of ecstasy stretching out into eternity. The world may very well have not existed.

He felt himself rushing towards something then, like a light in the distance coming closer at increasing speed. He felt her wetness flooding over him, felt her spread her legs wider and push him deeper. She groaned from far away. He felt her spasm and that sent him reeling. The light rushed over him as he heard himself gasping, equally from far away. His whole being seemed to disintegrate even though he felt his physical body thrusting of its own accord.

A long time seemed to pass as he floated in the light, his spirit free in bliss. *Have I known Jarlain before?* He asked of the light, but all he felt in response was the knowledge that, yes, he had.

He was partially aware of a hand on his cheek and a voice drawing him back. He did not want to return, but he wanted to be with that voice. He took the hand and kissed it, feeling his body return to him once more. Tears ran down his cheeks, the grief of a hundred lifetimes had somehow lifted a little.

He blinked and the jungle around him materialised. He looked down at her, she stared up at him in wonder and maybe a hint of fear.

'Is it always like this?' she breathed, her face and breasts were flushed pink.

He smiled and shook his head. 'No.' He lay down beside her suddenly spent.

'I've never felt like that before,' she breathed and stroked his cheek. He drew her close, laid his chin upon her head, and she curled her arm around him.

'I felt my soul lifting from the emptiness,' he tried to explain. 'I have not felt such release, only in battle, but that is very different.' He didn't know what had happened either, but he felt better than he had for a long time.

'They say a healer can do that when they make love. The energy is shared and healed,' she said, also trying to explain. 'I saw you, a powerful old soul. I felt like a butterfly when compared to a magnificent eagle.'

'Beautiful if not more so,' he said, stroking her hair.

'You took me higher than I ever thought possible. Maybe I helped you heal but you have opened up doorways within me to a higher place,' she said.

He did not quite understand what she meant, but heavy sleep was fast descending. They lay there by the sea in each other's arms until Doon's silver light on their flesh became Feygriene's golden light and the night slowly turned to day.

Marakon lay there for a moment as the dawn light increased, Jarlain curled up under his arm, her hair spilling over his chest. He felt the most content he had in a long time. The last time was when he'd awoken with Rasia in his arms.

Guilt, the pang hit him and was gone again in an instant. His love and desire had not diminished for his wife, he found he loved her more, just as he loved Jarlain beside him.

Yes, he decided, it was possible to love two people, but he doubted two people would share his love.

He held her there for a long moment, then gently kissed her and got up quietly. She did not even stir as he dressed. He decided not to wake her, she needed sleep to heal her injuries and he hated goodbyes, especially when it was forever.

With a lingering look at her, he forced himself to turn away, and walked along the beach to where his knights were gathering.

CHAPTER 9

Friends of King Thaban

HAVING had a hot bath and a good night's sleep, Issa, Asaph and Coronos waited in a stifling reception room outside the ornate wooden doors to the mayor's office. They had been up at dawn and arrived here before anyone else, and yet still they had already been waiting an hour. Two guards stood nearby, overdressed in stately royal-blue uniform and impervious to the heat.

Issa had her hair tied back and was dressed in her new tunic dress, but even that felt hot and uncomfortable. They were all washed and dressed in their new cooler clothes, but Asaph's and Coronos' faces were already covered in a sheen of sweat, and they looked as hot and uncomfortable as she felt.

'Some air in this stuffy place would be nice,' Coronos huffed and tried to open one of the windows. It opened only half an inch. After years of never being opened, dirt and grime had all but sealed it shut. A tiny breeze came through and he sighed in exasperation.

'I can't stand this place,' Asaph whispered. 'Is Castle Draxa like this? Because if it is then my place is back in the tree houses with the Kuapoh, and by Feygriene's fire do I miss that place now.'

'Draxa is not like this. It's not nearly as stuffy or musty,' Coronos said in a raised voice, and poked a heavy, garish curtain with his staff. 'The halls are wide, the ceilings high and the rooms big. Fresh mountain air circulates the city constantly,' Coronos explained casting a scowl at the guards.

A guard glanced at him, sniffed in disdain and turned back to stare at nothing.

'Sounds freezing,' Issa commented. 'I can't stand it here either,' she huffed, wanting to be far away from this place, or at least to stop wasting time sitting here. 'Surely a matter of utmost importance, of impending attack, would have all the bells ringing?' She turned to scowl at the guards. They did not even look at her.

Finally, the doors creaked open and a tall, thin, pale-faced woman walked out. She carried herself pompously and had permanently half lidded eyes.

'The mayor will see you now,' she said magnanimously, glancing down at them through her half open eyes. They all jumped up.

'Finally,' Coronos said under his breath as they were led into the mayor's office.

The office was a mess to the eye. Wooden bookcases lined one wall from floor to ceiling, and books overflowed the shelves. The other was covered in garish gold-framed pictures of various pompous and stately looking people. There was not a bare bit of wall left to ease the menagerie. The room itself was long and at the far end before the huge window was a large mahogany desk, behind which sat the mayor donning his customary cloak and long chains over his shoulders.

The mayor was everything his assistant wasn't; short, fat and red-faced. He puffed on a stubby cigar that only served to make the room even more stuffy and uncomfortable, especially when he hadn't bothered to open the window. There was a glass of something pale red on his desk and a whiff of alcohol in the air. He pushed his glasses back up his fat nose and looked every bit like a pig squinting up at them. Issa tried not to laugh.

He signalled his assistant to close the doors. 'What are these matters of utmost importance? The mention of war?' He stood up and leaned on his desk, eyeing them up and down more thoroughly.

'You may or may not know but the Isle of Celene has fallen to the Maphraxies,' Coronos said, stepping closer. The mayor didn't even flinch at the news. 'And we suspect an attack is imminent upon mainland Frayon.'

There was silence for a moment. Asaph's face shone with sweat and he had a desperate look, like a caged animal frantic to be out in the fresh air.

'We have heard rumours,' the mayor said, and took a sip from his glass. He winced as he swallowed—whatever was in the glass was strong and certainly not water. 'But here we are in South Frayon, not West Frayon. So it is of no worry to us.'

Asaph snorted and the mayor scowled at him. Coronos stepped as close to the desk as possible, his face reddening in anger, his tall Draxian frame towered over the short man.

'We must tell every major town and city about the destruction of Celene and warn them. The Feylint Halanoi stationed in the north must be warned immediately!'

' "We?" Sounds very like me,' the mayor retorted. 'So you want me to raise panic and alarm by sending out warning of a *possible* attack on Frayon? Do you really think you know more than the Feylint Halanoi? With their hundreds of years of experience, do you really think they don't know what is going on? Do you think you know better than all the wizards in the land?'

'Yes I… We do,' Coronos said. 'We have seen first hand the devastation that is left of Celene, and we know the Maphraxies will not stop there. We were lucky to escape with our lives. How they have come so far south should be of grave concern to you. If the Feylint Halanoi knew this they would already have set up a base on the south-west coast, something they have not done.'

'Yes, yes I suppose you are right,' the mayor said thoughtfully, sinking back into his chair.

Coronos sighed, clearly hoping he was getting through to the semi-intoxicated mayor.

'But I will not be responsible for spreading fear and panic across the kingdom,' the mayor continued. 'And neither could I be so arrogant as to warn the army of attack ahead of the king's warning. That could get me killed by the crown. I'm sure you understand.' Coronos began to speak, but the mayor talked over him. 'And besides, Master Wizard Freydel would have already warned us if there was cause for alarm.'

'Freydel is missing,' Issa blurted out. Everyone looked at her.

'And who, my dear, are you,' the mayor breathed nasally, eyeing her up and down in a way that made her skin crawl.

'I'm Freydel's friend, but I haven't seen or heard from him since

Celene was attacked. We are all worried and pray he is still alive,' she finished abruptly as an unexpected choke worked its way up her throat. *Please, Zanufey, make sure he is all right.* The thought of him being dead along with Ely was too much.

The mayor finished his glass noisily. 'Indeed, well, you can keep your prayers for the goddess, for all the good they will do you. Freydel is, of course, a Master Wizard, and no doubt fine.

'But back to the matter at hand. It's an impossibility that a big enough force of Maphraxies could strike with any permanency this far south. I would call Celene a one off, and if the goddess were truly here then her most sacred isle would not have been destroyed, as you say it was. To respect your efforts of bringing me this unfortunate news I will send a carrier pigeon to the king in Carvon, and leave it in his capable hands…'

A "one off"? She couldn't believe what she was hearing.

'That's not enough. We need more warnings sent on faster birds,' Asaph said, stepping beside his father.

The mayor scowled up at the young man, clearly feeling somewhat threatened. 'I've honoured your request, and now I must get on with more pressing business. If you hound me anymore, I'll have you thrown out of the city.'

'But your lives are at risk…' Asaph began, but Coronos laid a restraining arm on his. The mayor gave them a dangerous look and called for his assistant.

'One more small thing,' Coronos said mildly. The mayor sighed and looked up from the papers he'd begun thumbing. 'We shall travel to Carvon, and speak to the king himself. I'm a friend of King Thaban.'

The mayor paled a little then laughed. 'Where have you been for a decade? King Thaban died ten years ago. His son, King Navarr, now rules.'

Coronos looked away for a moment, masking his emotions, then spoke wistfully. 'Ah yes, we have been travelling foreign lands for a long time, and my memory is not what it once was. King Navarr was a promising young lad, my favourite. He'll be a good king, and he will remember his favourite Draxian visitor.'

The mayor paled even more as Coronos continued.

'I shall tell him how you honoured our urgent warning, and how much you care for your people and the protection of the Southern Kingdom.' There was nothing but sincerity on Coronos' face, and Issa marvelled at his diplomacy, wishing she'd had that skill when talking with the elf-king Daranarta.

'Thank you,' the mayor said tightly and cleared his throat.

'But we'll need two horses, fast ones, and some supplies. You'll still need to send carrier pigeons, they will be faster,' Coronos said. The fat man was beginning to sweat now.

'Yes, yes, fine. Geralda, see to it will you?' he said to his assistant lurking at the back of the room.

Issa grinned at the mayor's discomfort. He was clearly keen to get rid of these people who were friends of the old king.

'Oh, is there anything else you would like me to say to the king when we get there?' Coronos added with a sweet smile.

'No, nothing. All is well here,' the mayor all but squeaked.

'Good, well, let's be on our way. Good day, sir,' Coronos smiled, bowed and twirled away from the desk and the sweating man.

Only when they were outside the city's main walls with their new horses and breathing the blessedly fresh morning air did they start laughing.

'It's always good to play that card last,' Coronos said, 'and it has never failed before. As a Draxian, when you live some fifty years more than other people, you can remember grandparents and great grandparents and all the embarrassing mishaps of the past.'

'Were you really a friend of the old king?' Issa asked.

'Yes. And I'd sorely hoped my friend was still alive,' he shook his head. 'This is a problem my parents spoke of that only now am I beginning to understand. When Draxians get old, all non-Draxians who are your friends die so much sooner. It's heart-breaking and often the reason why we keep ourselves to ourselves. Anyway, talking to that half-drunk idiot of a mayor was going nowhere. I always suspected we would have to get to Carvon to spread our warning, but it's a long way even on horses, and I fear we're already too late.

'I could fly,' Asaph said.

Coronos shook his head. 'It's best you stay hidden for now. If people knew another Dragon Lord lived, the news would spread like wildfire, and I don't think it would do you any favours. You would have to travel and land at night, and a day away from the city where there would be no horses to buy. I was also hoping to spread the warning through towns and villages along the way, but I think the mayor is right. I don't want to spread fear and panic in the kingdom, not when I'm unfamiliar with King Navarr.'

'There's no point avoiding raising panic when panic is upon us. The Maphraxies could strike at any moment,' Issa said. 'Don't forget the ravens I sent. They will find any Daluni and tell them about Celene.' She wondered how far they had flown. She could reach them if she tried, especially with the raven talisman that made scrying that much easier.

'Let's hope the Daluni of Frayon are still held in as high esteem as once they were,' Coronos said. 'As you saw back there, belief in the goddess is becoming extinct. People seem to think that everything happens without a purpose and without a reason. What a chaotic, meaningless world they must live in.

'Come, let us start this journey. We'll have to take the main roads for speed. Always be wary of vagabonds or worse.'

The men strapped their packs onto the new horses. Duskar was already carrying her and her stuff. He'd accepted the saddle but refused the bridle until she'd cut off the bit and other unnecessary straps. He didn't like either of the other horses and created as much space between him and them as possible. He would snap his teeth if they got too close, and then sulked when she told him off. She hoped he would warm to them eventually. Surely he missed his friend Izy, Ely's gentle mare that must have shared the same awful fate of the people of Celene.

Issa shivered and turned to watch Asaph struggle with his horse. The new horses were especially fearful of Asaph as if they could smell the dragon within him.

'I don't trust these animals,' Asaph said, eyeing them suspiciously, 'and I much less enjoy riding them.'

Issa laughed. 'They are equally nervous of you. They must sense your dragon self. You need to get to know them better and build up their trust. Then they'll be loyal to you, but not too much.'

'I'd be afraid of me too,' he added and reached to stroke his horse who flicked her head nervously. She was a big palomino mare. After Coronos' horse, the only other animal available in the stables turned out to be the biggest.

Asaph managed to get his foot in the stirrup. The horse walked forwards causing him to hop along too. He gripped the saddle and struggled to get on her back. He grappled for the reins and nearly fell out of the saddle. Issa suppressed a giggle. The horse surprisingly waited patiently as she suffered her inexperienced rider. Issa could tell she was well trained. At the slightest motion from Asaph, she started to trot, her muscles rippling beneath her yellow coat. He managed to pull her to a stop.

'She's a frisky one. Looks like she needs a strong hand,' Coronos noted. 'Draxian horses are bred to be fearless of Dragon Lords. But still, her fear of you will also make her obedient.'

'I spoke to the stable boy about them,' Issa said. 'It helps to know a horse's history if you are to understand them or help them heal. He said she was a war horse but her master sold her when he was injured in battle. No one seemed to want such a spirited and powerful horse, which is why we got a good price for her.'

'So that's why she's called Ironclad,' Asaph shook his head and tried to calm his prancing mount.

Coronos chuckled and mounted his own horse. His horse was exactly the opposite, a calm mild mannered grey stallion.

'Old and docile like myself,' he joked and patted the horse's neck. 'But we're still nimble and quick when we need to be.'

Asaph snorted. 'You're anything but docile. Stubborn more like.'

'We don't need to listen to this nonsense do we, Socks,' Coronos said to his mount and began trotting up the dusty road.

Asaph frowned at her. She laughed.

'He's called Socks because it looks like he's got socks on.' She pointed at the horse's long white legs that abruptly turned into dappled grey over the rest of his body.

She nudged Duskar to follow Socks, and he did so but kept his distance. A moment later Asaph went shooting past them at a canter he could barely control. He pulled up short a few yards ahead, cursing loudly. It was going to be a fun ride, Issa grinned to herself.

They left the city from the North Gate and took the long dusty road leading north. She was very used to riding horses, and it turned out Coronos was well-ridden too. Together they helped Asaph learn the different gaits of his horse. He struggled at first, cursing all the while, but eventually he picked it up. She cheered when he got it right, pleased to see he was a fast learner, it meant the journey would move swiftly.

Inch by inch she managed to move Duskar closer to Socks until they walked side by side but a good two yards apart.

After an hour of riding, they'd settled into a shared pace. Duskar was slowly getting used to the other horses now they had learned not to get too close to him. The horses seemed quite content to trot up rolling hills and canter down the other side. Asaph was either in front or behind, but always just close enough to join in the conversation.

Coronos took out the map he'd sketched from the huge map hanging in the hall of Corsolon Castle.

'As planned, we're on the Old North Road. This wide dusty road can be seen for miles around, and it leads north-west all the way to Carvon,' Coronos said.

'It's a busy road,' Issa said, noting the increasing number of soldiers, merchants, couriers and everything in between moving along it. All on their errands between the two busy cities.

'Yes, which makes it safer, thankfully. I've not travelled this road for a long time, but I think it will take three days of non-stop riding to get there, or four with rest,' he judged.

'A long journey, given the message we deliver,' Issa said, feeling the haste of impending attack hanging over them.

'They may attack now or in a month, but attack they will,' Coronos said, putting the map away in his shirt pocket.

'Do you think they will attack the Uncharted Lands?' Asaph asked, worry creasing his brow.

Coronos nodded. 'They will attack everything and anything, and take over the whole of Maioria if they are not stopped. Perhaps they are attacking the Uncharted Lands as we speak. If they are not, then they will soon. Our freedom is all but a matter of time.'

'If every man, woman and child fought, we could drive them from Maioria,' Issa growled.

Coronos shook his head. 'Even then I don't think it would be enough. The simple fact of the matter is we don't have enough people or power to stand against the Maphraxies.'

'We don't if they are scattered all over Maioria,' Asaph said.

'Perhaps,' Coronos shrugged. 'Maybe if the elves returned. Maybe with all the tribes of the Uncharted Lands. Maybe with the goddess on our side.'

Issa chewed her lip. 'We have to fight, we have to try. We have to mean something, why else would Zanufey speak to me? Why else would Feygriene speak to and guide the last Dragon Lord? It cannot be for nothing, and I don't believe in coincidences.'

'There's much to be done, but first things first,' Coronos said. 'We must get to Carvon and speak to King Navarr. We can do no more and no less. An army must be formed on the western coast, but only the king has the power to command soldiers in his land. At least the mayor was right about something.'

Issa nodded. She felt frustrated and impotent. If the Maphraxies attacked now they would not be able to stop it.

CHAPTER 10

Freydel Returns

'CAN one sleep in the astral planes?' Freydel's voice echoed around him. He was meditative, almost in a trance.

'I guess one must if one has a physical body,' he mused. His answer to his question seemed to come from further away as if he were two people talking amongst themselves. When he was trying to work out something complex he would often talk to himself this way, questioning his higher self for answers. It worked so effectively here beyond the physical world that he began to feel that he was indeed two people.

'But to separate mind from body, must the mind go higher than the astral planes to sleep?'

'Higher than the astral planes are the ethereal planes. Maybe that is where the mind must go whilst the body sleeps,' he replied to himself.

'Am I asleep?'

'Yes,' his own voice replied, but from further away.

'Ah, then it is not so dangerous,' he breathed and relaxed, feeling himself drift.

'The body cannot survive, especially not without the mind,' he spoke to himself aloud, the sound of his own voice brought him back again. 'It will soon disperse into pure energy and become part of the astral planes.'

He came awake fully then as his voice of reason faded. He blinked in the growing light that finally gave him a visual reference. He was walking, or more like floating weightlessly, across a vast sea of pinkish-white clouds of energy. All around moved nothing but pure energy just like when he stepped into the Flow, only this was far stronger and far purer.

To his consciousness, everything was dreamlike and surreal.

'Have I died? Maybe I'm still dreaming. Or am I moving in the ethereal planes?'

He went to reach into his pocket, but only when he looked down did his physical body materialise as if thinking he had a physical body made his body appear.

'Thought precedes creation,' he murmured. He hoped to the Great Goddess that he would remember all this when he got home. *When I get home… I'm trapped here. My body is probably already dead.* The thought made him sad, briefly. The peace and infinite knowing of this place flowed through him and everything else was insignificant, even his physical body. Here he was unfettered by the chains of his cumbersome mortal self. *If I die here, it would be a welcome thing.*

He pulled out the orb. It was still black but much less solid. The energy around him responded and began to pool around the orb in swirls. He watched entranced. Was the energy of the orb communicating to the energy of the ethereal planes? He felt tired and laid himself down upon the flowing energy, still watching the orb. 'I shall stay here, where it is calm and peaceful.'

A voice came from far away, a rich, female voice that he could not quite make out.

'Leave me, I'm tired,' Freydel breathed, and felt himself drifting.

'Freydel.' The voice was right beside him. He sat up and stared up at the woman that had appeared before him. She was a little like the beings he'd seen in the pyramids, only her skin was pale pink, and she had hair. She was not as tall as the other beings, but still she moved with grace.

'You are an Ancient,' Freydel whispered in wonder. 'The orb has shown me the Ancients of long ago.' He held it up to her but she moved away from it. He did not quite believe she was real. All of this could be just one long strange dream.

'How can it be? How can you be here? How can the orb be here physically?' Her eyes were wide, making them seem even larger than normal.

'I *am* here physically. I am dying,' Freydel said, but he wasn't sad, and instead he smiled. 'Baelthrom trapped me in the astral planes and I cannot return. The orb is protecting itself, it has a will of its own.' He spoke openly, still only half believing the woman before him was real.

'Hush, never say that name here,' the woman looked about herself and shifted. 'He must never discover the planes beyond the astral.'

'Ah,' Freydel breathed as understanding dawned upon him. He *was* beyond the astral planes. It was the pure energy of the place combined with the power and memory of the orb that helped him to make sense of everything he had seen and experienced. 'I have seen him, Bael…'

'Shhh,' the woman warned again.

'I saw him in another time, another place, long ago,' Freydel continued, feeling lucid and dreamlike, and yet understanding many things. The woman's face was a mask of fear and wonder. 'The orb took me to a place where it could be safe, before the creation of Bael… Before he fell.' A different thought occurred to Freydel. 'How do you know my name?'

'I too am trapped here,' she said. 'But I'm cursed by *him*. A powerful curse that I can't break because I cannot set foot upon the physical world for long. I am Yisufalni.'

Freydel frowned. He knew the name, it was important, but he could not bring it to mind. 'I think my body has already died, Yisufalni.'

Her face wavered before him, and he felt himself drifting away again.

'Freydel.' The word brought him back. 'You haven't died, you could not be here if you had. There's still time. Return to the physical world, return now.'

He laughed. 'But I don't know how, and perhaps it is better if I stay here. You know he was not called Bael… He was called Ayeth.'

He learned then the power of calling aloud a name, and like waking from a dream into another dream he felt himself falling fast and darkness engulfed him.

'I know you are there, hiding in the shadows. Show yourself to me,' a man's voice demanded.

Freydel did not understand the language, but he understood the words that formed in his aching mind, and that voice he'd heard before.

'Where are you? Do you really think I—or any of us—cannot see you? Why are you here?'

Freydel blinked in the dimly lit place, feeling so utterly lost and confused as to where he was and what was going on that he began to think his soul was trapped. He was a ghost forever trapped in a time and place in which he did not belong.

He found himself in a blue crystal cavern, deep cobalt crystals covered the walls and ceiling of what seemed to be some sort of natural cave. The crystals glowed and gave off a soft light. There was one crystal unlike the rest and set apart from them. It was about twelve feet tall and as thick as an ancient tree trunk. This crystal was translucent white and it did not glow.

'There you are,' said the being standing beside the crystal.

Freydel recognised Ayeth. His blue stone amulet shone like the other crystals and his eyes were dark as they watched him. Another figure stood beside him. Delicate and slender, smaller than Ayeth, and stunningly beautiful. Her face was smooth and silver, and her lips were soft pearlescent. When Freydel saw her eyes, he caught his breath and shivered. They were all black and made her look soulless.

They were both staring right at him, and he backed away. The Flow moved in great swathes around the beings, and his own magical powers felt minuscule compared to the magic they could command. The woman smiled, but the smile did not reach her eyes. Freydel distinctly felt immense sorrow and anger flow from her. *Feelings are energy, energy is felt stronger in the astral planes,* his reasoning voice reminded him.

'You do not speak our tongue. Where are you from and how are you here?' Ayeth demanded.

Freydel felt his heart pounding, making his head ache even more. He was positively feeling ill now, his body could take no more. He couldn't deny any longer that they could see him and so he spoke, wondering how they would hear him.

'I'm trapped here, I'm trying to return,' he said and swallowed.

'A ghost, trapped. That is a punishment we have on our world,' the woman said. Her voice was smooth and high-pitched. Freydel didn't understand what she meant, but she made him very nervous.

'Not a punishment. I was fleeing danger. Now my time is short.' Could they help him with their power and technology? Hope sparked within him.

'Where are you from?' Ayeth asked, coming a step closer. His alien form and the power that emanated from him were incredibly intimidating. Freydel felt weak and ignorant—the feelings were so strong he wondered if Ayeth and the female were somehow making him feel them.

'From far away. A place we call Maioria, but it is in the future and in a different galaxy. How far I do not know.' He didn't think about what he said, he only knew he had to speak the truth to this man and could not have spoken otherwise.

'So you do not lie. You come from the future…' Ayeth said, coming closer until he was only a few feet away. Freydel stared up into those dark blue eyes—eyes that glittered hungrily. The woman behind him came closer, equally intrigued. Freydel felt like a mouse cornered by cats.

Ayeth paused, and his eyes widened. 'I sense something. You have something of power on or within you. What is it? Show it to me.'

Freydel trembled. He felt sick and about to pass out, but he could not deny that commanding voice. He unwillingly reached into his pocket and drew out the orb. 'It seeks its own protection. It brought me here through its own will.'

'A crystal orb of power from the future…' Ayeth said, his eyes wide with wonder. 'We may have been denied access to the crystal pyramids, but this thing from the future could be what saves us.'

'It *can* lead us to the future by its very energy. The One Source has brought it to us so we may be healed,' the woman exclaimed and bent closer.

Ayeth stared into it to. 'Something from the future… Can it have power over the past? With it I can break into the crystal pyramids. I know how to and I have the power such a thing might require. Let me feel its power.' His long six-fingered hand reached towards the orb.

Freydel felt his hand unwillingly lift the orb towards him.

'It is not yours to take,' Freydel gasped, trying and failing to resist.

The orb pulsed. He could feel anger flow from it. The power of Ayeth forced his hand forward whilst the power of the orb drew him back. He couldn't breathe. He struggled to pull the orb and at the same time maintain his grip on reality. The orb pulsed again, its energy juddering through his sick and weak body. His body was collapsing, taking his mind with it. The orb pulsed furiously. There came a jolting release.

'Freydel,' a voice called to him. He knew that voice, a friendly voice. He drifted towards it. 'Freydel, come to me,' the voice said, closer. He moved towards it, but it was hard, like trying to swim in quicksand.

'I'm tired,' he heard himself say.

'I know, but it's not far.' The woman's voice drifted around him. 'Just a little farther.'

He struggled on. The darkness was brightening moment by moment, but nothing was revealed in the growing light. There was only the light and the voice in the distance. He fought forwards.

There came a rushing sound and then he was falling at an alarming speed. He flailed in the air and cried out. Wind rushed around him but there was nothing to see but light. A face appeared in front of him, the face of an Ancient. Yisufalni's face.

'Follow me,' she said and smiled, but there was worry and pain in her eyes, and she moved with a certain weakness. She reached down, a cool hand grasped his. Then he fell forwards a long way and landed on something horribly hard.

Freydel opened his eyes and felt weaker than he had ever felt in his life. He tried to lift his arm and failed. All he could do was lie there breathing. It took a long time for his breath to slow. He opened his eyes and looked around. Surrounding him were the familiar stone chairs of the Wizards' Circle. The stones were purple in the dusky light of evening.

'I'm... alive?' he blinked in disbelief.

Below and to the west of the Wizards' Tower, the glittering waters of a river ran to meet the sea beyond the hills. The sky was dotted with clouds that were red in the setting sun, and the river was painted orange to create an exquisite sunset. Grassland and then forest extended either side of the river and continued for miles. It had been a long time since he'd last stood, or lain, in the Wizards' Circle, and he'd forgotten how beautiful this secret place was, so far east beyond the Known World.

The orb. He frantically searched for it, felt its cool surface in his pocket and relaxed. His staff, sadly, was still gone, probably for good. That realisation did not sit easily with him. Baelthrom had something of his, it created a link between them, a link he did not want. But he was alive and he had the orb, that was all he cared about.

'Oh great mother goddess…' he wheezed and lay back, letting the tears of relief fall down his face. 'I thought I was dead.'

I was dead, or dying. He'd nearly lost the orb and his life, but thank the goddess he had not. He breathed in the rich air of Maioria. It was heavy and sluggish, just like his body felt, and for a moment he missed the lightness of the astral planes. *But I never want to go back.*

He winced and turned over onto his side, his aching body protested at the slightest movement. There, not two feet away, was a small curled up child dressed in a grubby white dress. She had her back to him and was not moving. He blinked in surprise and struggled to remember what had happened. He inched himself up onto his elbow and reached out to squeeze the girl's shoulder. She groaned and moved under his touch, then turned to look at him. Her large pale eyes blinked back at him and her white skin seemed to glow in the dim light.

'Arla,' Freydel gasped. 'How did you get here?'

Her eyes were wide and fearful. She spoke in stutters. 'If I hadn't reached you and led you back here, you would have died. That was him wasn't it?'

Freydel stared at the child. He knew she had strange powers, but being so young he had never really thought much on it. He nodded slightly as he remembered Ayeth.

'You saw him? Yes, I think so. Baelthrom before he fell. I'm certain the orb took me there to show me, maybe to somehow protect it from the Baelthrom we know now.' Freydel frowned. He would need to write down everything he'd witnessed and ponder on it deeply.

'He's very powerful,' Arla said. 'He followed us almost all the way, but in the end, he had to turn back. It was so close. I'm afraid that he's seen me,' Arla trailed off, her grown up words strange in a child's voice.

'You brought me here? How? I saw a woman, like an Ancient. She, we, were beyond the astral planes,' he shook his head trying to clear the fog.

'I've seen the ethereal planes, but to return to the body and remember what you saw is very hard,' Arla said wisely, pushing herself to sit up.

Freydel stared at the child, trying to piece it together. 'Arla how did you reach me? How did you bring me here? How did you escape Celene when Cirosa was taken?' He wished he'd spent a lot more time with this strange child and her peculiar powers.

The girl looked at him and stammered. 'I can go places, like when you dream. I knew you were in trouble. I was hiding near the temple when they came. I asked for help and… She came and I followed.'

Arla shrugged as if it were a normal thing. There was more to this story, Freydel was certain, but either the girl was hiding something or she couldn't articulate what she wanted to say. She would not be the only one to talk to beings and ghosts beyond the physical world, many people had that gift.

'You can trust me Arla, if there's something I should know then you need to tell me.'

Arla nodded. 'I couldn't stay by the temple, they would have found me and…' tears filled her eyes.

'It's all right,' Freydel sighed. He pulled her into his arms as she cried, and rocked her gently. 'We're safe now. Was this woman you asked for help an Ancient? Is her name Yisufalni?' Arla nodded.

Freydel stared off into the distant green hills. *The girl speaks to the Ancients. They may be ghosts but they have not left us completely, and with their great powers they are able to help even now.* The thought warmed his weary heart and he smiled, tears filling his eyes. *There is hope, always.*

Arla stopped crying, and he held her away from him so he could look at her directly. 'Arla, where we are now is a very secret and special place, you must never tell anyone about it. Baelthrom must never know where it is. Can you keep it a secret?' Arla nodded again. 'How you got here I do not understand, but only a true wizard can come here, and only then by invitation from a member of the Wizards' Circle. No woman has been here since the orbs split the powers of the world. Since…' Freydel frowned, there was something he should remember.

'Our records speak of a priestess, a high priestess of the original holy order of the Great Goddess. She was also a princess and an Ancient,' he blinked in surprise. 'It could be her. I cannot be sure… I need to look at the records. But anyway, she was the last. No woman has been powerful enough to pass the Wizard's Reckoning since the orbs were divided.'

Arla yawned and shivered.

'Come, let's go and get water from the river. We might find some blackberries as well, and a better place to sleep,' Freydel said, feeling utterly spent.

CHAPTER 11

Raven Messenger

EHKA circled high above the three riders, then swooped low and landed on the pommel of Issa's saddle, making her jump.

'Where have you been?' She asked and stroked his feathers. She had not seen the bird since they'd entered Corsolon. The pressure in her head came on swiftly, drowning out the voices of Coronos and Asaph talking in front her. She closed her eyes and allowed Ehka's message in.

The brightly lit day on the road to Corsolon dimmed and a different world took shape. A world lit by a sky of murky orange and green. She saw through Ehka's eyes and he was flying. He came to land on a rocky hillside. It was covered in strange trees that were massive but stumpy. They had long thick branches that reached horizontally across the ground for several yards.

Something moved in the shadows. Then a dreadful face appeared before her in a swirl of black. Red eyes—not unlike Baelthrom's—glowed, illuminating a large, flat face, squat, upturned nose and a long wide mouth filled with inch-long fangs. The horrific thing's bat-like ears twitched, and a blood red tongue whipped out to lick its grey lips.

Demon. She shivered. She had never seen one, but she knew it was a demon. Only its grey face appeared out of the shadows, and somehow that was more terrifying than the whole of it appearing. If its face was as hideous as that then what did the rest of it look like?

The demon spoke in demonic, and her soul shrank from it, but Ehka was not afraid, only curious of it. The demon lunged out of the shadows. Thick muscles bulged over its chest, huge hairless wings stretched wide and its clawed hand reached forwards so fast it was a blur.

She screamed as its claws touched her feathers, then the images flooded into her mind. It took her a while to realise that what she witnessed was Ehka giving the demon a message, a vision of the future. Her breathing came fast and shallow as she struggled to focus on what she was seeing.

An empty plain loomed so fast she could only make out a black spire of rock. The same spire she had seen after entering the sacred mound. There came a flash and then light blinded her. The wailing howl of a demon scoured her ears as she squinted into the light. A long thin spear formed and she blinked in surprise. *It's that spear, the one in Zanufey's hands and in the sacred mound.*

Then the spear was gone and an immense battle was taking place below her; thousands of demons battling against each other. Demons of all sizes and shapes, black and grey and brown, winged and wingless, were locked together in a vicious struggle. Blinding explosions rocked her vision and demon magic surged. Black blood splattered the barren ground and the screams of demons tore at her soul.

'Please stop,' she rasped. She had to get away from this demonic place.

A blast shook the earth and she screamed, demon magic rumbled. Then there was nothing. Instead of howling demons and blinding explosions, there was deafening silence and darkness. A large crystal shard filled the dark and glowed green. That same hideous demon face appeared above it. Its eyes were flaming yellow and its face was a permanent scowl as it hungered for her soul. She choked down terror and shivered uncontrollably under the demon's gaze.

The vision swirled into a vortex of energy. Lightning and storm clouds spun in a maelstrom, making her sway sickeningly. The demon's face was the only thing that remained static in the vortex, its eyes never leaving hers.

'Issa?' Asaph's voice called from somewhere distant.

She blinked open her eyes and stared up into the worried faces of Asaph and Coronos. Duskar's long face loomed over them both, ears pricked forward with interest.

'I'm fine,' she said, but her voice was weak. Asaph helped her to sit up and scowled at the raven that always seemed to be the cause of their problems.

'It's not his fault,' she gasped. 'He is only delivering messages.'

'Some message,' Asaph grumbled.

They were on the grass to the side of the road. Passers-by looked at them curiously but didn't stop to offer any help.

'Drink some water,' Coronos said, passing her a flagon.

She drank and felt better. 'I'm fine,' she repeated, her voice stronger. 'What happened?'

'You went quiet and pale. Then you nearly fell off your horse,' Asaph explained. 'Duskar tried to keep you mounted long enough for me to grab you. Otherwise, you'd have another nasty bruise.'

She smiled. 'Thanks. I... Ehka showed me a vision. I don't understand yet. But I keep seeing demons...' an uncontrollable shudder made her stop. 'But I don't know why. They are horrifying.'

After she had caught her breath she insisted they continue. The men were dubious, but they helped her remount Duskar, and set off at a slower pace.

'Do you think the raven went to demon world, to the Murk?' Coronos asked when they had settled into the pace again.

'Yes,' Issa said. 'I'm sure of it. I've seen that awful place twice in the last few days, but as usual I don't know why or what it means.'

'It will no doubt become clearer in time,' Coronos said.

'Hmph, hopefully it won't be too late for whatever it was supposed to mean,' Issa said. Why did her visions and Ehka's messages always have to be so cryptic? Or perhaps they weren't, but she just didn't understand what they were trying to say.

'Do you know anything about a white spear? I keep seeing it. It seems magical, it's definitely powerful, and it glows and hums. I see it whenever I see the demons,' she looked at the men hopefully.

Coronos frowned in thought, then he shook his head. 'Nothing comes to mind. I know little about the demons, only that there was a great war a long, long time ago. The lands to the west were lost and many perished until the demon gates were sealed shut.

'It's interesting because the Kuapoh on the Uncharted Lands also know about the demon wars. They say their ancestors came from the land in the sea, and there were great wars against them. The demons still plague the Kuapoh now and then. They call them incubi and succubi. They are their ancestors who became possessed by demons long ago.'

'Why would demons be of concern to us when our enemies are the Maphraxies? Why would the raven go to the Murk anyway?' Asaph asked.

Issa shook her head. 'It doesn't make any sense and we already have enough on our plate. I don't want to see anymore demons.'

And what of the knights? She hadn't mentioned them. *"The raven searches for the Cursed King..."* Edarna's words spoken so long ago. She looked for Ehka, he was circling high above them. Had he somehow found the Cursed King? Was she supposed to find this strange white spear? She chewed her lip in frustration. She hoped Coronos was right, and it would become clearer in time.

CHAPTER 12

Against All Odds

BOKAARD swung his axe. A roar of fury exploded from his lips as he struck down two of the slimy fish bastards at once, their blood spraying all over him and the decks. He spun fast, ducked, and sliced the webbed feet off a third. His blood was alive with the fire of life, his heart pounded in his chest as he prepared himself for a rush of four more Histanatarns. Four was too many but what else could he do? Fight to the end.

At the stern on the higher deck, he glimpsed Marakon cornered by two fish bastards. Bokaard laughed, his voice mingling with the clash of metal and screams of soldiers. *Two of us sea dogs overwhelmed by an army of fishy devils. I'll bet you'll cut down fifty before they take you, you lucky one-eyed bastard.*

Bokaard grinned back at the four approaching. They didn't have the facial features to mirror his expression in mockery. They just snarled and ran for him.

'I thought that was it then,' Bokaard said, sipping his steaming hot chocolate, trying to control the tremor in his hands that had never quite left him since that day. 'I was ready for it, for death, as I always have been. So many of us had fallen by then anyway…

'But that was when the real terror came, when death on wings made of the night filled the sky. The Dread Dragons of Baelthrom blotted out the sun and filled me with terror worse than any demon out of the Murk.

When I saw those Dread Dragons above us… For the first time in my life, I prayed to Doon. I knew it was probably too late to ask him to give me favours, but it was all I could think to do.'

Rasia sipped her hot chocolate, spellbound as Bokaard told his story.

'None of us could move, not even the Histanatarns. We were frozen to the decks in dragon fear. They were so huge, their eyes burned red, and their screams ripped right through you. For a while they flew low and circled the ships. I don't know why they didn't attack us immediately. It seemed they were waiting for something, maybe for a command from that immortal bastard through their cursed amulets. Again, I thought, this is it, my life is done.'

Rasia took his cup, refilled it, and sat down again silently, not wanting to interrupt the big Atalanphian man in case he forgot any part of the story. She had to know what happened to Marakon. Her hands were trembling in hope or fear or both. Bokaard continued, his brilliant blue eyes looking into the past.

'The Dread Dragons all screamed at once—a terrible sound—and we fell to the decks, soldiers and Histanatarns alike. Then the fire came and the whole world turned red.'

He rubbed the bandages around his hands. Though it had been well over a week ago, maybe more, maybe less, he'd lost all track of the days since, but the burned skin on his hands was still painful. Rasia had salved and bandaged them as soon as he'd arrived. Somehow his face was not as bad, though patches of red and white marred his shaven scalp.

'The fire got me up onto my hands and knees, I mean, the whole deck was alight. The heat was so immense, my sun shields were melting on my face. The four Histanatarns I'd been fighting now ran at me, four flaming balls of fire desperately trying to get into the sea. They were quicker than me at reacting, no wonder they are so good at surviving, tough, slippery buggers. They didn't even care I was there and ran straight into me. We slammed into the burning rails and became entangled in rigging. The rails gave way, and we fell into the sea.

'The feel of that cold water on my burned skin was like Doon answering my prayers. I think I became a believer at that moment,' Bokaard sighed and smiled, wiping his eyes in remembered relief.

'Now my world was no longer on fire, but filled with water. I was not going to burn alive, I was going to drown with the sinking rigging and dead Histanatarns. Ha-ha, how hilarious I find it now. Looking back. How many times I thought I would die, and each time a different death confronted me. First, it was the Histanatarns, then it was the Dread Dragons, then it was the fire and now I would die by drowning.'

Rasia smiled at him. 'It's incredible. I don't know if you are blessed or cursed to survive all that.'

He smiled but then saw the tears in her eyes. He reached forwards and took her hand in his. 'Marakon has luck on his side, more than I ever had.'

'No, please.' Rasia shook her head and looked away, a tear escaping down her cheek before she could stop it. 'Please don't stop, don't let me break your thoughts. Tell me everything you can remember.'

Bokaard let her hand go and tried to remember what happened next.

'Everything was a blur. I hurt in a hundred places and I couldn't breathe. All around me rigging and debris were falling into the ocean. I remember seeing wood burn under water and being fascinated by it. The ships' hulls were groaning and cracking under the strain of their burning topsides. A strange sound, like a tortured whale dying slowly.

'I managed to struggle out of the rigging, and searched for the surface. I found it, only to fill my lungs full of smoky air. It made me choke even more. Then my ship began to roll sideways, towards me. I swam harder than I'd ever swum in my life, but the mast and sail came down over me and the world turned black.'

He sipped his drink then shook his head. 'I've no idea how I survived that day or after it. All I can say is that when the blackness ended, I was not dead. Although I wished I was. I awoke on my back. Rope entangled my legs and dragged them underwater.

'Other ropes entangled my arms attaching me to a five-foot square piece of hull. That was what kept me above water. Both my arms and legs were dead. I don't know what was attached to me beneath the water, but I felt like I had been stretched two feet taller.

'I was desperately thirsty, more thirsty than when I'd trained as a soldier in the desert—and we Atalanphians have been trained to go for a week without water. My vision came and went and I was hallucinating badly. But in my clear moments, I saw nothing other than wreckage and an endless blue ocean.'

Rasia looked away and wiped at the tears falling down her face. She bit her nails. Outside the window, her two boys were playing chase. Bokaard found their laughter lifted the gloom a little.

'Look,' Bokaard began, 'it does not mean Marakon is dead. He may have survived, just like I did.' He wasn't sure if it was a good or foolish thing to say. That he survived was a miracle, to expect that miracle to be granted to another was a long step.

'I know,' Rasia breathed. 'I still hope,' she nodded, but continued to stare at her children playing outside.

Bokaard decided to go on with the story, just so it was told, even though he did not see Marakon again. It might help take her mind off her suffering, if only for a little while, and he wanted to tell her what he had seen.

'I had to get the rigging off my legs. I was so weak, it took me maybe an hour to work a hand free so I could reach my knife. It took another hour to cut loose that darn thick rope. I'd cut most of it off when the cursed knife slipped out of my hands and sank. Luckily I managed to wriggle out of the rest and dragged myself onto the wreckage. My legs were so numb I couldn't feel them, but it felt so good to finally be out of the water.

'By that time the sun was setting, and I saw the most beautiful sunset I'd ever seen. The whole sky turned from gold to red to pink—a sunset in the middle of the ocean is far more spectacular than on land. Then I realised that when it was gone it would be dark and I would be alone. Alone out on that vast ocean, on a tiny bit of wreckage waiting for my death. I think I was more scared then than when the Dread Dragons came. As it got dark, I prayed like I never had before. I think I prayed more that night than a priest does in his whole lifetime.'

Rasia laughed. It made him smile, glad to bring a little joy into her life.

'It's funny how terrified I was then of the dark and the sea. Me, an Atalanphian, afraid of the ocean and darkness. I've never felt so small and alone in my entire life. I couldn't sleep for the terror of what might be moving beneath me. It was only when those horrible long hours of darkness passed and the dawn came did I fall asleep.

'When I next awoke I faced my fifth death. I was dying. Ironically I would not die of drowning, but of dehydration. There was not a cloud in that beautiful dawn sky, nothing to even suggest the rain I so desperately needed. I remember feeling my body slowly shutting down. I wondered if I should take my own life and beat death to it. My situation was utterly hopeless, but at least I would be in charge of my final demise.'

He couldn't help it, but his voice broke at the memory of it. He put his head in his palm as the overwhelming emotions flowed through him. Rasia squeezed his shoulder.

The emotions subsided, and he continued when his voice was calm.

'I gave up. Every time I tried to drink sea water I choked it back up. I had no knife or weapon to cut myself. I had only two choices, jump off the wreckage and drown, or stay on the wreckage and die slowly. I decided to leave the wreckage, after all the efforts I'd gone through to stay on it.

'The sun was setting again by the time I decided to leave my home. Honestly, I was so delirious from dehydration, I could barely string two thoughts together. It was the delirium that blessedly numbed the fear. It would be a race to the death between the time it took to drown, and the time it took for dehydration to kill me.

'I slipped into the water. It was so cold. I clung to the wreckage for a long time. I couldn't bring myself to let it go. I hated Doon then, hated him for making me suffer all the deaths under the sun and moons.

'I actually don't remember letting go. I think I must have drifted off to sleep briefly when it happened. I don't know how long I was floating for. I remembered fading in and out of consciousness. I only really woke up when I slipped beneath the surface.'

Rasia was white-faced, clearly lost in the horror of his story.

'I remember seeing the brightest stars above the surface, so beautiful. I was too weak to swim, and I just sank into the dark without a struggle, but always I looked up at the stars as they dimmed. Then the stars grew brighter again, and they'd changed from silver white to purple and blue. They were moving too. They grew brighter and bigger, and then they were all around me. I closed my eyes then. I thought the stars had come to take me home, to the One Source—and by Doon was I ready.

'Everything was so strange. I remembered suddenly being able to breathe and yet I moved deep in the ocean. I just couldn't work anything out. The purple and blue lights were no longer stars but these beautiful fish dolphin-like beings. They had an intelligent human feel to them.'

'The Wykiry,' Rasia gasped.

Bokaard nodded and blinked back tears of wonder. 'Yes. But I did not realise that at the time, I was so delirious. I thought I had died, and these star-beings had come to take me home. Looking back, I realise it was the Wykiry. They had come to me.

'In Atalanph we say the Wykiry are angels, they come to help souls lost at sea. Now I believe those sayings. Whatever it is they do, magic or otherwise, I could breathe underwater in their presence. They carried me through the ocean, a long way it seemed. I wish I could have stayed conscious for it but I was spent.

'They left me on the shore where a river empties into the sea, and I think they knew to find me fresh water. I did awake again, alone, and when I gulped that water down, I felt life returning to me once more. The water gave me enough strength to find food. I ate seaweed and mussels. Raw of course, yum.'

Rasia grimaced, Bokaard laughed.

'They aren't too bad, just very salty. I knew I was on Frayon, but I had no idea where. All I could do was hazard a guess. It was overcast, and there was no sun, but what shadows there were told me I was on the west coast. I reasoned I must be far north because of where we'd entered the Lost Sea on our ships.

'I started walking due south as soon as I had the energy. I came across a hermit madder than I'd become. He pointed me towards the closest town some thirty miles or so away, and told me it was called Wenderon. I remembered Marakon saying that is where you and the boys were. It took me two days to get here without boots, and the rest is… Well, you know,' he smiled.

Rasia shook her head in wonder. 'Last night, you looked so exhausted I barely recognised you. The neighbours came knocking, said there was an Atalanphian man looking for me. I had no idea who it was.'

'It's been several years since we last saw each other, and I feel I've lost half my body weight since the Dread Dragons destroyed my ship,' Bokaard said.

'We'll have a roast tonight, as big as I can cook,' Rasia said.

'That would be amazing,' Bokaard said, already looking forward to it.

'All I can say is that I gave up hope so many times, and still I survived, against all odds. I'm not a wizard or a visionary, and I cannot tell if Marakon lives or not. But I know he is one lucky bastard, and if it were me I would not give up hope.'

Rasia smiled and blinked back the tears again. 'You know it's funny. He's a soldier, as was I before our boys came. I always knew he would likely die in battle, and had prepared myself for it over the years. But a ship wreck… Not knowing whether he lives or not, that is harder. I cannot mourn him or let him go. I can only live in hope, like you say.'

She stood up and tied her thick copper curls back into a ponytail. Her face was pale and drawn, but she was still handsome and held herself proudly. Her strong, broad shoulders spoke of her soldier's training.

'Stay with us, as long as you want,' she said. 'As you can see, we have plenty of room. It will do the boys good to have a man around the house'

'Marakon's done well for himself,' Bokaard agreed, taking in their big kitchen and large garden. He'd had his own room last night, and a big comfy bed to sleep in. The best rest he'd had in five years. They even had a complicated system of running water. From what he could tell it was certainly one of the bigger houses in town.

'I'd rather we lived together in a hovel than in this big house and me alone,' Rasia said.

'Of course,' Bokaard said. 'I'll stay until I'm fit, if that's good with you. After then I must return to the Feylint Halanoi in Port Nordanstin and report what happened.'

'If it weren't for the boys, I'd come with you. I miss being on the field. I miss being an archer,' Rasia mused, watching her boys still chasing each other in the garden.

'After everything that's happened I think I'd rather be here,' Bokaard said.

Rasia laughed. 'Maybe you're right.'

Bokaard lay awake in his big bed. His belly was still full after two heaped plates of the delicious roast dinner Rasia had cooked earlier. He was tired, but couldn't sleep at this time—most Atalanphians would be up and about right now. They lived and slept twice in a day. Sleeping from noon until dusk and then again for a couple of hours in the night. But he was still exhausted after his ordeal.

The muffled sound of Rasia crying in the next room kept him worrying. She would be all right, in time. He couldn't comfort her anymore than he had. For all the odds against him, he could still imagine Marakon walking through that front door.

With a defeated sigh he swung his stiff and sore legs out of bed and pulled on his clothes, Marakon's clothes that Rasia had given him. They would have been tight had he not lost so much weight, but they fit fine now. *Slender elves.* Bokaard grinned as he did up the shirt buttons. He pulled on his boots and coat in the kitchen and tiptoed outside into the night.

He immediately shivered. *This damn country is so cold this far north.* He pulled up his collar and breathed in the fresh salty air. Their big house was on a hill overlooking the town of Wenderon and Wenderon Bay. The town hugged the near perfect semi-circle of the bay, and most of the lights were off apart from some taverns. The house was dark save for a light in Rasia's window. He sighed, feeling sorry for her all alone here. He was glad he'd left no one at home. When you spent so long at sea, it was hard to find a partner anyway.

He turned away from the house and walked up the path that led to a low point on the cliff. He sat down on a cold slab of stone and closed his eyes, listening to the sound of the surf. It pleased him, that sound. It meant he was on land again. After all that had happened he didn't ever want to get on another ship. But it was unlikely the Halanoi would let him be anything else other than a captain. The night was overcast, but Doon suddenly appeared from behind a cloud.

Bokaard blinked up at the bright moon. 'You're late tonight,' he whispered. 'Thank you for hearing my prayers.' He felt silly talking to the moon, but if the prayers he'd spoken so fervently when he was dying alone on the ocean had been heard, then he was eternally grateful. He felt peace come over him then. A content kind of knowing he had not really felt before.

'If you're listening, then maybe you can help my friend Marakon if he is still out there. No matter how I think of it, I cannot imagine him dead.' He looked across the ocean. 'I survived against all odds, so too can he.'

CHAPTER 13

The Witch and the Seer

IT was the smell that drove Edarna on. Not a nice smell; a dead rotting putrid smell that wafted through the trees like a dense fog. It got her all excited.

'Urgh, what is this,' Naksu gagged, holding the hem of her blue robe over her mouth.

'Well, this is what you can expect whenever you *walk* anywhere; dead things,' Edarna scoffed.

'Whatever has died must have been huge. This stench has been around here for most of the day, and I think it's getting stronger,' Naksu said.

Over the next hour, as they followed the thin trail through the forest, the smell did indeed reach retching proportions. Even Edarna had to cover her face with her shawl. As the smell ripened exponentially, they began to pass broken and mangled trees. Huge pines and thick oaks were snapped in two like a giant had stomped on them.

'Look, this happened recently. The leaves on the broken bits are still green, and the exposed bark is fresh,' Edarna pointed out.

They carried on through patches of destruction. Here and there, black scorch marks seared the earth and trunks. The charred smell of wood smoke was a welcome dampener on the horrible rotting dead smell. Whatever it was, it was going to be useful to any witch, Edarna thought and grinned.

'There's a clearing up ahead.' Naksu pointed to where the sunlight was bright beyond the trees. Edarna hastened towards it.

'Wait,' Naksu said. 'We should be cautious. Whatever did this may still be here.'

'Whatever did this, is dead or gone,' Edarna corrected. 'I've seen Dread Dragon destruction on Celene, and it was just like this. The scorch marks, the broken trees—all the same. Dragons did this, and if they were still here, you would have seen them hours ago.'

Naksu swallowed audibly. Edarna wondered if the woman had ever seen dragons before. Maybe she'd never seen the dark hand of war. Perhaps she'd spent her life cosseted away on Myrn, Edarna tutted to herself. How can you learn about the world if you never see it?

They sidled towards the clearing. Edarna tried her best to tiptoe over twigs.

When they emerged into the sunlight, Naksu immediately turned and vomited. Edarna was struck dumb, a mix of horror and sheer excitement at what she saw. She moved towards it.

'A dead Dread Dragon,' she said, then gagged at the smell.

She tightened her shawl about her face. The corpse was in a rapid state of decay, collapsing in on itself so it looked like a leathery bag of flesh filled with putrefying mush. Nothing had dared to eat it. Edarna knew no living thing would touch the corpse of an immortal. She analysed the beast. Its scales were so strong and resilient that, whilst the gooey insides rotted away, the skin would take much longer.

'Do you know how many years it took me to get just one dragon scale? Now look at this, there are thousands just lying right there in front of me,' she said in wonder.

'Don't you dare touch it,' Naksu shouted between vomits.

Edarna was captivated by the dragon. She walked around the bulk and found its horrific head complete with the terrible injury that killed it.

'Its throat's been ripped out by something just as big. Probably another dragon,' Edarna shouted her report. She stood there trembling. The hideous sunken eyes would surely open any minute, and this immortal dead thing would reanimate. Edarna breathed deep and slow.

'Dragon fear, even when it's dead. How can we humans ever kill even one of these monsters?'

The thing was so huge and so ugly she began to lose faith that Baelthrom and his horde would ever be defeated. But then here it was dead, and something *had* killed it. Something was missing. Where was its rider? She whirled around, expecting to see a Dromoorai running at her swinging its claymore, but there was nothing, only the still forest and a warm late summer afternoon.

Edarna relaxed and turned back to the dragon. The beast's eyes were sunken in, and already its skeleton was visible under its flesh. Its blood had long since gushed out over the ground and dried, so that it lay on a huge black patch of earth. The grass beneath it was very dead.

Disgusting things, the Maphraxies. Their bodies, having died long ago, rotted quickly. Where they died nothing grew, they poisoned the earth. But what didn't decay so quickly, Edarna now learned, were the dragon scales. Mr Dubbins tentatively sniffed a black patch of earth then turned away with a hiss.

'Not so good eh, Mr Dubbins? Their scales must be tough though... Resilient to fire, hard as iron, and yet flexible enough for flight. Dragons really are quite something.'

She needed a good stock of dragon scales. The spells and potions she could create with them stretched beyond her imagination. Just five scales would be enough for a lifetime of complex spells, and here there were millions of them—ranging from the tiny scales at the neck to the massive scales on its flank. They glistened metallic greeny-black, like oil in a peat bog. She forgot all about the horrific sight of the decaying stinking Dread Dragon, and looked critically at the new project before her.

'Two scales of each, from the smallest to the biggest, and only the best undamaged ones,' she murmured to herself. 'Some from the neck, torso, stomach, back and tail. Just ten scales are more than a lifetimes' supply, Mr Dubbins.' The cat looked at her once, then turned around and left. She picked up a stick.

'Now then, hmm. What else can we use...' She poked the head and jumped back. The head did not even budge. It was still dead, good. Carefully she wedged her stick between its massive lips. She had to heave all her weight against the stick in order to shove the top lip up.

Viscous black drool splattered out onto the ground and a gust of stench exploded from the beast's mouth. Edarna heaved and turned green, almost losing her stick in the goo. Almost. Her intrigue was strong enough to overcome the smell of rotting stomach contents.

'Teeth, yes. Dragon fangs. Invaluable. But how to get them loose. Hmm. A little explosion goes a long way. My oh my, I could take a week on it. Where on earth do I begin? We could be rich, Mr Dubbins. I could sell those scales for pure gold. I could... I could...' she stopped, suddenly stumped.

What the hell could she spend gold on? She couldn't even think of anything. She let the lips slop back and put her hands on her hips, analysing the huge bulk.

'It doesn't matter, Mr Dubbins, we'll be rich and that's it.' She had an idea, a thought that cut through her dreams of wealth. It made her stop and think.

'I found it,' a strained voice came from over the other side of the Dread Dragon. Edarna tried to ignore it so she could focus on the idea. Fire resistant clothing, oven gloves, shields, even armour. It would be the first of its kind ever to be seen. Edarna chuckled and clapped her hands

'It's here, come and look,' Naksu called. The idea wavered then was gone. Edarna sighed. She'd better see if the seer was all right. *She's probably never seen a dead thing, not even a rat.*

Naksu was bent cautiously over something black and part-hidden by long grasses. Edarna stepped on a twig, making the seer jump backwards in fright.

'A Dromoorai, eh? I wondered where he'd be.' Edarna nodded knowingly as she looked at the huge body on the ground. Everything that had been inside the armour was gone, and the ground beneath it was black.

'We've seen these, in our sacred pools,' Naksu shuddered. 'I hope I never see one alive.'

'Well, if you really want to save the planet, as you seers say you are trying to do, then you undoubtedly will meet one. Best get used to what they look like now.' Edarna offered her words of wisdom.

Naksu ignored the witch and continued examining the remains. 'Now the question is, where is its amulet?'

'What amulet?' Edarna said, peering closer, hoping she hadn't missed a trick.

'They all wear Shadow Stones. You know, those bloodstones mined from the bowels of the Maphrax Mountains.'

'Oh, *those* amulets,' Edarna chuckled. 'Well, it probably disintegrated like the rest of it when it was killed. And besides, an amulet's not that important.'

'It can't have disintegrated, not when every other piece of metal still remains. And something which connects all who wear them to the mind of Baelthrom is not to be taken lightly,' Naksu frowned.

'No, I suppose not,' Edarna conceded. She didn't know the amulet connected the thing directly to *him*. 'Does it really connect right back?' she asked shrilly.

'Yes. Whenever Baelthrom wishes he can see through any amulet, maybe all amulets at once. This is how he is able to move his Maphraxies so quickly, so precisely, and with devastating results,' Naksu said.

'Hmm, so you do know or thing or two then, back on Myrn,' Edarna said, nodding her head in a random direction meant to indicate Myrn. Naksu ignored her again.

'Somebody has taken the amulet, but who and why?' She stood up and looked into the distance.

'Well, whatever killed it most probably,' Edarna shrugged. 'And whatever killed it was pretty powerful. It ripped its throat clean out.'

Naksu grimaced. 'Without the body, I cannot tell how this one was killed, but look at the fresh scrapes of metal on its helmet and armour.' She pointed out the long gashes on the metal that only another metal object could create. 'Suggests it was killed by a sword or similar.' Naksu stood deep in thought, while Edarna poked around the Dromoorai.

'Nope, nothing of use here really. And I'm not lugging a dirty black claymore around,' Edarna said.

'When you spend weeks travelling in a forest, it all looks the same,' Naksu said. 'But I was hoping to come across the path I walked recently. There should be a Karalanth settlement near here, I'm sure of it. I had not recognised the place because of the destruction, but it could be where I helped to heal a young man. Oh of course,' Naksu breathed in sharply, a look of wonder on her face. 'Come on, it's around here somewhere.' The seer grabbed the reins of her mule and ran off.

'What's 'round 'ere?' Edarna said. 'Wait, I need to get some scales.'

But Naksu didn't wait and she disappeared into the trees, leading her mule behind her with Mr Dubbins in quick pursuit.

'Great,' Edarna huffed, and ran after the woman. 'I'm coming back you know. No witch in her right mind would miss a dragon scale collecting opportunity.'

Edarna found Naksu in a second clearing before another big patch of charred earth, but this time there was lots of ash and charred wood.

'Something big has been burnt,' Edarna said. Naksu looked around.

'There,' she said triumphantly and pointed to a well-worn path leading into the trees. Edarna followed the seer along it until they came to a wide, open space. It looked deliberately made, and either side of the path were big round patches of bare earth. There was a third patch of blackened ground, and she toed at the ashes thoughtfully.

'Burned until nothing remained. Looks like a cremation if you'd ask me,' she sniffed.

'This is it, this is where the Karalanths lived, a group of them,' Naksu said. 'Clearly, they were attacked and left. But why would they have been attacked? Can Bael...' she stopped short as if not wanting to speak the name aloud. 'Can he have known?'

'Known what?' Edarna said. 'And stop running off like that, it's no good on an old woman's knees.'

Naksu looked at her and seemed like she wanted to say something. Edarna raised an eyebrow. Hopefully it would be interesting.

'There was a sick human man here with the Karalanths. He had a terrible mortal wound made by Keteth. I helped to heal him and what I learned about him shocked me. He had an aura, very distinctive, an aura of a Dragon Lord.'

'Oh, 'im.' Edarna sighed. Did seers only get old news? 'Yeah of course it's 'im. The last Dragon Lord and all that,' she wafted her hand in front of her face dismissively, then stopped and looked worried. 'She would be with him. That's why they came. They're hunting her.'

'She who?' Naksu frowned, now confused.

'She *her*,' Edarna said. 'Issa, the Raven Queen one. That Dragon Lord is her bit of stuff, I'm sure of it. Don't see too many Dragon Lords kicking around these days. I scryed for her and saw her riding this huge golden dragon.'

Naksu's pale eyes went wide. 'Then he survived, praise Feygriene. I cannot be sure how long ago this happened, but the Karalanths have obviously left. Less than a week ago for sure. If I can find some pure water, I can use the Presight to see when they left, maybe even where they went.'

'Oh really?' Edarna was intrigued. The Presight was the same as the Sight, but it was the ability to see specifically into the past. 'I don't suppose you can show me how to see into the past?'

Naksu shook her head. Edarna's shoulders slumped. 'Few seers have the gift, and it's really hard to train. The past is the observer's interpretation of the events everyone at that time is experiencing. It is very personal and subjective, and takes years to learn. I'll do it now and do it quickly before this stench kills me.'

Edarna grinned. 'Perfect. Gives me some time to collect a few things.' She glanced back the way they had come to where the corpse of the Dread Dragon lay beyond the broken trees. She began to shuffle off in that direction.

'Great, then you can help me collect foxbane and wild fennel,' Naksu said. 'And keep your eyes peeled for a clear running stream, a pool of water would be best.' Edarna hesitated, licked her lips, and sighed.

'Fine, but afterwards I'll need to collect a few things for myself,' she said, but Naksu showed no signs of having heard her.

CHAPTER 14

Not a Moment Too Soon

'MURLONIUS, Murlonius, Murlonius,' Marakon spoke the boatman's name aloud three times. His voice seemed loud in the stillness of dawn. He only needed to speak it once, but he wanted to be sure, and three was very sure.

The knights clustered around him, each straining to see what would happen. Marakon was also captivated. The first time he'd met the boatman, he'd done nothing other than find him. It seemed like a lifetime ago.

He began to wonder if it had all been a strange dream and that he wouldn't come. They'd all be standing there expectantly on the beach, and he would look like a right idiot. But if it had been a strange dream, then he had been dreaming his whole life. Perhaps he'd left it too late, and now he was stuck here. At least he'd be with Jarlain, but what about his knights? He owed them everything and, by the goddess, he would kill Karhlusus to set them all free.

The sea had stilled since he'd spoken the name, the water was flat as glass and mirrored the pink-tinged clouds above. Awed murmurs came from his knights as the waves ceased completely. Mist formed on the horizon and billowed towards the shore. In that mist, the prow of a boat materialised. He could make out its ornately carved sea serpent head with the swinging lantern held in its clenched teeth.

Marakon grinned, between calling the boatman and his arrival, only moments had passed. The boatman must have been waiting for him. Could he still be too late? Had the hourglass run out of sand already? The boat neared the shore and the bent over old man struggled to stand up. With his oar, he pushed the boat forwards until it reached the sand. Lan raised an eyebrow at Marakon.

'He's more than just an old man,' Marakon reassured.

'I hope so,' Lan sniffed.

As soon as the boat touched the sand, it changed from a beautiful shining dark wood design to an old creaking thing that looked as if it could barely keep the water out. Marakon stepped forward. The boatman said nothing as he reached a wrinkled old hand into his sack, his face remained hidden in his hood. Carefully he pulled out an hourglass and showed it to Marakon. All that was left at the top was a pinch of pink sand that did not fall. Marakon looked from the hourglass back to the boatman with a frown.

'I had given up hope, King Marakazian,' the boatman said in a wheezy voice. 'But once again the goddess reminds me that when all seems lost amazing things can happen. Despite what you might think, time does not move in equal linear chunks—it speeds up or slows down depending on what the soul has to do. The sand stopped falling when you reached your knights. Not a moment too soon. You really surprised me,' he nodded and laughed.

'What if I had failed?' Marakon dared to ask the question.

'Then you and your knights would never be free, King Marakazian,' the boatman replied.

'I was King Marakazian once, a long time ago. But now I am not a king. I am simply Marakon Si Hara, a commander in the Feylint Halanoi,' he said.

'Indeed you are, Marakon. Time to let go of the past. Now you know what you must do to be free.'

'I must kill Karhlusus, once and for all. Then we can be free,' Marakon said and clenched his fist.

'Karhlusus resides in the Murk, I have seen him there, but the pathways to the Murk are closed. You yourself closed them,' the boatman said, leaning on his oar. 'You will need to open them to reach him. I cannot take you there directly until this is done. But by the time it's done you won't need me to give you passage there.'

'I do not remember closing them. Nor do I know how to reopen them,' Marakon frowned. He looked to his knights, but they only shrugged with blank faces.

'The Master Wizards of Maioria know of a gateway to the Murk, and only they can tell you, *if* they will tell you,' the boatman said.

Marakon inclined his head. 'I will find out how. Where can you take us now?'

The boatman raised his hands. 'Wherever you choose. Across the Sea of Opportunity the destination depends upon those I carry. If you wish you may stay here, though you will not find those wizards or reach the Murk.'

Marakon considered this for a moment then shook his head. 'I would stay here, but I want to be free. We want to be free. The chains may have loosened, but they are still there. I will go where I'm needed most, and I must see my boys and my Rasia.' A gut-wrenching longing to be home overcame him and he choked back the pain.

'So be it, Marakon Si Hara,' said the boatman. He gestured to them to get in the boat. The knights looked at each other, frowning.

'How can we all get in? We'll have to travel one at a time,' Marakon said.

The boatman laughed. 'Yes, I can see why you would think that. I do not exist upon the physical world as you do, things are different where I reside. Step into the boat and you will see.'

Still holding his horse's reins, Marakon stepped over the edge and steadied himself in the boat. He pulled his unwilling horse forwards, and it clumsily clambered into the boat. Immediately the boat stretched to accommodate the horse comfortably. Marakon laughed in surprise.

Next came Oria, equally dubious as she stepped into the boat and pulled her mount with her. Seeing the other horse in the boat made her horse less reluctant.

Again the boat stretched without so much as making a creak. One by one the knights stepped into the boat pulling their horses with them, and each time they did the boat stretched. When they were all in they looked at each other in astonishment and laughed. The boat was now massive and the boatman positively tiny.

'How can you row now?' Marakon asked, ready to believe the unbelievable.

The boatman chuckled. 'It might surprise you to know that millennia ago I transported a whole army this way. No less than a thousand soldiers. It matters less that I row, and more that I'm here directing the boat according to the wishes of those aboard.'

'You must tell me more of that story,' Marakon said. He wanted to hear everything about this man's extraordinary life.

'In good time, Marakon,' the boatman replied.

Once they were all in, the old man somehow managed to push them all from the shore with his oar. They moved easily across the flat surface of the ocean, and soon they were engulfed in that gleaming mist. The knights seemed pensive and their horses jittery, but as the boat moved without rocking, they began to relax.

'How long will the journey take?' Hylion asked Marakon.

Marakon shrugged. 'Maybe an hour, maybe a day. The last time I travelled this way I fell asleep.'

The shore was lost from view. When it had gone Marakon took out the stone Jarlain had given him with the bear marked on one side and the sun on the other. He smiled, brought it to his lips and kissed it. He sighed and tucked it back into his pocket. He knew she would be fine without him, but that didn't stop the pain of leaving her. He yawned and settled back in the boat, noticing that the others were yawning too, even the horses drooped their heads and closed their eyes

Jarlain opened her eyes to see a sky brightening with the dawn. She was alone and the emptiness tangible. She touched where Marakon had been laying and stroked the flattened ground. It was cold now. She'd heard him get up, felt him kiss her lightly, heard him leave, but could not bring herself to watch him go.

For much of the night, she'd watched him sleeping and had only managed a couple of hours sleep herself. She felt exhausted and, for the first time in her life, afraid to face the world alone—as if a brief moment with the man she loved had rendered her incapable on her own.

She looked out across the sea. The brightening dawn hurt her eyes. It was not a rising sun of love and life this morning. Her wounded leg was sore and stiff, and she struggled to stand up. It hurt a lot more today than it had yesterday. Limping, she made her way along the shoreline towards what remained of her home.

She walked around thick ferns and saw him ahead at the shore-edge with his knights. He was taller than most of the knights, his dark hair and beard worn so differently to how her people wore theirs. He was graceful despite his broad, muscular stature. She knew now that his grace was part of his elven heritage.

Her heart leapt at the sight of him, and she quickened her pace. She would have called out, but he was talking to a very old man in a simple wooden boat. The boatman, she thought. He was bent over and seemed old even though she couldn't see his face. She went closer to hear what they were saying.

All she wanted to do was call out and rush into his arms. He could take her with him, she would willingly go wherever he went. Just as she was about to call, he spoke of his wife and family, and the words died in her throat as her world crumbled. *He wants to be with his wife and children, he doesn't want to be with me.*

Jarlain stopped in her steps and leaned against a tree, her heart falling into the pit of her stomach. He wanted to go, and she had to let him. In a daze she watched the knights climb aboard the boat. She was only vaguely surprised when the boat grew in size to accommodate them.

Emotionlessly, she watched them leave the shore until the mist engulfed them. When the mist dissipated, the boat and Marakon were gone, and the sea returned to its usual lapping at the shore. He was gone, gone as easily as he had come into her world.

Jarlain stayed there for a long time staring out to sea wondering what now to do with the rest of her empty life.

CHAPTER 15

Hunting Her

BAELTHROM stood before the great iron ring. He released his clenched fist. The black Orb of Death had been so close to his grasp, but it had slipped away. It was not so much the losing of the orb that angered him, it was his inability to claim it. He glanced at the wizard's staff propped against the altar. That wizard was powerful. He would be found via his staff. Once he was turned into one of them, he would lead his necromancers.

'I must become more powerful. I grow bored with this unending war,' he rumbled. Kilkarn, the dark dwarf, nodded beside him.

'You will become ever mightier, my lord,' he grinned.

'We must strike harder and faster. Maioria must fall to me, and that girl must be found. She carries a power that is unlike any wizard's magic. I need her essence. She must become part of me.'

'When Frayon is surrounded, there will be no place for her to run,' Kilkarn said, creeping closer.

Baelthrom stared into the swirling grey clouds within the suspended iron ring. Through it he endlessly searched for her, but despite his efforts, and for all the Life Seekers he'd sent she had managed to evade him. He'd come close, but she destroyed his Life Seeker, and the Dragon Lord destroyed his Dromoorai. He'd glimpsed her power then, and he had to have it. Where did she hide? The question burned in his mind. He barely admitted it to himself—that he desired her like nothing other—her power, her life force, it was everything he did not have. It was everything he needed to take this world utterly.

'I will find you myself in the end,' his words echoed around the chamber. The iron ring pulsed briefly. Baelthrom recognised the energy.

'What is it, Hameka?' he asked, feeling slightly irritated. Hameka was more than capable of commanding the war on his own whilst he sought other ways to find this girl. Why his second in command had not captured her yet was a complete frustration to Baelthrom.

'Lord Baelthrom,' Hameka's voice intruded upon his thoughts. The man's thin grey face appeared before him within the iron ring. 'Our new bases on the Isles of Kammy are doing well. However, the place is small and our resources are limited. Draxa had many more resources and our prisons were full there. I hope that Vornus is managing the place wisely. I have requested that he send more ships filled with Maphraxies, but that will take time and there's little space to put them.

'Put simply, my lord, our resources here are wearing thin. The attack on Celene filled our prisons for a short time. We need more prisoners to create more elixir, as well as more space to house the new Maphraxies. I think we should attempt a permanent base on Frayon sooner than planned.'

Baelthrom considered this. Hameka was right, their resources would be stretched thin now they had spread from Drax. It took time to set up a fully functional elixir plant, and a vast number of prisoners to create the first pure batches.

'It's as we expected,' Hameka continued. 'As soon as the Feylint Halanoi are cornered they fight more ferociously. But now we have surrounded the western coast, we can expect a bitter struggle on their part before the end. We need more Maphraxies than we've ever had. Especially now with that girl and cursed Dragon Lord inciting the people.'

'Good, Hameka. Then we shall attack Frayon immediately. We have enough ships for a raid and scouting mission. Focus on the closest biggest town. My spies inform me that the Feylint Halanoi are only just learning of our attacks on Celene. Even our taking the Isles of Kammy, remote as they are, has yet to be discovered by the people.'

'Thank you, my lord,' Hameka inclined his head with a subtle smile. 'We have enough ships for a swift attack. We must continue to strike them before the Feylint Halanoi has a chance to send an army west. That way we can weaken the western front, and take their resources before they even set up base there. I just feel time is running out, and I'm keen to claim the main continent.'

'If you would only fully imbibe the Elixir of Immortality, Hameka, you would not feel so keenly the pressure of now. We have the time and the power to destroy Frayon, and though I too grow bored of waiting, we must strike with absolute precision.'

Hameka swallowed. 'We must not let news of this girl and Dragon Lord spark an uprising. That and this damned blue moon has already caused… ripples.' He wiped his forehead.

'Come, Hameka, the girl is close. We will find her before she does any more damage. I will find her myself. Now, there's another thing of interest. I have seen tribes of people to the West.'

The iron ring clouded over to reveal an image, the same image Hameka would be seeing in his Shadow Key amulet. A brown skinned woman with thick black curls looked in terror back at him. She backed away shaking her head, and then the image was gone.

'That is all I had at first; a glimpse from a spy coming to me from far away. After, I looked to my Histanatarn spies, they have proven useful if only for this.'

Another image formed in the iron ring, this time they saw through the eyes of a Histanatarn. Nutmeg-scaled and webbed hands hurled a spear into a mass of white-skinned people brandishing blades. The spear embedded itself in a man's throat and he fell. The people rushed forwards. The image ended when the Histanatarn was cut down with a blade.

'Both these peoples live upon the Uncharted Lands,' Baelthrom said.

He wanted to get his Maphraxies over there as soon as possible. The more lands he controlled, the easier it would be to take control of all Maioria. 'The Histanatarns are skill-less, and poor fighters against these warrior tribes. It is only their numbers that prove a threat. But these people, though skilled in battle, are no match for the Maphraxies. They are spread out and few in number. As soon as Vornus' ships reach you, we must send a legion there and bring back prisoners. Then we'll have more than enough resources.'

Hameka smiled and looked relieved. 'This is all pleasing news, my lord. I will ready our ships immediately to attack Frayon.'

Baelthrom nodded and ended the communication. The iron ring turned dark. He breathed deeply and entered the Under Flow. It was sluggish as if it was being drained by someone or something. It angered him. He should be getting stronger and he wasn't. He let the Under Flow trickle away and resumed his searching.

One by one he looked through the amulet of each of his Dromoorai, searching for the girl. Some fought battles whilst others slept. Though they never truly slept, they simply stood still in a dark place, be it cave or dungeon, and were always ready to fight. They were his greatest creation and he wanted more of them.

Another Dragon Lord walked the earth, a powerful one at that, but it was a shame there were not more to take. Perhaps this one could be bred from and therein he could create more Dromoorai.

Hameka sighed, grinned and leaned back in his chair. He always felt drained after talking to Baelthrom, but at least this time his lord was understanding, and the order to attack was good. After seeing the lack of resources on the Isles of Kammy he'd been worried. They would not be able to take Western Frayon with what they had. They needed to double their numbers, and he hated human breeding pens, it took far too long and he didn't like having so many stinking, disease-ridden prisoners to look after.

Hameka tapped his chin deep in thought. He still needed more capable commanders. Vornus was a self-serving traitor and always would be a traitor, but for now, it was in Vornus' best interests to manage Drax whilst Hameka was away. Him and that priestess bitch Cirosa—both self-serving bastards that could never be trusted. Even after the consumption of the Elixir of Immortality, the woman was mad and bent on revenge. They both needed to be kept on a tight leash. He would have to pick his own commanders himself, especially when more continents came under Maphraxie control.

He stood up and stretched his back. At least he was off that cursed ship and his feet on solid land. He went over to his desk and poured a glass of Davonian red wine. A decent crate of the stuff had been found in the storehouses on Little Kammy, much to his delight.

Taking a sip, he pulled out his map of Western Frayon and began to look for appropriate towns to attack.

CHAPTER 16

Creating from Memory

FREYDEL sat with Arla by the river, not far from where the wizard's tower rose. They had satiated themselves with clean water from the river, and Arla had helped him gather what berries, nuts and mushrooms they could find in the forest. Being the end of summer, food was abundant, and they foraged enough to make a simple dinner with some left over to spare.

Both of them were worn out. Arla's eyes had shadows under them, and Freydel felt like he could sleep for a week. Neither of them spoke, not whilst they collected food or now whilst they ate. Freydel was busy thinking over everything that had happened to him. He sighed as he washed down his last mouthful of berries with water. He would have preferred wine to water. The food helped to restore some strength, but his hands still trembled now and again. He glanced at Arla. She had barely eaten anything.

'You won't grow up to be big and strong if you don't eat,' he said with an encouraging smile.

She glanced up at him with those strange big eyes. 'I get sick if I eat too much.'

'Ah,' said Freydel, that would explain why she was so small and scrawny. 'Well, do what you can, it will help you feel better.'

She sighed and stuffed a blackberry in her mouth. A tortured look clouded her eyes which made him worry. She'll be all right after food and rest, he told himself. Freydel reached for the orb in his pocket, hesitated with a look at Arla, then took it out anyway. The girl knew he had the orb.

She glanced at it, then looked away without much interest.

The orb was heavy in his hands, heavier than he remembered it being in the astral planes. He sat there for some time staring into its black surface, but without commanding it. With all that he had learned, what should he do now? Facing Baelthrom, being trapped in the astral planes, seeing his entire life's work destroyed, travelling back in time, meeting Ayeth, going into the ethereal planes and then returning. So much had happened he needed time to catch up. It *had* changed him forever. He felt the most learned and the most powerful he had ever felt in life. And the most exhausted.

'We've been through a lot together, you and I,' he murmured to the orb. 'Do you remember the writing on the pyramid walls?' The orb responded immediately, faster than it had ever done before, and he saw the symbols and beautiful letters made of flowing curving lines on the side of the pyramid, just as he remembered them. Freydel laughed aloud, Arla looked at him.

'I guess that was an easy one,' Freydel said with a grin and stared closer into the blackness wondering what to try next. 'Let's try something else. Hmm. Remember my book of spells, the purple one? Remember I spoke aloud to you its entire contents? Can you show me that book even though it has been destroyed?' The orb swirled, Freydel licked his lips. It pulsed a flash of black light, making both him and Arla fall backwards.

He sat back up and stared at the book on the ground before him. The purple book, with its torn pages and frayed edges, lay on the grass in front of him just as he remembered it. Freydel stared at the book open-mouthed. He'd expected a memory, the pages of the book shown within the orb, not an actual physical thing. He was too shocked to be ecstatic.

'It created it from nothing...' he whispered. 'It created something from nothing.'

Arla stared at the book, a look of surprise on her face as well.

'Not nothing,' she corrected, 'from your memory.'

'What?' Freydel looked at her as if seeing her for the first time, 'Yes, from memory, you're right. All right then, something else. Ah hah. My staff, I lost it.' He closed his eyes and formed a very clear image of his staff.

'Recreate my staff,' he commanded. The orb did nothing. 'Create for me my staff. You know, the one I always carry around?'

Nothing happened.

'Please?' he chanced.

Nothing.

'Hmm.'

'Maybe it won't create it because it still exists?' Arla said, crawling closer to inspect the purple book on the ground.

'How can that be?' The very thought of Baelthrom still having his staff, or anything of his, chilled him to the bone.

'Don't touch that,' he said as she reached to touch the book. She pouted and drew her hand away. 'There's powerful stuff in there, enough to hurt people. Hmm, why would it only recreate things that have been destroyed?'

'Because it's the Orb of Destruction?' Arla chanced.

'Pah. Nonsense. It would destroy stuff, not create stuff,' he laughed, and then stopped. The girl was right, somehow. *Could it undo undoings?* His head hurt at the thought. Arla yawned. The sun was setting, and soon it would be dark.

'Well, I have a few blankets in my study. Or rather, I had until they were incinerated in dragon fire. Those blankets would be nice to sleep in. Let's see if this really works the way we think it does.'

He looked into the orb, 'Create my two blankets. The brown ones I left on the bed.'

The orb swirled and pulsed as before. Atop the book now appeared two wrinkled brown blankets.

'Hah-hah.' Freydel laughed aloud. Arla giggled.

The tiredness hit him then and he yawned, suddenly struggling to keep his eyes open. Commanding the orb always used a bit of his own reserves, but he'd not felt this tired from using magic since he was a young wizard.

'Oh my, maybe I should be more careful what I ask for,' he said between yawns.

He heaped together the twigs and dead leaves they had collected, surrounded them with stones, and set light to them. Around the fire he pushed together two piles of fresher leaves and settled Arla down on one of them with a blanket wrapped around her.

Before it was dark he found himself drifting off to sleep wrapped in his own blanket.

Freydel awoke before dawn. Arla still slept soundly. After a drink of water he sat in the growing light thinking. The orb had become more powerful than before, or rather his ability to interact with it had increased dramatically. All keeper's of orbs had very little knowledge of their potential. He doubted even if the ancients knew the full power of them.

With the orb now he knew he had become more powerful than any wizard in Maioria. What were the limits to the orb's power? What if he could time travel at will, with a far greater understanding than Grenahyme had ever had. He could recreate everything in his study that had been destroyed, as long as he could remember it. He'd have to be careful of course. Doing too much wiped him out. Plus it would be useless to recreate all his things here in the middle of nowhere. But still, his life's works were not lost. He almost laughed out loud.

He should call the Wizards' Circle again, just like he had tried to do before Baelthrom trapped him. He would tell them everything that had happened. No, maybe he should wait until he'd thought about it more. They would think him crazy for time travelling, let alone seeing Ayeth. What if he could go back in time to where he'd left Ayeth. Maybe he could stop him from ever becoming the Baelthrom they now suffered. Ayeth was very powerful. Freydel could learn many things from him.

The Wizards' Circle must know of Celene, which was why he tried to call it in the first place. The orb and he were stronger now, and he was already in the tower. It would be safe to call it now he did not have to travel through the astral. He shuddered at the memory. Perhaps he wouldn't travel in time again.

Arla remained sleeping as the sun rose, and so Freydel had his breakfast of forest berries alone with his thoughts. Afterwards he recreated his purple wizard's cloak and hat, a clean shirt, his teapot and herbal teas, and his water flask. After a wash in the river he put on his clean clothes.

It was when noon approached and Arla still didn't awaken that Freydel began to worry. He squeezed her shoulder, but she only gave a weak groan.

'Arla, wake up, have some food and water. It's time to get up.'

But she didn't awaken, not fully anyway. He laid a hand on her forehead, it was cold and clammy. Poor child is sick, he thought. She needed water so he pulled her limp body into his lap. She groaned in protest, but when he held his open flask to her lips she drank noisily. Her eyelids flickered but she did not perk up. This was not a good place to be sick in, not when he had nothing to give her. She needed to be inside and given hot food and herbs.

Though it was warm he wrapped both blankets around her and gathered his things. He would call the Wizards' Circle right away. They could help him get her somewhere safe. They would be worried that the child had managed to get into the Circle, but he'd had no control over that, and if it weren't for her he'd be dead right now.

He put his remade belongings into a blanket and slung it over his shoulder. Next he scooped Arla into his arms, amazed at how light she was, and made his way to the Wizard's Tower.

Reaching the tower, he carefully scaled the stone steps that wound around the outside of the tower. There were no railings to stop him falling, and the steps were only thin slabs of stone jutting out from the wall. He had to stop several times to rest before he reached the top, and by the time he got there he was sweaty and breathless.

He dropped his things, laid Arla down beside his stone chair, and looked long at his western seat that symbolised Celene, the goddess's Sacred Isle. Celene that was no more. He looked at the others. Twelve grey stone pillars with hollowed out seats and thin high backs all carved out of a single stone. Twelve seats to mark the twelve continents of the Known World, twelve seats to mark the twelve months of the passing seasons and twelve seats to mark the hours on the clock.

He took a deep breath and stilled his mind. Usually, he would call the circle with his staff and the orb, but without his staff, he would have to use his skill and the orb alone. Because he was already within the Circle he would not need to use the long spell, even though it was his favourite. Being physically present also meant he could create a far stronger and secure call for those wizards travelling here. He held up the orb and called the Flow to him.

'I, Master Wizard Freydel, call the Wizards' Circle.'

At his will and direction, the Flow swirled into the orb, and then pulsed out in a wave of dark energy, sending out the call. With Baelthrom ever watching the energies of Maioria, calling the Wizards' Circle carried some risk no matter how secure he made his spells. He prayed the wizards would also respond with a safer spell for transport. It was always more dangerous for the one calling the Circle to travel in the astral planes, as he'd woefully found out when Baelthrom detected him.

He looked back at Arla. She hadn't stirred. Worry furrowed his brow. He took his seat and waited. Who would come? It had been so long since the last, he couldn't even remember how long. Would Coronos come? He was here in the Known World again and so he would have received the call, he must come. Not everybody on the Wizards' Circle had to be a master wizard, but they had to be a novice or a high wizard of a particular standing. They also had to be an Orb Keeper, a king or esteemed representative of a country or a people. Finally, they would have to have survived the Wizard's Reckoning.

In the past, every member of the Wizards' Circle had been a Master Wizard. But that was hundreds of years ago when the power of Maioria was stronger. Baelthrom constantly leached upon the magic life force of the planet so that it now dwindled alarmingly. Thinking of Baelthrom, he added strengthening spells to the protective shield surrounding the tower so that it faintly shimmered pink and silver.

He sat still and waited. At least one seat would remain forever empty. His gaze rested on the eastern seat, a seat that had not been filled for thousands of years. The seat of the Ancients, the eastern most empire, had been empty for a long time. The last person to sit upon it had been an Ancient—and she had been female, so the history recorded in the orbs told them. He gasped aloud as her name suddenly came to him.

Yisufalni, I'm sure that was her name, it is the same. He remembered the woman, the Ancient, who'd helped him. Could it be the same woman? Why would it be any different? How could she still be here? Was she trapped in the ethereal planes? She had been one of the last of the Ancients, a priestess, a princess and no less than the last female to grace the Wizards' Circle.

With the rise of Baelthrom and the splitting of the orbs, it was the female magic users who suffered the most. They found themselves weak where once they had been strong. The female life force, the givers of life... Baelthrom had the Orb of Life, perhaps that was why they were so affected.

Not that male wizards remained immune. Everybody lost strength, but women were no longer able to survive the Wizards' Reckoning in the Storm Holt—and few men were able to survive it either. Women with any magical ability became witches or joined the ancient, secretive yet tiny order of the seers.

In the end it didn't matter who was more powerful, the power of the Maphraxies increased as the power of the wizards decreased, and no one could stop it. The power of the goddess had waned in the world, but when Freydel thought about Issa it didn't add up. She wielded a power he could not fathom or fully understand. It was an old power and it came from the dark moon.

The seat next to the Ancient's, the one that stood for Tusarza, was broken. For one strange moment, emotion welled up within Freydel. Maybe it was the memory of something pure and beautiful destroyed, like his Celene. The seat was split in two by a great force. A force driven by the axe of the dwarf wizard Hadden some five hundred years ago.

Hadden, in his fury and gut-ridden guilt, had smote the chair with rage and magic—as if by destroying the chair of Tusarza he somehow thought he could destroy the Maphraxies themselves that now occupied that land. It still lay as he'd left it, split and crumbling—a sad sight serving to remind them it would take more than a dwarven axe to destroy the enemy, and that all they really sat on were stone chairs.

The other seats were as fresh and pristine as when they had been made. No weather or time could wear them, protected as they were by magic. Freydel sat up straight and smoothed his purple wizard's robe. He put on his hat. The others would be arriving soon.

No sooner had he thought it than the air shimmered blue in the centre of the circle. Freydel wondered who would be first.

CHAPTER 17

Dreaming of Home

ASAPH looked at Issa for the fiftieth time in half an hour as they rode the long road to Carvon. His horse, Ironclad, was at last tired and walked placidly alongside the others. The colour had come back into Issa's cheeks, and he was pleased to see her skin gaining a tan from the South Frayon sun. She would never be as tanned as a Draxian, but he found her smooth pale skin and dark hair so attractive.

This time she caught his watchful eye and smiled. She was tired. Thankfully her eyes were no longer that luminous turquoise green that had scared him so much, though they still seemed abnormally bright. He had never seen anyone with eyes like that before and she had been so pale and weak. The bloody wounds on her shoulders made by the harpies had healed well, thanks to that bracelet of hers, but still, she carried the fine lines of scars. He would have to do more to protect her and somehow make sure she never left his side.

She dropped her gaze and carried on with her thoughts. She hadn't said much since the raven had given her its message. Why was she seeing demons? No matter how much he thought on it, he couldn't find a reason.

'Could demons be after us?' Asaph spoke his thoughts aloud.

'Those kinds of demons are in the Murk, they cannot reach us easily. I think it's something else,' Coronos replied. 'A message, a warning, I don't know…'

Issa remained silent, deep in thought.

'Well, we can add them to the long list of our enemies. A few more won't hurt,' Asaph laughed.

'No,' Issa said but continued to stare into nothing. 'I mean, yes. They were frightening, and yes, I saw war, but it was a war between demons. The demons I saw meant me no harm. It's like they are trying to communicate or something. That white spear. I don't know why it's important. I don't think the demons mean to attack us.'

'That would be a first,' Asaph scoffed. Demons have always attacked humans. 'Demons walk the forests of the Uncharted Lands. The Kuapoh spare no human possessed by a demon incubi or succubi. The dangers are just too great. They hate and fear any shape shifter and consider them all demons even if they're not.'

'That must have been hard for you,' Issa said, looking at him.

Asaph shrugged. 'Yes. No one knew about the dragon within.' He was surprised to feel pain then. That he'd had to keep his dragon-self hidden in shame his whole life was raw even now. One day he would fly free and far wherever he wanted, proud to be a dragon once more. He fell into silent reverie. Would he ever feel settled? Would he ever find a place to call home, a home like the one Issa had mentioned?

He felt a sudden need to see Drax. It might very well be that he wouldn't like the cold mountainous place he'd seen in The Recollection. The place that Coronos had shown him in the orb and spoken of so many times. But he had to know for sure. Even if it meant he went straight into enemy territory and never came out alive, he had to see it before he died.

And what of Issa? Maybe she wouldn't want to live there either, being as she was from a small temperate island. Would he give her up just to be in Drax, just to see Drax? No, he definitely wouldn't. But the thought of never seeing Drax was almost a physical pain.

'Please may I see that old map of Maioria you sketched ages ago, father?' Asaph asked Coronos.

Coronos fumbled around in his pockets and drew out a torn and crinkled piece of paper.

'It's not in the best condition. I'll try to draw another at Castle Carvon, or perhaps King Navarr's cartographer can sell us one. He passed the map. Asaph unfolded it and stared at the rough drawing Coronos had scribbled down. Holding map and reins in one hand, he traced the outline of Drax with his finger. The familiar outline of the dragon tooth-shaped land was so familiar to him even though he had never been there.

In his minds' eye, he felt The Recollection stir, and through it he saw huge grey mountains capped with snow. There was snow there even in summer. *The Grey Lords.* The mountains protecting Draxa stood like ancient warriors; proud, majestic and ready for battle.

Beneath them stretched a plain of grass dotted with purple, yellow and white mountain flowers. The grass billowed in a gentle breeze. A single wide river flowed fast with snow melt in the middle of the plain, and hugging the mountain slopes were thick forests of hardy evergreens. The sky was clear and deep blue, and for a moment he fancied there were two bright suns and not just one shining down.

He closed his eyes and breathed deeply. The rich smell of grass, pine and snow filled his lungs. It reminded him so much of the Dragon Dream, and it whispered the very essence of freedom.

'Asaph?' Coronos' voice drifted down into the meadows of Drax. 'Asaph?' he opened his eyes, feeling the Recollection close like a book.

'Huh? Sorry, I was drifting.' He blinked trying to get his bearings.

Issa was grinning at him. 'I guess I'm not the only one who gets visions,' she said.

'I was thinking of Drax, I'd like to see it one day,' Asaph said.

'Me too. But for now we are tired,' Coronos said. 'It's getting late and I'm hungry. I think it'll be safe to camp in the woods, hidden from the road but not too far from it.' They all agreed and spent the next half an hour riding along the road looking for a suitable spot to stop.

'With two orbs we should be able to create a very safe protective field to shield us from view. Vagabonds, cut-throats, ogres or Life Seekers. Hopefully even demons won't know we're there,' Coronos said.

'And bugs,' Issa chimed in. 'Please keep those big ants away from me. We never had such huge insects on Kammy.' She shook her head in disgust.

They found a small animal track leading into the woods across a brook where a curve in the road came. Pretending to look at the map, they waited for the last merchant to disappear along the road to Corsolon.

'The road is empty, let's go,' Asaph said. They trotted along the animal track into the woods.

'It pays to be cautious when travelling and sleeping in the open,'

Coronos said with an approving nod.

In the wood they found a dip in the bank and flat grassy ground surrounded by trees not far from the brook. There they dismounted and unpacked their things.

Issa filled up all their water canisters in the brook, whilst Asaph and Coronos looked for wood to light a fire. The mayor's kitchen had kindly given them several bags of dried roots, beans, herbs and spices, and after a few copper coins from Coronos, a lightweight crockpot to make a stew.

'Avernayis,' Asaph said a while later when they were all slurping down hot stew. The horses were tethered, apart from Duskar, and busy dozing or munching on the grass. A soft glimmer over them reassured that the protective shield was in place. The sun had set, but the sky was not yet fully dark. There was a slight chill in the air now they were further north, and everyone had wrapped themselves up in their cloaks.

'What was it like? Avernayis. It's in the south, isn't it?' Asaph said.

Coronos nodded. 'The home of my birth is south of the Grey Lords. Warmer and wetter than the north, Avernayis was just a small coastal town in South East Drax. It would have been the first to be crushed under the Maphraxie invasion. It was unremarkable, but as a boy it was fun to be beside the sea, crabbing and hunting for limpets.

'As a boy, I thought I'd be a fisherman. I had no idea I would one day become a Dragon Rider, or climb so high as to be the protectorate of the King and Queen of Drax. All I knew is that when I saw the dragons and Dragon Riders flying, I just had to be one. Even now I have dreams of flying; the freedom and wonder, nothing can beat it.'

'No it can't,' Asaph smiled.

'When I fly as a raven it seems different,' Issa said. 'I guess it seems so natural, the wonder is a little lost to me. It's totally different to flying on the back of a dragon, that's quite frightening.'

'You'll learn to love it in time, and walking around on two feet will feel so cumbersome,' Coronos said.

'Can I see the Orb of Water?' Issa asked him. 'I want to feel if it can shed any light on the demons.'

'Of course,' Coronos said and passed her the orb. 'You are its true

Keeper now, I only carry it. Sadly I cannot tell you how to use it. Everything I know about my orb was passed down to me from my predecessors, and a few other tricks I learnt along the way.'

'It's all right,' Issa said, taking hold of the beautiful turquoise orb. It glowed brighter as she took it, responding to the touch of its Keeper. Asaph hadn't seen her do anything with the orb until now, not that she was doing anything, she was just sitting there staring into it. Coronos busied himself cleaning his pipe and filling it with lintel weed.

Asaph set his bowl down and sat back on the sloping grass, arms behind head, eyes never leaving Issa. He liked the way her long shiny hair fell over her shoulders. Her pale slender hands that held the orb—hands that knew how to wield a sword and were becoming calloused like his own. He would like to practice sword fighting with her sometime. He yawned and his eyes drooped down to the swirling blue within the Orb of Water. Like the Orb of Air, if you stared into it, it became mesmerising, just as Issa was currently mesmerised by it.

To visit a liberated Drax with Issa, that was his ultimate dream. He would hunt for the sword, the great Sword of Binding. It could still be there, hidden deep in the underground tunnels of Draxa, he would find it. He fancied he could see the sword in the orb then, floating within its blue surface.

The Recollection opened easily to him in his semi-mesmerised state and he saw the sword's long greyish-blue blade shining brightly, the blood red pommel formed from the blood of Slevina, the dragon queen slain by it. The sword was surrounded by darkness.

"The great sword is hidden deep within the fortress of Drax, or was. Only myself, and the King and Queen ever knew where it was and how to find it." Those were Coronos' words. He reached out to touch that pommel. As soon as he did memory that was not his own flashed before his eyes.

'Die you bitch!' he screamed and plunged his long blade deep into the gigantic chest of the dragon queen.

Asaph's memory switched. An agonising, poisoned blade was embedded deep into the shining green scales of his chest. He glared down at the hateful human and screamed in rage and agony. He lifted himself up, bringing into his belly all the fire he could muster. He belched it forth along with blood so that he sprayed the human with flames and gore. He felt himself collapsing, his punctured heart pouring away its life.

Again his memory changed. He was human, on fire, and writhing in agony. He fell forwards into the blood of the dragon. His own blood poured from a hundred burning wounds. The blood extinguished the flames, but his life was spent. There he lay on the frozen mountainside, bleeding and dying beside his enemy—the bleeding and dying dragon queen. The blood gurgled into his nose, he tried to roll onto his side.

Asaph awoke with a jerk. His heart was pounding and his chest hurt from the memory of the sword embedded in it. He blinked into the blackness trying to remember where he was. Coronos and Issa were sleeping beside him. His arms were dead from having fallen asleep with them behind his head. He lay back down waiting for the blood to come into them and the pain to go. He had been dreaming, dreaming of Qurenn and Slevina. Great Feygriene, those memories were so vivid. He gave a long sigh, still shaken.

Coronos was snoring softly and Issa snuffled now and again. They must have left him sleeping. He hadn't realised he'd drifted off. He felt wide awake now though. Finally, his arms were functional again and he eased himself up to sitting. He took a long drink of water from his flagon, and his dragon sight adjusted to the darkness. There was a little starlight coming through the trees so it wasn't pitch black.

A movement to his left captured his attention. He peered into the forest, then stood up and picked up his sword silently. It was probably just an animal. Nothing would see them encamped here unless it was a magic wielder up close. The hairs prickled on the back of his neck. Something was watching them. Could it see through the shield or was it just looking in their general direction? He came to the edge of the shield, just a subtle shimmer in the air.

Something white moved amongst the branches in the distance. He strained to see, but it was gone. If he left the safety of the shield, whatever it was would see him and their presence would be known. Unless, of course, they could see him already. Why would he feel eyes upon him if he was shielded? Only a hunter could have that affect on him, the prey. He gripped the hilt of his sword and pulled it a little out of its scabbard.

An owl hooted in the distance. Another owl, this one much closer, replied. There came a distant rustling, a flicker of white in the trees far away, then the sound of a bird taking flight.

Asaph sighed and slotted his sword back into its scabbard. *Just owls hunting.* He sat back down, plumped up his cloak into a pillow, and lay down. He kept his sword close as he drifted into a deep sleep.

CHAPTER 18

Project Dread Dragon

EDARNA couldn't get to sleep, her mind was filled with Dread Dragon scales and all the things she could make from them, not to mention the gold she could earn. She could advertise in Carvon, stick posters up around the city. Word would spread quickly amongst scrying witches.

Dragon scales could be the one thing that reunited all the witches together. Imagine that, the Coven rekindled. She could start a movement, Rekindling The Coven. No witch in her right mind would ever turn down the opportunity to get her hands on incredibly rare dragon scales. She would become Grand Witch just for restarting The Coven, hah.

She twitched her toes and twiddled her fingers with what could be. Nope, there was no question about it, she'd have to get those scales no matter what. The body of the Dread Dragon was decaying fast, though the scales would decay last, their condition would already be deteriorating. Her livelihood depended on it.

The embers of the fire still glowed, but Naksu hadn't moved for a good half hour, the seer had to be asleep by now. Edarna sat upright, startling Mr Dubbins who was curled up beside her.

'Shouldn't you be hunting mice at this time?' she whispered to the cat. 'I'm going back to the Dread Dragon.' The cat's eyes narrowed to half-slits. Edarna interpreted that clearly as, *'I can't be bothered.'*

'Come or not. Do as you please as always,' she huffed and stood up.

A Quick-Walk spell would get her there in half an hour, and if she worked fast, it wouldn't have worn off by the time she returned. She had one night to do this, and this was that night. She highly doubted the seer would agree to her going back to the dead Dread Dragon, and certainly wouldn't want to come with her. Nope, she was on her own on this one, and she worked better that way anyway.

They had camped several miles north of the beast where, finally, the smell of death and rotting had disappeared. Mr Dubbins yawned, stood up, and went over to the sleeping form of Naksu. He curled up beside her and went back to sleep.

'Fine, lazy cat,' Edarna hissed. People thought it was all very nice and cute when cats curled up next to you, or let you stroke their fur, but all they really wanted was to steal your heat and get a massage. Edarna knew their ways very well, and she was not fooled.

'You'd better look out for her while I'm gone. Or else.' The cat opened one eye, rolled it up to look at the witch, then slammed it shut.

'Hmph!'

Edarna put on her green witch's robe and instantly felt ready for work. She stuffed her wooden chest under one arm and crept into the forest. There were no moons tonight but the sky was clear, and the way was lit by starlight.

She walked some twenty yards away from the sleeping seer, opened her chest, and pulled out a green vial half the size and width of her little finger. Scrawled in barely legible writing were the words *"QUICK WALK."* She unstoppered it and downed the sour liquid.

'Urgh. Great Goddess. Why can't they add a little sugar. Damn novice witches. No one to teach 'em anymore.'

Regardless of the foul taste the potion worked immediately. She felt strength and energy flood into her legs—a feeling she'd not felt since she was a young witch. She grinned wickedly. 'Let's go fast.'

She set off at a stomping walk-run, covering the same ground in ten minutes that took an hour before. She did not even sweat or get breathless as she followed their tracks back the way they had come.

Soon she was engulfed in rotting stench, and in less than an hour she burst through the trees to stare again at the horrific massive decaying body of a Dread Dragon.

Edarna slapped her mouth shut and got down to business right away.

'So, hmmm,' she surveyed the beast. 'Let's start on the hard bits while we're fresh.'

The old witch set down her chest, and with a word it expanded to its normal size of about three feet long by one foot high. She whispered her secret spell to unlock it, and it undid smoothly even after all these years and a recent dunk in a lake. She lifted back the lid and rummaged around inside. She drew out a long knife with a serrated edge close to the hilt, a thin reel of elven rope, and her prized hazel beam wand. At a word the tip of the wand began to glow white and illuminate the area nicely.

'Uh huh,' she nodded with a smile, then began to work out how she would get on top of the dragon to reach the largest, toughest and unblemished scales flowing along its horny spine.

Wand between teeth, she hooked the so far indestructible elven rope that had never let her down around the furthest horn and pulled herself up onto its head. She stood there balancing for a moment, half afraid the thing would wake up.

Moments passed, and nothing happened. She breathed a sigh of relief, and hooked the rope around the next reachable horn, leveraging herself onto a flat bit between its horns and its spine. With a loud belch, the scales gave way and her foot sunk an inch into bloody puss.

'Urgh.' The sudden stench of rotting flesh made her gag, and she wrapped her shawl around her mouth forcing the bile back down. She struggled to pull her foot up, and it slowly released with a loud sucking noise. Carefully, she scraped the goo off her boot onto one of its horns and began to leverage herself up again, choosing her footholds more carefully.

'Oh, my.' She bent over breathless at the top of the beast's bulk. A particularly shiny scale caught her attention, and she bent closer to inspect it. 'A little blemish on the side, but nothing major.'

Satisfied she took hold of her wand and placed it against the scale's edge where it overlapped the next. 'You remember this part from before, don't you, Wandy.'

Carefully she traced the wand around the scale, and where it passed a thin line of orange glowed. Next, she took her knife and carefully prised the loosened scale free. It took some tugging, then suddenly came free. Edarna sprawled backwards clutching at her elven rope and the scale for dear life. She held herself still for a moment, then grinned and tossed the scale down onto the grass beside her chest.

She pulled herself up and continued the increasingly tiring process of extracting scales. The hours ticked by as the witch worked over the body of the Dread Dragon, selecting the finest scales of all types and sizes. It wasn't until the light of dawn blushed the sky pink that she realised how long she'd been working. She stretched out her aching back and yawned, but the thought of more dragon scales drove her on. Just a few more, it was always just a few more.

When the sun burst over the top of the trees, Edarna pulled the last tiny neck scale free with a yawn. Her legs were also beginning to ache— the first sign that her Quick Walk spell was beginning to wear off. She sighed, she wanted more, all of them. Reluctantly, she made her way to the ground and packed the horde of scales into her chest.

'Now for the fun finale,' she grinned, pulling out a small black pouch.

Using a stick she lodged the pouch into the beast's lips, held her wand close and whispered a spell. A flame ignited at the end of the wand and set fire to the pouch. Edarna pelted it behind the nearest tree.

An explosion rocked the ground and sent every bird in the vicinity screeching into the air. A few moments and lots of smoke later, huge chunks of rotting flesh began to splatter down around the corpse. When the last chunk of flesh had fallen, she ran over to the beast and squealed in delight.

'One fine dragon tooth.' She clapped her hands and reached down into the gore where she extracted a tooth thicker than her wrist. Carefully, lovingly almost, she wiped the black blood and drool off onto the grass, and stuffed the tooth into her chest. With a word the chest shrank down to its travel size, and she tucked it under her arm.

With a last reluctant look at the mutilated Dread Dragon corpse, she sped back through the forest, consoling herself that she'd harvested the very best scales she could find and a dragon tooth.

By the time Edarna arrived back at their camp, Naksu was already up and heating tea over a fire. The albino seer looked at her with a raised eyebrow as she nonchalantly slipped from the trees into the clearing. Edarna smoothed back her hair and sniffed proudly.

'I was up early collecting herbs for my supplies,' she said. 'We witches must be disciplined with our sleeping. You need to be up at dawn or before to get the freshest ones.'

Naksu snorted, and Edarna noticed her hair was wet.

'Has it been raining?' Edarna looked up at the clear sky.

'No, I had a swim in the river at dawn,' Naksu said stiffly.

'Oh. Hah. Must be a seer thing. Is that necessary so early?' Edarna gave a sweet smile. *They swim at bloody dawn in a freezing river?*

'If you want to exercise and cleanse your body, mind and soul, then yes,' the seer replied.

'Oh,' Edarna nodded, feeling more than a little unfit. She sat down with a yawn. 'I just need to stretch my back out, not as young as I used to be,' she lay down and stretched.

In less than a minute, she was asleep and snoring deeply. The seer looked on with a wry smile as she stirred her tea.

CHAPTER 19

The White Owl's Prey

THE next morning everyone was up early with the dawn. They were just about to mount their horses when Issa felt the orb pulse. She pulled it out of her sack, it was flashing blue. Duskar sniffed it with interest. She looked back at the others with a frown. Coronos pulled out his orb. It was flashing white. He cupped the orb with both hands and stared into it. She copied him, but couldn't see anything other than swirling turquoise. She felt out the magic flowing into it.

'I can feel a presence as if the orb is communicating with somebody or something far away,' Issa said.

'My oh my,' Coronos said with a smile. 'If I'm not mistaken I think someone is calling the Wizards' Circle. Something I have not seen or felt since we fled from Drax. If I had more skill with magic I would know who called it. I must answer the call. Our journey must wait.'

'What happens now?' Asaph asked.

'We re-tether the horses and I accept the call. I will then be transported to the gathering of wizards,' Coronos explained, he seemed excited and eager to be gone. He retied Socks to a tree.

'Do we all go?' Asaph asked hopefully.

'No, we cannot. Only initiated members of the Wizards' Circle can answer the calling. It's not a denial of entry,' he added, obviously seeing the disappointment on Asaph's face, 'but a matter of your physical encryption. If you are not a member, then you simply won't be able to be transported there.'

'But I am the Orb of Water's Keeper,' she said. Surely she'd be able to go. 'And it's clearly calling me.'

'Of course, I understand that, but you won't be able to accept the call even if you tried. You still need to be a member of the Wizards' Circle.'

'How do I become a member then?' she felt a little miffed. She *was* an Orb Keeper now, and she *could* use magic, and the orb *was* calling her.

'You must be invited by the Circle to undertake the Wizards' Reckoning,' Coronos said. 'But it wouldn't matter anyway. They will not ask you.'

'Why?' she huffed, folding her arms. There better be a good reason. 'I've proven myself to be good with magic, Freydel said so himself. I killed Keteth when no one else could. And now I carry an orb, entrusted to me by the Wykiry. *And*, what other wizard can turn into a raven?'

'All these things are true, but it's not about any of that,' Coronos shook his head with a sigh. 'They won't ask you to join because you are female.'

Issa scowled. 'So what?'

'Well, I don't really know the ins and outs of it,' Coronos said awkwardly.

She caught Asaph grinning at his father's discomfort and pinched him. He forced a straight face and turned away to tether Ironclad as Coronos continued.

'Women haven't been members of the Wizards' Circle for… I don't know how long, maybe since the Ancients. It's not that they are denied entry, it's just that few survived the Wizards' Reckoning after the magic of Maioria was split apart. And when Baelthrom took the Orb of Life, none survived the testing. It seems the magic ability of women was hit terribly hard. Many no longer tried to wield magic and instead turned to witchery. The strongest of them became seers, of whom we wizards know very little.'

Issa looked at the ground. Hearing this made her sad and annoyed. She knew she could wield more magic than Coronos, and she had an orb. She was still developing her magical skills too. Maybe she would even be as strong as Freydel. She couldn't be the only woman skilled in the magical arts. How strong were the seers? Were women really not as strong as men?

'What if I took the test and survived?' she said, glancing at Coronos to gage his reaction.

He looked at her. 'If the Wizards' Circle agree a person has magical ability, and that person wants to take the test, they cannot be denied.'

'No way.' Asaph came over to them shaking his head. 'It's not worth risking it. We have more important things to do, and our lives are threatened enough as it is.'

Issa ignored him. 'What happens to me if I take the test and survive?'

'You will become stronger in every way, particularly when it comes to magic. You will understand yourself better than ever you did before, and you will know your deepest darkest fears, your flaws and weaknesses. Obviously, this test will take you to your very limits and beyond,' Coronos said. His face had paled, perhaps in memory of his own Reckoning.

'But Asaph is right. It's not worth the risk. And anyway, I'd better get going.' He set his pack and cloak on the ground and sat down beside them.

Issa wanted to know more about this Wizards' Reckoning, and for a moment wondered what would happen if she somehow accepted the orb's call. In the end, it was respect for Coronos that made her relent, but she was not happy.

'I guess you should take this with you then.' She pursed her lips and handed him the Orb of Water.

He smiled and took it. 'It would please the wizards immensely.'

Issa and Asaph watched Coronos as he settled down with the orbs.

'How long will you be gone?' Asaph asked.

'As long as it takes, but never more than a few hours,' Coronos said without breaking focus on the orbs. And then, with a flash, he was gone.

'Wow,' Asaph said. 'I've never seen him do that.'

Issa grimaced, unable to stop the intense feelings of jealousy.

'Don't worry about it,' he said, placing a hand on her shoulder. 'I wish I could go too.'

She sighed. 'Yes, but, it's more than that. We need wizards, witches, seers and all magic wielders working together, not separated into their little groups. As one we are strong, apart we are divided.' Her own words surprised her. 'I wish I knew how to fight this war to be rid of the Maphraxies for good.'

'We all do,' Asaph agreed. 'But at least this gives us some time alone together,' he pulled her close, 'to chat,' he stroked her cheek, 'and to…'

The butterflies in her stomach began to dance as she looked up into his blue eyes. '…kiss.' He bent to kiss her.

She found her anger dissolving as their lips touched. He hugged her close and rubbed her back gently as they kissed. She returned the touch, the muscles of his back hard and firm under her hands. His hands moved to her hips, and she found herself suddenly giddy. His kisses became more intense, and his tongue touched hers making her shudder in delight. He gently stroked her bottom, and she sensed he was losing himself too.

All of a sudden she began to feel out of her depth and afraid. He was too close, not just physically. She couldn't make sense of her feelings. Like shutters coming down, she felt herself close up. She pulled away with a gasp.

'Are you all right,' Asaph said, blinking.

'Yes, sorry, I… Just too much right now,' she tried to explain.

'I'm sorry—'

'No, it's me. I got scared. I don't know why.' She cut him off before he could apologise.

'I got carried away. You are so divine,' he smiled.

She grinned back feeling her cheeks redden. 'I need some water.' She wiggled out of his embrace and went to find her water flagon.

'Why don't we do something fun,' he said. 'Like hunt for truffles and nuts. We might even make something tasty for lunch. After I can show you the best way to clean your sword, or something.'

'Sounds like a good idea,' she said. Glad to do something else rather than sit there feeling awkward. 'The shield will hold until we take it down or the magic wears thin. The horses and our stuff will be safe here without us.'

All awkwardness forgotten, she followed him into the forest.

Cirosa had not left the place by the stream where she'd sensed strong magic and smelt that odd scent. Remaining in owl form she'd been hunting her prey for days, and come across that scent a day ago outside of the gates of Corsolon. Human, definitely human, and something else she had not smelt on a human before. Dragon. It smelt like Dread Dragon, only alive. It could be him, the Dragon Lord she'd been sent to find.

She had not seen the owner of this scent yet, despite diligently following the trail along the road north out of Corsolon. It was probably because she only hunted at night. An owl in the day was ripe for hunting, especially a white one. Besides, the bright sun really hurt her eyes now, though it didn't used to. The smell was strong here in this place by the stream, and at first, it had confused her, for she couldn't see any people and yet the scent stopped here.

Many times she'd circled above looking for where the people were or where the scent led off but found nothing. Only when she had flown close had she felt the energy in the air, the familiar feel of magic like static on the skin making her feathers feel fuzzy. They could be using magic to hide, so she stayed close, waiting to see if they revealed themselves, and now she dozed in the hollow of a tree.

'See who can find the most mushrooms.' A man shouted below startling her awake. Seeing it was still day her owl-like mind tried to drift back to sleep.

'Ha-ha. I've found another one.' The man's voice prevented her from falling back to sleep.

'That's not fair, I've only found one.' A female voice came from afar.

Suddenly remembering her pressing task, Cirosa looked out of the hole. Below her, a reddish-blond haired man was on his knees digging out mushrooms. She stared at him transfixed and moved a little further out of her hole to get a better look.

It was him, it had to be. He fit the description Baelthrom had shown her in the amulet, a tall, blond, long-haired Draxian. And that strange smell, a mix of human and dragon, was coming from him. She stared at the man, unable to believe she'd found him. She drew the Under Flow to her. She couldn't hold much in this form, but it was enough to see the man's aura. It was like fire, vibrant and alive. *The powerful aura of a Dragon Lord. You cannot escape me now, stupid man.* Baelthrom would reward her well.

She thought upon all the ways she'd planned to trap him, and how she would bring him triumphantly before Baelthrom. There were so many things to try, men were easy to seduce. That would be the best way to take him. Then she would tell her lord that she had him. It would be easy.

The man stood up, rubbed the back of his neck, and looked around. The smile on his face became a frown. His hand went to his sword. The white owl slunk back. The man turned to stare straight up into the trees. She froze. He seemed to be looking right at her. For what seemed like a minute they stared at each other. She couldn't be sure he could see her through the leaves, and she was a long way up. If she moved he would definitely see her, so she stayed there frozen to the spot.

'Hah. Look I've found four now.' A young woman with long black hair ran into view and the man dropped his gaze.

Cirosa shuffled backwards, angling her head so she could just about keep her prey in view. Hatred for the woman surged in her veins, even in owl form, and a bitter taste flooded into her beak. She wanted to screech her hatred aloud, and only sheer hard will stopped her from doing so.

That bitch. For a moment she couldn't remember why she hated the woman, then she remembered Rance, *idiot of a boy,* and her life back on Celene. Her name was foggy in Cirosa's memory like so much was after her rebirth into the arms of her lord. It didn't matter who she was anyway, Cirosa wanted to kill her, and could imagine the satisfaction of doing so right now. *Claw out her eyes and rip her flesh apart. I'll take her man as she took mine and rip her apart in front of him.*

'What's wrong?' she asked the man.

'I don't know, I...' he began, looked up again, then shook his head. 'I think we're being watched. I felt it last night when everyone was asleep, but I only heard owls. Then I felt it just now, something watching us.'

The woman looked around the forest. 'I don't know, now you've said that I think I feel it too.'

'Let's get back under the shield and make some lunch. I hope Father isn't gone too long,' the man said and turned to go.

'Good idea. Race you there.' The woman laughed and sped off.

'Hey, not fair, I wasn't ready.' The man tore after her.

Cirosa slunk back into her hole, seething with hatred. She consoled herself with a victorious feeling at having found her prey. She would not let them out of sight now. All she had to do was plan her attack. It would have to be perfectly timed. No mistakes or unforeseen things could destroy her chance to take her prize to her lord.

CHAPTER 20

The Wizards Arrive

FIRST to arrive was Haelgon, dressed in purple silk robes that put Freydel's own to shame. They billowed in a non-existent wind as his form took shape in the centre of the circle. His black skin glistened, and his blue eyes blinked as he took in the surroundings.

'Freydel.' He grinned and walked over to him.

Freydel got up to greet the Atalanphian High wizard and shook his old friend's hand.

'It's been a long time since last we met in person.' Freydel smiled up at the tall man.

'Indeed it has. I felt a faint call some time ago, but when nothing more happened I ignored it,' Haelgon said. He glanced down at Arla in surprise. 'How did a child get here?'

'She is sick, it's a long story, but I'll explain everything when we're all here,' Freydel said, and indicated to the centre of the circle where the air began to shimmer again. Haelgon nodded and went to take the southernmost seat that symbolised Atalanph, glancing back at the curled up child as he leant on his mahogany staff.

Drumblodd's unmistakably squat but strong dwarven stature wavered before them. The exiled Venosian dwarf leant not upon a staff but upon a long bladed axe. A short purple cape draped across his wide shoulders. His red beard was heavily entwined with white—more so in the six months or so since Freydel had last seen the dwarf. His hard face was set in a familiar scowl that hadn't softened with age. His scowl always made Freydel think that it was to hide the sadness and guilt that plagued the dwarves, knowing as they did that it was their kin the dark dwarves who'd helped Baelthrom rise to power.

Venosia had fallen to Baelthrom over four hundred years ago, and the dwarves had fled. They were tough. They managed to thrive wherever they went, even in the harshest of places. Some went to the sweltering deserts of Atalanph, but most went to the frigid Everridge Mountains that separated Davono from Lans Himay, and spread the entire length of the Frayon continent. In both places, they built cities underground and managed to make a home.

Drumblodd blinked at Freydel and then Haelgon. 'It's good to see you both again,' he said in a gruff voice and bowed to them. For all the months they'd not seen each other, the dwarf was, as always, of few words. They hailed him back, and he turned to take his seat, heavy dwarven armour clanking.

Freydel wondered, and not for the first time, if the dwarf slept in his armour. He always seemed to be dressed in it, and it surely took more than half an hour to put on. Drumblodd was a novice magic wielder and had little patience for the arcane arts, preferring instead to skill himself in weapons. However, he was the current king of the exiled dwarves living in the Everridge Mountains.

Third to arrive was the elf, Averen. His violet eyes appeared in the mist before anything else. He was tall and pale with long coppery hair tied back in a silver cord. His face had not aged in fifty years, blessed as elves were with a long life and youthful looks even until death. Freydel was surprised to feel a pang of jealousy, knowing grey flecked his own beard now, and that lines creased his face. The elf had that usual amused look in his intelligent eyes, and he took the longest to marvel at their surroundings.

'It's been so long... Woetala's beauty is so pure here,' he said, then saw Freydel.

'Freydel.' He came over and shook his hand. Averen's purple robes shimmered with a silver hue, again putting Freydel's own to shame. 'Haelgon, Drumblodd, how wonderful to be together again. We really should meet up more often.' His eyes rested on the sleeping child, and he raised an eyebrow at Freydel.

'All will be revealed,' Freydel reassured.

The elf travelled a lot, frequently moving between the courts in Atalanph, Davono and Frayon, where his wisdom and music were always welcome. He needed no fixed abode or books or scrolls but kept his wisdom in his remarkably sharp mind—managing to memorise a great many things just once and recall them easily. High Wizard Averen gave a graceful bow and seemed to glide as he took the Elven seat of Intolana, a land also lost long ago to the Maphraxies.

Averen had been one of the few elves to stay behind when his people withdrew into the Land of Mists. Though he wasn't as strong as the elf wizards before him, he was powerful enough to be a high wizard, just one rank below a master wizard. Of the elves that had remained, most found homes in the forests of Davono and Lans Himay that clustered around the mountains where the dwarves now lived. The truce between all three races; dwarf, human and elf, held only under the shadow of their shared enemy, Baelthrom. Freydel was aware that peace between them was a small blessing to take from their shared dire future.

Young Luren from Lans Himay was next to arrive. The scared-looking, mouse-like man was a novice wizard, but his ability was such that he had the potential to become a high wizard, maybe even a master wizard with hard work. The man had been a young boy apprentice to Master Wizard Grenahyme, and was the most suitable person to take his master wizard's place. His purple robe hung limply on his shoulders.

'Greetings, fellow wizards.' He smiled nervously at everyone, bowed deeply to Freydel and scurried to the seat of Lans Himay.

Navarr, King of Frayon and also a novice wizard, was next to arrive. The man was tall and stern with a short brown beard and hair. A scar ran down his cheek gained from a battle against the Maphraxies. It served to add to his ruggedly handsome looks but was also a tribute to his bravery. Navarr was always keen to fight alongside his soldiers against the Maphraxies. Navarr would never be more than a novice wizard, and like Drumblodd he respected battle skills over mastering the Flow. This made the human king and the dwarven king great friends and strong allies. What skill he lacked in magic, he made up for in the sword.

'Freydel,' he beamed, grasped his hand, and then stared down at Arla. 'How did she get here?'

Freydel smiled. 'There's a lot to tell, we're nearly all here.' Navarr raised an eyebrow, nodded, and turned to greet the rest of the Wizards' Circle.

When his father King Thaban died, no one wanted the heir to the throne of Frayon risking his life in the Storm Holt, but the prince was adamant and no one could deny him entry when he chose to face his demons. Navarr was as impatient as he was ambitious. To say he had barely survived the Wizards' Reckoning would be correct. But they'd all barely survived. The testing took you beyond sanity. It was up to you to return. And the prince had. And soon after became king.

The air shimmered. Next to arrive was Master Wizard Domenon. Quiet, handsome, ambitious and untrustworthy Domenon. The man was dark-haired and bearded, and as tall as Averen and Coronos. His eyes were a strange smoky grey, and they darted everywhere taking in everyone, measuring up everyone, missing nothing.

Freydel composed himself. He did not like the only other master wizard in Maioria. As far as he was concerned, the man cared only for himself and was always looking for opportunities to further his own ends at the expense of others.

Dark within as well as without, so Freydel had always thought. He just knew Domenon begrudged all Orb Keepers, the way he looked at the orbs hungrily, clearly longing to have one in his possession. If he owned one, he would be as powerful as Freydel was. Something that did not sit well with him at all. Apparently, he was a wizard who came out of nowhere, long before Freydel was born, and he rose rapidly to the rank of Master Wizard. He said his parents were killed by Maphraxies after he was born, and he was just a poor scullery boy living on the streets before a kind wizard saw his skill with magic and took him in.

One thing was clear, there was more to Domenon than was known, far more. Like Averen he never seemed to age, and had been a member of the Wizards' Circle long before even Averen was on it. That he did not inherit the Orb of Death, or any other orb, was a huge source of anger to the dark-haired man, and possibly a wise move on behalf of the orbs' previous Keepers.

'Greetings, wizards and powerful men. How wonderful it is to be all together once more after so long.' Domenon bowed low as they greeted him back. He turned to Freydel.

'Freydel, how good it is to see you. I felt you call the Wizards' Circle some time ago, but when there came no final confirmation in the calling, I began to worry.'

'Greetings, Domenon. When we're all here I shall explain everything,' Freydel smiled.

Domenon frowned and took them all in. 'All here? We are all here.'

Domenon was the only wizard Freydel had not spoken to since Coronos had returned. Freydel's smile deepened. The man had clearly not felt or sensed Coronos' return, let alone contacted him.

'Not all,' Freydel said. 'But goodness, every time I see you, I'm reminded of how little you've aged since we first met decades ago.' The observation was a challenge or more a query on his strange past that no one seemed to know about.

'As you well know, it's a tribute to the Draxian and Elven blood that runs in my veins,' the man smiled proudly.

Freydel was suspicious. Apart from his height and agelessness, the man had nothing about him to suggest he was a Draxian or an elf. Freydel suspected age-defying magic, which always ended up being black magic. But to talk about it to the others would be to accuse and smear another member of the Circle. Something that was unacceptable unless absolute proof was discovered. And anyway, they needed peace amongst them, not more divisions.

Master Wizard Domenon was powerful and skilled even if he was twisted wrong somewhere, and the Circle could not afford to lose a master wizard. Besides, he'd never actually done anything wrong. He watched the man take the Davono seat next to Navarr, who smiled tightly at him. Domenon had the ability to make everyone feel uncomfortable.

The last to arrive was Coronos. The sight of the old Draxian warmed Freydel's heart, which had been left cold by Domenon. All the wizards' eyes went wide in shock. They laughed and got off their seats to greet him.

'Coronos.' Freydel said. He hugged the old Draxian.

Coronos looked old. Deep creases lined his face like canyons where once only crevices had been. His hair was ivory white and wispy, no longer thick and full, and his grey eyes, though still clear, were filled with sorrow. Something deeply troubled the man, and as weary as he looked he had all the attributes of a tightly coiled spring.

Coronos smiled and squeezed Freydel's shoulder. 'You don't know how much it pleases me to see you all here.' He took them all in and nodded. 'After all this time.'

The wizards spoke at once.

'Tell us where you've been?' 'Freydel told us you'd returned.' 'We thought you were dead.' 'What happened to you?'

Coronos shook his head and held up his hands. 'So much has happened... over twenty-five years. I cannot even begin to explain all. We fled Castle Draxa, just a handful of us, and we barely survived the Lost Sea. But though Feygriene was not with us when the Maphraxies took Drax, she was with us on our journey to the Uncharted Lands. The few of us that survived the journey, found lands inhabited by strong, honourable people. Amongst them, we thrived for twenty-five years.'

Looks of amazement and wonder spread across their faces as Coronos spoke at length of his time away; from the fall of Drax to their arrival in the Uncharted Lands, and the people they lived with for a quarter of a century.

Freydel was well aware that no one had ever travelled to the Uncharted Lands and returned, mostly because of Keteth and the vast distance across the sea between the continents. All he'd ever heard were myths and legends of lands beyond the Lost Sea, but now he had proof of those unknown lands, the world suddenly seemed a much bigger place.

He listened enthralled as Coronos told them of his and Asaph's life with the Kuapoh, and their treacherous return and run in with Keteth.

The wizards clustered closer, and he felt his orb grow warm and hum a beautiful sound, like the low note of harp strings. The other wizards' orbs also began to hum as if in greeting to each other. He smiled, and everyone laughed, wonder mirrored in each other's faces as the Flow moved pure and strong around them.

'The orbs,' Averen said. 'They sing stronger than they ever have. Stronger even than when we last met with Coronos.'

'The orbs sing stronger because I bring the Orb of Water with me.' Coronos pulled from his cloak a stunning turquoise orb.

Freydel's eyes went wide and everyone gasped except Domenon, he couldn't help but notice the hungry look on his face. He'd felt a shift in

magic when Coronos had arrived but was so taken up with the return of
the Draxian to the Circle that he'd paid it no heed. Now he understood
why the Flow moved so powerfully. The orb was strikingly beautiful, and
tears came into his eyes as it glimmered and sung in Coronos' hands. He'd
never seen it before except in the memory of his own orb. None of them
had seen it before.

'For so long this orb has been missing from the Wizards' Circle,'
Averen breathed, speaking Freydel's thoughts aloud. The elf frowned and
shook his head. 'Poor Wykiry.'

'I'm not its Keeper. For protection, Issa, to whom the Wykiry gave
this orb after she finished Keteth, entrusted me as its Secondary Keeper. I
don't know why the Wykiry passed on to her the orb, surely it would be
more protected beneath the ocean, but they have their wisdom.'

'They would have done it with good reason,' Freydel nodded
thoughtfully. 'And what a gift to the Circle it is.'

'I think they may have wanted to return it to the people of the land.
Maybe even for it to be with the other orbs,' Averen said. Freydel
considered that. The elf was probably right, the reasons to give it to Issa
would be many fold. It also made her very powerful, and he was pleased
about that, she needed all the strength she could get. But he wasn't sure if
she was the right person to be an orb keeper.

Coronos grasped the elf's hand. 'Averen, you've not changed in all the
long years I've been away. Nor you, Domenon,' the Draxian turned to
shake the Davonian wizard's hand.

'But you.' Coronos gripped King Navarr's hand. 'You certainly have
changed from a boy into a man, and congratulations, I never thought I'd
have the fortune to be with you on the Wizards' Circle. I'm deeply sorry
about your father. He was a dear friend of mine.'

'I know, Coronos. He passed peacefully,' Navarr said and nodded to
reassure. Freydel looked at the ground. King Thaban had been a good
friend of everyone.

Coronos smiled. 'I'd hoped to see him again, goddess rest his soul.
I'm looking forward to chatting with you before a good fire and a nice
bottle of wine. We were in Corsolon, and told the mayor to send carrier
birds warning of Maphraxies on the West Coast. Something we must all
talk about urgently. We're on our way to you right now, and travel the

road between Corsolon and Carvon.'

'We've heard rumours of Maphraxies but received no official warning yet. I'll send riders to the coast and inform the Feylint Halanoi immediately. You are always welcome at my court, Coronos Dragon Rider.' King Navarr addressed him formally, making the old Draxian smile. 'Everything that you left with my father is still locked away in the vault untouched. When will you arrive?'

'Thank you, that is comforting news,' Coronos said. 'Hopefully in a day or so.'

'There is much we all have to discuss,' Freydel chimed in, 'especially about the enemy drawing near. Let us place the orbs and be seated so we may talk in turn about all that is important, and why I called the Wizards' Circle.

'The orbs sing louder for I too bring an orb not seen in the circle for a long time,' Drumblodd piped up just as everyone turned to their seats. The wizards hesitated and stared at him as he drew out the Orb of Fire.

'You bring the Orb of Fire?' Freydel said. He actually felt faint with elation, that and the powerful magic coming from all the orbs. The wizards clustered close again to look at the flaring orb in Drumblodd's thick-fingered hand. It looked like a ball of flowing lava and flared the colours of fire; orange, yellow and red. It flashed red several times as if it was communicating with the other orbs.

Drumblodd nodded. 'I bring it with me, finally, to its rightful home. I never agreed with Obearn's hiding it away. As you know he named me Secondary Keeper before he died, but then he passed away without telling me where it was. I'd been the Orb of Fire's Second Keeper for nigh on thirty-five years. After years of searching, we found it deep in a vaulted molten chamber.'

Freydel nodded. 'Obearn's ways were always… difficult. Keeping the orb from the Circle, as he kept himself away, was the source of many disputes amongst us, but we could not force the issue. We are just lucky it is with us and not with Baelthrom. But anyway, four orbs together in our possession; this really is a cause for celebration. Now the shield will be impenetrable.'

He looked at the subtle transparent rim of the shield surrounding the Wizards' Tower, like a huge bubble around them, its edges visible every now and then. He began to relax. He'd felt pensive ever since calling the Circle.

One by one the wizards placed the orbs in the six indents hollowed out in the stone at the centre of the Circle. Seeing the blue of the water orb contrasted with the red of its sister the fire orb warmed Freydel's soul. From the smiles of the other members, even Domenon, he knew they felt the same.

'If only the elves would bring to us the Orb of Earth rather than hiding it and themselves away in the Land of Mists,' Averen sighed. There was sadness suddenly etched in his smooth features.

'At least the orb is not in *his* hands,' Freydel said. The only orb truly lost to them, and a major hole in their power, was the Orb of Life. *You may have stolen the Orb of Life, and by doing so kept us all in chains, but you have not, after thousands of years, managed to steal the others from us, Baelthrom.*

They all took their seats. Freydel's heart went out to Coronos as he watched the older man lean heavily on his staff and take the northern seat of Draxa. He sat in it wearily and wiped a hand across his brow. Coronos was wise and learned but always remained a novice wizard. Still he had power beyond his own skill because he held the Orb of Air, and more so now that he was Secondary Keeper to the Orb of Water.

He dropped his eyes back to the orbs; black, white, blue and red. These past few days he'd learned more about his orb than he had in a lifetime of studying it. He was already the most powerful wizard here, and yet he'd unlocked more power within his orb and within himself, and there was still more to learn.

Perhaps he should be the Orb of Water's Primary Keeper now. He was strong enough to hold two. It would certainly be the safest thing for it. Issa could not take the burden of looking after it herself as well as everything else. He'd have to think about how best to broach the topic with the other wizards. For now, there was a more pressing issue at hand, and he didn't look forward to discussing it.

'Four orbs and eight members of the Wizards' Circle now together, where once we would have been six and twelve,' Freydel said ceremoniously. A hushed silence fell upon them, and he swallowed. 'My friends and fellow wizards, I have some terrible news. I dread to inform you that Celene has fallen.'

CHAPTER 21

Maggot

A deafening roar shook the ground and walls of the demon hall within the rocks and earth of Eastern Middle Murk. All of the Shadow Demons gathered there cowered back from their rage-filled king. Even the wings on Maggot's back trembled with the sound.

The crystal shard dimmed and darkness fell upon the hall. King Gedrock's roar seemed to echo for hours. Stillness crept forwards and eventually silence descended upon the shaken demons who stood frozen. Fearful eyes glowed red as they looked at each other, all wondering what horrific things the king had witnessed in the crystal shard to make him howl. Maggot pulled on his ears and twitched.

Gedrock's eyes flashed, wild with rage and fear. A green ray of Zorock's light pierced through the highest round opening into the cave, illuminating the underground hall and the huge gathering of Shadow Demons. The king gave a look of pure shock and horror—a look so unnatural on any demon's face. Unrest like a cancer spread through the crowd. Maggot was afraid.

'The raven did not lie. Our end, the end of the Murk, is coming. I have seen it in the crystal shard.' As the king of the Shadow Demons spoke, more of Zorock's green light fell in through the opening, by design cleverly illuminating the great stone chair upon which King Gedrock sat.

Maggot cowered and shivered. He had heard about the awful raven that had come from the higherworld foretelling their king of their doom. Gedrock continued, his deep voice rasping and constrained.

'But more than that, the Demon Slayer returns, and with him his

Banished Legion,' veins bulged on Gedrock's neck as he spoke. He dropped his hands from the jagged crystal embedded in the waist high stone before his throne. It was taken from the crystal caverns beneath Carmedrak Rock when the Shadow Demons fled thousands of years ago. The crystal shard pulsed green in Zorock's light, reflecting the moon of the Murk even as the moonlight cleansed and charged it.

The hall was the busiest Maggot had ever seen it, and like every other Shadow Demon here he bustled close to see their king. The demons shuffled nervously, but not one of them dared utter a sound. Usually they'd all be chattering when great gatherings such as these took place. The gathering had been called because of the king's vision, and they had all felt it—something bad had happened. Something terrible to cause such a disturbance in the energy of the Murk. It seemed to be coming from that awful bright place above; the higherworld called Maioria where extremely dangerous, but very tasty beings resided.

The larger demons in front of Maggot shuffled forwards and blocked his view so he had to squeeze between their legs and wiggle closer to see the throne. Whilst the tallest demons in the room reached up to ten feet high, Maggot was barely two feet tall and numbered amongst the smallest of the lesser demons. King Gedrock rubbed his face with a clawed veiny hand. Maggot shivered again as the fear in the room slithered over him, a horrid alien feeling.

'Our mortal enemy can only have returned for one thing, to claim the spear and destroy us utterly.' Gedrock's muscles bulged on his arms as he clenched his fists and hunkered back in his great chair. Sweat gleamed on his grey skin and all over his bald scalp little veins stood up. The demons around him whispered and shuffled.

'The crystal shard does not lie. Even as our destroyer returns, our own kin are turning upon us, led by one that is not even our own. The Grazen and the greater demons are organising themselves. As I speak, they are preparing to attack us, to wipe us out completely, so that the greater demons can take all. But we will never submit ourselves to that demon-human half-breed, Karhlusus.' Some Shadow Demons howled out in agreement, whilst others shook their heads with worry. They all were in agreement in their hatred of the demonic wizard Karhlusus.

'The greater demons want nothing more than to take our home, the

Murk. They have already enslaved our kin, the Grazen, and they will not stop until we are all slaves to them. Our troubles are dire, and they are many.' Gedrock's eyes turned hard as he surveyed the Shadow Demons standing before him, all looking to him, their king, to lead them, to protect them.

Maggot caught the king's gaze and dropped his eyes to the floor. His king was awesome but also scary. After a moment he peeked a look. Gedrock's eyes had returned to the glowing crystal. It made him shine green too, making him seem even more so their great king. He leaned upon one hand and scowled in thought. The crystal shard pulsed and the Shadow Demons clustered around him even closer, wondering what it was their king would see, for only the king of the demons could access the crystal shard. Gedrock's eyes gazed far into other planes.

'I see our utter annihilation.' Horrified chattering filled the hall in response, but did not disturb Gedrock's spoken thoughts, 'and I also see our freedom.' All mutterings ceased. Gedrock frowned in confusion and his voice dropped to a whisper. 'I see the spear of death. I see Velistor.'

The demons hissed. Their red mouths filled with fangs opened wide and snapped shut. Some shook their heads and tugged on their ears. Maggot felt sick and belched loudly. His stomach was the first thing to suffer the effects of fear and nervousness. The gnashing of teeth calmed as a look of understanding spread across and smoothed Gedrock's face. His long flat nose twitched.

'The Demon Slayer will hunt for Velistor, but in his finding it lies our freedom,' Gedrock's eyes shone brighter.

The king's advisor, Wekurd, a gangly demon whose skin was sagging and pale with age, bent close to Gedrock's large ear and spoke, his voice thin and whining. Maggot was close enough to hear what he said.

'We all know Karhlusus has Velistor under lock and key, and protected by greater demon magic such that none of us could possibly undo, even if we could find the spear.'

Gedrock looked away from his advisor and nodded slowly, his lipless mouth taut and grim. He remained that way for a while, long enough for ideas to form and whisperings to begin amongst those gathered. Then he spoke in a hushed voice that still managed fill and echo within the hall.

'If the Demon Slayer does not find the spear, the crystal shard says we are doomed.'

Maggot began flapping his wings, trying to ease the tension and intense emotional heat that filled his body. He struggled to take everything in. Freedom from the greater demons, freedom from the detested Karhlusus who had enslaved their cousins and ever threatened to enslave the Shadow Demons. Freedom from those upon the higherworld with whom they had warred for eternity. Freedom or utter annihilation. The extreme options were just too hard to comprehend. He listened pensively for his king to say more.

'We cannot fight greater demons, and we cannot fight our kin chained by them. We never could,' Gedrock's advisor said, coming closer to the king.

Gedrock side-glanced at him, nodded slightly and rested his eyes back on the crystal shard. The light of Zorock fell fully through the opening now and illuminated all the Shadow Demons in green. Zorock was full tonight, and the crystal shard would be at its most powerful, another reason why they gathered now. Gedrock lifted his arm and laid a hand upon the crystal.

'Our death awaits us in all directions but one. That's what the raven showed me, and the crystal shard confirms it. The Demon Slayer, our mortal enemy, must find the spear, and with it slay our other enemy. He will not stop until Karhlusus is dead, he cannot for it's the only way the Cursed King can be free. And it's the only way we can be free. All else is our annihilation.' Gedrock took a deep breath and let his hand drop from the crystal. 'We must open the demon tunnels.'

Shock and horror filled the voices of the Shadow Demons as they dared to disagree with their king. Such an act of dissidence would be crushed painfully, but to Maggot's surprise, the king ignored them.

'And we must make a pact with our ancient enemies.'

The hall hushed into stunned silence. Maggot's wings beat faster, lifting him off the ground. He opened and closed his mouth, struggling to comprehend what he'd just heard. The demon tunnels hadn't been opened since the Demon Wars over three and a half thousand years ago, long before his soul had been dug out of the rocks of the Murk. Since then the tunnels had been sealed by the Demon Slayer who supposedly now walked again upon the higherworld.

'They'll destroy us all,' the King's advisor breathed, his eyes were wide. 'The Demon Slayer will destroy even lesser demons on sight. We cannot possibly make a pact with him.'

Maggot's wings beat faster than his heart and he struggled to control his height, having to roll head over tail to drop lower in the air. Not that it mattered what he was doing, every demon was struggling in their own way and no one was looking at him. All eyes were locked onto the king and his advisor.

'Not with him,' Gedrock shook his big head. 'We make a pact with another, the one who speaks with ravens. We must make a pact with the Raven Queen.'

A squeak escaped Maggot, and he clamped his hands over his mouth. How could they even think about talking to one of those ugly, painfully bright, higherworld beings? Humans—their most hated enemy who'd destroyed thousands of demons over millennia and wouldn't hesitate to do so again.

Maggot's head bonked the ceiling and made his vision go blurry. He did another cartwheel to drop lower in the air, nervous energy refusing to let his wings slow their frantic beating.

'Even so, we cannot open a demon tunnel. Only a greater demon has the power and even they could not break King Marakazian's seal. Not even Karhlusus could.' The king's advisor continued to dissuade him, but Gedrock's face was firm.

'The crystal shard never lies,' Gedrock repeated. 'There is one gate they did not close, and it is hidden by the wizards of the higherworld. There is still one gateway into Maioria. Protected by powerful magic, yes, but closed, no. Once there were even ancient demon tunnels within the earth of Maioria, tunnels that the humans never discovered.'

'But my great King, *that* gateway also leads downwards to the greater demons in the Pit. It is simply too dangerous, we cannot enter it.' The advisor shook his head but backed away when Gedrock's ears began to twitch and his eyes narrowed, a sign he was getting irritated. 'Perhaps we should speak on this in private?' Wekurd posed in a high-pitched voice.

'Enough,' Gedrock roared, and every demon took a step back. 'All must hear this for it concerns our very future. The crystal shard never lies, and only before the King of the Murk, the true king, does it reveal our destiny. I have seen our future, and there is only death and the sinking of the Murk into the Pit to become one with the greater demons. And we the Shadow Demons, all of us, their slaves. This cannot happen.

'Only a pact made with the one I have seen in the crystal shard, the one they call the Raven Queen, can bring us close to the one that would destroy us all. Through the crystal shard, the Storm Holt gate can be reached, and only this gate still links us to Maioria. The wizards of the higherworld never closed this gate because they knew that once they had, they would not be able to test their magic and power against the demons in the underworlds, they would never know how strong their enemy had become if they shut that gate. So they left it open. To reach the Pit they must first reach the Murk. I shall send one of us through the Storm Holt gate to find the Raven Queen. One of us that is the least frightening to the humans '

Silence descended upon the Shadow Demons as their king spoke. Maggot did another frantic cartwheel, the action only making him feel even sicker. A belch clawed its way up his throat and out his mouth. It echoed loudly in the silence. The king glanced at him. Maggot clamped his hands over his mouth.

'I shall send Maggot.'

Maggot's wings finally stopped beating and he dropped to the stone floor with a thud.

CHAPTER 22

Remembering the Prophecies

THE wizards looked at each other, their faces a mix of sadness and confusion. Freydel frowned. He'd been expecting a reaction of shock. As if seeing his confusion Haelgon spoke, his deep voice was soothing.

'Master Wizard Freydel, we know the devastating news of Celene. We are all still reeling from it.'

'How do you know?' It was Freydel's turn to be shocked.

'The first to know were the Daluni,' Averen said, worry for Freydel vivid in his face. 'They said ravens told them. Then we confirmed it for ourselves.'

'But how can you know so soon?' Freydel struggled to make sense of what he was hearing.

'Freydel, are you all right? Where have you been? Celene fell a week ago,' Navarr said.

Freydel sat back in his chair. How could that be? He shook his head as the other wizards looked at him, worry now mirrored in all their faces.

'I've been gone only half a day, a day at most since I first tried to call the Wizards' Circle.'

'Freydel, my friend. Tell us what happened. Why did you call the Circle, and why did the first call fail,' Averen said gently, sensing that was the heart of the problem.

Freydel nodded and considered where to begin. 'Initially, I intended to call the Circle to discuss Issa, the young woman I talked about when we last scryed together and discussed the rising of the dark moon. As I mentioned then, to put it simply, the events that I witnessed over the past few months all fit exactly with what I knew of the Prophecies of Zanufey.'

Several wizards raised sceptical eyebrows now as they had when he'd last spoken to them through the orb. For a moment it seemed all the ancient prophecies swam in Freydel's mind, and he wished he had the time to tell them and show them everything he'd witnessed. He raised his hands in placation.

'Before you judge, I would ask you to be open-minded and try to recall all that you can of the ancient scriptures and prophecies, whether you believe in them or not. You all know the prophecies about the dark moon even though you might have forgotten them. Grenahyme was particularly versed in them, and I too became well-versed after he entrusted many of his prophetic books to me. It was a raven that led me to Issa, ship-wrecked as she was on Celenian shores. You know that the raven is the messenger of Zanufey. But few people now remember what once our ancient ancestors knew.

'That the planet, our Maioria, has cycles, just like each moon has a cycle and the sun too. We vaguely manage to track these cycles by using the term "Ages," but our efforts are not so accurate. Nevertheless, my friends, I believe a new age is dawning upon us other than the "Last Age" that was forced upon this planet by Baelthrom. The new age is coming with the rising of the dark moon, and the goddess Zanufey oversees this new age.

Navarr shook his head and spoke his mind. 'I don't believe this goddess is with us, if there ever was such a goddess.'

In the past, such open denial of the goddess, in any of her guises, would have caused gasps of disbelief, but the learned men said nothing. Luren and Domenon even nodded in agreement.

"But the wise men will not believe…" written translations of the Nameless One came to him then. Freydel sighed. Losing belief in the goddess, and the hopelessness that went with it was a sickness spreading across the known world. Baelthrom's coming had planted the seeds of doubt, and it had been growing steadily ever since as the prayers of his victims went forever unanswered and the future turned dark.

'A month ago I would have agreed with you,' Freydel began. 'But the extraordinary events that have come to pass involving the dark moon and Issa I cannot easily ignore. I would be a fool to ignore. When the raven tapped on my window at dawn all those weeks ago, everything changed.'

Freydel took a deep breath and told them everything that had happened since he had found Issa and everything that he knew of the young and naive woman from the Isle of Kammy.

'I did not want her to face Keteth, despite knowing the power she could wield,' Freydel concluded. 'But my hand was forced by Cirosa, the High Priestess of Celene—and next in line to the Oracle might I add. In matters of the goddess, and of course the goddess's chosen one, the Temple has the final say.'

Averen and Haelgon looked intrigued, whilst Luren, Drumblodd and Domenon looked unmoved.

'There are three potential Children of the Raven,' Domenon said, and everyone looked at him in surprise, including Freydel. 'But only one will be strong enough to become the Raven Queen. Should such a warrior exist, of course.'

Freydel gave a half smile, allowing the man a little more respect for his knowledge of the prophecies.

'I, too, am well versed in the prophecies, *many* prophecies, not just those of Zanufey and the dark moon,' Domenon said, his eyes lingering upon Freydel. 'The Raven Queen of prophecy will bear a mark somewhere upon her body. A mark neither there from birth nor made by any weapon. A mark that appears when she's coming into her power.'

Freydel swallowed. He did not know these prophecies, and he had not seen a mark upon Issa nor had she mentioned one. Domenon was sceptical about her, so it was unlikely he was making these prophecies up. Though the man would support anything that served his own interests, whatever they might be.

' "The mark of the goddess, the mark of the messenger, the mark of the alter self," ' Domenon recounted from scripture.

'I'm not familiar with these scriptures. Who wrote them? Where are the texts?' Freydel said.

Domenon smiled as if he'd scored a victory. 'As I said, I'm well-versed in many prophecies. I have a collection of some of the most ancient books upon Maioria. That quote is from the Book of Ages. A book that compiles pre-ancient literature and fragments of history from ancient inscriptions found on long-lost temples. There is only one copy of this book, and I keep it in my private library within Rebben Castle. Perhaps we can arrange for you to visit it sometime?'

Freydel grimaced then forced a nod. 'I would like that.' How he could have missed any book on the topic of the Raven Queen was a source of dismay. That Domenon had such priceless information at his fingertips left a bitter taste in his mouth.

'I choose not to believe in the goddess,' Domenon continued, adjusting the ruby ring on his finger. 'At least not in order to enrich my life or bring me the things that I desire. It follows, then, that I am not one for prophecies. The thought of fate makes me feel... unwell. I prefer to live my life as I wish, and learn from my own mistakes and experiences regardless of there being a deity to guide me. Destiny is simply a choker on a spirit who longs for freedom. Whether or not the prophecies are true remains to be seen. Personally, I'd prefer not to believe in them or waste my time with them, but it does not make them false or non-existent. I have enough of an open mind to realise that.'

'It's all nonsense,' Drumblodd scoffed.

Luren yawned, and Navarr fidgeted as if wanting to get back to his tasks.

'Gentlemen, whether you want to believe them or not, that is up to you,' Freydel addressed them all. 'This young woman, barely a beginner in the arcane arts, destroyed Keteth with her abilities. This cannot be denied. In truth, I did not want to believe the ramblings of mad men and women, and on this topic, I had many discussions with a similarly sceptical High Priestess of Celene.'

The wizards began talking to each other all at once so that Freydel could not make out what was said. Only Coronos remained silent. Frowns and nods, sighs and laughs of disbelief filled the air. It was Coronos' quiet voice that stilled them to silence again.

'It's very clear to me and all that I've witnessed, that Baelthrom and Keteth both felt the power in her, and perhaps the threat or asset she might become to them. Baelthrom desires her so much that he would strain his forces this far south and risk his lands up north.'

Freydel smiled at the wise man's words. 'Indeed, Coronos. Baelthrom is no fool. Perhaps it is foolish old men like us who don't want to believe there could be powerful magic moving in the world once more.'

'There is a new magic moving in the world once more,' Averen said. 'Or perhaps it's an old magic rekindled with the blue moon that rises. But talk of prophecies aside, for we have talked much about them before now. Freydel, you suggest there is more to your calling the Wizards' Circle.'

'Yes, I digress,' Freydel agreed. 'After Issa arrived, much happened in such a short amount of time…' He thought back to the time just before he called the Wizards' Circle. It seemed so long ago now.

'I was in my study on Celene as normal. Everything was as it should be, *everything was fine*. I used the orb to scry for her, for Issa. I knew Keteth was gone; the Flow told me that. I saw her alive, and the Wykiry were with her. Then I saw Maphraxie warships and Dread Dragons. They were so close to Celene, it had to be an attack. I had to warn everyone. I called the Wizards' Circle to warn you all of Celene and to ask for your assistance…' Freydel's voice wavered. Coronos watched him, seemed about to speak, then looked away with a frown. Freydel dropped his gaze to stare at the four orbs, hoping to seek strength from them.

'Freydel, we are all deeply saddened by the loss of Celene,' Averen breathed.

'Aye, there was little we could have done,' Drumblodd said.

'What is done, is done,' Freydel said and told them why the call failed.

The wizards listened silently as he described how Baelthrom had chased him, and how he'd lost his staff and become trapped in the astral planes. He told them of the purer power of the orb in the astral, and how he travelled back and forward in time. Worried glances were shared when he spoke about the High Priestess of Celene, and that she may have betrayed them, and of how Yisufalni came to him when he was dying. He wouldn't be here if Arla hadn't reached him, and that was how they were both here, thankfully alive.

The one thing he did not tell them, for good or ill he would never know, was meeting the beings beyond the stars, and of Ayeth. For some reason he could not bring himself to do so, he needed more time to think about what had happened. Perhaps he also did not want them to know that travelling to another planet entirely could be done. He finally fell silent, and the other men looked at each other dumbfounded. Even impassive Domenon looked shocked as he stared at the orbs.

'Can it really be Yisufalni?' Averen said.

'She was most certainly an Ancient, such as the orbs have shown us of their makers. What do you know of her?' Freydel asked.

'Yisufalni was the last female to sit upon the Wizards' Circle, although in the Ancient's days it wasn't called that, though I don't remember what it was called. She was a High Priestess and a princess, daughter of King Fulucia of the Usteralax people. That's all I know of her for that is all that's recorded in the old records. Perhaps she watches us from afar, whether from this life or the next, who knows,' Averen replied, his eyes shining with wonder. Everyone seemed to be considering what it meant.

Arla stirred and gave a small murmur, bringing Freydel back to his responsibilities.

'The child is sick, maybe with a cold or fever. I have not the necessary herbs and potions to treat her here.' He frowned down at the child curled up in blankets. Deep worry for the girl nagged at him. It seemed more than just a fever. 'I don't know the extent of it, but she communicates with this Yisufalni. Perhaps she can tell us more when she's well again. But I must get her to a better place and soon. Maybe when we're done here I can take her somewhere with good healers. I have no home to return to…' he trailed off into little more than a whisper.

'You are welcome at Castle Carvon,' Navarr leaned forwards. 'There is plenty of room. And since Coronos is joining us, maybe we should make of it a celebration. But for now, my worry lies on what the enemy plans next. They won't stop at Celene, that was just a warning, a show of might. I must ready Frayon's western coast for attack immediately.' Navarr clenched his fists and scowled.

'I shall take you up on that, Navarr, your healers are skilled,' Freydel said. 'As soon as we are together we will plan how to protect Frayon. Warn the Feylint Halanoi as soon as you return.'

He wanted to set the king's mind at ease but could think of nothing to say. An attack was imminent, there was no ease to be found.

'It would be good to spend some time with you, Freydel,' Coronos said. 'And you needn't worry about Issa, she's safe and well. My son looks out for her, and has taken quite a shine to her.' There was a twinkle in Coronos' eye.

'Son?' Freydel asked, and the others looked at him in surprise.

'Adopted son. It's a long story.' Coronos smiled and hesitated. A frown of pain or concern crossed his face, 'but he is as dear to me as my own daughter was. It's been so long since I have been in the Old World, and even then I never really talked to the Circle about my love life, so you may have forgotten that the Lady Eleny of Celene was my daughter.' Coronos' voice did not break, remarkably, but his sorrow was tangible.

Ely. Freydel gripped the arms of his chair so tight that his knuckles cracked. He'd driven down his feelings for Celene so that he could survive up to this point. With everything that had happened, he'd not had a chance to think about anything other than his own desperate survival. Now Coronos' words seemed about to break him. It hit him at once, and he would have fallen had he been standing. Ely was gone. It didn't feel true. The other wizards looked at the ground and shook their heads not knowing what to say.

'I hadn't forgotten, Coronos,' Freydel lied, his voice barely a whisper as their eyes met. For a moment the two men shared their silent sorrow.

'If there's anything I can do, please let me know. Ely was a dear friend of mine.' Freydel's voice cracked. He tried to think of Ely now and found he simply couldn't bring her face to mind. He couldn't bear to think about the fate of the people of Celene. *I should have died with them…*

'Sometimes I wish I were back there, on the Uncharted Lands with the Kuapoh people,' Coronos spoke wistfully as if to himself. 'It was a hard but happy twenty-five years of my life away from the scourge that eats Maioria. Now I'm back I don't know if I can cope with witnessing those I love taken from me again. But then I knew Baelthrom would go there too, in time. There's no safe place in the whole world.'

'Tell us about your time with Issa,' asked Freydel, desperately needing to break his thoughts of Ely. 'I would like very much to know your experiences and opinions. Tell us what happened after Keteth was slain. We must know everything there is to know.'

CHAPTER 23

The Shores of Home

MARAKON drifted and awoke many times in the journey across the Sea of Opportunity, as the boatman called it. His knights and their horses all dozed too, most slept now whilst others blinked blearily across the ocean. Nobody spoke, it seemed wrong to break the silence. Something about the place, the smooth, silent travel across calm waters, the hypnotic glittering ocean and the perfectly timed rhythmic rowing of the boatman, made sleep steal across you before you even knew you were tired.

'Are we near yet?' Marakon whispered, leaning forward to Murlonius in front of him.

'Only you can decide when we are there, Marakon,' Murlonius replied without breaking rhythm.

The cryptic answer initially annoyed him. He wasn't inclined to mysteriousness and demanded clear answers as any commander might. But then he remembered the boatman's words, *"the destination depends upon those I carry."*

'But what if we all choose different places?' Marakon asked, then he noticed the old boatman's hands were no longer wrinkled and aged, but smooth and pale like an elf's.

'What trickery is this?' he started, and his hand instinctively dropped to his sword.

'No trickery, Marakon.' As the boatman turned to look at him, the hood fell back from his face. Marakon gasped at the man's smooth features and strangely long skull. Murlonius continued without breaking the rhythm in his rowing. 'We've simply left the physical planes of Maioria and now my true image, the body I had before I was cursed, is revealed.'

Marakon shook his head in disbelief. The elven ancestry was definitely there but this man was indeed an Ancient.

'I told you I was cursed, and I'm cursed to never set foot upon Maioria. I am indeed an *ancient* Ancient, as you people call us,' he chuckled. 'After Baelthrom destroyed my people, he bound me with magic I could not break. Never able to die, but trapped forever here in this place.'

'Where is this place?' Marakon asked

'This is no place. It is simply the space between places, and I have been here for eternity,' Murlonius said. The weariness in his voice made Marakon feel tired, and he let go of his sword feeling a little ashamed at himself. 'And regarding your original question, who ever calls me decides upon the destination. You want desperately to see your Rasia and to go where you are needed most, so that is where we are headed. And now, it seems, we arrive. Look there.' The boatman raised a hand and pointed ahead. 'The mist clears.'

Marakon stared ahead as a dark patch of clearing formed in the mist. The sea began to lose its sparkle and the waves became choppy, waking the knights and horses. Marakon squinted through the mist, trying to make out what was beyond it. Then all at once the mist disappeared and a cloud covered scene took shape.

On the horizon, a hump of land rose above dark ocean. The sky was filled with heavy clouds and rain began to splatter on his face. He shivered. Though it was the end of summer, this place felt frigid compared to the heat of the southern Uncharted Lands.

Marakon glanced at the boatman. The man had his back to him as he continued to row, but his hands... They were changing from smooth, pale skin to what they had been before, shrunken and shrivelled and covered in age spots. *A man as cursed as I am.*

'Is there any way to end your curse?' Marakon asked.

He shook his head. 'Only when Baelthrom is dead and gone can we be free.'

' "We?" There is another?' Marakon frowned. The boatman nodded but said no more.

The boat began to pitch and roll in the unsettled water, and Marakon's attention turned back to the scenery unfolding around him.

The familiar pale grey cliff of Wenderon Bay stood out against the darker grey cliffs that bordered it. The cliffs undulated up and down the north-west coast of Frayon for miles. A lump formed in his throat. Rasia was here, and his boys, just the way he'd left them. Finally, after so long at war, after going through hell and back, he'd come home.

'We arrive at dusk, but there will be no sunset this day,' the boatman said looking up at the heavy sky. His old man's voice was weak and raspy, and he'd pulled his hood low over his face.

A few lights of the town glinted in the dullness. The town nestled into a dip in the cliffs and Marakon fancied he could see their house at the highest point at the back of the village, a light in the window still on, though it was too hard to see that far ahead.

They neared the shore from the south, following a fast-flowing current. Marakon couldn't stop staring at the town. He searched everywhere for a glimpse of Rasia or the boys amongst the grey buildings, but he couldn't make anyone out, the people were probably all huddled inside away from the wind and rain.

When the boat touched the sand of the southern most beach, it was no longer an ornately carved masterpiece with a sea serpent's head at the bow. Instead, it had become an over-sized, aged and warped boat that barely kept the water out. He was keen to jump off the creaking old thing. He came close to the boatman as the knights disembarked.

'Thank you, Murlonius the Ancient. If I ever survive long enough to lift my curse, I'll do everything I can to help you lift yours.'

The boatman's face was hidden in his hood, but Marakon heard a smile in his voice.

'May you have what you seek, Marakon Si Hara. I look forward to when the rest of your days are filled with peace and light.'

The mist came, and with an oar, Murlonius pushed his shrinking boat back into the sea. Marakon watched him disappear with sadness in his heart. The man who was cursed to live in no place for eternity. Hope, both a poisonous thing and a saviour. When there is no other choice hope was the only thing to cling to. He wasn't sure if he liked hope.

He turned back to his knights. Ghenath's face turned to horror. She pointed northwards out to sea. Marakon whipped his head back towards the ocean and his stomach lurched.

'Maphraxies, lots of them,' Marakon growled, taking in the familiar spider-like shapes of the ships speeding towards the shore. There were four that he could see clearly. Their black masts splayed wide and their thin hulls slicing through the surface.

'These are the Maphraxies you told us of?' Cormak asked, gripping the haft of his axe. Marakon nodded grimly.

'They're coming in fast. We should raise a warning,' Lan said, and mounted his horse.

'Ready yourselves for a long a bloody battle. Spare no enemies, they are not alive anyway,' Marakon said, and pulled himself into the saddle. 'Especially protect the children, they'll want them for their Black Drink. And for goddess's sake do not get captured.'

The knights galloped along the sandy beach to the harbour. Marakon was hoping to be stopped by a guard or town's officer, but there were only two fishermen sorting through their nets. They turned to look at the fast approaching knights on their white horses. The first fisherman fell back from Marakon as he pulled hard on his reins to a walk.

'We mean no harm,' Marakon cried out before the man turned to run.

The fisherman hesitated and then stayed, eyeing them nervously as Marakon came closer. Rain ran off the man's grey beard, his wide yellow hat was unable to keep the weather completely out. His younger apprentice came to stand beside him, hugging his long yellow coat tight around his neck to shield against the wind.

'There's danger. You must go from here immediately.' Marakon pointed back towards the black ships approaching. The fisherman's eyes went wide in horror.

'How many?' he gasped.

'Four, at least. That's far more than we and the whole of Wenderon can fight,' Marakon said. He had no idea how they could possibly fight four ships full of Maphraxies, but he had to warn them, and he had to get Rasia and his boys safe. 'Go now, tell everyone to run, or fight if they wish.'

The two men ran off, shouting their warnings to the other fishermen. Marakon turned back to the ships. There looked to be five now, gangly spiders looming close.

'We'll protect the townsfolk as best we can, but in the end, we'll flee,' he said.

Ironbeard nodded. 'Then let's not make it easy. Lan, Drenden, Meyer, help me close the port gates. The rest can spread the warning.'

Marakon nodded his approval, remembering the dwarf was always quick thinking. The four knights galloped off towards the port. Marakon and the rest cantered through the cobbled streets, the sound of their horses' hooves echoing loudly.

The fishermen managed to spread the alarm quickly, and soon scared and bewildered people began to flood out of their houses, shops and taverns, clutching their children and belongings to their chests.

The knights weaved their horses amongst them, yelling their warnings. Their cries were taken up by the people, and soon screams of "Maphraxies" and "run" filled the air as panic brought the whole town to life. Those who were young and fast were already running to the hills, or bareback on horses and donkeys, whilst others locked themselves away in their houses and basements.

Those who stayed would not survive, Marakon knew, but he could not force people from their homes. The situation was hopeless enough as it was. All the while he shouted warnings, his eyes travelled to the east of the town where the hill rose, and where Rasia would be with his boys. He had to get them out and get them out now. A glance behind him told him the ships had reached the shore. It would not be long before he'd be face to face with his most hated enemy once more.

He felt it moments before the shadow engulfed the town. A shiver of deathly cold ran up his spine, his heart skipped a beat, and all the noise and mayhem dimmed to silence. His white eye throbbed and his hands trembled. His horse pranced to the left and slipped on the wet cobbles, almost throwing him off. The other horses reared and the fleeing people stopped in their tracks and fell to their knees.

Marakon could do nothing as the dragon fear gripped him in terror. A screeching roar ripped through him and wind gusted as great wings beat down from above. His horse suddenly bolted. All he could do was grip the reins until the fear strangling his body loosened its hold. His white eye throbbed so painfully that even when the fear began to subside he couldn't think or see clearly.

'Slow, calm.' He shouted the words to his horse as soothingly as he could and began to regain some control over himself and his mount. He brought his horse to a shifty stop behind the back of an old barn on the edge of town. He was alone in a dark, dead-end alley, the screams of people came from somewhere ahead. He blinked through the rain, struggling to get his bearings in the growing dark of dusk. *Rasia.*

He moved along the alley and turned a corner. The spewing fire of a Dread Dragon lit up the town, igniting several houses despite the soaking rain. At least it gave him enough light to see where he was. He couldn't see any of his knights, but they would be far better prepared and armed than the townspeople. The town rose high ahead and to his left. He'd have to go forwards and take the main road, that was the quickest way home from here.

Thirty yards ahead was a wide cobbled high street lit by street lamps. People were fleeing up it and a few Maphraxies followed them, running in their lumbering gait. Even as he watched, more Maphraxies filled the street.

Behind was a dead end, the only way was forwards. With a deep breath, he urged his horse forwards fast into a gallop and drew his sword. At the last minute, he spotted a tiny alley to his left and took it. It was so narrow, his boots scraped along the walls.

The alley came out into the town square. People fled in a wave of screams and panic as Maphraxies spilled into the square. Lots of them. Their disgusting nets drawn at the ready. This was a raiding party and they were here to collect mostly children.

Rage, made stronger by the dull ache in his white eye, coursed through his veins and he charged into two Maphraxies. His horse's hooves slashed at the undead as he hacked his sword down, half beheading one and slicing the hand off another. Black blood oozed from its wound. The shocked Maphraxie had no time to raise its mace as Marakon's sword thrust straight through its throat. It convulsed to the ground, blood spewing from its twisted mouth.

Marakon's gut clenched in disgust. The sickly-sweet smell of Sirin Derenax combined with the putrid smell of death made him sick to the stomach. He strengthened his senses and let the cold hard warrior within consume him. His single-minded purpose: get to Rasia and kill as many

Maphraxies along the way as possible.

He hacked and slashed his way forward. This was a far bigger and tougher enemy than the Histanatarns. Already his sword arm ached from striking against armour and parrying heavy weapons. His arms would get used to it, and he would fight until exhaustion made him slow and a quicker enemy's weapon sunk into him.

The other side of the square he glimpsed two of his knights, unrecognisable in the gloom and rain. Seeing them alive gave him strength. Strong hands gripped his leg, almost wrenching him from his horse. Blindly he arched backwards and stabbed whatever was behind him. There came a grunt and his leg was released.

Dread Dragon fire lit up the sky in a blaze of red. More houses ignited and thoughts of Rasia drove him on. His horse reared as a Maphraxie lunged towards it. Hooves struck the Maphraxie down, and with a powerful leap, it cleared the rolling enemy.

It took Marakon some time to get through the square, and by then half the town was ablaze. The rain came harder, soaking everything and blessedly slowing the spread of the fire. Screams came to his right. A woman was struggling against two Maphraxies who held a wriggling bundle of children thrust up in a net like fish. Behind her lay two unmoving bodies. Blood covered half her face but still she fought. Marakon cried out as the Maphraxie's club smashed down on her head. There was a spray of blood and the woman collapsed atop the other bodies.

Marakon lunged his horse forwards, spun his sword, and beheaded the one holding the net with its back to him. He punched the face of the other with his pommel, feeling bone crack under his fist. The net dropped and Marakon sliced it open. Three terrified children scrambled out.

'Get to the trees,' he said. Their faces were covered in dirt and blood, and they had all soiled themselves.

'Run to the trees and don't stop,' he shouted. 'Take the quietest streets and stick to the shadows. Don't stop or look back.'

The eldest girl finally nodded, grabbed the other two by the hand, and dragged them into a dark alley. He should go with them to protect them, they would probably only be caught again. But even as he thought it he saw another struggling bundle, bigger than the last, and being carried by four huge Maphraxies. To his right Cormak bounded into view, his blade a blur as he wielded it.

'Cormak, here,' Marakon shouted.

The knight looked up, saw him, and headed forwards. They met with the four Maphraxies between them. Metal scoured against metal in a clash. Cormak felled the one with his back to him whilst Marakon took on the largest that had seen him coming. This one was big, a foot taller than the others, and armed with a short sword as wide as his head.

Marakon side-stepped his horse and eyed it up more cautiously. Most Maphraxies were dumb but strong and violent, so they were armed with simple weapons like clubs and maces that required only brute force to wield. That it could wield a sword was a surprise. Only Dromoorai had swords, massive two-handed claymores. Baelthrom's horde was getting smarter, he thought grimly.

Marakon swiped his sword at it in a test swing. It fell back dodging his blade easily. *Interesting.* Then the Maphraxie lunged with incredible speed. Marakon reared his horse back and took the devastating blow full on his buckler. The force of it juddered his arm and shocked his body for a moment.

A moment too long, for that black iron short sword was already on its way down. He flung himself forwards, barely staying mounted as he dodged the blow that glanced off his horse's armour. He sprang back up, stabbed, ducked and stabbed again, fast as an elf, and finally sinking his sword in deep. The Maphraxie howled and thrashed madly as it fell to the cobbles. Without hesitating, he wrenched his sword free and stabbed the neck of the Maphraxie trying to unhorse Cormak. It fell without a sound. The two men sat back panting.

'The horses are a hindrance in these close quarters,' the dwarf gasped.

Marakon nodded. 'I need to get to my wife, but you must help the people. Help free the children. Get the other knights together. We cannot risk being taken alive.'

Cormak nodded. 'Goddess protect you,' he turned his horse around and shouted for the other knights.

Marakon whirled away at a gallop. *Rasia, I pray you and the boys are safe.*

CHAPTER 24

Seat of a Lost Land

'THE Wykiry came for Issa, they protect her,' Coronos said.

'She said the Wykiry brought her to Celene,' Freydel nodded. He gasped then as if remembering something. 'In the orb, I saw a golden dragon.'

Coronos held the master wizard's eyes for a long moment, struggling with indecision. He couldn't keep Asaph's identity secret, not from the most learned men and powerful protectors of Maioria.

'What is it, Coronos?' Freydel asked, and all eyes looked at him. 'You are safe to speak your truth here, we are all under oath that nothing leaves the safety of the Circle.'

Coronos released a long held breath. 'Yes, you are right, and I should not keep secrets from the Circle. My adopted son, Asaph, is the son of Queen Pheonis and King Ixus of Drax, and he is a Dragon Lord. The last.'

Domenon snorted, and Coronos glimpsed a peculiar look of disgust on the man's face before he smoothed it over. Domenon said nothing, however, and returned his gaze back to the orbs.

'I'm stunned,' Freydel said. 'And I thought this would all be about Celene and Issa. So, then, that is why I saw a dragon in the orb when all the dragons are gone.'

Coronos shook his head. 'The dragons are not gone, not all. They're sleeping, Asaph has felt them. It is hard for him, there is no other Dragon Lord to train him. We have kept his identity and his gift secret all his life, but it will not remain so for long.

'Baelthrom will hunt him now just as he hunts Issa. He will not let the heir to the throne of Drax live to stir up rebellion, and not a Dragon Lord at that either. His Maphraxies already hunt us. Issa holds a power I don't understand, but I agree that it's linked to the blue moon. Soon after the attacks, the raven came to her and told her of Celene. We left that same hour on the back of a dragon.

'I'm sorry Freydel, we were too late. All we found on Celene was utter destruction… and the body of my daughter. Celene was a burning barren ruin and all the people dead or captured. When we reached the destroyed Temple of Celene on the eastern side, the harpies attacked us. I've never seen anything like it. We were outnumbered, but Issa called the ravens—so many I could not count them. They drove back the harpies until they fled.

'When I saw that, I knew she was the Raven Queen of prophecy. For one night we tended our wounds, and in the early hours of dawn, the land itself began to quake and tear itself apart. Asaph carried us away, and the last I saw of Celene was molten rock and fire as it crumbled into the sea. I wonder how much of it is left. Perhaps the goddess herself destroyed it because it was no longer pure.' Coronos finished and stared into his lap feeling numb.

'It's all gone…' Freydel whispered, not realising he spoke aloud as he answered Coronos' question. The silence that descended upon the Wizards' Circle was palpable. His eyes drifted over the empty stone seats and rested on the Ancient's chair.

'Celene is gone. Sharing the same fate as the land of the Ancients. Another land to count along the lost. Tusarza, Venosia, Drax. Now I sit upon a seat whose land is no longer there.'

'We all long for a time when peace reigns throughout all Maioria,' Averen said.

'Am I to believe hope for peace is purely the iconic ambition of the young, and the forgotten dreams of old men?' Freydel said.

'We must be content with each day and grateful for what we do have, rather than dwell upon the things that cannot be.' Drumblodd's voice was gruff as he stared at the broken seat of Tusarza.

For a moment Freydel forgot why he was here, what the point of it all was. For all his power and knowledge, what had he achieved? If he could not save Celene, or Ely, or even warn her people, what use was such power? He wiped a hand across his brow and looked out towards the glittering ocean. The beauty of the land reminded him of Celene, and for a moment he loathed it.

'The Immortal Lord takes all.' Averen's melodic voice drifted over them, unshed tears glistening in his eyes. 'Another land is lost as his noose tightens around us. We must all ask; "What are we to do?" More will be lost before our end draws near. Fear will only make us hesitant and dim our senses. Frayon will undoubtedly be our last stronghold. Perhaps a Dragon Lord and a Raven Queen can be a light to spark hope in the hearts of the people. In *our* hearts.'

'I know nothing of the power of this dark moon, but it flows through her like magic flows through the orbs.' Freydel forced himself to speak, to bring himself back to the world. 'So you see, gentlemen, I'm not alone in my thoughts. Coronos, too, has witnessed the power she holds.'

'If this woman is who you say she is, the Raven Queen of prophecy, then we must see her in the flesh and decide for ourselves,' Domenon said, a sceptical look on his face. The others murmured agreement. 'Perhaps having a female on the Circle would be a beneficial thing for us all. Some female company would be nice here for a change,' he smiled. The wizards shifted uncomfortably.

'Yes, you should all meet her, as I have proposed,' Freydel said. He agreed with Domenon, even though he didn't like agreeing with anything the man said. 'But what are you suggesting, Domenon? Only a wizard who has passed The Reckoning can sit upon the Circle. We all know how many women have entered the Storm Holt and died never to return. That is why we put a stop to it.'

Domenon merely raised his eyebrows. 'Well, if she is so powerful, how could she fail? Are you afraid of women on the Circle, Master Freydel?' he said the last with the hint of a sneer. Freydel was irritated, wondering if it was deliberate or just the way he spoke.

'Of course not. It's been so long, I'd be concerned to risk it. The Storm Holt that is,' he snapped, his emotions were fraying. He knew it would eventually come to this. It was only a logical progression of the conversation between the wizards; to suggest one powerful in magic be tested in the Storm Holt. It was a conclusion Freydel dreaded. He didn't want to put the girl's life in danger again. *She is a woman*, he corrected himself. He tugged on his beard.

'We lost so many women in the Storm Holt, even in our lifetimes,' Haelgon shook his head. Drumblodd closed his eyes with a sigh.

'But if she is the one of prophecy…' Navarr began, 'Domenon *does* have a point.'

Freydel shook his head. *Now Domenon has got Navarr thinking his thoughts.* 'I'll not agree to put her through another dire test.'

He felt guilty; that was it. He felt tricked by Cirosa in some way to send Issa to her death against Keteth. It had tested his faith in the prophecies and the goddess herself to its limits. The worry and guilt for her had made him sick. Who knows how long Cirosa had been communing with the enemy. Perhaps it was all by design to get rid of Issa from the start. He couldn't agree to endanger her life like that again.

'But she did survive, Freydel,' Averen smiled. 'And much more than that, she destroyed Keteth. If Zanufey protects the Raven Queen, as surely she must, then what are you afraid of? Surviving the Storm Holt gives one so much control over their talents no matter what their ability, and not to mention a deep inner strength that no experience in the normal world could ever give us.'

'He's right,' Luren and Drumblodd agreed simultaneously.

'There is no way on Maioria *I* could have faced Keteth and survived, and yet I survived the Storm Holt,' Navarr said. 'And I'm no master wizard.'

Freydel rubbed his chin as he took in those before him. Clearly seeing Freydel's anxiety, Haelgon spoke.

'There is nothing to fear, Freydel, we all have the girl's safety at the forefront of our minds. If she is strong enough to slay Keteth, then she will pass the Wizard's Reckoning. If she does that, then she should be here amongst us upon the Wizards' Circle.'

Averen agreed. 'That is what the Circle is supposed to be; the most adept magic wielders brought together for the greater protection of the orbs and Maioria, and for the sharing of knowledge and the advancement of our skills. All those things regardless of gender or race.'

'She must take the test which we all have taken—' Luren piped up but fell silent when Freydel gave him a look.

The young man was so impressionable, and Domenon made sure he had his impression upon him. This whole thing was Domenon's suggestion anyway. It was going from bad to worse. Merely a suggested idea was now becoming reality. The thought of Issa entering the Storm Holt made the blood drain from his face.

A memory forced itself upon him, only a glimpse of a still picture that broke him out into sweat.

His parents stood in the kitchen of his childhood home. The wooden beams of their ceiling, the hob with something always cooking upon it and smelling divine, the warm fire in the hearth—it was all exactly as it had been when he was a child. Only something was horribly wrong with this fond childhood memory. Now his parents held long sharp knives. Blood smeared the walls, the hob, the chairs, the floor. He didn't know whose blood it was in his child's mind, but he remembered the terror as he looked up into their smiling faces and all-black eyes. They came towards him and he had screamed.

The memory released its grip and he wiped the sweat from his forehead. It was not a real memory, at least not one that came from his childhood. It was a memory of his time within the Storm Holt. There he re-experienced many things he'd already experienced in his life, only this time they were distorted and sick, a horrific demonic replay of his otherwise happy life. Now many of his happier memories were tainted. Real memories of true events overshadowed by his re-experiences in the Storm Holt, leaving them impure in his mind.

He'd nearly died in there and the experience taught him that perhaps he was not as powerful as he wanted to be. Doubt was a far deeper and lasting wound than any bodily scar. Poisonous doubt in his power and abilities that his magic might fail him at any moment, just like it had failed him in the Storm Holt. He knew from their silence that the other wizards had been maimed in some way by the Reckoning; physically, mentally, and emotionally.

'Are you all right, Freydel?'

Freydel looked into Drumblodd's eyes and saw understanding there. Drumblodd carried the scars from the Storm Holt on his cheeks. Several white lines marred his face, making him look meaner than he was. It had taken three of them to drag his kicking and screaming bloody body away from the gate. It had taken a week for him to walk and another week before he would speak again. He'd never talked about what had happened, though, never uttered a word. None of them did.

'Yes, I'm fine,' Freydel nodded.

Averen was the only other who had visible signs of his maiming, he'd lost the last two fingers on his left hand. Of those who entered, less than half returned. No one knew what happened to the others, perhaps they remained in the demon worlds, living out their own torturous nightmare. He prayed they died swiftly in there.

'Entering the Storm Holt to prove her strength is not necessary. Slaying Keteth is proof enough,' Freydel said firmly.

'If she did kill the White Beast,' Domenon said, spreading his doubts. 'We have no proof.'

'Are you calling me a liar?' Freydel glowered.

'No, Freydel, I'm simply wondering about the proof of it,' Domenon sighed. 'Baelthrom has no use for the White Beast if he cannot control him. He let Keteth live simply to keep us hemmed in in West Frayon. Who can say that the Maphraxies didn't have a hand in his destruction? It means more power released to the world and the removal of an entity that was getting in their way.'

'She can tell you about it herself when she is here,' Freydel said in finality. 'When Coronos and his party arrive in Carvon, I will again call the Wizards' Circle and bring Issa here. But I will not agree to the Storm Holt and will advise her against it. The final decision remains in her hands.'

The wizards agreed. Navarr fidgeted. 'This meeting must draw to a close. I have many things to attend to, and we've already been here over half a day. Time is short. Who knows when and where the Maphraxies will strike. Being prepared is a matter of great urgency.

'Indeed, Navarr.' Freydel said. 'I'm keen to bring Arla to you and your healers.'

'Of course, Freydel. There is a room for you in the west wing for as long as you desire. Arla can have the room next to yours,' Navarr said.

'Thank you, it means a lot. If the Circle will kindly assist in transporting the girl and I to Navarr's hospitable home, the journey will be much more pleasant and less taxing on my weakened energy reserves.'

Freydel stood up, retrieved his orb and lingered a thoughtful look at the Orb of Water. Then he turned and gently picked up the sleeping Arla. She curled up in his arms but did not awaken. Her body was so light he worried immediately for her wellbeing.

The wizards rose and chatted briefly with each other before saying their farewells. Beside Freydel, Drumblodd gripped Navarr's arm.

'You will have dwarven warriors whenever you need them, Navarr,' Drumblodd said. 'You have but to ask.'

Navarr tapped his hand upon the dwarfs. 'Thank you, and I shall need them Drumblodd, be sure of that.'

'There is one more thing we have not discussed; the safety of the orbs,' Domenon said, gaining everyone's attention. He eyed each Orb Keeper purposely. 'If Baelthrom can get so close to taking another, we'll need to reconsider their protection. Wouldn't it be safer to leave the orbs under high protection in the safety of the Wizards' Tower? If Baelthrom is hunting Orb Keepers, maybe both Keeper and orb would be safer apart?'

The wizards frowned, uncertain. Freydel didn't like the thought of that at all.

'Leaving the orbs altogether just waiting for him to find them is by no means safer and possibly sheer folly. Why do you think Orb Keepers exist? To protect the orbs at all costs, not leave them lying around,' Freydel said.

Domenon smiled and spread his arms. 'Let us hope then that the Orb Keepers are strong enough, and can be trusted to protect them... at all costs.' His look lingered on Freydel who held his eye unsmiling.

'We Orb Keepers will do whatever we can to protect the orbs,' Drumblodd said, 'as we've always done.'

'Come now, gentlemen, we must get this child to a healer,' Navarr said.

The wizards formed a circle around Freydel, Navarr and Arla and spoke in unison a transportation spell. Shimmering light engulfed the forms of the three, and then they were gone. One by one the other wizards left until Domenon was alone. He took one long look at the empty hollows where the orbs had been.

Coronos was far too old to carry two orbs, and being only a novice wizard he was far too weak to protect them should anything happen. If this girl needed a Secondary Keeper, then he would be the best choice by far. The girl would know nothing of orbs anyway. Perhaps he should become a mentor to her just as Freydel had. He drew his gaze away and then left the Circle as the others had done.

CHAPTER 25

The Battle of Wenderon

MARAKON turned eastwards to where fire filled the sky. Though the street ahead was clear of Maphraxies, Dread Dragons massed in the sky above.

His horse hated the flaming buildings and shied away if he got too close, but the blaze formed a weak kind of cover from aerial attacks as he cantered up the cobbled streets. People fled everywhere, some almost running under his horse in their panic.

'Run to the trees, run to the hills,' Marakon screamed at them, never knowing if they heard him or not.

He came to the last row of houses. The road led to the top of the hill, and their house was at the end on its own. He turned onto it and galloped as fast as his horse could go.

He crested the hill, almost holding his breath. His horse screamed and reared. His house was a roaring blaze, and not three yards above it was the heaving mass of a Dread Dragon's airborne underbelly, its scales gleamed red in the firelight.

Smoked filled his lungs and he choked. Terror made him weak and he battled with his horse to keep it from bolting. He stared from the Dread Dragon back towards his house, his horse squirming beneath him, desperate to get away from the dragon. A window exploded outwards as the heat within grew too much. That would be the expensive kitchen, he thought numbly. *Rasia, dear goddess I hope you got out!*

'You bastards,' he breathed. 'You bastards!' he screamed and raised his sword at the Dread Dragon. It turned easily in the air, and two huge red orbs for eyes looked at him through fire and smoke.

'Fight me, damn you.' he forced his frantic horse forwards, ready to take on the giant beast as it snaked towards him. He saw another smaller set of red eyes on its back. The Dromoorai rider. Its amulet sparked into life and Marakon was distinctly aware of three beings looking at him.

'Come on then, you cowards. You've destroyed me before. You won't destroy me now.' He raised his sword high as the dragon's head snaked towards him. His mount reared and slashed its hooves. He lunged upwards to meet the head that was twice the size of his horse. His sword sliced against unbreakable black teeth and scales, making sparks fly in the dark. A fleck of black blood splattered his face, telling him he had nicked it at best. But then the Dromoorai pulled the beast's chains up, and the Dread Dragon lifted into the air, never taking its eyes off Marakon.

'What's the matter? Are you afraid of fighting armed soldiers? Would you rather fight children?'

The dragon turned away and left him standing there stunned. Why didn't it kill him? *What am I, insane? I should never have tried to take on a Dread Dragon…*

He turned to look at the ruin of his house. The roof creaked noisily then collapsed inwards. Thick smoke billowed out and he shielded his eyes. His thoughts turned to Rasia.

She would have fled with the kids. The burning house didn't mean she was dead. He had to find her. He turned his horse around and galloped back towards town.

The town was filled with death, screaming and mayhem. Most streets were overrun with Maphraxies. It seemed like a grotesque dance; the ugly, black-armoured, deformed Maphraxie giants fighting against the smaller town-folk in the firelight of their torched houses.

Marakon slowed to a walk, and whirled his horse around in a circle, wondering what to do before he lunged straight into battle and his mind turned only to fighting. The rain continued to pour down, making the streets shiny and slick. Anything other than Dread Dragon fire would have been extinguished by now, he thought sourly.

It was time to gather his knights and fall back. Despite wanting to help the people, Rasia and his knights were his priority. It would be stupid to think they might be invincible. Even if they were somehow immune to death, it didn't mean they couldn't be captured. It didn't bear thinking about. He raised his sword high and urged his horse into the fray, yelling.

'Knights. Knights of the Raven.'

He hacked into the first Maphraxie, dismembering its arm as it wielded a studded club. Black blood spurted in goblets over his horse and leg. He thrust it through the throat in disgust and moved forwards, shouting as loud as he could, hoping his knights could somehow hear him above the chaos of battle.

'Ghenath,' he cried out as the elf knight rounded the corner. She drove her curved, slender sword easily into the neck of a Maphraxie, then looked at him, her eyes wild.

'Fall back, there are too many,' he yelled. 'Tell everyone to fall back and take cover. We cannot risk being captured.'

She nodded and turned her horse back the way she had come. Marakon tried to follow, but his path was immediately blocked by a beast of a Maphraxie. This one's eyes gleamed, and it looked at him with more intelligence than most.

He adopted a different tactic. Rather than hack and slash at the brutes like he usually did, he treated this one as if it had human cunning. He pulled his horse back as if afraid. The Maphraxie came on emboldened. As it lifted its axe he reared his horse, and to his surprise, it slashed out its hooves into the enemy's face. He thrust his sword in a killing blow.

'Good boy.' He patted his horse's neck.

He'd ridden horses into battle many times but never had he experienced this level of teamwork. His horse always seemed to know what he wanted it to do and responded without pause. He wondered if it had been so in the past when he was king.

'I wish I could remember what I called you back then.'

He darted into an empty street and turned to survey the battle. The market square was heaving with Maphraxies. There were several bundles of children being tossed between them. Screams of terror filled the air, but between him and the net of children, there were at least twenty Maphraxies. He could not reach them.

A snarl came from behind and his horse skittered. Two death hounds bounded towards him, not quite managing to stay abreast of each other in the narrow alley as they struggled to get to him. Drool slathered their drawn lips and fangs. Their eyes were wild, like rabid dogs.

He drew his dagger and hurled it, kicking his horse forwards at the same time. The first beast fell instantly, the dagger embedded between its eyes. The other hound leapt over the body of its companion only to be slashed down by his sword. He reached down and pulled his dagger free of the twitching corpse.

The alley was empty for now. Ahead was a wide, fire-lit street, and beyond it were more dark alleys. They would eventually lead out of town and into the woods. He glanced back at the market square filled with Maphraxies. He grimaced. Today was not a victory.

Fleeing from battles were always the hardest decisions he felt he ever had to make. He preferred to die fighting than to flee. He would have felt better if he'd managed to gather all of his knights to him. But then he couldn't fight a hundred Maphraxies and still consider himself sane.

There came a scream, and a young boy staggered into the alley. The child pressed himself up against the wall trying to hide from whatever was coming. Marakon trotted forwards, sword at the ready.

The boy trembled and stared up at him. Marakon motioned for him to get behind his horse, and the boy slunk back. A wiry Maphraxie hurtled round the corner, rope at the ready. Marakon's sword decapitated him instantly. A second Maphraxie tried to enter more cautiously but met the same fate as its comrade. He listened for footsteps but heard none.

'Come, up behind me.' He pulled the boy up onto his horse.

'My sister,' the boy wailed.

'We'll try to find her,' Marakon said, and urged his horse forwards into the brightly lit street. Fire flared around them, even the wet cobbles seemed to be burning. The instant wall of heat that hit him made him gasp. He heard a scream in the next alley.

'Kelly,' the boy squealed.

Marakon galloped forwards. Thrust under the arm of a Maphraxie was a small blonde girl screaming. The Maphraxie was running and had its back to Marakon. It didn't even see the sword that ran it through. The girl scrambled free and Marakon pulled her up in front of him.

Protecting the children now became his priority. He had to get them to safety. The next street was empty and he glimpsed the dark shape of trees at the end. He cantered along it into the forest beyond and didn't slow his horse for a good few yards even after they had entered the trees.

Moving through the thick foliage quickly became difficult on horseback. He had a thought. Perhaps he could help more people this way, carrying them on his horse one by one.

'Hey, boy, what's your name?'

'Ben,' the boy replied.

'Ben, I need you to do something brave. Take your sister as deep into the woods as you can. You have no need to be afraid. Scouts keep these woods clear of wolves and bears. But if you look after your sister, I can go back and help more people.' He helped the boy onto the ground followed by his sister.

'The monsters will be gone before dawn, but do not return to the town until sunrise. You hear me? Go now, quickly, as far and as fast as you can.'

The boy nodded.

Marakon turned his horse back the way he had come. Weariness filling his mind as it drained the strength from his body. If he helped the people, he might find Rasia and his sons. He urged his horse faster through the trees. He didn't even see the dark shape moving at the edge of the forest until it was upon him.

His horse screamed as a foltoy the size of a bear pounced on top of them, sending them all to the ground. The wind was knocked from Marakon's lungs and he struggled to keep from being crushed by the beast. He struck at it with his sword and fist as best he could from his prone position, managing to shear off a chunk of flesh from its back.

It screamed. He rolled to his feet as it twisted to face him. His horse staggered up and seemed to limp. He hoped its armour had stopped a mortal wound.

'Run,' he screamed at his horse. To his surprise, it obeyed him and ran back into the woods.

The foltoy turned to follow it but Marakon leapt in its path.

'No you don't,' he growled. 'Now you get to fight me.' The foltoy hissed, green eyes cunning. He lunged at it and sliced another wound along its side. It howled, but still hesitated to retaliate.

'Fight me,' he screamed. He ran at it. The beast was fast and dodged his sword. Claws flashed towards him. He fell back as they narrowly missed his face. In the same instance, he flicked his sword up and sank it shallowly into its shoulder. The beast screamed, staggered back, then ran towards him, maddened by pain.

Marakon stepped to the right as it came on, raised his sword and slashed a deep gash down its side. But to his surprise, the foltoy did not stop, and instead carried on past him into the woods. The beast was wounded, black blood oozed from its side, but he couldn't let it get away, he had to be sure it was dead.

He chased after it, slashed at its tail, taking the end off. The foltoy made an awful sound, and quick as lightning turned and swiped at him. Marakon took the full force of the blow on his chest. Claws scraped along his breastplate, and if he hadn't been wearing armour he would be dead.

Before he could recover the foltoy struck again, putting all of its weight behind the blow, sending him sprawling down the bank. He hit his head hard on a tree trunk as he rolled. The last thing he saw was the foltoy bounding off into the forest.

It seemed only moments later when Marakon swam up through a woozy fog of pain. He was alone and all was silent, apart from the noise of his rasping breath. He could barely breathe against the constriction of his damaged breastplate that had also twisted in his fall.

He reached aching arms up to find the straps and undid them. It came free and he sucked in lungfuls of air. He sat up wincing. His body was sore all over, cuts and bruises were everywhere, but none of them appeared fatal. Waking up feeling like this was becoming annoyingly normal.

He blinked, trying to get his bearings. The soft light told him it was dawn. The overcast sky was a mass of grey clouds but at least the rain had stopped. He flinched as movement caught his eye, but then laughed as his eyes fell upon his horse munching on grass at the forest edge.

He eased himself up onto leaden legs and hobbled over to it. There was dried blood on his flanks but he otherwise seemed fine. From his pack, he took long dregs of water from his water flask. The water helped clear his woozy head.

Dried blood, both red and black, covered the ground where he'd fought the foltoy. He glanced into the forest. In the distance lay an unmoving black shape. He smiled grimly. At least that foltoy wouldn't kill anymore. He strained to see more in the forest, hoping to catch a glimpse of the children, but there was nothing. *They'll be far from here if they have any sense*, he consoled himself.

He glanced at the town. Smoke billowed up into the sky from many places. The Maphraxies would be gone by now, along with however many unlucky people they'd managed to capture. Rasia…

He tied his breastplate to the saddle and, feeling saddle sore, decided to walk. His muscles screamed for rest as he made it back into what was left of Wenderon.

CHAPTER 26

The City of Rivers

THE sun was setting when Coronos finally returned. There came a shimmer in the air in the same place where his father had left that morning, and then there he was again. He looked weak and tired.

'Father, are you all right?' Asaph took hold of Coronos' arm as the old man swayed.

'Asaph?' He blinked. 'There you are. Yes, I'm fine. I was never very good at transportation, and now I'm older it hits me hard.'

'Maybe you shouldn't do it again,' Asaph said and helped him sit down upon his folded cloak.

'Well, I never felt I fit on the Wizards' Circle, not with my skill in magic. But being an Orb Keeper and advisor to King and Queen of Drax, I felt obliged. I didn't think being an Orb Keeper was a good idea either,' he puffed then chuckled.

'Goodness, what have you made for dinner? I'm famished,' he said, eyeing up the huge mushrooms sizzling on a hot stone in the fire. A pot of soup hung above them, along with a pre-cooked load of roasted roots and truffles and some more of the mayor's kitchen's bread.

'Well, you were gone ages, and we got bored. We couldn't leave the camp for long because we didn't know when you'd be back. Issa has gone to find some berries for pudding,' Asaph said.

'Wonderful. I guess you two had some private time together?' Coronos wiggled his eyebrows.

'What?' Asaph felt his cheeks grow hot. 'Uh, we just foraged for food, nothing more.'

'Really,' Coronos said, completely unconvinced as he settled himself before the food.

'And maybe a little kiss,' Asaph added quietly. Both men laughed.

'He's back,' Issa said, bounding over with a small sack full of berries, and surprising Coronos by bending to hug him. She then set about finding plates and spoons in their packs, humming a song neither man recognised.

'Just a kiss, you say?' Coronos said with a raised eyebrow.

Asaph shrugged innocently.

When they'd finished filling their bellies and packed everything away, Issa began questioning Coronos about the meeting. Everything from how the transportation worked and how it felt, to the contents of the meeting and who everyone was. Asaph could see the weariness in Coronos' face, and he would have suggested they talk about things tomorrow had he not been so fascinated about it himself. Besides, Coronos seemed like he wanted to talk despite being tired.

'Only high wizards and master wizards can call a full Circle and transport people to it. The orbs make it easier too for they were keyed to the Circle back in the time of the Ancients. I could, if I wanted, use the orb to return me to the Wizards' Circle alone and at any time. But it is very taxing for me, especially now I'm old.'

'So, only wizards who have passed the Wizards' Reckoning sit upon the Circle?' Issa asked.

'Yes,' Coronos said.

Asaph could see the cogs working in Issa's mind, could sense that she was seeing an obstacle to overcome. Before she could ask any more questions, or start thinking ridiculous thoughts, he voiced his thoughts.

'Where is this place?'

'It's east of Maphrax, a long way east, and in warm oceans. That's as good as I know. We know that the island was chosen by the Ancients as a safe protected area where meetings, magic and artefacts could be discussed and kept safely hidden. It's veiled from view, much like the elven Land of Mists. Anyone passing would see only ocean and move right through it.

'I have not seen those men for over twenty-five years,' Coronos said wistfully, stuffing his pipe with lintel weed. He sighed. 'Master Wizard Grenahyme was a great wizard and a good friend. Still, he was old when I knew him. Luren, Grenahyme's apprentice, is young and nervous, but I'll bet his tutor taught him well. He'll make a powerful wizard.'

'How was Freydel?' Issa perked up. She'd been quiet, probably musing over Coronos' words. Asaph had not met the Master Wizard that she spoke of so frequently. He was keen to meet him.

Coronos looked at her with a held breath that he let go slowly. 'He's drained, but thankfully he's all right—and my what a story he has to tell. He is already at Castle Carvon, so he can tell you all about it. Let's just say he's lucky to be with us. He had a sick child with him. Arla I believe her name was.'

'Arla? Sick?' Issa said.

'Yes, maybe with a fever, Freydel isn't sure. He's taken her to Carvon, to King Navarr's healers.'

'I can't wait to see them,' Issa said. 'I've been worried sick about Freydel, and all I've heard from Arla was that strange note she left me. But what happened to Freydel? I just couldn't reach him through scrying.'

'He tried to call the Wizards' Circle when the orb showed him Maphraxie ships close to Celene,' Coronos said.

He put a small stick in the fire, set light to it, then brought the flame up and sucked it into his pipe. 'It was after he'd initiated translocation to the Circle that things went wrong. Baelthrom happened to have his attention fixated on the Flow and Celene, that was how he sensed Freydel's passing in the astral planes. It was close, too close for an Orb Keeper, but he got away. If it weren't for Arla, I don't think Freydel would have made it back easily, if at all.' He took a deep pull on his pipe and Asaph watched the smoke rise up into the night sky.

They talked about the members of the Wizards' Circle and where they came from until Coronos' pipe was empty and cold and the fire just a small patch of embers. Asaph considered all this talk of magic. He had magical abilities, amazing abilities, but only in his dragon form. Using magic came second nature to a dragon, so he understood all that Coronos spoke of. He could feel magic in his human form, but only weakly.

'There's one thing I should mention for you to think upon,' Coronos looked at Issa, she raised her eyebrows. Asaph watched her face, hoping she wouldn't get any more ideas. 'You mentioned you would like to meet the wizards. Well, it seems that they would like to meet you too. Anyone powerful enough to defeat an ancient beast like Keteth surely deserves the Circle's attention.' Coronos smiled.

Asaph frowned, though no one was looking at him. He didn't like the thought of wizards giving her attention, or any magic wielders for that matter—especially not male ones. She'd been through enough already and this just sounded like trouble.

Issa stared at the ground. 'It was the Raven Queen and the dark moon, I couldn't do it now.'

'They do wonder if you really did overcome Keteth,' Coronos said. 'So you'd better tell them about it yourself. They are also all far better versed in the prophecies than I am. Perhaps they can help you understand this Raven Queen better.'

Issa darted a look at him. 'I would like that. Sometimes I feel a mystery to myself,' she said. Asaph felt she was a mystery to him too, an intriguing mystery he longed to learn more about.

'Well, that brings me to another thing. It has not been decided yet, and it will probably end up in a vote, but it looks like they may invite you to undertake the Wizard's Reckoning and enter the Storm Holt.'

'Enter the Storm Holt?' Issa almost jumped up.

'Enter the Storm Holt?' Asaph scowled. 'You nearly died in there.' He felt his face flush with anger. There was no way he could agree to this, and to his chagrin Issa was already excited by the prospect. Why did she always find danger? It was like she deliberately put herself in harm's way. Did she care so little for herself, or how others felt if she got hurt?

'She has no need to do anything of the sort just to prove her worth to a bunch of old men,' he blurted. He couldn't bear the thought of Issa going into the demon worlds, especially not with him.

'Asaph,' Coronos said reproachfully.

Asaph looked away embarrassed. Coronos went on. 'It's not up to you or me, but up to the Circle, and in the end the choice always remains with the invitee. Issa doesn't *have* to do anything.'

Asaph caught Issa's eye. 'Don't do this. It's not worth it. We have other things to do. Coronos told me some of his experience in there, but it was so bad that he never told me the whole lot.'

'Asaph, don't worry so soon about me, touching though it is. I have to think about it at least,' Issa soothed.

'I knew you'd say that. You don't need to think about it. Just say "no",' he advised. 'I'm going for a piss.' He stalked off, but he didn't go so far as to not be able to hear their conversation.

'He cares about you, that's all. The decision is up to you. If they invite you of course, and it's not a decision to be taken lightly,' he heard Coronos say. 'But what it has given us, everyone who has survived the Reckoning, is a greater understanding of ourselves, both the good and the bad. Thus you would be less of a "mystery to yourself," as you put it. Some return with greater magical abilities, others come back with new gifts, such as the Daluni talent or the Sight. Others, such as Domenon, claim they live longer. Nevertheless, what didn't kill us made us stronger. We have all come back stronger.'

Asaph shook his head as he listened. It was all so unnecessary. Why did she even think she needed to agree to other people's tests? He just knew she would accept the invite if they asked her. First Keteth and now the Storm Holt. He didn't understand. It seemed that she liked a challenge, no matter how dangerous it was. Sometimes it seemed like she wanted to die. He sighed. He could feel the anger in her, and the need for revenge, he had those feelings too. But he wondered if it made her do these crazy things. If, somehow, the need for revenge was taking over her reason.

He buttoned up his trousers and began to make his way back when movement caught his eye, something bright disappearing through the trees. He followed where it had gone for a few paces and then peered around the trunk of a large tree. He gasped.

Partially hidden in the trees, not twenty yards ahead, was a woman of such beauty it took his breath away. She seemed made of white and silver light glimmering in the darkness as she half hid behind a tree. Her long platinum hair flowed over her shoulder, naked breast and down to her slender waist. He couldn't stop his eyes travelling over the perfect curve of her hip and her long legs, graceful as a deer's.

He felt his cheeks reddening, realising she was naked. His eyes travelled back to her angelic face, red lips and cool, blue eyes. She seemed frail and vulnerable shying behind the trees. She smiled fearfully back at him. He went towards her, dazed by her innocence and beauty, and wanting to touch her to see if she was real.

As he neared, she became scared and disappeared behind the tree.

'Don't go,' he called out, and ran towards her. When he got there she was gone. He whirled around looking for where she might have trodden, but there was no sign of her passing, not even with his experience in tracking.

He blinked, feeling his captivated daze wearing off. She was so beautiful and pure, how could he not be dazed? Was she a fairy or wood sprite? Maybe she was his imagination. He sighed and turned back, feeling a headache coming on.

'Did you see something?' Issa said, and added when he frowned, 'We thought you said something.'

Asaph shook his head. 'No, it was just an owl, I think. Nothing to worry about. I've got a headache for some reason though. I think I'll get some sleep.'

'We should all sleep,' Coronos yawned. 'If we're up early we might be able to reach Carvon tomorrow night.'

By the time Asaph lay down his head was positively pounding. He drifted into a lucid, disturbed sleep filled with dreams of a beautiful pale woman driving his lust for her, and a white owl fleeing through the trees.

They were up early and left their small encampment as the first hint of light touched the skies. They'd all slept well and Asaph's headache had almost gone, though he still felt a bit dazed as if his dreams hadn't fully left his waking life.

They covered a lot of ground that day. It was easy to travel along the well-worn Old North Road as it led across gently undulating countryside filled with deciduous forests and a few farmers' fields scattered here and there. He didn't feel like talking much, content enough just to enjoy the ride.

Coronos and Issa, however, chatted for hours about the wizards again and the Storm Holt.

Asaph only half listened, finding himself drifting inwards and focusing on his own thoughts. Thoughts that often turned towards a beautiful woman with platinum hair. He felt excited every time he thought of her, which was embarrassing. It worried him also—Issa was the only one he'd had eyes for. He tried his hardest to push thoughts of the woman to the back of his mind. She probably wasn't even real, she could have been a ghost. It was towards sunset that he glimpsed the beautiful city of Carvon.

'Is that it?' he asked, marvelling at the majestic twin peaks of Castle Carvon as it stood upon the most elevated part of the city.

The city was on a high hill, and part of the hill had collapsed a long time ago so that a long white cliff formed beneath the city. Subsequently, the land they currently travelled upon was a few hundred feet lower than the land atop the cliff where the city was. A huge gushing waterfall tumbled over the cliff, along with many other smaller ones. It seemed strange to see a cliff here in the middle of the land where they had mostly seen rolling hills and forests.

Issa stared in awe. 'It's huge, and look at the size of that waterfall!'

'Yes,' Coronos said with a smile. 'It's called the City of Rivers—for the number of rivers that flow through it. Though there is really only one river, the Arin Flow, split into many rivulets. The castle itself is divided by the river and split into two parts, as you will soon see for yourself. It's my favourite place after Draxa. Mind you, we'll not get to see much of it today, for though it looks near, the distance is deceptive. We'll be lucky to make it to the Lantern Road before full dark.'

Coronos was right, it seemed to take an age to close the distance between them and the city, and it was almost full dark by the time they reached the "Lantern Road" as Coronos called it.

Indeed it was a lantern road. They rounded a copse of trees along with other late travellers barely lighting the way with their torches, only to see a double line of bright lanterns leading up the hill through the trees. Asaph blinked, his eyes adjusting to the sudden brightness.

'It's rather pretty,' Issa said, and gave an approving nod.

'They lead for a mile, all the way to the city gates,' Coronos said.

'They light all these lanterns for travellers?' Asaph said. He'd not seen anything like it.

'Yes,' Coronos said. 'They begin lighting them every evening at sundown. Carvon is a large city, the largest in the Known World actually, and trade is big business with people coming and going through the night. This is a city that never shuts its doors, and whose gates are guarded all through the night. They also call this road the "Mile of Light," for it is a welcome sight to weary night travellers such as us.'

Asaph nodded. 'Will there be food? I'm starving.' His belly had been rumbling for a good hour. To keep a fast pace, they'd not stopped and eaten nothing but dried fruit for dinner.

'Me too,' Issa said.

'Oh yes,' Coronos nodded vigorously. 'You can expect a meal fit for a king at Castle Carvon. It's tradition. The King and Queen of Carvon have always prided themselves on lavishly welcoming their guests, and I suspect nothing has changed since King Navarr took the throne.'

They made their way along the Mile of Light towards the City of Rivers, the light of the lanterns and the grandeur of the city seemed to energise Asaph's weary body. From the smiles on Coronos' and Issa's faces, he could tell they felt the same.

That same say, Edarna first glimpsed the twin spires of the City of Rivers early in the afternoon.

'Oooo look, there it is,' she squealed. 'I've not seen it for, er, well, a few years,' she trailed off realising her age. She took in the glorious site of the city's light grey walls shining in the sunlight and set against a blue sky. The rich forest hugged the city and waterfalls cascaded down the cliff in front of it.

Naksu smiled. 'It always was a particularly handsome city—my favourite, really. Although I don't relish the thought of meeting the Oracle for some reason.'

'You and me both,' Edarna tutted, but nevertheless strode grinning along the winding road.

She was more excited about the food she could find within its walls than the actual grandness of the city. *No, I'm more excited about the amount of gold I can make selling dragon scales.* She corrected herself with a smile, her fingers drumming the lid of her travel chest.

There was no easy way to find a witch these days, not after the Derobing, but a city was filled with everything and all sorts, and she knew that if she asked the right questions she'd find someone who knew a witch. Or, if she managed to find herself a place to set up a base, she could advertise around the city and bring the witches to her.

Naksu trotted to keep up with her, her mule following behind. Despite Edarna's complaints of sore ankles, Naksu had refused to let the witch ride her mule. Edarna thought it rude to deny an old woman an easier mode of travel but the look in the seer's eye had silenced her. Edarna hadn't quite forgiven her.

'What are you grinning about?' Naksu asked suspiciously.

'Ohm nothing.' Edarna turned her grin into a frown. 'I was hoping to meet a fellow witch, maybe.'

'Sounds like trouble,' Naksu muttered. Edarna ignored her. 'Where's your cat anyway?'

'Goddess knows.' Edarna rolled her eyeballs. 'He's probably already waiting for us at the city's front gate.'

Naksu nodded but didn't seem convinced. 'Don't you worry about him?'

'Not about *him* never. Ungrateful sod,' Edarna said.

'Oh,' Naksu said in surprise. 'I thought witches cared a lot for their familiars.'

'It's give and take,' Edarna explained, and that was all she said on the matter as they made their way to the capital city of Carvon.

CHAPTER 27

Old Friends

'WE are guests of King Navarr,' Coronos said politely to the two guards at the gate. 'Please tell him Coronos Dragon Rider and his party have arrived, he is expecting us.'

One of the guards looked at them wide-eyed, bowed to Coronos and scuttled off through a small door to the left of the main gate.

'Probably the mention of "Dragon Rider," ' Coronos winked back at them.

Moments later the guard scuttled back. 'He says to take you to the West Gate where it's quieter and closer to your rooms.'

Coronos nodded, and the guard scuttled up a small track leading them a hundred yards or so to the West Gate. The gate was closed and unguarded apart from the guards walking the ramparts.

'Thank you, sir,' Coronos said, and bowed slightly to the guard. The guard unlocked and opened a smaller wooden door within the gate, and let them through. He gave a sharp nod and stood to attention as they entered.

Asaph glanced back into the darkness of the forest. He was reluctant to leave the trees and enter the closed-off world of a city. He realised he'd hoped to catch one last glimpse of the pale woman, a realisation that concerned him. He turned away from the forest as the door shut.

Inside the city walls, the streets were brightly lit with lanterns, the smooth cobbles gleamed orange in their light. A nearby tavern had its doors open and a barman was trying to eject the last of its drunken patrons for the night. The thought of a drink seemed appealing to Asaph, perhaps it would help clear his brain fog or at least help him relax. He felt strangely wired but befuddled at the same time.

'King Navarr,' Coronos said, immediately catching his attention. He hadn't noticed the man that had stepped out of the doorway to their right. He glanced over at Issa. She hadn't noticed him either.

'How good it is to see you in the comfort of your home.' Coronos bowed. Issa and Asaph looked at each other, then copied Coronos, bowing awkwardly in their saddles.

'I would never have expected the King himself to greet us out on the streets, and especially not this close to midnight,' Coronos said, smiling as he dismounted. Three stable boys came running over to take their horses. Duskar immediately flicked his head as a boy approached. Both horse and boy stepped back from each other.

'Duskar, easy, it's all right. You get to sleep in a nice stable tonight,' Issa said, patting his neck. She dismounted. 'He's a bit wary of anyone else other than me He's had a troubled past,' she said by way of apology.

'Haven't we all,' Navarr retorted.

Everyone laughed. Asaph found himself relaxing under the king's humorous smile.

'Perhaps I'd better take him to the stables myself,' Issa suggested when Duskar continued to eyeball the boy.

'As you wish. Let's all go, we can chat on the way, and the stables are just around the corner,' Navarr said.

The stable boy led the way. Asaph turned his attention to the King. The man caught his eye and Asaph dropped his gaze feeling nervous, but not before he caught a glimmer of respect there. He wondered at it.

I might have been a king, once. But that reality was as far away as liberating Drax. His heritage of a kingdom and the life he might have led was for someone far grander than he. Coronos and Navarr talked about their journey as they entered the castle through a rather unremarkable wooden side door. Asaph was unable to concentrate on what they were saying. Instead, he found himself drifting in his own world again.

They arrived within Castle Carvon too late to wash and change clothes before eating and risk waking everyone up, so Navarr had the night kitchen staff set up a table in a smaller room on the ground floor.

Only half an hour could have passed since they'd stabled their horses and been shown their rooms, to when they arrived in the dining room. But when they arrived the fire was already ablaze, and the eight-person table had so much laid out on it that not an inch of tabletop could be seen.

Asaph lunged for the bread—freshly warmed in the oven—and took a hunk of cheese, a brimming bowl of yellow sweet-smelling soup, and two handfuls of grapes.

'Hungry?' Issa asked lightly.

'Mmph,' he mumbled through a mouth stuffed with food. For some reason, he was famished and he began to wonder if he was fighting off a cold. Food, a few glasses of wine, and a decent bed would see him right again, he was sure of it. Coronos and Navarr were deep in conversation about the old king, and what had changed in the Known World since he had died.

Issa took her bread, soup and glass of red wine and sat down beside him with a sigh. She smiled at him, and for one horrifying moment he felt he had to force a smile back. She looked pretty in the firelight, if a little tired from travel, but now he thought about it, she was not as beautiful as the pale ghost woman he had seen. He felt disturbed by the thought. Issa, to him, had always been the most beautiful woman he'd ever seen, so how could that have changed? Her smile wavered as if she sensed his uneasy thoughts.

'Asaph what's wrong? You've been quiet since Coronos returned,' she sipped her wine. It had already brought colour into her cheeks in a way he used to find attractive.

'I'm fine,' he began defensively, surprising himself. 'Well, I have a headache, but the food is helping. I think I might be coming down with a cold.'

She smiled and relaxed. 'I thought you were cross with me about deciding to enter the Storm Holt.'

'You haven't decided yet have you?' He suddenly felt cross again.

Coronos and Navarr paused their conversation to glance at him. He must have raised his voice. Perhaps tiredness was getting the better of him.

'Well, not exactly, but I've been thinking about it,' she replied.

'Well, it's up to you,' Asaph said more softly, and the other men continued with their conversation.

'Ahh, there you are.' A voice Asaph didn't know spoke, breaking off what he had been about to say.

'Freydel,' Issa gasped and jumped up to meet the man standing in the doorway.

He embraced her like a daughter and then came to join them at the table. He had a neat, trimmed beard and warm hazel eyes. He looked younger than Coronos but older than Navarr. Asaph immediately sensed a powerful magic wielder and his dragon self stirred in response to it.

Freydel greeted them all, but refused food, saying he'd already eaten with King Navarr. Instead, he filled a glass full with red wine. His smiling gaze rested on Asaph.

'Asaph.' The wizard reached to shake his hand. 'In the short time I've been with Coronos, he spent most of it talking about you.'

Asaph shook his hand and smiled back at the man. 'Only good things I hope.'

Freydel laughed, 'Of course, and I'm sure there is so much more to tell.'

'How is Arla?' Issa blurted. 'Coronos told me she is sick.'

Freydel sighed and worry creased his brow. 'She's not getting better as we'd hoped. If anything she has fallen into a fever. Luckily Navarr's healers are excellent, so she is in the best hands.'

'I should see her, maybe I can help.' Issa began to rise, but Freydel put a hand on her shoulder.

'No, you need to rest too. And besides, Arla has just fallen asleep. You can see her in the morning.'

Issa relaxed and began to question him about everything that had happened since they'd last seen each other. Asaph was interested to begin with. It was exciting hearing about what a wizard got up to, and how he'd used magic to call the Wizards' Circle only to become trapped in the astral planes. The Kuapoh often talked about the dimension above this one. But as exciting as it was, he soon found himself drifting.

He poured another glass of wine hoping it would perk him up and was just thankful that everyone was busy with their own conversations without needing to converse with him. The wine had the opposite effect and made him sleepier, before long he found his eyes beginning to shut of their own accord.

'I'm sorry,' he said and stood. 'I need to sleep. I can barely keep my eyes open.'

He said goodnight and left them chatting. With a sigh of relief he closed the door to his own large, but blessedly quiet room. The four-poster bed was huge and the mahogany desk and wardrobe so big it must have taken ten men to carry them in here. He sat on the lavish velvet-covered bed and barely got his boots off before he sank back and fell asleep.

Not long after, Freydel said goodnight to a yawning Issa and Navarr—the king graciously offering to escort her to her room.

Freydel filled up his and Coronos' wine glasses, and sat back down, enjoying the way the firelight made the shadows dance in the room. He glanced at Coronos. Though he looked tired and it was late, the wine had perked him up, and he insisted on talking for a little longer. So they sat and talked non-stop about pretty much everything that had happened since Coronos had fled from Drax with the heir to the throne in his arms.

'It is my fervent hope,' Coronos said finally. 'To see Asaph take back the kingdom of Drax, but such dreams may never come to pass, and yet still we must hope and still we must dream. I've lived a long life—longer than my father's—and I feel Feygriene calling to me as my days dwindle. At least I saw Asaph to manhood, and I'm glad he's found his love, but I fear their days in this uncertain world will be hard and full of sorrow. What a terrible future the young of Maioria now face.' Coronos shook his head.

'Asaph is lucky, under the circumstances, that he has you to look after him. A loving and exemplary father,' Freydel smiled, trying to add a positive note to the conversation. 'But tell me, what do you think of Issa? I've worried for her safety ever since she left Celenian shores.' Shores now lost forever beneath the sea, Freydel sighed aloud as a pang of pain hit him.

'When I first met her in the desolation of the Shadowlands, I did not think she would live through the hour,' Coronos said. 'She was like a wraith; all skin and bone and deathly pale. And yet even then I felt a strange magic about her. Strange in a good way, but a rare magic that makes you stop and think. Now she has recovered she is strong, in magic and in body. Already she can wield a sword better than I could at her age.'

Freydel raised his eyebrows and laughed. 'I had no idea such things would interest her.'

Coronos nodded. 'She's very determined and high-spirited. Though I don't think she was always so driven,' his face darkened. 'Baelthrom and his horde have taken so much from us, they've made us all violent and vengeful. It's only in the little things... It's probably nothing to worry about, but I think she is driven by revenge. Well, of course she is, so is Asaph and so am I. But it seems, more so since Celene, that her heart has hardened a little, the joy in her now dampened and shaded with seriousness. It's not how a young woman should be.'

'She grieves, we all grieve, for Celene, for Ely, for her home and her people,' Freydel said. He had trouble pushing memories of Celene away now he was tired.

'Yes, that's true. My concern is that she dwells upon revenge. Yearns for it. Such yearning can become poisonous,' Coronos said.

'That too is true. I've not seen her since she left Celene to face Keteth,' Freydel replied. 'I shall see how she is, and consider all you have said. What are your thoughts on the Storm Holt? Do you think she should enter it?'

'No. I would not wish anyone to enter it. Especially not a woman when so many have... gone,' Coronos said.

Freydel felt relieved, at least he wasn't alone in his feelings. Coronos continued. 'As you say, she's proved herself already against Keteth and Baelthrom's abominations. But in saying that, should she decide to enter, we should not fear. If she fails, goddess forbid it, then no wizard will ever again pass.'

Freydel nodded and finished the last of his wine. 'I don't want her to enter at all, whatever the cost. But I've a feeling she will not shy away from this. If she is invited, then I think she will choose to enter, and none can deny her. I will not invite her, but that is my wish, and my guilt in agreeing to send her to Keteth.'

'Your wishes are honourable, Freydel, don't be guilty. I would only advise that if she does choose to enter, then she should do so when the blue moon is here and full. Do you know when that might be?'

'No, there have been too few moons for me to accurately chart its progress,' Freydel said. 'And now my study and its beautiful star gazing roof is gone, it looks like I won't be able to. But that moon, when it rises, it rises full and heavy and for a night only. Maybe Luren could dig out Grenahyme's model of our moons and nearest stars. Or maybe Domenon has something on the subject in that library of his that he's managed to keep secret from us. From my rough calculations, I counted at most twelve days between first rise and the next. Longer has passed since it last rose, so its orbit is not predictable to us yet.

'Hmm, that aside, does Zanufey's moon even rise in the Murk? I would think it doesn't. No moon of ours has ever risen in the Murk, let alone the Pit.' Freydel lost himself in thought for a moment, trying to reason it through, but tiredness gnawed at him. 'Bah, my brain is too tired and full of wine to think clearly now.

'Mine too, let's get some rest.' Coronos winced as he stood up. 'My oh my, I'm saddle sore all over.'

'Hah. A good night's sleep will help. Tomorrow, first thing, I'll call the Wizards' Circle again.' Freydel stood up as well. 'We'll bring Issa to the Circle. When she leaves, we'll vote on whether to invite her to the Storm Holt and go from there. Tell her not to leave the castle. I know how inquisitive she is.' Coronos laughed and nodded.

Freydel showed Coronos to his room, and then eagerly retired to his own. King Navarr had kindly given him a room at the end of the quiet west wing. It was a turret room, all round and cosy just like his study on Celene. But he sorely missed his stargazing window, and without all his maps and scrolls the room felt horribly stark.

He got into his bedclothes that the maids had given him, but still felt hot and sweaty. He flung open one of the windows and pulled up a chair to sit in the cool night breeze. Breathing in the smell of the forest beyond the city walls, he considered Coronos' thoughts on Issa.

Now he thought about it, the old Draxian was right, in a way. Issa seemed far stronger and confident than when he'd last seen her. She was colder and harder as if a resolve burned within her. He wondered if the girl he had saved on the shores of Celene was being eroded away with grief and revenge.

He closed his eyes and imagined he was back in his study in Castle Elune. Immediately he recalled his last moments with Ely and the grief welled up.

"I doubt very much that the High Priestess cares at all whether Issa lives. In fact, I should think she'd prefer her dead," Ely's words rang clearly in his head. *"…I'm suspicious that this was all a set up to destroy Issa."*

'Oh, Ely. Knowing what I know now… I think you were right,' Freydel breathed. 'I'm so sorry…'

Unshed tears forced his eyes open. He blinked them back, blew out the lantern, and let darkness fill the room. He could see the stars outside better without the light. They twinkled and shone, forever sending their light down to Maioria.

For a while he fought back the sorrow, trying to think of nothing else other than the endless stars out there, but it was a battle his old, tired and wine-filled mind could not win. Eventually, the tears won.

CHAPTER 28

The Soul Knows

THE vision of destruction that greeted Marakon as he walked through the town in the growing light of dawn was one he had seen many times before. But this time it was the town in which his wife and children lived.

'Rasia,' he called out.

His voice echoed off half-destroyed buildings and blackened walls. Burnt bodies littered the streets, and it took an enormous effort to force himself to look at them without emotion. He *had* to see if they were Rasia or his boys.

He came to a corpse, half crushed under a fallen wall. There was no hope of recognising it or any of the dead, they were so burnt they no longer looked human. Smoke still flowed from the smouldering ruins, and every so often caught the back of his throat causing a fit of coughing.

'Rasia,' he choked out louder, but there was no answer. He'd yet to see anyone alive.

He took a narrow street leading back up the hill to his road. He knew what he would find, so when he saw the crumbled mess that was his and Rasia's home, he wasn't surprised. The dragon had torched it good last night. He dared to look in the hot ash for any signs of his wife and children, but there was none. She wouldn't have hidden or stayed in a burning house. She would have fought and sent the children running. Just like he'd sent the children into the woods.

'Rasia,' he shouted into the desolation. Only the wind answered his call, whistling through the broken stone. He turned from his destroyed house and led his horse into town towards the port.

'Hylion, Hally,' he called out the names of his knights as he walked, but again there was no answer. There had to be someone alive. He refused to think that his knights had been killed. In the distance, he heard coughing. He strode towards it. In the smoke, a figure moved.

'Marakon?' a woman called.

'Oria.' He made his way over to her. Her plaid, fair hair was all a mess, and her face was smeared with blood and dirt, making him wonder how he must look.

'Thank the goddess, Marakon.' They embraced in relief.

'Where are the others?' he asked, stepping back.

'We've made a hospital down in the old warehouses by the harbour. The only buildings that are still standing whole. There aren't many survivors,' she said.

'Many fled, they will return,' Marakon said.

'We're missing some knights,' she said, fear in her eyes.

'Who?'

'Drenden, Hally, Meyer and Konnen. Have you seen them?'

Marakon shook his head and pursed his lips. 'They may have run helping the others.'

Oria looked away, pain in her eyes. 'They took Hally. Ghenath saw her captured. Ironbeard saw Drenden. Drenden was with Meyer, they had trouble closing the east port gate, then the dragons came. Ironbeard was nearly captured himself. Konnen is missing, maybe he will return…' the hopelessness was clear in her voice.

Marakon looked to the sea in the distance as if hoping to see them there. But there were no ships, the enemy was long gone. He knew with dreadful certainty that there was no hope for them. They might not be able to die but they could certainly be enslaved.

Marakon gripped Oria's shoulders and looked into her green eyes. 'Then they are gone.' The hope that had been there dimmed and instead her eyes filled with tears. She bit her lip and dropped his gaze. 'Let's pray they take their own lives before they are… changed,' he said grimly. *Has all that I've done been for nothing? Have I brought them back from the Drowning Wastes only to be enslaved again?*

'We, the Knights of the Raven, must never become separated from each other again. We must fight this enemy as one. We cannot be captured by those bastards. I couldn't find my wife or children, but I haven't stopped searching yet.' Marakon let go of her shoulders.

'Come to the hospital, they might be among the wounded,' Oria said, linking her arm through his.

Marakon let Oria lead him and his horse through the rubble-filled streets down to the harbour. He was in a daze, partly from the need for food, partly from battle exhaustion, but mostly faced with numbing fear and worry for his wife and children.

The old warehouses were smaller than the newer ones that had stood to their right, but the old ones were made of solid stone, and unlike their inferior part-wooden replacements they had withstood time and the attacks of Dread Dragons. He peered inside. It was cool and dimly lit by as many candles and lanterns as could be salvaged. There were windows, but these were covered in moss and dust from age and lack of use.

The warehouses were filled with people, young and old, injured and walking. Those that were well enough were tending the wounded. Moans of pain and hushed voices filled the air. A few people had sheets of blankets drawn up over their faces. These were quietly being carried away through a door at the back of the room that led into the next warehouse.

'Only days ago a similar scene was before me,' Marakon whispered, remembering the Elder's house filled with wounded Gurlanka.

'Come,' Oria retook his arm when he hesitated and led him further into the building.

He darted his eyes over the women tending the wounded. No one had the copper curls or the cherub-like smiling face that matched his Rasia. Oria led him through the half of the room where the injured women were. Some had terrible wounds, and blood soaked the sheets that covered them. He tried to keep his face a mask though he knew they would not see the day through. Beyond those more seriously wounded were those sleeping. His eyes rested on a woman whose copper curls flowed over the pillow, her face was turned away.

'Rasia,' he gasped and ran to her.

She shifted at his voice and as he looked down into her pallid face she opened her eyes.

'Marakon?' she blinked, her eyes were big and brown just as he remembered them, but there was pain in them, and deep circles under them.

'Yes, it's me. I'm here,' he took her cold hand when she raised it and kissed it tenderly.

'Marakon,' she breathed and began to cry. She repeated his name many times. He bent down and hugged her gently, trying and failing to stop the tears flood from his own eyes. 'I missed you so much. You came back to me. Don't leave me again.'

'I won't,' he promised and stood up, stroking her hair back from her face.

'I tried to…' she said the last part so quietly he couldn't hear her. Her lips were blue and she looked so weak. Her eyes fluttered and he thought she was going to fall back asleep.

'Tried to what, Rasia?' he bent closer.

'Tried to save them,' tears ran down her cheeks. Marakon gripped her hand and held his breath.

'They came for them. They didn't want me, but I fought them. There were eight of them and two of us. I killed two before they struck me down. We chased after them, but it was too late. A building collapsed on me. I made him leave me and take a horse to chase them down. They took our boys, Marakon,' she trailed off into weak sobs.

Marakon gripped her hand and hung his head. 'My children are gone,' he breathed. His utter hatred of the enemy rose to poisonous levels. Rasia began to cough—a cough that shook her whole body, forcing his attention back to the present.

'Rest, Rasia,' he soothed, but her coughing only got worse. 'Do you want some water?' Whether she nodded or shook her head he couldn't be sure. He tried to hold her as the coughs racked her body. Blood patched on the sheets above her stomach where she'd been wounded. Healer women hurried over and helped her sit. Blood flecked her lips and the nurses wiped it away as best they could, glancing at each other with concern. He stood there horrified and useless as they helped Rasia drink water, then laid her back down to sleep.

Marakon stayed by her side for hours, listening to the rattling of her breath, opening himself to the blessed numbness of grief that stole over his weary body. Everything he did in his life was a failure. His curse was not over, his life was still filled with misery.

About mid-day Rasia came round again, and she seemed stronger than before. There was a little more colour in her cheeks, and her lips were more pink than grey. She smiled at him, her brown eyes warmed his soul, just like they always used to when they awoke together in the morning. At least he still had his Rasia. He returned the smile and for a moment felt the shadows inside draw back into the darkness. He took her hand and held it against his cheek.

'You look terrible,' she said.

He laughed. 'I'm not the one in a sick bed.'

'True,' she smiled. 'But you should get some food and rest. I'll be fine right here. Has he returned yet?' she asked faintly as if speaking exhausted her.

'Has who returned?' he asked, but she seemed to be drifting. Did she mean the children or had she found herself a new lover? He couldn't bear to think the last. 'Rasia, who fought with you to save the children?'

She roused again and looked up at him. 'Bokaard. He came back. He's alive.'

Marakon stood up straight, stunned. It took him several long moments to put it all together. 'That's incredible,' he said.

'No more incredible than you surviving,' Rasia smiled. 'I think he knew you weren't dead. He longed to see you. Maybe he'll return with the children. Go now, eat and rest.'

'I'll not leave you again,' Marakon said firmly.

'I'm not going anywhere.' She shook her head. 'And I need to sleep myself. I'll still be here when you return. Go, I insist.'

Marakon felt the exhaustion as a physical thing dragging him down, but he didn't want to leave Rasia's side. She was right, though. She needed to rest peacefully without him worrying beside her. His stomach rumbled. She was already asleep when he reluctantly turned to go. He decided to get some food and take an hour's rest at most.

The townsfolk had gathered food from the few surviving stores and placed it in the smaller warehouse next door. There he found Ghenath and Cormak. They talked about what had happened as he made a meal of seed bread, apples and a vast array of pickled and salted items. To his empty stomach, it tasted like a meal fit for a king.

Afterwards, he took off his armour and found a quiet place in the corner of the storeroom atop a pile of hay. He immediately fell into a deep sleep and did not awaken for several hours.

When Marakon awoke, Rasia was gone. They had moved her body to the next warehouse where the other people now lay in permanent rest.

'It is often the way,' the old female nurse smiled at him sympathetically. 'It's as if their soul knows. They live just long enough to say goodbye to their loved ones, and leave when they are free to go.' She squeezed his arm gently, and then left him alone with his wife's body.

Rasia's once tanned face was now grey-white and her lips a shade of slate. He stroked her cheek. It was so soft under his hand, and so horribly cold. He didn't bother to wipe away the tears that flowed down his cheeks.

'You told me you would still be here,' he whispered, 'but it turns out you had to go.' He knelt down beside her and buried his head into the sheets, letting the grief consume him.

Marakon stayed there for a long time, stayed even when the tears had gone and the grief turned to numbness once more. Slowly he stood up. There was no point staying here, Rasia was not here, she was gone never to return. There was no point to anything anymore. He gently drew the sheet over her face, a face he would never see again.

Marakon left the warehouse of dead and wounded and stood outside in the fresh air. His knights were gathered beside the harbour wall. They had eaten, rested and cleaned their armour. It gleamed in the sunlight that fell now and again through the clouds. They were only eight now. Four were gone and he doubted he would ever see them again either. The knights smiled at him, concern and sorrow shared in their faces.

'We're sorry, Marakon,' Lan said. 'We did what we could, but there were too many of them.'

Marakon said nothing, but gripped the big man's shoulder and squeezed.

'We cleaned your armour and tended your horse,' Ghenath said. He thanked her. They looked at him expectantly, waiting for him to tell them what to do, what their next task would be, but he had nothing to tell them. He had no desire to do anything.

'The Maphraxies will not return, not immediately anyway,' he said, his voice hoarse and cracked. 'So you may as well stand down and rest and help the people here. Where's my horse? I need some time alone...'

They brought his cleaned and rested horse to him. Luckily his horse's wounds were little more than a few grazes on its hindquarters. He put on the saddle and bridle but left the armour where it was on the stable floor along with his own freshly cleaned and fixed armour.

He eased his aching body into the saddle and trotted along the coast road leading north out of town. He didn't know where he was going or what he was doing. He couldn't just sit in that destroyed town. He had to feel the wind in his hair, the sun on his face, and perhaps, for a moment, he thought he could outrun his life.

The road ran upwards and along the cliff edge with thick forests to the right. There was no one on it as he galloped along, and he focused on nothing else but the ride. The sun was beginning to set through the clouds, turning them orange and pink. The air was fresh and filled with the smell of the sea. He came to a high point on a cliff that jutted outwards and stopped to give his horse a rest. He patted his neck and stared out to sea for a few minutes.

He'd just started off again when he saw a dust cloud in the distance coming towards him. Marakon slowed his horse to a trot. He wore no armour, but he still had his sword. *No Maphraxie rides a horse,* he laughed and let his hand drop from the pommel. The other horseman closed the gap between them, dropping to a trot as he neared. His face was covered with a scarf to keep the road dust out.

'Marakon?' a muffled voice came from behind the cloth and he pulled it down.

'Bokaard?' Marakon said in shock as he looked back at his friend.

He'd only half believed Rasia when she'd spoken of Bokaard surviving. He'd thought she was delirious with sickness.

They dismounted and embraced roughly, laughing like they used to do over a beer in a tavern.

'Praise the goddess, you white belly, you're alive. I knew it.' Bokaard grinned.

Marakon shook his head. 'You would not believe my story even if I told you.'

'Well, you're gonna tell me, you lucky bastard, and then you can disbelieve mine,' Bokaard said, his grin infectious and white teeth gleaming.

'I'd like that. Over a beer of course,' Marakon nodded.

'They came by surprise, destroyed the town.' Bokaard dropped his smile and became serious.

Marakon reached over and gripped his shoulders. 'My children. Rasia said you chased after them. Did you find them? Did you see anything?'

Bokaard looked away and shook his head. Marakon suddenly saw the man's exhaustion. Blood soaked his leather jerkin from a wound.

'I tried,' he grimaced and blinked back tears. 'I have not stopped riding until now, searching for them all this time, though I knew it was helpless. They destroyed the house, came right for the children. We fought them, Rasia and I, but there were far too many. We chased them, then Rasia was trapped. I would have stayed with her, but she made me go after the boys.

'I took a horse and found them again, but then was attacked. I lost them going right out of the town. I followed where they might have gone. I thought maybe the boys could have escaped and run away. I thought the knights on white horses might have freed them. I thought and hoped for many things, but I never found the boys again.'

Marakon dropped his hands from Bokaard's shoulders. It had been a poor hope at best. 'You did what you could. You have my deepest gratitude.'

'Did you find Rasia?' Bokaard asked.

'Yes, I found her. They were looking after her and I…' he trailed off as a painful sob caught his throat. 'She's gone, Bokaard.'

'Oh no,' Bokaard stared out to sea, his dark skin seemed to grey then. 'I promised myself to protect her, to protect them all.'

'It's not your fault,' Marakon tried to appease the anguish in his friend. 'We arrived too late to do much. There were too many of them. They came here with a purpose, and many Maphraxies. That anyone survived should be considered a miracle.' His own words of consolation sounded hollow in his ears.

'Come, let's find a beer and talk.'

In silence, they rode back to the smoking ruin of Wenderon.

CHAPTER 29

Demon Dreams

'RAVEN Queen.'

The voice called to Issa in the darkness of her dream. She spun around to peer into the blackness from where the voice had come. It was a strange voice, one she had never heard before, deep and gravelly and not human.

'Raven Queen.' She spun around again as the voice came from directly behind her.

'Why do you call the Raven Queen?' she asked, hating her trembling voice.

'We must speak with her,' the voice replied.

'Who are you? Reveal yourself.'

'We know where the spear is.' Red eyes gleamed in the black, and she fell back, immediately thinking Baelthrom. But then she saw these eyes were different and they had pupils with a vertical slit, just like a cat's.

'I've seen you before,' she said. 'I saw you in the sacred mound, in that vortex. What do you want from me?'

The eyes disappeared and in their place, a glowing spear formed.

'The white spear,' she breathed.

'Yes,' the voice hissed. 'We know where it is.'

'What is it for? Why do I keep seeing it?' Issa said.

'Come to us, and we'll tell you. There's a man who searches for it. Only he can kill the Demon Wizard.'

'I don't care about the Demon Wizard. Leave me alone,' she shouted. She wanted the darkness to go away and the demons to leave her alone.

'You will care. The greater demons from the Pit are coming.'

Horrible forms moved in the dark. Long, pitch-black faces with hungry eyes that bore right into her soul. They clustered around her, their sharp claws tearing at her skin and pulling her hair. She beat them back with her fists.

'Get away from me. Go away,' she screamed.

Issa awoke choking on her scream. She sat up gasping. The sheets were wrapped around her and she was covered in sweat. She kicked them off and glugged down a glass of water. The dream faded and the quietness of the room crept in.

'Uh, Zanufey, please tell me why my mind's plagued with demons.' She dropped her face into her hands. From the gap in the curtains, it was still dark outside. She flopped back onto the bed and shoved aside the smothering velvet covers. It took a while for her racing heart to calm again, but eventually she fell back into a dreamless sleep.

Asaph was also having a difficult night. Whether it was the late night food and wine giving him nightmares he couldn't be sure, but in them, he was being hunted by a white owl the size of a dragon.

It swooped and struck him as he fled through the trees. Whole branches were torn from their boughs and thrown around him. Talons longer than his hand snatched at him, and the owl's eyes were hungry all-black pits. Asaph could not end the nightmare but spent the whole night suffering.

When he finally awoke well after dawn, he felt more exhausted than he had before he'd gone to bed. The door to his room opened and his father peered in.

'I did knock,' Coronos said apologetically.

'Ah.' that must have been what woke him up. 'I overslept,' he mumbled, propped himself up, and drained the water by his bed.

'Issa said you might be coming down with something. How do you feel?'

'I had a rough night of tortured dreams. Now I'm awake I feel exhausted. But I think my head is clearer,' Asaph said. Indeed the fog that had stuffed up his mind all of yesterday now seemed to be clearing. He sat back against his pillows with a sigh of relief. The fog had been so bad, he realised, that it had even blurred his feelings for Issa. That realisation worried him.

'Good, maybe it's passing. We're doing nothing today, but resting and eating,' Coronos grinned. 'Well, you and Issa are, Freydel and I will be attending another meeting.' Asaph nodded, relieved not to have to do anything.

'Breakfast is being served downstairs where we ate dinner. You'll have to be quick if you want any hot chocolate as Issa is about to finish the lot.'

Asaph struggled out of bed to the sound of Coronos laughing. His father turned to go.

'Oh, one more thing,' Coronos paused in the doorway. 'I've told her to stay in the castle until the orbs call us, but you know how her inquisitiveness drives her. Try to keep her here. If she tries to go into town, we'll not find her again until dinner time.'

'I'll do my best,' Asaph frowned. 'Getting her to do anything she doesn't want to do, or trying to stop her from doing the things she does, is virtually impossible. I guess you'll be taking her to the Wizards' Circle?'

'Yes, but none of this should be of any worry to you,' Coronos reassured him. 'The Wizards' Circle know what they are doing.'

Asaph slumped, he felt left out, but also too tired to put any emotion into it.

'What if they decide to invite her to take that stupid test? How can I protect her if I can't be with her,' Asaph sighed.

'No matter how you feel for Issa, you cannot stop her making her own choices,' Coronos said. Asaph pulled on his trousers. He really didn't want to think about it right now. 'Now be quick if you want some breakfast.'

Asaph slipped on his sandals and hurried out the door still on his shirt.

An hour after breakfast, Issa felt the Orb of Water calling her. Knowing she would be called she had placed it on the bed whilst she washed and dressed. Her linen clothes had just been delivered by the maid, all clean and pressed. No sooner had she dressed than the orb began to glow.

She watched it, admiring the swirling turquoise within it as it throbbed and hummed. She went to touch it then hesitated and chewed her lip. She didn't feel ready to meet the most learned and powerful magic wielders on Maioria. Right now she wished she was the Raven Queen. Why did the warrior woman only seem to come to her when she was in battle or when Zanufey's moon was with them?

She checked her face again in the mirror. Her luminous eyes were nearly back to normal, just a subtle glow that no one would notice unless they were really looking into them. She didn't want to be seen as a reckless over-user of magic, or a novice—all of which those strange turquoise eyes surely meant.

As a last thought, she quickly buckled on the short sword that Grast'anth had given her. It would probably look strange, but it immediately gave her the confidence she needed. The last time she had felt this nervous and flustered about meeting people was at a summer fair on Little Kammy where, as a child, she'd had to act in a play with the other children. All those faces looking at her had made her faint, and she never acted in a play again.

'I'm not a child anymore, I'm an adult,' she said firmly to her reflection in the mirror. Saying it to herself didn't make her feel any better.

She picked up the raven talisman. *I could show them it. Perhaps they will know something about it.* She went to stuff it into her belt and paused. Maybe she should wait to see who they were before she revealed too much about herself. She set the talisman back down. Taking a deep breath, she stilled her mind.

There came a squawk at the window making her jump out of her skin. 'Ehka. Great Goddess,' she cursed and stared at the bird. He opened his mouth as if laughing. 'Where have you been? How do you always know where to find me? Anyway, I've been called to the Wizards' Circle.'

He hopped in the open window and jumped onto the bed, staring into the orb with intrigue. She picked up the orb and gripped it in her hands. It was warm and tingling with static energy. Suddenly she realised she didn't know what she was supposed to do. Was that part of the test?

To see if she could do things intuitively? Or maybe Coronos just forgot to tell her how it worked.

She couldn't explain it, but she could feel the orb calling her, just like when a friend called out your name. She mentally accepted the request. Air rushed all around and through her, making her tingle with energy. It was exhilarating and yet exhausting at the same time. It felt as if every cell in her body had separated and energy was moving right through them. Then they were drawn swiftly back together and in moments she felt solid ground beneath her feet.

CHAPTER 30

Powerful Men

ISSA swayed, and stood blinking up at Freydel. He had a warm smile on his face.

'Next time it will be much easier,' he assured. 'Take a moment to get your bearings.'

She took a deep breath. Everything became solid and stopped swaying. She looked around. The place was beautiful. A lone mountain towered to the south and green forests blanketed rolling hills. Sparkling rivers flowed through the forest and fed into lakes, then wound onward to the sea in the north. The sun was high and would have been strong, but she could see the protective shimmer of a magical shield surrounding them.

Twelve stone chairs ringed the turret that raised them off the ground to a dizzying height. The stone turret and chairs felt ancient, much like she felt the sacred mound to be. But despite their age, except for the broken one, they were in pristine condition. There was a great sense of something missing from the circle, or a sense of loss as if it were broken and incomplete. She couldn't quite put her finger on it.

Eight of the chairs were occupied by the most powerful and learned wizards of Maioria, who all now sat staring at her with intrigue. Once there had been twelve, six men and six women, so Coronos had said. She caught his eye and he smiled encouragingly back at her.

'You may place the Orb of Water alongside its sisters,' Freydel gestured to the floor and she saw three other orbs had been placed there.

She stared in absolute wonder at the red orb she had never seen before.

'The Orb of Fire.' She bent close to it as she placed her orb next to it. Its rich swirling mass of fiery reds and oranges was mesmerising.

'Indeed. Come, stand beside me.' Freydel took her hand and led her back to his seat. She felt less nervous as he held her hand. She stood beside him while he sat and then spoke.

'Issa, please meet the members of the Wizards' Circle.' Freydel introduced the wizards, and she nodded to each of them, feeling her cheeks grow hot under their gaze.

'Members of the Wizards' Circle, please meet Issa, Zanufey's Chosen and slayer of Keteth,' Freydel said proudly. The wizards nodded and murmured. Her stomach lurched and she stared at the floor, wishing Freydel hadn't called her that.

'I should like to know how you did that,' the tall, dark-haired wizard Freydel had introduced to her as Domenon, said. The only other Master Wizard in Maioria asked in a tone that suggested he did not quite believe what he had heard. His dark grey eyes were guarded.

'It was the Raven Queen,' she blurted, then grimaced—she'd shown her nervousness. For some reason, the wizards looked astonished at her reply. Freydel said he *had* told them everything she'd told him.

'I don't quite understand it,' she added, annoyed that her voice wavered, she wanted to appear strong in front of these men. 'But when the dark moon rises, its power is somehow available to me. It fills me. The last time the dark moon rose, the Wykiry took me to him, to Keteth. I would have died but the raven came, the same raven that helped me on Little Kammy.' She stopped abruptly. She was describing it all wrong and confusing herself. She clasped her hands behind her back to stop them fidgeting.

'How very interesting.' Domenon rubbed his chin thoughtfully.

'Where are you from, Issa?' the black-skinned wizard asked.

A man from Atalanph, she thought intrigued. She stared into his incredibly blue eyes. He was tall and broad and seemed made of solid muscle. There were battle scars on his bare arms and a hardness in his face that demanded respect.

'From the Isles of Kammy, west of central Frayon.'

'And who are your parents?' he asked. Despite his hard looks, his tone was gentle and reassuring.

'My adopted mother told me my real mother was a seer. I don't know for sure but I think my father may have been a Daluni. My father is dead and I don't know if my mother still lives.' She replied honestly seeing no reason to hold back. Perhaps these powerful men would be able to shed light on her heritage and her abilities. 'My adopted mother was killed when the Maphraxies came…' she trailed off, not wanting to bring up painful memories here. The wizards nodded and shared a frown of sadness; hers was an all too common tale.

'What do you know of Zanufey?' the elf man Averen asked.

Issa looked at him, probably for too long before she answered. She was so unused to seeing elves, especially not in Maioria, and she found him stunningly beautiful, which only made her shyer. His face was much kinder than Daranarta's.

'She talks to me sometimes, or rather, shows me things,' Issa admitted reluctantly. She never felt comfortable talking about Zanufey to others. It felt too personal and she assumed that they would not believe her, especially when she sometimes doubted it herself. She still didn't quite understand why Zanufey talked to her.

The wizards looked at each other in amazement, or disbelief, except Freydel who remained expressionless as he watched the reactions of the other men. She carried on, trying to find a better way to explain herself.

'I don't know why or how, but when my mind is still and I will it, I see a sacred place, a mound surrounded by ancient stones. There is an entrance to this mound, and it leads to other places, sometimes other planets. I imagine that I'm entering this mound and it seems I go there truly. Sometimes within it there is this desert. On this desert, there is a doorway made of giant stones and she is there. Zanufey is there. She calls to me, she calls me *Maion'artheria.*'

'It sounds like mind travel, or translocation,' Freydel nodded.

The wizards began talking amongst themselves, all except Freydel and Domenon. She noticed his dark eyes never left her. She swallowed. Did the wizards not believe her? For a brief moment, she sensed something strange about Domenon, or was it something familiar?

She focused on him with her mind, like she did when healing sick animals, but avoided looking at him. Immediately she sensed the briefest feeling she had when she was around Asaph. It was a subtle awareness that this person was not wholly human. Just as quickly the feeling was gone before she could get a handle on it, and she felt her mind shut off from him as if he'd shoved her away.

She glanced at him. There was a surprised look on his face that turned to amusement. He smiled at her in a way that made her cheeks grow hot. He seemed to look at her the same way a wizard treasures a magical object, something that is owned and used, or at least could be. She felt very small and looked away from him back to Freydel.

'It means "My Sacred Daughter" in a tongue that precedes the Ancient's,' Freydel explained, silencing the other wizards. 'So you see, gentlemen, there is a lot that fits with the ancient prophecies.'

She had a thought and thought it wise to ask a question of them. 'Do you know of this sacred mound? Of where it is or what it might be or mean?' She hoped one of them would know something about it, but the wizards simply looked at each other, frowned, then shook their heads.

'Never mind,' she sighed. Maybe the Oracle or the seers would know, if she ever got to meet them.

'Why do you think Zanufey talks to you?' the dwarf asked, he sounded sceptical but not unfriendly.

'I don't know.' Issa shrugged. 'It's like she is trying to guide me. I also get visions of this Raven Queen. She is a warrior skilled in the sword and magic. I don't quite understand it, but when the dark moon rises it seems I am her, or when there is danger and my life is threatened, this warrior takes over me.'

'It's no different to my soldiers at war,' King Navarr said. 'When on the battlefield, well-trained, skilled and experienced soldiers find themselves committing amazing feats of bravery. After the battle, they always say they've no idea how they did it and are adamant they don't have the courage or the skill to do it again. Until the next battle comes of course, and they act the same way.'

Issa nodded. 'Yes, I suppose it feels a little like that.' She smiled at the king, glad to have someone help explain her feelings. He smiled back. Perhaps the Raven Queen was always with her then, a warrior sleeping within ready to awaken when needed, much like Asaph's dragon self.

This Daluni talent you have, is it like this?

The unspoken question made her jump. Only Asaph had ever spoken to her telepathically in that manner, and he could only communicate that way as a dragon. It seemed far too intimate.

'Didn't you know that Daluni can talk to each other telepathically?'

The voice, or the sound of the voice in her head, was Averen's. She looked at the elf, colouring a little under his violet gaze.

'I didn't know. The only other Daluni I knew were the Karalanths,' Issa said. The words flowed far more quickly and easily than having spoken them aloud.

'Ah, well, most elves have the Daluni talent too. Karalanths will only speak this way with other Karalanths, and their talent is different, they use pictures rather than words,' Averen said.

'The animals mostly use pictures when they talk to me, it can sometimes be difficult to interpret,' Issa said, realising then the similarities and differences between speaking with animals and humans in this manner. *'But the Wykiry used words.'*

'Yes, that's right,' Averen said. *'It gets easier communing with animals, but takes lots of practice. The Wykiry can use any form of mind communication. They still remember being human despite being permanently in a non-human form. And don't worry, you can relax, I'm not here to interrogate you.'* Averen smiled at her and turned back to listen to Freydel.

Issa felt his mind distance itself from hers, and a wave of relaxing calmness spread over her, leaving her to wonder how he'd done that. These wizards were masters and she could learn so much from them.

'Daluni mind-speak is best left for later, don't you think, Averen?' Domenon said.

Averen replied, completely unfazed. 'Not between Daluni, Domenon.'

Domenon smiled at her again, and Issa wondered if he'd somehow been able to pick up on what was said between them. He made her nervous and yet the unease he deliberately seemed to spread intrigued her at the same time. There was definitely something odd about him, possibly dangerous.

'I would like to see how she is in the Flow. Just like we ask all novices before they undergo training in the arcane arts,' Haelgon said, and the others nodded in agreement. 'Issa, would you mind? We shall all enter the Flow first and then you can follow, all right?'

Issa nodded and hid her reluctance. She didn't like to do anything with the Flow when she was even slightly nervous and unsure—erratic feelings caused erratic energy—and she really didn't want to look like an amateur. But she was still a novice, she reminded herself, and had barely had any training in using magic. Yet she had already used it so many times to save her own life. It was strange, but in this pure place of power, she could sense the other wizards enter the Flow, even though she was not in it.

'Enter now, Issa,' Freydel said. He had his eyes closed beside her.

She shut her eyes and tried to still her nerves as she focused. Gently she stepped into the Flow. Her heart began to pound, reminding her that she had barely recovered from her overuse of magic. She hoped they wouldn't ask her to do anything too strenuous with it.

'Good, Issa,' Freydel said.

She could see the others in the swirling mass of energy that moved and billowed around and through them. Entering the Flow was always like looking at another reality overlaid upon the physical world. The magic that swirled around the two master wizards was immense. The Flow pooled around Domenon in waves of blues and reds, whilst the energy that pooled around Freydel was lighter and more varied in colour—like the colours of the rainbow, but just as powerful, if not more so.

Averen and Haelgon pooled their magic, though it did not move around them as strongly or in such quantities.

She chose not to pool the Flow, and instead let it flow through her easily as it wanted to do. She felt exhilarated in the magic once more, and besides these powerful magic users, the Flow was an awesome flood of power.

'See and feel how the Flow wants to go to her?' Freydel said, his voice echoed a little.

'The energy around her is indigo, like the blue of the dark moon,' Averen said, a hint of wonder in his voice. 'Can you pull the dark moon's power to you now?'

'No. I can only reach it when it is rising full over Maioria,' she said.

'Can you try?' It was Domenon.

'Maybe.' She was wary of doing anything she had not done before, but she had to try in front of the wizards. She heard herself say, 'I'll try.'

She let her mind expand, searching outwards for the dark moon. Somewhere out there in the deepness of space, she knew the dark moon moved.

'It's a long way away,' she said. Could it feel her searching for it? Could she reach it? She stilled her mind further, focusing only upon the dark moon. And then, yes, she felt it. It was far away, but then she felt it drawing her to it faintly.

I don't understand the connection we share. If you can touch me with your power just a little. There came a movement of energy, and then the faintest feel of its power filled her. The Flow around her shimmered, and she stared at it in shock along with the surprised voices of the wizards. She now felt tired.

'Very good, Issa,' Freydel said. 'I think that's enough for now?'

There were murmurs of agreement.

'I would like to see how much of the Flow she can pull to her.' It was Domenon again.

'Domenon, I think that has been enough,' Freydel said. 'Issa has suffered much lately. I don't want her to exhaust herself with magic again. Despite how powerful she might become, it's still very taxing for a novice user of magic.'

There came mixed murmurs. 'I don't know, Freydel, I think Domenon is right,' said Averen.

'Pooling the Flow is not the same as using it,' Haelgon added.

'I agree with Domenon,' Luren said. It was the first time she'd heard the young man speak.

'All right,' Freydel sighed. 'Issa, if you want to, call the Flow to you, as much as you feel comfortable with.'

She nodded, feeling like she was performing on stage and about to be judged. She remembered Freydel's lessons and began to draw the Flow to her. *I must not let myself get carried away in its ecstasy,* she reminded herself. The first time she had pooled the Flow in company, she had nearly lost herself and exploded Freydel's entire study. Not losing the self and not pooling too much too quickly were both tests in themselves, and she realised that was why they had asked her to do it.

In this place of power, the Flow came willingly to her, like reaching out and grabbing long strings of ribbons billowing in the air. The stream she held quickly became a river, and then a torrent flooding through and around her, and yet she stood firmly and easily within it. She grinned, nothing came close to the feel of magic flowing through you.

She reached for more until the torrent doubled then trebled in size. Still more she could hold and soon it seemed as if all the Flow was coming to her, a great tide of exhilarating energy that was a roar in her ears and a rush in her body. If she thought about it, it would overwhelm her and wash her away. She just had to be it and experience it without thought.

'All right Issa,' Freydel chuckled. His voice seemed to come from far away. 'You can let the Flow go now. Gently.'

With utter reluctance, she let go of the Flow until she held nothing. She felt empty and normal without it. With a forlorn sigh, she stepped out of the Flow and stood there feeling sluggish and dizzy, glad to steady herself on Freydel's chair. Everything in the physical world seemed so solid, heavy and boring when one left the energy of the Flow.

'Thank you, Issa. As you can see, Issa has enormous potential,' Freydel smiled at the others.

Issa caught Domenon's gaze. He was not smiling now—actually he was frowning. Whether he was angry or not she could not decipher. He stared at her deep in thought. She looked away.

'Yes,' Navarr agreed. 'Issa, do you mind telling us how you overcame Keteth?'

'All right,' Issa sighed. She hated talking about her battle with the monster Keteth had become. She wanted only to remember the good man he had once been. Nevertheless, she began a succinct recount of the events that occurred when the Wykiry came, and the struggle she had nearly lost against Keteth.

'In the end, it was the dagger Karshur that delivered the killing blow, I simply held it.' She pursed her lips, watching their reactions, but only the elf man showed an element of surprise.

'So, the infamous dagger finally fulfils its destiny,' Averen said, and then in her mind. '*When there is time, you must tell me how you came to find that dagger.*'

Issa nodded at him, but said nothing. Would he believe her if she told him a fairy found it for her?

'And what about Celene? Coronos told us about it. How did you defeat the harpies?' Haelgon asked.

Issa wondered how best to explain. 'When Keteth was… freed, he imparted to me his *gift*. I don't fully understand it, but he gifted to me the ability to reach the land of the dead and return, alive. After that I could see how he got there, I could feel it. Maybe it was possible because I had been to the Shadowlands and survived, I don't know. But to enter the land of the dead. It's not a gift I wanted or would ever use. I never want to meet the Forsaken again.

'Karshur, his spirit, witnessed this gift. When the dagger was returned, Karshur added to Keteth's gift with his own. Perhaps he knew I would never use it, I don't know, but he gave to me a spell that would take me to the realm of the dead easily and in an instant. Still, I never thought I'd use it, but then I found the raven talisman he mentioned. Somehow he knew I would find this talisman, and when I found it I could use the spell.'

The wizards were frowning. Issa carried on awkwardly, finding it difficult to articulate everything that had happened. It sounded so silly, so crazy when she tried to put everything into normal words.

'It's a raven made of glittering black stone, and it's about this big.' She made a circle with her hands. 'Have you seen or heard of it?' The men shook their heads. If the most powerful and learned wizards of Maioria didn't know of the raven talisman, then what in the world was it?

Issa sighed. 'I know nothing about it, only that it's powerful, like an orb but different. It's possible its power is linked to Zanufey's moon, but until it rises again, I cannot know. With this talisman and the gifts given to me by Keteth and Karshur, I had greater power. I went into the realm of the dead and called the ravens to me. I could not have defeated the harpies without the ravens or the talisman or the gifts,' she ended in a quiet voice.

'Where is this talisman?' Freydel asked, completely intrigued.

'I didn't bring it. I decided coming with the orb would be enough, and I didn't yet know who I would be speaking with,' she answered honestly.

'Can you call the ravens to you now?' Luren asked. His furtive features were excited, he clearly wanted her to perform a magic trick.

'I guess I could, but I won't. I will only call them when they are needed,' she said. He looked disappointed. She had a thought. 'But I might be able to call one, the one that came to me in the beginning.'

Luren nodded and grinned. Even Freydel seemed intrigued. She closed her eyes and focused on the Flow again. The faint energy of the dark moon still moved around her. *Ehka, I know you are linked to the dark moon too.* Could she reach him and call him to her this way? It seemed like an easy and simple thing to do, though she had no idea how to do it. She stepped into the Flow and gathered up the indigo energy.

'*Ehka,*' she said with her mind. '*Come to me, follow the power of Zanufey's moon.*' She willed the indigo magic from her and imagined it searching for Ehka. She thought she heard a caw come from far away but couldn't be sure. She stepped out of the Flow, half expecting Ehka to be there beside her, but he wasn't. She felt her cheeks going red, suddenly feeling silly as the bemused faces of the wizards looked on. Luren's excitement faded into disappointment.

She shrugged and gave a sheepish grin. 'I guess it didn't work, or he didn't want to come. He's not a dog that comes when I call, he has his own strong-willed mind.'

'I think we have interrogated Issa for long enough,' Freydel said, clapping his hands together with finality. She gave him a grateful smile, feeling worn out.

'One more thing,' Domenon said. Freydel gave him a withering look but Domenon was staring only at her. She shifted uncomfortably under his heavy gaze. 'It's written in the Book of Ages that the Queen of Ravens will bear a mark, not a mark from birth or battle, but one that comes of a sudden when she comes into her power. "The mark of the goddess, the mark of the messenger, the mark of the alter self." Do you have a mark, Issa?'

She swallowed. She didn't want to reveal her personal mark to these men. But rather than honour her dignity the wizards only looked on with more intrigue. Freydel gave her an apologetic look. She could lie, but they would most definitely sense it.

'I do have a mark,' she said after a long pause. This caused murmurs of surprise amongst the wizards. Perhaps that is what they needed to see to believe she was their fabled Raven Queen. A mark like a clear and unquestionable label detailing a product in a market stall. Maybe she needed that too, to believe in herself. 'It was Karshur's gift to me for fulfilling his purpose.'

'I think we need to see it,' Domenon said.

She felt herself colour and frowned her disapproval at him. It felt like a battle of wills, his against hers, and he'd won. He had exerted dominance over her and she hated it. She could not *not* show the expectant wizards the raven mark. It proved to them without question that she was the one spoken of in the prophecies. She was beginning to hate those prophecies. *I am Issalena Kammy too, dammit! I have a life of my own, not just to fulfil the stupid old prophecies.*

Trying to make nothing of it, she reached up to the cords on her tunic dress and untied them. The wizards shifted uncomfortably, except Domenon. She pulled the neck of her tunic down just enough to reveal the shimmering blue mark on the centre of her chest.

Domenon seemed taken aback at that, and she suddenly realised he had not believed her the entire time. She smiled, the final victory was hers.

In an instant and quicker than a bird the tall man jumped off his seat, strode over and gripped her shoulders. He stared closely at the mark. She was too stunned to move, and his iron grip was painful and unyielding.

'Domenon!' Several shocked voices commanded the wizard at once. At the same time, she felt the Flow suddenly jerk or snap. There was a flash of indigo light, and through it, Ehka burst into the circle. The big bird tumbled left then right, struggling to keep airborne as he fought to overcome his disorientation.

'It's a raven, it's the mark of the raven,' Domenon said in shock, not even noticing the squawking bird or the protesting wizards. He lifted his eyes and stared into hers with a penetrating gaze. Though it was he who was scrutinising her, for the briefest moment, she saw something move within his eyes. Her eyes went wide in surprise and she strained to see further.

He released her suddenly and snapped his head away. Whether he was trying to prevent her from seeing anymore or realised the error of his actions, she couldn't be sure. Freydel steadied her as Domenon strode back to his seat without an apology, and sat there staring at the floor deep in thought.

'I must apologise for our *Master* Wizard,' Freydel said in a raised voice, glaring at Domenon. 'He's renowned for having strong emotions and acting on impulse. It's both his power and his weakness. He will apologise at some point no doubt.'

Domenon ignored him and continued his deep reverie.

'Are you all right?' Freydel asked.

Issa retied the cord of her tunic, shaken by Domenon's actions, and whatever he seemed to be hiding. One thing was for sure, he was not entirely human, and that was not just because of his supposed elven heritage. He didn't feel elven at all to her.

'I'm all right.' She tried to compose herself. 'Ehka,' she called to the bird circling wildly above her. He landed quite unsteadily at her feet.

'This is Ehka,' she said and bent to stroke his neck.

'It worked,' Luren laughed aloud.

She smiled, surprised herself. Stroking his soft feathers and having him here, immediately comforted and calmed her. Ehka looked at each of the wizards, stared hard at Domenon, then lost interest and began preening himself.

'I think Issa has suffered us more than enough,' Freydel said, and laid a reassuring hand on her shoulder. The other wizards agreed and began to stand. 'I'll help you return, but don't forget to take the orb. It's always better to return to the place you physically transported from with the stuff you left with. It creates calm and balance in the energies.'

She took note of his advice and stooped to retrieve the Orb of Water. 'Sorry, Ehka. Looks like we're going straight back.' She scooped the bemused bird up into her other arm and said goodbye to the other wizards. She was very glad to be leaving.

CHAPTER 31

The Vote

RETURNING took only moments. Freydel was part of the way through the spell he was weaving when the world turned hazy and a rush of air blasted through her. In a blink she was back in her room in Castle Carvon, swaying and utterly disorientated as Ehka squawked in her arm. Thank the goddess she was home and away from all those wizards. She plopped Ehka and the orb onto the bed and sat down to stop the room spinning. But, after a moment, she conceded Freydel was right, this time she recovered much quicker. There came a knock at the door.

'Who is it,' she called out after a moment. She wanted to pretend she wasn't here. She hoped it wasn't Freydel returned from the Circle to ask her more questions. She wanted to be alone.

Asaph poked his head around the door and grinned. 'I sensed you were back, or perhaps it was that noisy raven.'

She smiled at him. She hadn't expected him at all. 'Oh, it's you. You can come in. I thought it might be someone else I'm too tired to talk to.'

'You can tell me everything, and I promise not to get cross. I brought you some lunch,' he said, coming fully into the room. He carried a tray filled with fruit, freshly baked rolls and ceramic pots filled with something.

'Wow, I'm famished.' She eyed the rolls realising how hungry she was. Using magic always made her hungry. She patted the bed for him to sit beside her. 'You seem better today,' she said.

'I'm sorry for my behaviour. I don't know what came over me. Some strange sickness or just fatigue, I'm not sure,' he said with a guilty look.

'But I feel much better now.'

As they ate, Issa told him what had happened at the Wizards' Circle.

'If I meet Domenon I'll make him apologise,' Asaph growled.

She giggled. 'Hopefully, he'll feel guilty enough after today. He's a strange one. I think I'll keep away from him. Now the elf man Averen, he was nice…'

'I don't want to hear about the elf man,' Asaph scowled. He caught her grinning at him, and laughed. 'I guess I fell for that one. When you've rested, why don't we explore the castle and grounds? Coronos said to try to keep you in the castle until he's back. So I thought this way you would satisfy your curiosity and I get to be with you alone. The river really does run right through the castle's centre and there are these beautiful bridges going all over it.'

'Sounds stunning, although I'm too tired right now. I don't think I can rest with you here though can I?'

'Are you sure?' he bent closer to her and smiled in that way that made butterflies dance in her belly. His lips brushed hers and she parted them as her passion quickly rose. As they kissed that out-of-depth feeling began to grow and she felt herself tense up. Asaph must have felt it for he gently let her go, leaving her almost shaking with desire and confusion.

'You can relax,' he smiled. 'I won't overpower you. We can just rest together.' He lay back on the bed and then drew her down with him.

Despite the desire she felt for him she could not seem to stay relaxed when they kissed. She began to wonder if it would always be this way. Would she always be afraid to let anyone get close to her like that? Would she shy away from intimacy? Ehka flew to the nearby chair with a strange caw. He sat there eyeing them suspiciously. Issa laughed and found herself relaxing.

'I think you should take your belt and sword off, though. It can't be very comfortable to lie on,' he said. He undid them and let them drop to the floor, then smoothed the creases on her tunic. His touch on her stomach made her tingle again, but instead of doing anymore he let his hand lie lightly across her and closed his eyes. She sighed and closed her eyes as well.

'Bah, I have no time for prophecies and such nonsense,' Drumblodd scowled. 'But she *has* mastered the Flow, whether or not what she said was true, about killing Keteth and all.'

'She didn't lie,' Averen said. 'I would have felt it.'

'She didn't lie,' Haelgon seconded him.

'I think little of prophecies too. I agree with Domenon. I'd rather be free from fate and destiny to forge my future,' King Navarr said.

'We are all free to forge our own futures. The prophecies merely speak of one particular timeline that may be followed. There are many possible timelines,' Freydel said. He wondered then if he had changed his own timeline by seeing Baelthrom in the past as Ayeth. Thoughts that certainly deserved more time to think upon.

'So, let us finish why we came here, and decide whether to invite Issa to undertake the Wizard's Reckoning and enter the Storm Holt.' He said it curtly, wanting the dreaded outcome to be over. 'We will first discuss any questions the Circle has, and then cast a vote—a simple show of hands. Are there any questions?'

'What happens if she passes and wants to become a member of the Circle?' Drumblodd dived straight in. The other wizards shifted and frowned at his words. 'It may have been forgotten that not only have women *not* sat upon the Circle since the time of the Ancients, but neither have they been Orb Keepers. Issa is an Orb Keeper.'

'I have considered this,' Freydel began, 'but to become a member of the Circle also requires an invitation. If we should reach that point it would also have to be decided in a vote. Those have been the rules since the Circle was created. But even so, there is another issue, upon whose seat would she sit? The Wykiry have no seat, not since the time of the Ancients or maybe never.'

The wizards began to chat amongst themselves, such questions had not been asked before.

'How can we trust her?' It was Domenon. He hadn't spoken since his embarrassing actions towards Issa and had instead sat there in brooding silence.

'Explain,' Freydel said.

'I wonder if we should ever have brought her to the Wizards' Circle, not with Baelthrom's spies everywhere. You say the High Priestess may

have betrayed Celene, may have joined ranks with the Maphraxies. But
what if Issa has as well? It could be that Issa was captured on the Isles of
Kammy, turned into a spy and then brought the Maphraxies to Celene.'

Freydel sighed. Why did he always have to cast doubt and waste time
in meetings?

Averen shook his head. 'I would have felt it, the taint of Baelthrom.
We all would have.'

'Even if she is genuine,' Domenon continued, 'it appears that the
Maphraxies will stop at nothing to capture her. She is the one bringing us
all this trouble. If it weren't for Issa, Celene would still be with us. Why
not just let the Maphraxies take her and spare hundreds, maybe
thousands, of people?'

Gasps spread across the Circle.

'Domenon, how can you say such things?' Coronos said, a look of
shock on his face.

'I am talking about the greatest good for the greatest number of
people,' Domenon said, a touch of anger in his voice. 'If they have her
perhaps they will leave us all alone. It would give us much needed time to
prepare the Feylint Halanoi, and spread the army to every major town
along the shores of Western Frayon.'

Luren, ever ready to listen to Domenon, raised a thoughtful eyebrow
on the subject, and the wizards began murmuring to each other again.

'Enough.' Freydel held his hands up and rested back control of the
meeting. 'We will not sacrifice *anyone* by sending them to their deaths.
Such preposterous ideas belong to Baelthrom's own.' He glared at
Domenon. 'Now enough of this talk. Gentlemen, time wears on, let us
cast a vote. All those in favour of inviting Issa to the Wizard's Reckoning,
please raise your hands.'

Haelgon, Navarr, Averen, Drumblodd and Luren raised their hands.
Coronos did not and, much to Freydel's surprise, neither did Domenon.

'Five against three, Issa will be invited to enter the Storm Holt. But
the decision is hers. No one can force or deny her now,' Freydel said. The
end vote hadn't surprised him, but at least he wasn't the only one against
it. 'If I may ask, what are your reasons for agreeing to invite her?'

'She is more than strong enough, and we need more adept wizards,'
Averen said passionately. The others agreed with him.

Freydel nodded, it was fair enough. 'As you know I'll have no part in testing Issa after sending her to Keteth. Coronos, what are your reasons for denying?'

'I too believe she has proved herself more than capable. I only hope the Storm Holt will bring her greater peace of mind and understanding of herself,' Coronos said.

'Domenon? Please share your reasons,' Freydel asked stiffly.

'I don't want to risk sending another woman into the Storm Holt,' Domenon said. 'The magic of the world is different of late, and it's been many years since the Storm Holt was used. How do we know it hasn't changed and become more deadly? We all know it is a gateway to the demon worlds, what if the demons have grown restless? There are too many unknowns.'

Freydel considered the man. Was there more to what he was saying? Domenon didn't care about anyone else but himself, so why did he care about a woman going into the Storm Holt? Perhaps he didn't want Issa to become more powerful. Perhaps he was already jealous of the powers he had seen in her. He already wanted the orbs, could he also want this raven talisman? He didn't seem that bothered about the talisman, seemed more upset about the mark on her chest. Was he afraid the prophecies were true? Surely he would be pleased there was hope, a way to end Baelthrom. He dropped his eyes from the brooding man and looked at the others.

'The vote has been decided, let's end this meeting and return home. Navarr, Coronos and I will pass the invite to Issa and leave it in her hands. If she agrees, we will call one more meeting.' Freydel stood up. One by one the wizards left the Circle, with Coronos, Navarr and Freydel leaving together to return to Castle Carvon.

Freydel arrived in his room alone. Worry for Issa clenched his stomach. He slumped onto the bed and buried his face in his hands with a sigh.

I'm sorry Issa. I know you will accept the invitation. There is nothing I can do to help prepare you for the Storm Holt. I hope Zanufey can reach you there even if her moon cannot.

'Yes,' Issa said to a sombre-faced Freydel. 'I accept the invitation to enter the Storm Holt. You know I couldn't refuse.' She spoke firmly.

'I thought as much,' Freydel nodded. She followed his eyes as he looked away out of the window at the darkening sky. The fire crackled in the hearth, and the room was dimming with the onset of evening. He stood up to light a few candles. He didn't want her to go, that much was obvious. He really cared for her. She found it touching and immediately didn't want to be a cause of worry for him.

Coronos smiled at her. 'I don't think we have anything to be concerned about. Though all of us—me, Asaph, Freydel—would prefer you not to risk yourself.'

'I'm touched by your concern, all of you. But we all know that I have to go,' she said with a half smile. She would go, even if all the men she knew and cared about didn't want her to. She had thought about it constantly, even before they'd invited her to the Storm Holt.

'I have many reasons. I don't care about sitting on the Wizards' Circle. I don't even care about proving myself to anyone anymore. Not after Keteth, not after the attacks on the Karalanths, and certainly not after Celene.' And she really didn't. She had a good sense of her strengths and abilities now. What the wizards thought didn't matter to her, only that they respected her enough. She'd like to prove her strength to Domenon though.

'The demons from the Murk plague my dreams every time I sleep, or when my mind is still, and I don't know why. There's something important happening, or that I'm supposed to do, but I don't know what. Through the Storm Holt I can reach the Murk, and find out why the demons are speaking to me,' she trailed off. In the Storm Holt, she would find her answers.

Freydel shook his head. 'I think the demons speak to you because they know you will soon be in their clutches. Never trust a demon. Everything they do is two-faced and double-edged. As much as it pains me to see you put yourself in danger, passing the Wizard's Reckoning will make you a stronger wizard, a stronger person.'

Issa didn't care about being stronger, though she didn't voice her feelings. Since her friends and family had been killed, she cared less for herself than she dared to admit. It was either run away or fight. She would either be a coward or face everything that came her way until it killed her. Entering the Storm Holt was a way to be fearless and fight back. A way to vent her anger, frustration and vengeance when she could not take it out on the real enemy.

'My biggest worry is telling Asaph. Perhaps I shouldn't tell him,' Issa chewed her lip. They'd had such a nice day exploring the grounds together, they'd really got on. She didn't want to upset him or cause an argument. She wanted to spend more time with him, to let her feelings for him grow naturally. Maybe then she could relax in his arms.

'You must tell him,' Coronos said. 'I understand how much he cares for you and wants to protect you, but the young man must learn that he cannot keep you under lock and key, or anyone else for that matter.'

A smile broke over Freydel's face. 'It pleases me greatly that he watches over you, but Coronos is right, he must realise everyone has to make their own choices.'

'It just seems so cruel,' Issa slumped her shoulders. 'I know he will be angry.'

Issa was right. Asaph was angry. Furious even.

'You just cannot accept this stupid invite,' he shouted. His handsome face flushed red as he towered over her.

Her temper flared. How dare he talk to her like that. Who did he think he was? She was vaguely aware of a servant closing the door to the dining room where they argued.

'I'll go where the hell I want. Even if it is to hell,' she shouted back and stood tall, folding her arms across her chest.

'This is madness. Why do you insist on throwing yourself in harm's way?' he whirled away and leant on the mantelpiece. 'How can I help you there if there is trouble? Do you care so little for yourself? Do you care so little for me and the others?'

Issa didn't know what to say, Asaph had spoken the truth. She *did* care little for herself. Her own desires just seemed unimportant for the tasks she felt drove her. Did she care so little for Asaph? She cared for him a great deal, too much, and that was the problem. She didn't want to get close to him and suffer losing him like she had Ely and Rance, her mother and all her friends. She cared more for Asaph and everyone else than she did herself. But if she was Zanufey's chosen, then her relationship with Asaph had to come second.

'I would rather you didn't care for me. Can't you find a nice Draxian woman to spend your life with?' she retorted. 'Being with me will only get you killed. Don't you see? Our time together is meaningless in the face of what we have to do. There simply is no time for us.'

Asaph paled. She immediately regretted her words. The stunned look on his face made her feel faint and her anger dissipated. She'd hurt him, deeply somehow. He stood up and stalked out of the room.

She struggled for words, trying to find something better to say, only to watch the door close behind him. She blinked back tears and slumped into a chair, rubbing her pounding temples.

CHAPTER 32

Into the Storm Holt

ISSA stood before the Wizards' Circle once more. After doing nothing but eating, sleeping and exploring the extensive castle grounds, she felt strong and ready for anything, even entering the Storm Holt.

She had not seen Asaph since their row. She'd been deliberately avoiding him since then and supposed he'd been doing the same. She wished he was here now, wished he could come with her. She didn't want to do this alone.

She began to wonder what she had got herself into this time. The wizards all seemed far more solemn than the last time they'd met. Freydel looked positively worried, but then he had actively opposed her entering the Storm Holt.

It was night but the shield above glowed softly pink and the gentle illumination of the orbs set them all in a calming soft light. She was dressed in her simple tunic, blacksmith's belt, riding boots and sword. She had wrapped the talisman in cloth and stuffed it into her belt as a last thought.

'You cannot take anything into the Storm Holt,' Freydel said, indicating her sword. 'Not the orb, jewellery, or even clothes.'

'Oh,' she said. So much for her sword, orb and talisman. And the dark moon couldn't even reach her there. Then perhaps it would prove whether the Raven Queen was always within her. She had not shown them the talisman yet but now didn't seem to be the right time.

'I'll just leave them here, then.' She put her sword on the ground along with the talisman and Ely's bracelet. She hesitated as she took off

Asaph's ring. Without it he would have no link to her, she would be completely alone in the world of demons. What if she never returned? She blinked back tears wishing she'd ended on a happier note with Asaph. She suddenly felt more alone now than she had ever done in her entire life.

'Everything except the organic, physical body is destroyed upon entry into the Storm Holt,' Averen said. His soft voice was trying to be reassuring. 'We tend to leave our clothes at the entrance for when we return. But don't worry, you will go alone.' He grinned.

Issa forced a relieved smile. At least she wouldn't have to be naked in front of these men. Doubt gnawed at her mind, fear clenched her belly. The Storm Holt was sounding more and more ominous.

It was the test of tests, but if Luren and Coronos could pass, two novice wizards who had nowhere near the level of control of the Flow as she had, then surely she could. She tried to console herself with positive thoughts. She licked her dry lips.

'We visited the place where the Storm Holt gate is before you arrived. The Storm Holt is ready and waiting, as it always has been,' Freydel said quietly, his face was pale and serious. 'There's nothing anyone can say or do to help you prepare for what is to come, and it's better they don't in case you expect something that does not happen. The Reckoning is different for everyone and it depends on what is to be found deep in your soul.'

'I'm ready, I think,' she lied. She could never be ready, but there was no point hanging around. She clenched her fists and tried to calm her racing heart.

Freydel laid a hand on her shoulder. 'You know you don't have to do this?'

Issa nodded. 'I know, but I can think of no good reason not to. And if I did not, for the rest of my days I would always regret it.' She did not mention the near continuous dreams about demons, white spears, and knights on white horses. If she turned back now they would think her a coward, she would think herself a coward. She looked at Domenon and hardened her resolve.

'That is how it felt for all of us,' Averen gave a knowing nod. 'I never want fear to make me live in regret.' She considered his wise words. As suffocating as fear was, she didn't want to live in regret either.

She expected them to all begin forming some spell to take her to the gate, but instead Freydel showed her to the stone stairs that wound around the tower leading all the way to the ground far below. She felt sick just looking over the edge.

'Some have quipped that surviving the stairs down is the first part of the test,' Freydel smiled, trying to lift the mood. He murmured a word and a soft ball of light appeared above her head about the size of her fist. 'The light will guide you. It's better for us to remain here where we can watch the energy of the Flow more clearly, though none of us can assist you or even reach you after you enter.'

'How long will it take?' she asked. The wizards laughed and her cheeks coloured.

'It takes as long as it takes, sometimes as much as three days,' Domenon said, his face unreadable.

'Three days?' she said in a raised voice. 'Is there food and water down there?' Again, the wizards laughed.

'You'll be unlikely to need food or water, much like you don't need such things in a dream, even though you will be physically there. You'll certainly need such things when you get back for your body will have been depleted and taken to the brink of its tolerance,' Freydel said.

She nodded, her nerves jittering. Domenon stood beyond the others looking off into the night sky. He had said little this entire meeting. She wondered then why he had not agreed to invite her. It's not like he had any fondness for her. Maybe one day she would ask him—if she dared to hear the answer.

She looked back down the steps. 'It'll take a day just to get down there,' she murmured. Coronos chuckled.

'We will be here when you return. We'll be ready to assist you immediately,' Freydel smiled and gave her a reassuring pat, but the smile did not reach his eyes and for a moment she felt comforted by the only father figure she'd had in her life. Two now, if she included Coronos, she corrected herself. She nodded, and without much ceremony began taking the steps down, the orb leading her on.

The steps were narrow and there was no rail to stop her should she fall, so she hugged the wall close. She turned back to look up at the wizards one last time. They were all clustered around the stair top looking down at her, their faces a mix of concern and encouragement. She turned away with a sigh and slowly made her way down.

Now she was alone she wished Ehka was here, but she had not seen him since yesterday. The night was dark and cool, but breezeless. When she reached the grass-covered ground she could hear the night sounds of forest animals. Above her came the high-pitched squeaks of bats, and in the grass, insects rattled their chorus. There was not much to see in the dark, and so she let the Freydel's ball of light guide her and turned inward to her thoughts.

They said the Storm Holt was a gate that leads to the underworlds, the demon worlds. The Murk was the closest and the first. Beyond it was the Pit—and that is where the danger began. Beyond the Pit no one knew, they called it the endless Abyss. They said she would face greater demons in the Pit, and they took all forms to try to destroy your mind and wrestle your soul from you. Was she ready to face demons?

She didn't feel courageous or powerful. She wanted revenge, she wanted to fight Maphraxies, not demons. The demons had not killed her mother and destroyed her home. The demons had not attacked and slain the Karalanths. The demons had not brutalised and murdered Ely and destroyed Celene. She had no quarrel with demons, only that they plagued her mind.

The ball of light lead her along a narrow path into a thick forest of deciduous trees, mainly old chestnuts and oaks. She could tell from the flattened grass that the wizards had recently been here. How strange that they took the risk and chose to keep one gate open to the demon worlds. One gate so that they could descend into hell and test themselves against their adversaries to keep them strong. Why didn't they guard it day and night? They said the demons couldn't come through it, only wizards could enter, but it seemed a bit of a risk.

Would she meet her equal in the Storm Holt? How bad would it be in there? It was frustrating no one could tell her what to expect, only that it would show her the deepest parts of herself, and make her overcome them, or not. How could it be any worse than what she had already suffered? She bit her lip, memories of those who had died swam before her. *If I am meant to live, I shall live. I'm done with fearing for my life when so many others have lost theirs because of me.*

She turned a bend and brilliant blue and white light broke through the dense trees. She peered ahead and stepped closer. The hairs on her arms stood up, responding to the static energy that now charged the air, just like it felt when caught in a thunderstorm. She emerged into a clearing and stared ahead. A concentrated oval-shaped light swirled in a circular motion that was slow near the rim and too fast to follow in the centre.

'It's the same one I saw in the mound,' Issa whispered aloud, staring in awe at the spinning vortex of energy. A storm of furious light hidden deep in the forest of an unknown and uninhabited island. It was made more impressive and bright by the darkness of the forest. Blue and white flares tumbled and spun around each other in a whirlpool of storm clouds. The vortex was at least ten feet high and six feet wide, and it remained suspended in the air about a foot off the ground, like a rip or a hole in the fabric of Maioria. And so, she supposed, it was exactly that.

A rip in time and space. No wonder they called it the Storm Holt. She stepped towards it, not wanting it to suck her in like before. For all the violence of the energy storm, there was no sound or wind. Actually, there was the opposite of sound, a strange deafening silence as if all noise was being sucked into it. Now and then silent lightning flared within it. The Flow between her and the Storm Holt moved erratically and in a wildly unpredictable manner. Fear knotted her belly.

'I have to enter that?' The first experience in the mound was terrifying enough. She swallowed and looked back the way she had come. Suddenly all her courage dissipated. *She could turn around. She could be a coward...*

'Hallo,' a small voice came from somewhere in the darkness, making her jump out of her skin.

The Flow was instantly at her command, her eyes strained into the darkness and her heart pounded. It took her a while to locate the small dark shadow a few feet away beside the Storm Holt. The shadow became more distinct as if it were somehow materialising, and what she saw she didn't quite believe.

She blinked twice at the ugly, pot-bellied, two-foot high creature. It was completely bald with thickly-muscled, stubby arms and legs, and toes and fingers complete with sharp claws. Its roundish face was wide with a big mouth and a single white fang protruded over its upper lip. It was mid-grey all over, except for its eyes which were yellow, and its tongue which was blood red. It sat on the bole of a thick oak and was more animal than human.

Now and then, the ugly creature flapped its bat-like wings, lifted a foot or so into the air, then settled back on the oak. She would have continued to be terrified, but the thing seemed more frightened than she was. Its eyes were wide and constantly darting left and right, and its tongue flicked nervously in and out of its mouth. They stared at each for a long moment.

'Are you supposed to be here,' she asked in a shaky voice, wondering if this was the thing that had spoken. Her hand went to her sword that was not there, but she was ready to use the Flow at any moment. The thing might start small now but grow into something monstrous.

'Yes,' it squeaked. She wondered if its voice was normally like that, or if it was just because it was nervous. 'Are you a wizard?' its voice trembled. The question took her by surprise. It could speak whole sentences and clearly had an inquisitive brain.

'Maybe. What *are* you?' She frowned, relaxing her stance and letting go of some of the Flow. The creature seemed quite small and pathetic.

'A Shadow Demon.' His voice trembled less and became a pitch lower—which was why she decided it was a "he." He forgot his fear and stood up proudly on his stubby legs.

'Oh,' she frowned. 'I've not heard of one before.' Were there different types of demons? She'd assumed they were all huge and terrifying. He seemed a little perturbed and folded his wings solemnly. The bemused look on his face almost made her laugh out loud. Did they actually have emotions and feelings? She was beginning to question everything she'd been told about demons.

'But it sounds quite frightening,' she added, the creature seemed to grin, although it looked more like a grimace that creased up his ugly face.

'Did you come out of that?' She pointed at the Storm Holt. The Shadow Demon nodded. 'Are they all like you in there?' If they were all so small and puny, she had nothing to worry about.

'No. Some have wings, some do not. King is ten feet tall, but he's not the biggest,' the Shadow Demon said. There was a hint of awe in his face at the mention of this King.

'Oh,' she said. A ten-foot tall one would not be nice. 'Well, I have to go in there, apparently. That way I can master myself and become a real wizard with lots of respect. Anyway, how did you come through it? I thought only wizards could enter, and no demons could possibly come here from there.' Could this demon really be trusted to speak the truth? No demon could be trusted, she reminded herself.

'King sent me. It wasn't easy, but I'm small and King is strong,' he said.

She frowned. The wizards had said nothing could come through, and yet here appeared to be a Shadow Demon.

'And you don't need to enter to become a wizard,' he said and stood proud again as if he knew more about it than she did. Which he probably did right now, she conceded.

'Yes, but it makes you strong and…' she had a thought and started on a different tact. 'Why are demons plaguing my mind and my dreams? And why did this "King" send you? Who is this "King"?' she should never be stupid enough to trust a demon, of any sort.

'Our great King Gedrock. King of all the Shadow Demons. He's looking for the Raven Queen, so he sent me to find her. But it took him a lot of effort, and me a long time to get through. Demons can't easily travel to the horrible higherworlds now most gates are closed.'

'Why is King Gedrock looking for the Raven Queen?' Now she really was suspicious. If they had a king, it meant they had order. It meant they had rules and leadership. That seemed far too advanced for what she'd been led to believe about demons. She'd assumed they were just a demonic force of chaotic beings. If they had order and feelings, that made them something else. She couldn't work out if she was worried or relieved.

The demon looked left then right as if afraid someone or something was watching. 'Because the Demon Wizard has opened the gates to the Pit, and the greater demons are coming to destroy us.'

'Why should I care about demon problems? I have enough troubles of my own.' She let go of the Flow completely. This silly creature was unlikely to hurt anyone.

'Because the Demon Wizard wants to return with his greater demons to here, to Maioria. Once he takes over the Murk, Maioria is next. He can come here because he's from here, he's part human,' the Shadow Demon said.

'So? What can I do about it?' she said. The last thing she wanted was to get involved in someone else's war, and she certainly wasn't about to start helping demons.

'King thinks you can help. King thinks you can get the spear and give it to the one who can kill the Demon Wizard.'

She stared into the Storm Holt. 'The Cursed King and his Banished Legion,' she breathed. Were they the knights riding on those white horses? Is that why the demons were reaching out to her? 'Why doesn't King just give it to them then?' What kind of powers did this king think she had?

'King says the Demon Slayer will kill all demons on sight. King needs an intermediar-aray,' the demon stumbled over the word.

'Is King the one who plagues my dreams?' she asked. The demon shrugged. 'Will the Storm Holt take me to him?'

The Shadow Demon looked concerned. 'Maybe. I can take you to him a better, safer way. Look, if you—'

Issa cut him off. 'But I need to enter the Storm Holt, regardless of what this king wants. That's what is expected of me. That's the test I've agreed to take. The wizards will know if I don't enter. I've already decided, I must undertake the Wizard's Reckoning.'

The demon swallowed audibly. 'No gate to the Murk, whether closed or open, is safe anymore. The greater demons are opening all the demon gates. They are doing something dangerous with them. Maybe this gate will get you to the Murk, maybe it will take you to . . . beyond the Pit.'

'Sounds bad,' she murmured, suddenly wishing she hadn't foolishly agreed to take the test. 'Still, it can't be *that* bad. If I don't do it, I'll never have the opportunity to take the Reckoning again. Besides, it sounds like this, er, king, is waiting for me.' The demon could be lying, it could all be a trick. The wizards would know, the gate had to go where they said it went. Maybe this was all part of the 'test' anyway.

'Who are you? Do you have a name?' she said.

'Maggot,' he replied.

'That's not a name, that's... that's disgusting.' She wrinkled up her nose.

'Thank you,' Maggot beamed.

She frowned at him. This all had to be part of the Reckoning. Maybe it started easy and got harder.

'Well, Maggot, I'm Issa, and I have to enter that gate.' She said it decisively, her mind made up.

'Issstha, Ithy, Issy,' he struggled with her name. 'But it's not safe...'

'It's never been safe, Maggot, that's the point. That's why wizards enter it. Tell your King Gedrock to meet me when I get there. Now, if you'll excuse me.'

She untied her boots and set them down in the grass. Next were her belt and tunic dress. She set these down by the boots and hesitated at her underwear. Did she need to be completely naked? It all seemed so wrong. She glanced back at Maggot who was flapping nervously in the air.

'It's not safe,' he shook his head and flapped his wings. Confusion twisted his face. Perhaps he was having trouble with whatever orders he had been given now she refused to follow him. 'King will be cross if you die, and I shall be punished.'

She took a deep breath. At least he was honest—something she had not expected from a demon. Actually, a lot of things she had not expected from demons had just happened.

'Well, you can come with me. No need to shake your head, it's up to you. I'm wasting valuable time here. Now, do you mind? I need you to turn around so I can undress.' She wafted her hand at him. The demon looked even more confused.

She sighed, what did the thing care if she was naked or not. She slipped off her underwear and shivered, suddenly feeling horribly vulnerable. A glance at Maggot told her he was still struggling with what to do now. She stepped forwards and reached a hand tentatively towards the swirling gate. Immediately she felt it pull on her and drew her hand back. Her heart pounded and sweat beaded her brow.

'The greater demons will kill you in there, you'll never get out,' Maggot suddenly wailed beside her.

He seemed quite pitiful and a desire to pet him almost overwhelmed her. He really wasn't helping her resolve to enter the gate. *Never trust a demon,* she reminded herself as he continued.

'I can take you another way. I'll be in trouble if you don't come back, I know it.' He had come close enough to lay a small clawed hand on her knee. He looked up at her with pleading yellow eyes.

'Isthy, it's not safe.'

'My mother used to call me that; Issy.' She smiled at him, a sad smile. 'You see, Maggot, I have to go, I don't have a choice. Not now. When I'm there, I will meet your King.'

She turned back to the Storm Holt, closed her eyes and stepped forward into the maelstrom. Maggot wailed her name as she fell and then was whipped up into the storm. She didn't know if he followed or not.

CHAPTER 33

The Wizard's Reckoning

ISSA spun over and over. She couldn't breathe for the panic that ripped through her, and the terrifying energies that shuddered around her. Where the Storm Holt entrance had been silent before, now the roar of energy filled her ears. The world was a blur of flashing lightning, howling noise, and spinning energy. Every cell in her body vibrated and screamed in pain. She began to feel herself fragment, just like she had when she transported to the Wizards' Circle, only this was violent and painful. She thought she was going to die.

The spinning slowed and the deafening noise dimmed a little. Her body pulled itself together and felt more solid. The air turned hot and heavy as she struggled to drag it into her lungs. She couldn't do anything to slow her movement in the flaring maelstrom of blue and white, she was trapped in the rapids of a flow of energy. Beyond the tunnel in which she was hurtling, she saw a sky filled with green-tinged clouds and a huge emerald pockmarked moon. The green moon of the Murk.

A face formed in the clouds, a demon face, the same demon she had seen in her dream. Red eyes with black slitted pupils watched her endless tumble through the Storm Holt. Its mouth moved as if it was trying to speak to her. She tried to slow her fall, but it was like trying to grasp at the wind. All she could do was focus on dragging air into her lungs and endure the forces battering her. She struggled to stay conscious.

'Raven Queen,' the demon's voice boomed around her.

'Help me,' she screamed. 'I cannot stop it.'

Far below she glimpsed the ground, a wide plain and a huge, black rock that stabbed into the sky. She'd seen that before, in the sacred mound. That was where the demon horde had flooded from. To her horror, she realised the Storm Holt was taking her straight to it. She grappled for the Flow, but it wasn't there. There was magic and energy in the Murk, but it was unavailable to her. She was not of this place, she could not use the energy here. How could she be tested as a wizard if there was no magic that she could use? Nothing made any sense. Her mind began to scatter.

The spire loomed close at a rapid rate. She covered her head and screamed as she tumbled towards the rock, only to find that she passed right through it unhurt. Darkness engulfed her. She blinked, trying to understand. Solid stone could not break her fall whilst her physical body was pure energy in the Storm Holt.

She was still being carried by the maelstrom, though. Now she spun through darkness flecked through with the blue and white energy. She burst into great caverns lit by flaming braziers. Things moved on ledges in the walls. Demons, thousands of them. Some were small and brown, like the demon she'd met at the gate entrance, but others were the size of dragons with enormous black wings made of the shadows themselves. They began to shriek at her presence, screaming and howling for her blood and soul.

'Get it,' they screamed.

'Fresh blood...'

'A living soul...'

Those with wings leapt into the air and flew towards her. She was soon followed by legions of demons following her downward plummet. Their claws flashed in the light. They gnashed their teeth, and their eyes... She tried not to look into their eyes. Faster, she begged. At first she'd wanted the Storm Holt to slow, but now she prayed it carried her faster. There was nothing she could do to fight them or run away, she was stuck in the maelstrom that drew her ever downwards.

Long black faces, more terrifying than the demons she had seen in her dreams, made her soul shrivel. Those faces were the length of her body, and their black fangs the size of her arms as they snapped at her. Though their fangs could not seem to hurt her physical body, she felt their teeth and claws tear at her energy and rip into her soul.

The flying demons followed her through rock and stone, they seemed to be made of energy just like she was. For a moment she was thankful that the tunnel did not stop, and her fall was fast enough to keep most of the demons from reaching her. She curled up in a ball to keep from seeing their horrific faces and prayed to Zanufey to end it.

Bright light on her eyelids forced her eyes open. She was falling through a cavern filled with light. She turned and saw the white spear directly beneath her, the source of the light. She reached to grab it as she tumbled past, but her hands were not solid and she could grasp at nothing. The spear passed harmlessly through her body, but its energy was like a breath of fresh air to her soul. She could feel the spear's power and it gave her strength. Could she feel the spear's magic because it was originally from Maioria?

The demons that had followed now fled in horror at the sight of the spear. The spear disappeared as she plunged through the rock floor and into a dark sea of nothingness.

So complete and empty was the nothingness that Issa neither knew if she fell or was still. The utter darkness was more terrifying than the demons that had chased her. Had she fallen beyond the Murk? How would she ever get back out? How would anyone find her? Cold fear spread through her. She wondered if this was what it was like to be buried alive, to die alone trapped in the darkness.

Red lightning flared, lighting up a sky filled with black clouds. It was a blessing to the nothingness. Lightning torched the sky again and again, and the scene brightened. Now she could see the tunnel of energy, only it was much weaker than before. The barest hint of blue and white swirled around her, and she could see through it clearly into the world beyond.

She appeared to be falling slowly through a red sky. Magenta clouds boiled around her, and it was hotter than any place she had ever experienced. Sweat soon rolled down her skin, draining the strength from her spent body. The air was thick as soup in her lungs, and she felt crushed by the pressure of the place. Her descent slowed so that she floated rather than fell through a world filled with boiling clouds. Her thoughts were slow too. She couldn't seem to think straight and strange noises came and went.

Then the madness came.

It came in the sound of voices whispering around her. Voices of friends she'd known came and went, snippets of conversations she'd had in the past talked around her as if she were having them now. Faces of people she'd once known formed in the clouds. They seemed to be able to see her, they were talking to her. She blinked. Were they real or was she making them up? She shook her head, trying to hang on to her sanity.

'Issy? Is that you?' a soft voice came.

'Ma?' she called out, desperately needing something familiar to cling on to.

'Issy, why did you leave me to die?'

'Ma? I did not. I came for you. I…' she gasped as Fraya's pale, sunken face formed before her. The unfathomable sadness in her eyes sent shivers through her body. Then her mother's eyes turned black and she scowled in a demonic way, her face a snarl of hatred. Issa slammed her eyes shut and clutched at her temples. The voices crowded around her.

'Why did you kill me, Issa?' A voice cut through the others.

'Rance?' She turned to see his handsome face smiling back at her in the clouds. There was sadness in his eyes. 'Rance, I did not. Keteth came.' His face disappeared and instead, she looked upon his body, all bruised bloodied and bloated. Cirosa was weeping over him. She looked up at Issa with a hate filled snarl.

'You did this,' Cirosa screamed, her blue eyes flared into red with slitted pupils like a demon's. 'You murdered him.'

Issa shook her head and tried to back away.

Keteth appeared from behind a cloud. Not the man, but the beast. He was huge in the sky, his great white bloated mass snaking towards her. He was as real now as he had been when she last saw the beast. She tried to move away from him but had no way to control her inexorable descent or any movement. He opened his mouth in a grin, revealing thousands of needle sharp teeth.

'None of this is real,' she screamed at him, at the voices. *How can this be a wizard's testing when I cannot fight and use the Flow?*

She shut her eyes and clamped her hands over her ears, but the voices came into her mind. She screamed, again and again, trying to drown them out. She couldn't fight them but she could refuse to listen to them. She had never before felt so helpless and pitiful. She understood then why no wizard spoke of their cowardly useless existence in the horrors of the Storm Holt.

What caused the voices to end she did not know, but when she stopped screaming there was only silence. When she opened her eyes there was black nothingness again. She could sense no movement, no Storm Holt tunnel. Nothing. It seemed to be like that for a long time, hours at least. Hour after hour of nothing.

With no detectable boundaries of any sort, she began to lose all sense of self, and with it, time and space became meaningless concepts. It could be said that, without her self-consciousness, she actually ceased to exist. She could not tell where she and the nothingness were separated, they seemed one and the same.

Slowly her world began to fill with the memories of the past as if her dissipating mind was scrabbling furiously to gather the parts of itself together. It seemed as if everything she had ever been and done was trying to arrange itself into some sensible linear pattern that made up her life, but the connections between events had been lost. Right now, everything she had ever experienced appeared to have happened at the same time. She latched onto a memory and focused on it.

Just like opening one's eyes after a long sleep, her awareness returned and with it the rest of the world. Or at least *a* world. When she blinked open her eyes she found herself sitting on her mother's bed, dressed in her usual sage coloured trousers and a white shirt. She touched her clothes, feeling a sense of normality return. She took a deep breath and let it out in relief. This was where she was supposed to be. She'd made it home where she belonged.

'Ma?' she said. Fraya was propped up by cushions.

'I'm sorry to tell you the truth, Issy,' she croaked, carrying on with the conversation they had clearly been having, 'but you must know before I'm gone.'

'Know what?' she asked, her head was pounding with everything she was trying to piece together. 'It's all right Ma. I understand everything. You need to rest and not worry,' she soothed.

Being here didn't quite seem right. She had been here before, so she shouldn't be here now, but she couldn't work out why. Everything she had been and done before this point was a mess in her mind. Her memory was like a puzzle all broken up and left on the floor. No two memories connected, no two memories made sense. All she knew was that she should not be here, and yet it all seemed so natural and *normal*. This was her home.

'Your mother just didn't want you,' Fraya sighed sadly.

'What?' She frowned in confusion. This wasn't quite how she remembered it.

'I'm so sorry. After your father left her, your mother didn't want to be reminded of him. Said he'd near as well forced himself upon her. In an act of mercy, she tried to end her pregnancy, but nothing worked. She couldn't afford to keep you, she was so poor herself. She said that, for your own sake, you should never have been born.'

Issa listened in numb silence. Somehow what she was hearing wasn't right, or was it? She was sure Ma had said something different. Or had she remembered it wrong? Why couldn't she remember what happened? Her mother continued, her voice weak and rasping.

'I couldn't bear to watch her let you drift away in the ocean, so I took you in. It was hard, I'll admit that. I suffered much in the early days… But now you're a full grown woman, and you can make of your life what you will with all that I have left. Leave me now Issy, I need to rest.' She sighed, rolled over and closed her eyes. Her breath rattled in her chest

Issa stood up and walked out the door in a daze. *My mother had been a seer, a seer, damn it.* But maybe she'd remembered it all wrong. Maybe she'd made it all up in her head. What in hell was going on?

'Where am I? How did I get here,' she whispered as she took in their familiar kitchen, her home on Little Kammy. The same painted yellow plates on the table, the comfy old chair with the rip in the cushion that was her favourite, the flowers on the window from Farmer Ged. 'It's all as I remember it, and yet something is different and I… I should not be here.'

She looked down and noticed her shirt and trousers were faded and patched. She smoothed her hair and found it was tied back, but cut short and limp. Her hands were covered with callouses and bitten nails from worry and hard work. She pulled down her shirt and gasped in horror. There was no raven mark upon her chest. She remembered it clearly, but now it wasn't there. Where was she? This couldn't be home, things just weren't right. What was happening?

A deafening roar came from outside and rumbled the floor. She screamed and covered her ears. Fire flared against all the windows, from the kitchen through to the adjoining sitting room as if the whole house had been plunged into a sea of flames. The glass exploded inwards from the heat, spraying her with shards. The roof began to lift up, wooden beams splintered and stone walls cracked. The entire wall in front of her collapsed as the roof supporting it was flung away.

She found herself staring back into the enormous eyes of a Dread Dragon. It breathed in. She collapsed onto the floor as dragon fear stole the strength from her legs. Fire exploded around her. Her clothes and hair burst into flame. She screamed as the burning agony scoured her body and drove all thoughts from her mind.

"You should never have been born," the words hurt her like physical blows as she floated in nothingness.

"Your mother just didn't want you."

'I had a life, it was different to this,' she said aloud, but doubt crept in. She was unwanted there too. She wished she'd never been born. Edarna's face came into her memory.

'Edarna,' she reached out to the witch. 'Is that you? Can you reach me? Are you scrying for me?'

She blinked and found herself sat with the old witch at her kitchen table, a mug of tea held between both their hands.

'It's all in your head, girl.' The old witch shook her head and sighed.

'Edarna?' she said. What did she mean? What had they been talking about? The witch continued.

'The goddess is gone if there ever even was one, and we'd all do well to forget about her. There's no prophecy of a Raven Queen, there's no blue moon, and there's no goddess called Zanufey. You dreamt it up, and I've never heard the like. You need to get your head checked to make up stuff like that,' she tutted.

'No, it's true.' Issa shook her head. 'You told me most of it. How did I get here?' She looked around.

Edarna scowled at her, her face filled with hatred. Issa jumped up, knocking her chair over, and backed away, her heart pounding in her throat. Edarna's eyes flared into red demon eyes and horrible feathers began to sprout out of her face. In the next moment, the witch had become a huge raven. It flew at her, its sharp beak and talons stabbed at her head and arms.

'No, Edarna. Stop. It's me!' she screamed and tried to beat back the huge bird, but it did not stop.

'Help,' she screamed. Talons and beak struck and sliced. Hot blood trickled down her arms. The raven was going to kill her. What was happening? This wasn't her life, this was something else.

All at once the bird was gone, and along with it Edarna and her kitchen. Instead, magenta clouds again filled the sky. She checked herself. Her arms were covered in dried blood, but they didn't hurt and there were no wounds. She swallowed and breathed. She was not falling through the maelstrom, but she had no idea where she was.

She stood on a plane of red earth and rocks. The ground was so hot beneath her boots she felt her feet beginning to burn. The plane was vast, spreading out for miles and miles. The air was hot and dry and parched her throat. She neither knew how or why her reality changed, she had no control over anything. All she could do was face each onslaught and pray she would find a way out.

She scanned the barren land. Whilst nothing was there, all the while she felt eyes upon her. The hairs prickled on the back of her neck. Something watched her, though she tried not to imagine what. She started to walk, she didn't know where to go, only that she had to move. The hunted feeling remained, but there was no cave or rock or tree to hide behind.

She saw a dark object lying on the earth in the distance and moved towards it in a lurching jog. It was a person lying still. Or a body. Her eager jog slowed to a tentative walk. The person was wrapped in black cloth that billowed in the wind. When she neared, her eyes fell upon a lifeless face.

'Maeve?' Issa stared in horror. The plump face of the Castle Elune maid was ashen and bruised in death.

'You did this,' the whisper came from her lifeless grey lips.

Issa swayed, feeling as if she would faint.

'You did this,' the body screamed and opened her eyes. They were black and shiny like onyx.

Issa ran. Other black-shrouded bodies appeared around her. One by one they sat up, their grey faces and black eyes following where she went. She recognised a stable boy who had looked after Ely's mare. Then there was the seamstress who had made her dress. And then, she dared not look harder, but she thought she saw Tarry. She forced her eyes away, she did not want to see the dead of Celene or Kammy. But then they stood up and began to follow her. They started shouting at her. She covered her ears and ran faster.

Beyond a pile of rocks, she glimpsed the white spire of the Temple of Celene. She ran towards it. It looked so pristine and pure in this desolate depraved place that she began to hope. She fell against the solid doors, turned the heavy handle and staggered inside. Thank the goddess it was not locked. She slammed the door shut, locked it, and leant against it with a desperate sob.

The temple was wonderfully cool and clean, and just as she remembered it before it had been destroyed. She slid down the door with a long relieved sigh. Her tunic dress was soaked in sweat and smeared with blood and dirt. She pulled the front down, but still there was no raven mark. At least she remembered it being there. That alone kept some of her sanity.

A groan came from somewhere followed by a long sigh.

'Hello?' she pulled herself up and tiptoed forwards.

A man moaned followed by a woman speaking softly. The sounds were coming from the far end of the temple around a corner.

'Who is there?' she said more quietly. Caution would be best in this place. Her breath came shallow and her hand dropped to her sword hilt. She looked down in surprise. She hadn't had her sword before. Otherwise she would have fought the raven with it. Quietly she pulled it free. More moans came, both a woman and a man, this time more urgent.

'Are you hurt?' she whispered as she came to the corner. Quickly she rounded it with her sword high, but the people she looked upon did not pay her any attention. It took her a while to take in what she was seeing.

Asaph was naked, and he had his back to her. Sweat rolled down his muscular body. Wrapped around his waist were long white legs, and his hands gripped the smooth bottom of a blonde haired woman. They both moaned again as he pushed into her, and together they writhed in ecstasy. She recognised that woman.

Issa gave a horrified gasp as she looked at Cirosa entwined around him. She covered her mouth and dropped her sword. It made a mighty clang on the marble floor. They both turned to look at her without ceasing their lovemaking. Asaph smiled at her pitifully as if she were a silly child. Cirosa's cold blue eyes stared at her, and then an impossibly long red tongue came out of her mouth and licked Asaph's arm.

'Stupid girl. Maybe she wants to see what a real woman looks like,' Asaph said and laughed. He thrust harder and together they groaned.

Issa grabbed her sword and ran out of the temple, her ragged heart pounding and her mind struggling to hold on to sanity.

'How can I fight this?' she cried. She was trapped here, far beyond the Murk, so far down no one would ever find her. Things happened so fast she couldn't think, she could only endure and pray she survived. She collapsed onto the ground with a sob. 'I would rather face the Shadowlands,' she screamed at the sky.

As soon as she thought it, the hot, red landscape turned cold. The colour leaked out of the sky so that slate clouds now filled it. The wind blew frigid and she hugged her bare arms against the sudden chill. All around her loomed grey trees, and ghosts moved between their trunks. The Shadowlands, how could it be? Sorrow gripped her heart and she dropped her face into her hands, trying to muffle the sobs that shook her.

She prayed the wraiths would not hear her. How could she ever find a way out of here? Was this place nothing but an awful twisted reflection of Maioria? Was everything she thought somehow created? She could not remember what was real anymore.

She closed her eyes and brought to mind the sacred mound as clear as she could. She forcefully willed herself there. After a moment she opened her eyes. She laughed aloud when she saw the mound ahead, but the laugh died in her throat. It was the sacred mound, but it was a mess. The huge stones that surrounded it were mostly knocked down and broken. From the look of the moss upon them and the signs of extreme weathering, they had been like that for a very long time.

The mound itself was still there, but it was sunken and collapsed on one side. The entrance was no longer an entrance, but just a dark hole, much like the entrance to fox's den. She heard footsteps running behind her. She whirled around, hand reaching for her sword, but she was too late.

The Raven Queen stood there, her pale face emotionless and terrifying, her sword already falling in a downward arc. The sword sliced easily through her body, from her left ear through her throat and exited above her right breast. The shock kept the agony at bay for only a moment and then she was collapsing, bright red blood—her blood—spurting from her neck. The last thing she saw was the dragon scale-armoured woman smiling down at her with black, slitted pupils.

CHAPTER 34

Demon Light

I surrender. It is hopeless. There is no way out, no way to fight.

In the darkness the voices came again, they raged around her, demanding, accusing, hating.

"Why did you kill me, Issa?"

"You did this."

"Stupid girl.'

"It's all in your head…"

"You should never have been born…"

Issa could not fight them or shut them out. She tried not to focus on any one of them, for fear of bringing up some distorted memory of the past in which she must act out her hopeless role. Her entire life had been a lie. Everything that she remembered was distorted. She wished she had never existed. If she had never been born, Celene would not have fallen. Ma, Ely, Rance, Maeve… they would not have died. She could not undo her existence, but she could give herself to Baelthrom and end this. He would be here in the demon worlds, she was sure of it.

The thought seemed horrendous, but to exist anymore in this hell was worse. She could not use magic or her sword, and she could not find a way back to the Storm Holt. There was no one here to help her, she was utterly alone. She closed her eyes and dared to turn her mind back to the very first time she had met the Dromoorai and had felt the terror of dragon fear.

The screech of a Dread Dragon filled her ears. She blinked and froze in terror. Below her, the sea crashed against the tall cliffs. Wind whipped her hair and above her the Dread Dragon came. She turned to jump from the cliff as she had before but then stopped. Her heart pounded in her throat and she thought she would vomit. She turned to face the dragon. Its horn-covered head snaked towards her, its red eyes mesmerising. She struggled to breathe against the panic.

The beast's giant claw reached down and grasped her waist in a crushing vice, forcing the air from her lungs. She gasped fast shallow breaths and went limp. The sea and sky rolled and rocked as the Dread Dragon carried her high. They went so high the air grew thin and her limbs froze in the cold. She passed out in the altitude.

'So, you come to me.' The voice that brought her round was so deep it was hard to hear, like the rumble of thunder coming from miles away and yet the vibrations are still felt.

Issa blinked into the darkness and shivered. She lay curled up and naked on a freezing stone floor. With leaden arms, she pushed herself to sitting, and hugged her knees. She had given herself to Baelthrom, the one she hated. It was a simple fact. She had surrendered and he had found her in the Storm Holt. It was over now, or would be soon. She began to cry.

Heavy magic draped around her in chains, sucking the strength from her body and the clarity from her mind so that she felt drugged. The memories of the recent events mingled so completely with her past that she no longer knew which ones were real. All she knew was that there was a huge presence before her and powerful alien magic moved.

'Yes,' she croaked, her throat was parched and bruised from the iron collar she wore. She wanted to face what was before her without fear, without trembling, but she could not even stand up. She could barely breathe, and sweat rolled down her temples despite the deathly cold.

'I knew you would come to me in the end.' The words wrapped themselves around her.

A giant moved in the blackness and two eyes flared into life, bright green and triangular in shape such as no human should have. Baelthrom, her heart shivered. A gauntleted hand gripped her chin and lifted her face up to look at him, she was too weak to lift it herself. Light fell upon his hideous form revealing a hideous mixture of creatures moulded together to contain his consciousness. Massive demon wings folded down against his human back, reptilian tail and legs bulged with muscles, but his face was forever hidden in his three-peaked black metal helmet.

This was the one who hunted her. This was the one who had destroyed everyone she had ever known and taken away her life. She lived only to destroy this being, but now she was here before him, she was as she never imagined being; naked, weak, powerless.

'What shall I make of you...' he murmured thoughtfully. His eyes changed to blue as they locked onto hers, flooding her brain with their painful light.

'Just kill me,' she shuddered. She tried to move her eyes but they were locked onto his.

He laughed low and deep. 'I do not like death, it is... wrong. No, I shall not let you suffer it. I need your power. I need to know you fully within and without. But I need you pure, I need you before the Elixir of Immortality changes you forever.'

He pulled her up and crushed her against his bare chest. She could feel his human heart thudding, though the life force that animated it was far from holy. He pulled her head back and looked into her eyes. She felt his mind probe hers and had no strength to stop him.

'Show me what you are,' he breathed.

He crushed her chest harder against his. The feel of his bare skin against hers made her shudder, she had no strength at all to resist. She realised he was relishing the beat of her own heart, that somehow he was drawing the strength of it into his own. Her heart pounded harder, aware of the life that was leaving it. Frantically she felt for the Flow, but it was not there. *Zanufey!* She screamed in her mind but there came no answer other than Baelthrom's laugh.

'Is that your goddess? A goddess that has never and *can* never help you? I will be your god.'

Heat began to leave her as he drew it into himself. In its place, his coldness seeped into her. The cold was deathly. It entered her mouth, her chest and her abdomen, his black alienness filling her body and soul. Pressure started in her head, which grew to excruciating levels. Black spots danced in her eyes. Pain exploded in her ears, she felt a hot trickle come from them. She was aware of moaning senselessly.

'Let go, give yourself fully to me.' His words whispered through the pain.

She was paralysed in his grip as he drew her essence, her life force, into himself to become one with him. She felt her body and soul dissolving in his grasp until she could no longer feel where she ended and he began.

'You are afraid of death. Are you not tired of seeing all those you love taken from you? I can free you from death. I can free them all from death. I alone can give you immortality,' he crooned.

Even though she had chosen to surrender, she began to struggle, her body and soul sensing the death that was coming. She fought to keep the pieces of herself together, to prevent her and Baelthrom from becoming one. For a moment he let her struggle as if he enjoyed it, and then he pushed harder, forcing himself into her, letting her know she could not be free.

I cannot fight. I am lost. I am so far away from the light.

She stopped fighting. She surrendered. He filled her completely. Everything that she was, had been, and wanted to be, was sucked away. Her whole being was turning dark. Pitifully she began to sob as she gave up her soul to the darkness.

In their hideous melding of minds, bodies and souls she caught a glimpse of his design, caught an image of the complete jigsaw. She saw that the undead Maphraxies were nothing more than the empty, soulless bodies of the living, willingly serving Baelthrom's vast army in exchange for the immortality of the physical self. An endless life in chains. Through the Black Drink, he trapped and consumed souls to feed his power. That was his strength. Their bodies he took for his army. His gift of immortality was a lie, even for those who willingly took the Black Drink. It chained their soul to Baelthrom forever and it could never be undone.

Unfettered, Baelthrom would consume all, the energy of everything would be drawn into his being. Soon he would be too powerful for anything to stop him. And then she realised he knew all of this, he had planned it. All the life of the world would become one in him, a life that was no life, a mindless existence of servitude. She saw the blackness of the dark rift that he always looked to rolling in Maioria's sky. He wanted to take Maioria and the whole galaxy into the place from which he had come.

As the blackness swallowed her, she saw the end of worlds, the end of days.

'Issy, go to the light,' a small voice called out, one she vaguely recognised.

There is no light, there is only nothing. I am nothing.

A faint green light glowed from far away, showing her that there was darkness and she was in it. At this moment in time she knew only three things; that there was a light, there was her consciousness, and there was the darkness. The voice she only half believed was real until it came again.

'Go to the light of Zorock,' a deeper voice boomed.

She reached for the light and it engulfed her, driving back the darkness. A being moved, bigger than a Dread Dragon. It had all-black eyes and green, hairless skin. Black horns twisted high above its elongated skull. Its face was long as was its nose, and its mouth was filled with fangs. Wings lay folded on its back and it crouched on thick-muscled arms and legs. The beast stared straight through her into her soul. It did something there that made her soul shiver, letting her know it could take it if it wanted to, but that it chose not to.

She felt something in her soul shaken free, and when it was gone she felt clean as if something dirty had attached to her. The being watched her unblinking with those all-seeing black eyes. It held up a hand, each finger had long black claws, and motioned her towards him. She moved fast towards the beast. She screamed.

The world came rushing back to her. In the next instant, she was coughing and shaking on a stone floor. She blinked and looked up. Everything was bathed in green light, the same light she had seen in the darkness, the same green as the light that came from the moon Zorock. It came from a large crystal set on a pedestal made of rock. Beyond the crystal, red demon eyes with slitted pupils glowed.

'No more. Please, no more. Just kill me, kill me,' she begged, and laid a sweaty cheek down on the cold stone.

Several feet shuffled close and the strange murmurs of voices not wholly human came from nearby. She was too spent to look at them.

'Are you sure she's the one?' a wheezy voice said. 'She seems a bit small and weak.'

'She was not supposed to go beyond the Pit. No wizard goes that far. Karhlusus has done more than just open the gates,' another deeper voice replied. 'She should have died, but she has not. She is the one. Look at the mark on her chest. The mark of the raven.'

A tiny finger prodded her. She groaned in response. 'It's all ugly, skinny and white,' a familiar voice said.

'Leave it alone, Maggot.' The wheezy voice scolded.

'Maggot...' she repeated the name, some memory forming in her mind.

'I told you not to enter the Storm Holt. The greater demons have done something,' Maggot huffed.

'Storm Holt...' she breathed and struggled to lift herself up. She could only manage propping herself onto her elbows. 'I'm in the Storm Holt.' She blinked, trying to see, but her vision kept blurring and everything was out of focus.

'You left the Storm Holt, now you are in the Murk,' the deep voice said.

'Maybe she needs wursel blood,' the wheezy voice said.

'They don't drink wursel up there, stupid,' the deep voice said. 'Find some water. Maybe there's some left in the lower caverns.'

Feet shuffled away and she closed her eyes and slumped back down, trying to breathe the thick warm air that managed to make her feel weaker than she already was.

Some time later, a blanket was draped over her and something was shoved against her lips. She involuntarily drank the old warm water that was poured down her throat. She choked and swallowed and blinked. The water was helping, despite being foul. She rubbed her eyes. She was wrapped in a rough stinking blanket, the smell of which she could not place and decided not to try, and in a very large room carved out of rock. The only light came from the green crystal, so she could not tell how big the room actually was, but it felt big.

She blinked up into the faces of three very different looking demons that, if she had not been so exhausted, she would have been afraid of. She instantly recognised the tiny, ugly demon with the protruding tooth and potbelly.

'Maggot?'

The little demon looked up at the other two towering above him. One demon was skinny and bent over and hung on to a gnarly staff. He seemed old, but they all looked similar with grey, hairless skin and wide, round heads, clawed feet and hands, large ears and long tails. The last demon was the most frightening. He had huge muscles and was big and wide, maybe ten feet tall. His wings were partially folded over his back. He watched her with a permanent distrusting scowl.

'You should not have entered the Storm Holt,' the big demon said. 'I sent Maggot to bring you a different way. That gate now leads straight to the Pit and beyond.'

She nodded and closed her eyes. 'It goes on and on and never stops. I had no idea it would be like that. I would never have gone.

'You saved me.' She suddenly realised. 'Why?'

The demon's scowl deepened. He looked away. 'We need help,' he said it quietly as if it shamed him. 'And so will you if you do not help us. The greater demons are coming. The only way to stop them destroying us, and to stop them entering your world where they will destroy you too, is to find the spear and kill Karhlusus. The Demon Slayer knows how to kill him, he also knows how to close the gates.'

She shook her head. 'I don't know who or where this Demon Slayer is...'

'We need you to find him.' The demon talked over her. 'We need an intermediary. He'll kill us on sight. Do not forget that we hate your kind and the world you inhabit, but we will help you find the spear and fight the greater demons. We will help you close the gates to the Pit and to the Murk if you destroy Karhlusus. Our only hope is to work together. '

She nodded. She was so exhausted and confused she could think of nothing to say except to agree. They had, after all, saved her. 'All right. I'll try. Why is the spear so important? Why can't you get the spear yourself?'

The demons looked at each. The big one spoke.

'In your world, the spear was turned into a weapon to kill demons. Demons cannot touch the spear without being destroyed.'

The skinny demon growled and spat at the wall.

'What was it before?' she asked.

'We don't know,' he shrugged. 'Perhaps the Demon Slayer does. You call the spear Velistor, and Karhlusus knows its worth. He keeps it locked away in Carmedrak Rock.'

'The black spire in the desert?' She remembered the hideous black rock.

The demons nodded. 'It's filled with greater demons and has become the entrance and exit to their world, the Pit. Find the Demon Slayer, and together we have a chance to drive back the greater demons.'

'I will try,' she said again, 'but only because you saved me. Thank you.' She looked up sincerely into the face of the big demon. She meant it with all her heart. 'The thought of being trapped down there, of never getting out... I surrendered everything. I gave up on myself—' she choked back a sob. Right now she had never felt so grateful to anyone, funny that she felt that way towards these demons.

'Hmph.' His face was expressionless.

'If the Storm Holt is too dangerous, how will I return?' she asked.

'Wekurd, show her,' the big one said.

'Yes, my king,' Wekurd said with a bow and limped forwards. So he was the king, King Gedrock, Maggot had called him. She was pleased some memory was returning.

'This is the Murk.' Wekurd scratched the shape of a waxing crescent moon on the floor with his staff. 'This is Zorock.' Next to it he drew the shape of a waning crescent. Finally, he drew a long straight line joining the mirrored crescents together. 'This is the symbol of the Murk and the line is the symbol of the gates to our world. All gates to our world come through our moon Zorock.'

She remembered seeing the green light of Zorock when she first passed through the Storm Holt entrance.

'When you step upon the symbol of the Murk, speak your intention and spill your blood. It will bring you here.'

'Spill blood?' She was taken aback. Were they joking? Their faces were serious.

'Just a few drops,' the skinny demon wheezed. There was a disturbing hungry look in his eyes as he looked at her. Keen howls came from somewhere, making her shiver.

'Enough has been explained,' the king said, he looked uneasy. 'Her presence is disturbing the demons. They can smell her. She is not to be harmed,' he said specifically to Wekurd. The skinny demon nodded, the hungry look was gone from his face and replaced with subservience.

'Bring her to the shard. Maggot, take her back to the higherworld,' the king demanded and turned away.

'Wait, please, not through the Storm Holt again.' She gasped and tried to get up as the big demon stalked off. He folded his wings down against his back, and his long thick tail snaked out behind him. Wekurd gripped her arm and helped her up. His cold grey flesh against hers made her skin crawl, but his grip was strong. She could barely walk and so had to let him half carry her as they followed the king.

'It's safe returning through the crystal,' Maggot said as he flew to catch up with the king. 'For you, it is, anyway,' a frown creased his already wrinkled face.

'Touch the crystal,' the king demanded when she neared.

She couldn't disobey that commanding voice, it vibrated right through her. She placed her hand on the crystal next to where he had placed his. She stared at that hand. It was big and strong enough to crush her skull in one grip.

Maggot flapped his wings and hovered close to the crystal. There was a reluctant look on his face and he grimaced as he placed his own stubby hand upon it. She swallowed. If the demon was afraid, then so was she. The king glared at her, those red eyes with black slits watching her from beyond a green crystal were becoming a familiar sight.

'We will meet again, Raven Queen,' he said and his voice was lost in a rush of air.

Issa and Maggot fell out of the Storm Holt in a heap on the grass beside her clothes. She shivered and trembled with cold, fatigue and a strange electrical disturbance in her body that made her twitch. She couldn't move a muscle with her own will. She wondered if this was how being struck by lightning felt. She breathed the cool, light air. Had she finally made it home? The thought brought tears to her eyes that spilled down her cheeks.

A raven cawed, she recognised Ehka's call. He landed beside her and waddled close to her face. He blurred in her vision. With another caw he flew off. *Oh Ehka, thank the goddess.* He was going to get the wizards, she hoped. Though the last thing she wanted was to see anyone. Not in this state, not with the things she had seen and done.

She realised then that she had failed, failed on every level. She had surrendered herself and given up her soul in the Storm Holt. She would have cried if she wasn't already. All she wanted to do was crawl away and die somewhere. It was lucky she could not reach her sword.

'Issy?' A small voice came from behind her and she felt small hands grip her arm. She couldn't even bring herself to speak. The hands left her arm and in the next moment, her tunic dress was dragged over her shivering body. That small gesture, coming from a demon at that, ignited a spark of wonder in the darkness of her mind.

'Your face is leaking,' he said. Was that worry in his voice? Cold hands touched her wet cheek. It made her cry even more.

'I thought demons hated humans,' she stuttered, trying to keep Maggot in her vision, but he kept blurring into a patch of grey.

'We do. So many demons have been murdered by humans. And you stink and look so ugly. But King needs you... and you liked my name... and you didn't kill me like I was told humans would.'

Men's voices came from afar and he stepped back in fear.

'Go, Maggot, they are coming to help me.' She shivered. 'But they might not like you, and though I want to I cannot protect you right now. Go and... Thank you.'

'For what?' The demon frowned, his face was an ugly scowl in her blurry vision.

'For finding me in the darkness.'

'We live in the darkness, Issy,' he said. He backed away towards the Storm Holt as the men's voices neared. She watched as he disappeared into a patch of shadow and then was gone completely.

There came loud excited laughter that hurt her ears, and then a soft blanket was thrown over her, bringing with it much needed warmth. Her body was gently lifted and a barrage of voices surrounded her.

'She made it, I knew she would.'

'I told you she would.'

'There was never anything to worry about.'

'She still might not live yet, her skin is blue and cold as ice.'

'You didn't tell me it would be like that,' she croaked. The voices went silent as she spoke. 'Everything I feared came to pass.'

'It is different for everyone,' Freydel said next to her. He wasn't carrying her and she strained to see who was.

It was Domenon. He looked down at her. There was a strange look in his eyes that she could not fathom. It was not surprise—he was not surprised she had returned, perhaps he knew she would all along. It bordered on concern, maybe worry, and certainly confusion. His eyes also bore the faintest tinge of brightness, proof that he had recently been using the Flow, and for a moment it seemed his pupils were longer than they should be. He looked away, and she focused on trying to say conscious.

'I used no magic. I lost everything, even myself. I surrendered my soul, willingly. I died,' she said, her voice ragged and painful in her throat. 'I did not pass any test,' she felt the tears fall again. They were so hot on her cheeks, they burned.

'Yes, Issa, yes you did pass. To return is to pass, no matter how it is done,' Freydel said.

'I would not have survived had the Shadow Demons not reached me. If they hadn't found me I would not be here. I didn't know I was so afraid. So afraid of everything. I went beyond the Murk, beyond even the Pit. I went so far I don't know where it was.' Her voice was barely a whisper.

The wizards were silent as she spoke, probably trying to hear what she said. Freydel spoke, his voice soothing and yet full of emotion.

'All that matters in this life is that we have the fortitude to face whatever comes our way.'

She felt herself drifting as she considered his words. After a moment she said, 'I have been to the bottom of the abyss and beyond, and I gave my soul away. How can I fear anything again?'

She would still be there if the demons hadn't reached her. But she had gone to them, she had chosen to trust them. What if she'd never met Maggot? No one would ever know what had happened to her if it wasn't for him. It was Edarna's words spoken so long ago that came clearly to her then and made her wonder.

"…Beware of the deceivers and their false gifts and broken promises. They would make you an enemy of yourself to break you so that you will serve them. Master yourself and know that true friends can be found in the most unlikely places."

Continued in *Demon Spear*

DEMON SPEAR

The Goddess Prophecies

Book 4

Araya Evermore

DEMONS. DEATH. DELIVERANCE

All these Issa must face as darkness strikes into the heart of their last stronghold. Greater demons are rising from the Pit, Carvon is brutally attacked, and a horrifying murder forces Issa and her companions to flee. But despite the devastating loss, she must keep her oath to the Shadow Demons and alone reclaim the spear that can save them all.

Struggling with failure and rejection, and doubting his feelings for Issa, Asaph finds solace in street fighting. Alone, he becomes an easy target for the snares of the white owl. His own destiny calls to him, but it will take an ancient, awakening dragon and a terrible price to free himself from Cirosa's chains.

All around there is devastation and loss, but the dark moon is rising once more to spread its light upon the world. With its power Issa has a chance to stand against the darkness, and fight the terrifying evil rising from the Abyss.

ALSO BY ARAYA EVERMORE

The Goddess Prophecies series:

Goddess Awakening ~ A Prequel

When darkness falls, a heroine will rise.

The Dread Dragons came with the dawn. On dark wings of death they slaughtered every seer and turned their sacred lands to ruin...

Night Goddess ~ Book 1

A world plunging into darkness. An exiled Dragon Lord struggling with his destiny. A young woman terrified of an ancient prophecy she has set in motion.

He came through the Dark Rift hunting for those who had escaped his wrath. Unchecked, his evil spread. Now, the world hangs on a knife-edge and all seems destined to fall. But when the dark moon rises, a goddess awakens, and nothing can stop the prophecy unfolding...

The Fall of Celene ~ Book 2

Impossible Odds, Terrifying Powers

"My name is Issa and I am hunted. I hold a power that I neither understand nor can barely control..."

The battle for Maioria has begun. Issa faces a deadly enemy as the Immortal Lord's attention turns fully in her direction. Nothing will stand in Baelthrom's way—he must destroy this new power that grows with the rising dark moon...

Storm Holt ~ Book 3

Would you sell your soul to save the world?

The Storm Holt… The ultimate Wizard's Reckoning, where all who enter must face their greatest demons. No woman has entered and survived since the Ancients split the magic apart eons ago. Plagued by demons and visions of a strange white spear, Issa must take the Reckoning to find her answers and fight for her soul to prove her worth to the most powerful magic wielders upon Maioria…

Demon Spear ~ Book 4

Demons. Death. Deliverance.

All these Issa must face as darkness strikes into the heart of their last stronghold. Greater demons are rising from the Pit, Carvon is brutally attacked, and a horrifying murder forces Issa and her companions to flee. But despite the devastating loss, she must keep her oath to the Shadow Demons and alone reclaim the spear that can save them all…

Dragons of the Dawn Bringer ~ Book 5

An Exiled King. A Broken Dream. A Sword Forged for Forever.

Issa can trust no one. Her closest allies betray her and nobody is as they seem. When a Dromoorai captures her and a black vortex to another dimension rips into her room, she realises the attacks will never stop and there is far worse than Baelthrom reaching for her out of the Dark Rift…

"Be the light unto the darkness…Be the last light in a falling world."

They had both been chosen: he to save another race; she to save her own from what he had become. Now, both must enter Oblivion and therein decide the fate of all…

BOOKS BY JOANNA STARR

Farseeker

Enlightened. Enslaved. Erased.

Earth, 50,000 years ago before the magic vanished. Invaded by aliens posing as gods, advanced civilisations crumbled. Now, these powerful off-worlders war for control of the planet, and the people who remain no longer remember what they once were. Seduced then enslaved, humanity has fallen…

Free Starter Library

Join the mailing list and get your FREE Starr & Evermore Starter Library available only to subscribers. You'll discover Issa's origin story in my prequel, *Goddess Awakening*, which is not available anywhere else. You'll also get a taster of my latest *Farseeker* series with extra scenes not included in the main story.

To receive this epic free gift, please go to my website below. As a subscriber, you'll also be the first to hear about my latest novels, and lots more exclusive content.

www.joannastarr.com

About the Author

Araya Evermore is the pen name of Joanna Starr - a half-elf and author of the best-selling epic fantasy series, *The Goddess Prophecies*.

Joanna has been exploring other worlds and writing fantasy stories ever since she came to Planet Earth. Finding herself struggling in a world in which she didn't quite fit, escaping into fantasy novels gave her the magic and wonder she craved. Despite majoring in Philosophy & Religion, then Computer Science, she left her career in The City to return to her first love; writing Epic Fantasy.

Originally from the West Country, she's been travelling the world since 2011, and has been on the road so long she no longer comes from any place in particular. So far, she's resided in the Caribbean, United States, Canada, Australia, New Zealand, Spain, Andorra and Malta. Despite loving the mountains, she's actually a sea-based creature and currently resides by the ocean in Ireland.

Aside from writing and working, she spends time talking to trees, swimming with fish, gaming, and playing with swords.

Connect with Joanna online:
www.joannastarr.com
author@joannastarr.com

Enjoyed this book? You can make a big difference…

If you love fantasy books and would like to bring this series to the attention of other fantasy readers, the best thing you can do to reach them is to leave a review.

If you've enjoyed this book, I would be very grateful if you could spend just a minute leaving a review, (it can be as long or as short as you like) on the book's Amazon page.

A heartfelt Thank You in advance.

Printed in Great Britain
by Amazon

79266763R00171